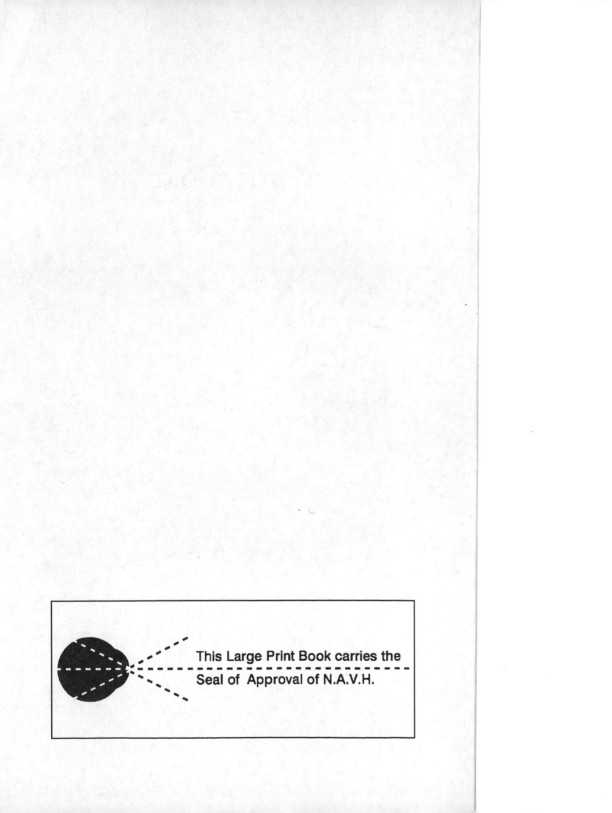

WHITE BONE

RIDLEY PEARSON

WHITE BONE

THORNDIKE PRESS
A part of Gale, Cengage Learning

GALE
CENGAGE Learning™

Detroit • New York • San Francisco • New Haven, Conn • Waterville, Maine • London

GALE
CENGAGE Learning

LIBRARY OF CONGRESS CATALOGING-IN-PUBLICATION DATA

Names: Pearson, Ridley, author.
Title: White bone / By Ridley Pearson.
Description: Large print edition. | Waterville, Maine : Thorndike Press, 2016. |
  Series: Thorndike Press large print basic | Series: A risk agent novel
Identifiers: LCCN 2016025681 | ISBN 9781410491527 (hardcover) | ISBN 1410491528
  (hardcover)
Subjects: LCSH: Large type books. | GSAFD: Spy stories.
Classification: LCC PS3566.E234 W48 2016 | DDC 813/.54—dc23
LC record available at https://lccn.loc.gov/2016025681

Published in 2016 by arrangement with G.P. Putnam's Sons, an imprint of Penguin Publishing Group, a division of Penguin Random House LLC

Printed in the United States of America
1 2 3 4 5 6 7 20 19 18 17 16

White Bone is dedicated to the thousands of individuals who have made it their life's purpose to protect and defend the elephant, rhino and other endangered species on the African continent. These people earn less than they could elsewhere; they sleep in tents or front seats or not at all. They battle the harsh conditions of the African environment, and the monetary conditions that create a market for elephant tusk and rhino horn: poverty, corruption and greed. They often spend more time trying to raise awareness and funds than they do on the ground battling poachers. They are unnamed, unseen and, in many places, unwanted. Without them, the African wild elephant and rhino will be gone forever within the next nine years.

An African elephant is killed every fifteen minutes.

ACKNOWLEDGMENTS

Special thanks to: editors Christine Pepe, Al Zuckerman, Genevieve Gagne-Hawes, Dan Conaway. In Kenya: David Drinker, U.S. State Department, Nairobi; Dr. Paula Kahumbu, Wildlife Direct; Richard Bonham, Big Life; Dr. Karen Ross, African Wildlife Foundation; Susie Weeks, Mt. Kenya Trust; Dr. Juliet King, Northern Rangeland Trust; Orfir Drori, Wildlife Law Enforcement; Dr. Cynthia Moss, Amboseli Trust for Elephants; Benson, Chief of Security, Solio Ranch; Rob Burnett; Sebnem Denktas, Robb Report, Istanbul.

Ground Logistics/Guiding, Kenya: Mikey and Tanya Carr-Hartley / Specialised Safari Company, Ltd.

Without Mikey and Tanya and their staff, there could have been no *White Bone.* They arranged every aspect of my extraordinary weeks in Kenya, including many of my interviews with "hard to get" sources. Their

7

lodges, guiding service and four generations of experience provided me insights and experiences I will never forget, as well as access to NGOs, and they looked after my personal security. I am deeply indebted to them.

Lodges: Ol Donyo Lodge, Solio Lodge
Guides: Olé, Laypeta

1

Seven men, armed with automatic weapons, phosphorus flares and patience, hunkered down on a craggy hilltop, training night-vision binoculars onto a savanna etched with elephant grass, thornbush and fever trees. They mentally mapped intersections of game trails and rutted vehicle tracks that read in their optics as green-black scars. A few of the men double-checked their weapons.

The leader of the men, Koigi, checked his watch. In forty-two minutes, a full moon would rise directly in front of them. It was a night ripe for killing. Poachers preferred full moons. One could nearly smell the elephant blood on the warm breeze.

"East, southeast," spoke Koigi. He was a big, solid man with exceptionally large hands, a growling voice and an even temper.

Six sets of night-vision binoculars swept to the right.

Koigi breathed in deeply and exhaled slowly. Mount Kenya's hilly terrain made for difficult surveillance. Twelve years of lying belly-down in the red, powdery dirt of his birth country, of squatting on his haunches until his knees froze with pain, of enduring all the elements, from mountain blizzards to desert dust storms — all to protect the elephant. He'd been hungry. Thirsty. Sex-starved. He'd put much aside to preserve and protect God's most noble creature.

The elephant was Africa. Kill an elephant and you kill a piece of the continent where all life began. To him, Africa was the heartbeat of the world, every elephant a shrine. Anyone intent on executing an elephant deserved the noose, the spear, the bullet. This philosophy simplified his existence, justified his actions. And though he was as hunted by the law as the poachers were by him, it allowed him to sleep at night.

Their binoculars revealed three adult elephants, their curving tusks appearing dark through the lenses. The beasts walked nearly trunk to tail as they lumbered silently into the open field.

Two of Koigi's rangers, uniformed snipers, lay prone. One of these was making small adjustments to his rifle scope. The other held a seventeen-thousand-dollar TrackingPoint rifle with a computerized scope. Koigi was viewing this man's targeting with his smartphone.

"All good, boss," the first reported.

"On my command," said Koigi.

2

Guuleed, whose ring finger was missing its final joint, signaled the driver to kill the engine.

The tip of his finger had been lost when caught beneath a hook-ended ladder that had shifted as he'd ascended up the hull of a container ship in a rolling sea. The missing piece of finger served to remind him to expect the unpredictable.

Along with the ladder — which had led to the deck of the container ship he'd eventually commandeered — he'd also climbed through years of blood and glory, scaling the ranks of the lawless and dispossessed to a place of prominence in a Somali syndicate known as Badaadinta Badah, which translated as "Savior of the Seas."

He pressed the TALK button on his walkie-talkie three times. Three clicks. Five minutes later, he heard three similar clicks confirming that his team had the elephants in range.

He set the radio down onto the dash of the twelve-year-old Toyota Land Cruiser.

Guuleed quietly climbed out of the doorless vehicle and waited for six of his men to join him. They were a somewhat sorry lot: young, greedy, hungry, foolish. Sacrificial lambs. Anything could, and did, happen in the bush. A lion attack. A Cape buffalo stampede. Rangers.

Patting the satellite phone clipped to his left hip, Guuleed silenced its ringer. He didn't need any interruptions, any reminder the world was currently upside down. No matter how rich or influential, no man should threaten another with wholesale slaughter of his extended family, wife and children included. Certainly not a slant-eyed foreigner. It was *išmata* — *yišmeti* — gloating over another's unhappiness. It was a burden no man could bear.

Guuleed hand-signaled three of his men to the right, two to the left. He and his driver would hold back. Not a word was spoken as the electric fence — currently without power — was cut. All movement was silent. Elephants had been sighted by a local tea farmer earlier in the day, headed toward this, a known watering hole. Guuleed had spread his money around wisely. Given the heat and the water, they would be moving north-northwest. Within the hour, as soon as the moon rose, the prize would be exposed.

3

One of only a few fifty-year-old bull elephants left in Kenya, Grandfather had been previously shot and wounded by poachers and was distinguishable by a large tear in his left ear. He was always seen in the company of a half-dozen females, and his arrival caused a moment of hushed reverence among Koigi's squad. The men were prepared to lay down their lives for the likes of Grandfather.

Koigi spoke Swahili, directing three of his best to take up a protective position. As his men deployed, Koigi monitored them, first with his naked eye, then through the night-vision binoculars. Good men, he admired them all.

"Boss?" the first of his two snipers asked.

Koigi answered flatly. "Provide cover if engaged."

The clouds on the horizon lit up like smoke in a wildfire. The moon was improbably the size of the sun.

By dividing his small squad, Koigi was taking yet another calculated risk. Such strategies could backfire. When the attack came — and it would come, as his source was reliable — it would be at the hands of an assortment of misguided, greedy locals under the direction of a well-trained Somali. Guuleed was a pus-oozing sore from across the northern border. Before an ounce of elephant blood spilled into this beloved soil, Guuleed's would flow freely, his head on a pike. Koigi lived for this moment.

"Boss, why does Grandfather not wear a collar?"

"Because the KGA has its head up its ass." The Kenya Game Agency, along with funding from private conservation groups, had begun collaring and GPS-tracking several dozen elephants. His men chuckled softly. "But more likely he's taken too many darts from treating his wounds." Repeatedly tranquilizing the elephants could turn them aggressive.

When the firefight came, shots rang out, sounding like the dull popping of firecrackers. It happened quickly — two or three minutes that felt like an hour. The bittersweet smell of cordite and gunpowder warmed Koigi's nostrils. The crack of gunfire sent the elephants running. Bullets whistled over Koigi's head. Chips of rock sprayed around him. An elephant dropped, first to its front legs, then collapsed and tumbled in a nauseating slow motion. Koigi, rifle in hand, screamed — an amateurish mistake. He caught a bullet in his vest near his left shoulder. Fell face-first in pain.

Dragged to cover by the ankles, Koigi saw his men kill at least two, including a driver. An engine revved.

"Retreating," his man announced.

"Stay with them!" Koigi ordered, but he could hear it was too late.

The sound of the engine faded.

"They fought longer than necessary. They could have escaped with fewer casualties." Koigi spoke between clenched teeth. "The first we've seen of this."

"Desperate," said his man.

"Yes, but the question is: why?"

Far below the hill, dust rained down onto the wounded elephant as she exhaled her final breath, her tusks spearing the rising moon.

4

Dear John (that's a funny way to start a letter),

We have not seen each other in over six months and the few e-mails we share are typically little more than simple greetings. I write to express my gratitude and appreciation for sharing with me your skills and experiences. They have taught me well and have provided great opportunity. I have gained from these.

I have now completed my first solo exchange, and I am most pleased to report a success. Perhaps the opportunity for sharing the details will arise in the near future. This would be most welcome.

John, as we've written to each other, we often joke. Of course. I have no problem with this. Now I must be more serious. I find in my heart both something missing and something fulfilling. Missing, when too much time separates us. Fulfilling when we are together. It is a small thing, perhaps. I cannot say. But its very existence interests me. Excites me, even.

Folding the overly creased letter and zipping it into an inside pocket of his windbreaker, Knox failed to appreciate the English countryside's mid-May blossoms. The breeze rustled branches twisted like arthritic fingers in an all-pink orchard. A pale dawn yawned dully behind a steady drizzle. The silent swipe of the Mercedes' wiper blades moved out of sync with the beat of The Killers in his earbuds. His reflection revealed a face hardened by the sun, by the stress of caring for his adult brother's special needs. And by his deep concern over the events of the past twelve hours.

He opened a phone photo of him and Grace, his sometime co-worker, in Istanbul's Inebolu Sunday market shot a year earlier. He leaned lower and angled himself to check the driver's rearview mirror, alarmed by his current state. He looked north of forty, nearly a decade off, enhanced in part by his hair having gone dark due to a long, snowy Detroit winter. He'd lost some weight, adding lines to his already leathery face. Grace looked out through those expressive Asian eyes of hers, modest, subdued. They hid her ambition well, disguised her unruly sense of superiority and often unearned confidence.

He touched his jacket where he kept her letter. He felt like he was back in high school. She'd probably tossed his return letter the moment she'd read it. Their contact over the year had amounted to some random texts and the occasional video chat, prompted by loneliness or friendship or whatever force binds one person to another in confusing ways.

Their recent letters — one in each direction — were something altogether different, all the more profound. And now Knox was traveling — all on a hunch. The last-minute ticket had cost a small fortune; leaving his brother would cost him sleep.

The cool English countryside was nonetheless in bloom. Forty-five minutes from Heathrow, the Uber car exited the M25 for the A41 and finally headed west of Northchurch, down a hedge lane called Cocksgrove. The parallel lines of towering trees gave way to a manor house and a loose-stone horseshoe driveway that fronted an ivy-covered, three-story brick spectacle. A backdrop for a costume drama. Water sprayed over the Italian fountain's four horses ridden by trumpeting angels.

Knox heaved the oversized brass knocker, forgoing the electronic call box. Paused. Pounded it down again impatiently.

A manservant answered. A black tuxedo with a white vest. Eight thirty-six A.M. At six-foot-three, Knox towered over him.

"Mr. Winston," Knox said, stepping past the man and into the foyer's cathedral ceiling and checkered marble floor. "Mr. *W-i-n-s-t-o-n*?" His voice echoed. The manservant's expression did not vary.

"You will find him in the breakfast room, sir." The manservant directed with an open palm. "He's expecting you."

"He's what?" Knox moved more reluctantly down the portrait-lined hall. The place was a costume drama cliché. He passed a nine-foot-tall Siberian bear rearing on its hindquarters, and Knox hung his small duffel bag over the bear's right forearm without breaking stride.

The manservant picked it off.

Knox stopped short when he saw the man at the end of the long and perfectly polished dining table. "Sir."

Graham Winston was far younger-looking

than Knox had imagined. Mid-fifties at the most. Not quite leading-man handsome, but attractive. Strong shoulders, soft hands with manicured nails, Beretta country clothes, including bush-brown, narrow-wale corduroys and a heavy gray sweater that nearly matched his hair.

"You were expecting me?"

"Sit down, please," Winston said, having stood to shake hands.

"How? Dulwich?" The only connection Knox had to Winston was through his Rutherford Risk "control," David Dulwich — aka Sarge — certainly had the means to track his international movement.

"How may I help you? No, no! First, let's get some food in you. How's that sound?"

A footman approached and pulled back a chair. Knox sat. A place setting was airdropped around him by two others.

"Coffee?"

"Please." It was poured for him, along with orange juice and a glass of ice water. Sugar and cream appeared. All this in fifteen seconds. Knox studied the dignified man at the head of the table in silence and sipped his coffee. He had an appetite brewing.

"I tried to reach Sar— Dulwich — but ended up speaking to Brian Primer, who, in typical chief executive fashion, left things fuzzy around the edges. I don't like fuzzy. I need a couple of answers."

"Long way to travel for a few questions."

"Important questions. You wouldn't take my call, as you'll remember." Winston showed nothing. "Straight answers would be appreciated."

Again, no reaction.

"Grace and I — Grace Chu, Rutherford Risk — stay in touch. We didn't used to, but you know . . . things change." He was experiencing the uncomfortable mix of jet lag and coffee. "I guess you could say we've become friends. So anyway, maybe three or four weeks ago, I caught up to her on a video call. She was on her phone, Heathrow in the background. Said she was visiting a friend of ours. That's all she said. Well, you're the only person she and I share in England, so I understood the context. An operation. Solo. Important, because you're an important client of Rutherford Risk. I wasn't involved. No harm, no foul. End of discussion. But then her texts stopped. Not that I get that many anyway. But one a week. Maybe two. You know? Contact. Of course they would stop when she was on an op. I've got no problem with that. I knew she'd make contact when she resurfaced."

"If you have come to ask me for specifics . . . I don't mind sharing, if the proper paperwork's taken care of."

"I finally got a text," Knox said. "Yesterday." He paused, taking note. Winston hadn't expected to hear that. "Yesterday," he repeated. "London time, at any rate. There are a couple things you need to know. One, when we're in the field we don't send casual texts, unless the op isn't classified or an at-risk. Texts leave contrails, meaning you can be sourced. Two, if you do text or call, you take a number of precautions, including using pre-paid SIM cards, ghost protocols, VPNs. You know most of this. So, here's the situation. Grace texted me from her number. Now, that's intentional. That's telling me something. Her text was an emoji and a question mark. That's all. The emoji was a bomb. A tiny little bomb followed by a question mark. Any guesses, sir?"

"Terrorism? A drone strike?" Winston lifted his cleft chin in consideration. "Not sure what you're playing at."

"Blown," Knox said. "She's worried she might have been blown. Discovered."

"I am aware of the expression, John."

"Yeah, well, so the thing is, the only reason she would involve me is because she doesn't trust her communication lines with you. She knows what kind of events a text like that sets into motion. She will send me an abort the moment she's in the clear. She hasn't done that, meaning she's not in the clear."

Winston looked as if he'd been sucker-punched.

"You're paying attention," Knox said.

"No reason to be rude, John. Hungry yet?"

Knox reached to refill his coffee but was beaten to it by a pair of arms leaning over his shoulder. *This could become habit-forming,* he thought. He addressed the man connected to the coffee urn, requested four eggs, sunny-side up, dry wheat toast, lean ham and smoked salmon.

"I can't trace calls. Rutherford Risk can, so I called Sarge, but no joy. I wanted access to the company's Digital Services department. There's a tech there, Vinay Kamat. Vinay will do anything for me. But not this time. He stonewalled me."

"No one likes being stonewalled."

"You see? I knew I should come here, straightaway. If it's your op, Mr. Winston, then you can request whatever you want from tech services, including putting a source on the text sent to me to confirm beyond a doubt it was from Grace."

"She's fine." The deep voice came from behind Knox. It belonged to David Dulwich. Prior to joining Brian Primer's security firm, he'd been Knox's supervisor for contractor work based out of Kuwait. In recent years, Dulwich had hired Knox on a freelance basis to perform dead drops or kidnapping extractions. Most recently, Dulwich had betrayed Knox and Grace during the Istanbul op, something nearly but not entirely forgiven by Knox.

"What the hell?" Knox barked at Dulwich. "You're tracking my reservations now?"

"I look out for my friends," Dulwich said. He sat down and waited to be served. "Don't read too much into it."

"Where is she? Did you hear what I told him about her text? A bomb and a question mark." He closed his eyes to calculate. "Ten, maybe eleven hours ago." Knox paused. "You got the same text, didn't you?"

In the silence, though, Knox reconsidered. Among Dulwich's many skills, he was completely unreadable, even by a close friend and associate like Knox. "No, you didn't. And why would that be, one might ask." He directed this to Winston.

"I'm merely an observer at this point," Winston said. "Carry on."

"You want to tell him?" Knox asked Dulwich.

"John's implying Grace wouldn't contact me if she feared she'd been blown because it might compromise the op if traced to me or, God forbid, you, sir."

"Ah!" Winston said.

"Loyal to a fault," Knox said. "That's our Grace. Contacts me because I have nothing to do with anything you two are up to. Me, because if her text is traced, the trouble stays away from you, and she knows I can handle it."

"If you say so," Dulwich said.

"So? What now? You call Vinay. We get her twenty and you or I, or both of us for that matter, hunt her down and get her out of whatever hellhole you have her in. Why? Because that's what she'll expect."

Dulwich sat stoically. The kind of stoicism Knox had no room for. Not when this tired, this concerned.

"Kenya," Dulwich said. "The op is in Kenya."

"She wouldn't leave me hanging like that. I should have gotten a second text. Something. Anything."

"It is disturbing," Dulwich said. "Not alarming. Not yet, but disturbing. We both know there are a hundred reasons for it — dead phone battery, loss of reception, loss of phone — none of which are worth getting too worked up over."

"Ten, eleven hours."

"Understood. But, John, it's the first I've heard of it. Give me a moment, would you?"

"You wouldn't take my call! You'd have heard of it sooner if —"

"Easy!"

"Primer wouldn't give me the time of day. Kenya? What the fuck?"

Dulwich had a gnarly, road-rash kind of face. It looked as if some of his medals for heroism might have been pinned to his right cheek at one point. The scars were, in fact, the result of field sutures and subsequent skin grafts to repair fourth-degree burns over 60 percent of his body. Knox had dragged the man from a burning truck cab in the middle of a desert; that act of selflessness hung between them always, like something ready to detonate.

"It's a solo op," Knox said. "That's fine. It's Grace, so it's mostly forensic accounting. Help me out here."

"You're doing fine on your own. No reason to panic, John," Dulwich said. "I should have taken your call. Mea culpa."

"I can't take another Istanbul, Sarge. We put that behind us. You fuck with me now and we've got problems, you and me. Big problems."

"The two of you need a moment? I can leave the room."

The eggs were delivered.

"Well, maybe not." Winston stabbed a piece of sausage and stacked on a slice of tomato. He lifted it to his lips but did not take a bite.

"I have many resources within the government," he said, "including Number Ten, if I must play that card. I'd rather not. My contacts are not without substantial resources in Nairobi."

"Is that a double negative?" Knox asked. Some egg yolk leaked from his lips. He wiped it with a starched and ironed piece of cloth. "Are you talking about British Intelligence? Bring 'em on. Let's trace that text."

Winston gave no acknowledgment. He might not have heard.

"We'll await this evening's contact," Dulwich said. "She'll post on one of two websites. Nothing coded or tricky, just a post to let us know she's still going good."

"Every night? Did she post last night?"

Dulwich wasn't pleased. "Solar flares or something. Murphy's Law, right? We'll give it the rest of the day."

"Not I. No way. A bomb with a question mark. What was she into?"

"Is," Dulwich emphasized.

"You don't know that. We don't know that. *Is,* if we're lucky. If we're fast. *Was,* if

29

we're slow to respond. You know the drill, Sarge."

"Hello?" Winston said. "I do not know the drill. Please."

"John believes she's been abducted, which would explain, to his way of thinking, both the text sent to him and our not hearing from her last night."

"But we were told —"

"Yes. Tanzania, all the way up to Israel. A satellite failure or something."

"I'm listening through Grace's ears and I'm not hearing what I want." Knox drank more of the coffee. *Who could make a cup of coffee this good in their home?* he wondered, envying Winston's wealth. Odd, that wasn't his way. "If she's blown, then by whom? Cops? Spooks? Mob? The original job was . . . ?"

Knox worked on the smoked salmon while keeping his eyes on Dulwich.

5

"Last year I made a donation," Winston said, "of over a million pounds to fund measles vaccinations at the Oloitokitok Clinic in southern Kenya. The clinic is privately funded. It services a sizable geographical area, including northern Tanzania. There's a long version if you want. But you strike me as an impatient man, John. So. About two months ago, data started coming in showing we had made one hell of a lot of people extremely ill with our vaccine. We now suspect the original measles vaccine was stolen in shipment and replaced with one to prevent leptospirosis in cattle. We caused meningitis, lung infections and quite possibly worse. We were told that in all probability the original vaccine was resold out of country at a high price, and that the cash funded terrorism. I sent Grace to find out where my money went, who took it and, if possible, to undermine whoever stole it. If

31

the clinic is directly or indirectly involved with terrorism, then it's also connected to the poaching of elephant tusk and rhino horn, another pet peeve of mine. I want that made public."

"Follow the money," Knox said. "Her specialty. By 'undermine,' you mean get it back."

"Yes."

"You asked her to steal money from terrorists." Knox grimaced. "Nothing risky about that. You know her," he said accusingly to Dulwich. "Shit!"

Silence.

Knox addressed Dulwich. "Her daily reports?"

"Not reports. Just confirmation she was on the right track. Two sites to check for posts. If one, things were moving. The other, a setback. Two weeks ago, the clinic shut its doors unexpectedly and without explanation. It was empty, all equipment gone, within days."

"She scared someone," Knox said.

"Indeed," Winston said.

"And you honestly believe she hasn't been kidnapped or killed? Jesus, Sarge."

Dulwich twitched. "It could be coincidence. However unlikely."

"She turned over a rock and the bugs ran

for cover," Knox said. "I don't buy you had her working in a vacuum. Why no calls? Grace can encrypt anything."

"Metadata," Dulwich said. "The call, sure. But not the origin or destination tagged onto that call."

"Kenya is a place of corruption by degrees, John," Winston said. "Phone lines. Airwaves. The Internet." He shook his head. "We all agreed up front: it wasn't worth the risk."

"The first forty-eight," Knox said, referring to the critical hours after a kidnapping.

"Not there yet. It's not a kidnapping," Dulwich said. "It's not anything. It's a fucking solar flare knocking out the Internet."

"Because you're prescient."

"Because I only heard of this text ten minutes ago. The Internet being down, that's for real, John."

"She's been blown."

"We don't know that."

"We're going after her, you and I, Sarge. That's what we do. If we're wrong, we get a round-trip on our host here. But we're not wrong."

"I'm out," Dulwich said. "We — Rutherford — did a thing there, not even a year ago. Pissed off the Chinese — those guys are so in bed in Kenya that they've got monogrammed pillows. I'm tagged — no good. They have facial recognition at Jomo Kenyatta. Lots of terrorism they're dealing with. I might make it into the country from the Ugandan side, but that'll take days. A week, maybe. It's overland shit."

"How convenient! When I just happen to be available."

"You don't put an operative in jeopardy by running after him or her. If Grace is nearly blown, the worst thing we can do is show up looking for her."

Knox knew it was true, but was loath to admit it. *How could Sarge sit there so calmly?* he wondered. How could these two not see the obvious? She'd thrown up a smoke signal and they were turning a blind eye. Her letter warmed in his pocket.

"Fuck," he said. "I'm going down there. Today. Now. If you hear from her tonight, fine. I'll ride a giraffe or whatever one does in Nairobi, and return in a day or two. Agreed?"

"Our people can look into it, John. No need for that," Winston said.

"British Intelligence? And you don't want me giving her away? Tell him, Sarge."

Dulwich looked trapped. He wasn't one to play lapdog. He'd pop a nun in the nose

34

if she held out on him. But a client as important, as wealthy and powerful, as Graham Winston kept Sarge on a short leash.

"You know the sign in the petrol station window?" Winston said in his buttery accent. "Ten bob an hour. Twelve, if you watch—"

"Fifteen if you help," Knox said. "Yeah. Ha-ha. So, I'm paying twelve. I'll take a look, and then I'll turn tail. No spooks. Don't do that to her."

"What exactly would you need?" Winston asked.

"A full download." He addressed Dulwich. "I'm assuming tech services is tracking her mobile, her movement. If not her mobile, then her log-ins. Expenses? Credit cards?"

"Cash," Dulwich said.

Winston took a neat bite of toast. "It's toxic there, John. Corrupt police. The military, government, wildlife service, health care . . . there are degrees of corruption in every institution."

"You sent her in alone," Knox said to Dulwich.

"For computer work, John. Follow the money, like you said."

"And you thought, what, she'd just sit around her hotel room?" Indignant, Knox spat out pieces of food unintentionally as he spoke. "You know her! She's been sucking up to you for two years! She wants to run the company someday! So, one or both of you provided her with local contacts and connections. I'll need that same information, exactly what she got."

Knox looked down at his plate; he was eating off china, with actual silverware, and where was Grace? Tied up in some Kenyan warehouse? "I need to get down there." He pushed back his chair and stood. "I'll stay away from her, contact only the people you trusted, but I need that list. Hotels you may have recommended, restaurants. Bars. Coffee shops. I don't care. Anything. Everything."

Now Knox spoke directly to Dulwich. "My flight shouldn't originate from here, just in case she's already talked. Route me through Frankfurt. A puddle jumper to Berlin. Berlin to Nairobi. All separate tickets, no code sharing. Paid for on my company card. I go in on business. Same as always: I'm on a buying trip."

Dulwich nodded. He spoke to Winston. "As you know, John's business is . . . world arts and crafts. Import/export. It gives him good cover in situations like this."

Sarge was coming around to Knox's way of thinking. Knox kept the smile off his face.

"If and when I track her down, I will stay away from her and whatever she's chasing. I get a visual and I'm back on the plane. She'll never know I was there. To everyone else, I'll be my usual annoying self, a two-bit hack looking for some Maasai necklaces. If they run a background check, I'll pass with flying colors."

Dulwich glanced at Winston, who nodded. "I'm counting on her making contact tonight, but I don't disagree with you."

Another double negative, Knox thought.

"I'll make every effort to enter from the west," Dulwich said. "We'll set up a web code."

"Every name you gave her, and in the same order," Knox said, repeating himself. "All I've got is her footsteps."

6

The smells hit her first. Dust. Sticks. Dry grass. A bitter taste, staining her mouth.

It took her some time to come to grips with what had happened, to realize the taste was left over from whatever drug he'd stabbed into her. She was sore, but didn't bother checking for a bruise. Instead, she focused on an undulating reddish brown line a foot in front of where her cheek lay on the powdery dirt.

Safari ants. The column of workers was an inch wide, protected on the outside by an interwoven network of sentries a half-inch thick.

Grace sat up slowly, overcome with aches and pains. She must have been thrown from the vehicle. She wiped mascara from under her eyes and searched for the Jeep. But she saw only endless savanna.

Why was she waking up at all? If someone wanted to kill her, why not just do it? Why dump her instead?

She took in the sameness of the savanna, which stretched before her, an endless plain of auburn grasses, stunted trees and coiling shrubs. In the distance, smooth gray hills rose slowly to join verdant mountains. The expanse left her feeling inconsequential and meaningless.

Her few safari rides had instilled in her a respect for the scope of the African bush. Open, unfenced space to the horizon. Wild animals, elegant and bold. But that had been from the cushy backseat of a Land Cruiser, a thermos of tea within easy reach. She recognized immediately that there might not be any kind of structure for a hundred kilometers in any direction. Somewhere in the distant mountains stood Ol Donyo Lodge, where she was currently a registered guest. But where exactly? How many days on foot would it take to reach those hills?

There had to be an explanation for her current situation. Was she a victim of an accident? Had the truck hit a ditch? An animal? Had she hit her head in the collision and wandered off into the bush? Her short-term memory was fleeting and confused.

She would sort out the cause later. An

aboriginal instinct was spreading from her belly through her chest and into her extremities.

Two days earlier, while being guided in the Solio reserve in the north, she'd found herself uninterested in the big game, but fascinated by her guide and driver, a Maasai in full tribal costume. He'd been willing to indulge her.

"On one's own," Olé, the guide, had told her, "a stranger to the bush won't last a single night."

"But the Maasai," she'd countered. "You have lasted thousands of years."

"It is true. We have lived here, hunted here, survived here, for thousands — tens of thousands — of years. We have learned from our forefathers. We can survive for weeks, months."

"Teach me."

"Excuse me, Miss Grace?"

"Olé, we see a rhino and he runs away. Giraffe, busy with eating. We spend forty minutes driving dusty trails searching for a lion that I honestly, sincerely, do not want to disturb. I feel in the way here. I'm intruding. Please, tell me about your life, the lives of your tribesmen. Help me understand the humans in this place."

He'd started with the obvious: what to eat

— roots, mostly. But not all! Particular berries for particular purposes; how to find water; methods to prevent bug bites and to treat those that bite anyway. Set snares. Take shelter. Avoid being stalked and hunted by jackals and cats. Some of the information was new; some similar to lessons given by her grandmother while tending their family farm in central China.

Safari guests were constantly cautioned to never leave the vehicle without instruction to do so. When allowed, Grace had always been accompanied by a guide. Cape buffalo were the animals most feared. Not rhino or jackal or hyena. Not elephant. Cape buffalo were known to charge without provocation. The safari vehicles were reinforced and fitted with roll bars and all manner of defense, but out of the vehicle? That was another story. She was one woman, one small woman, alone in the bush and with no form of self-defense.

Grace's thoughts circled back, unable to let go of the need to understand what had gotten her here. It had been nearly four weeks since she'd arrived to investigate Winston's bad vaccine. During that time she'd felt little if any personal threat. Her most recent visit had been to an NGO called Larger Than Life, not the type of people to dump you in the bush.

Her only reasonable concern had been the discovery, days earlier, of someone attempting to breach her computer. Though a virtually impossible task, it had been enough to scare her, to put her on the move.

She reviewed the past few weeks, looking for a misstep. She'd begun with interviews of the activist, the old reporter. She'd moved on to some early success behind her computer — she'd breached a shipping company's servers. Various pieces of the investigation had begun to fit together. She'd covered her digital tracks well, had taken extra precautions — but had sent John a red flag when someone tried to hack her. She thought if there was to be trouble, it would be in Nairobi, not a tiny village on the Tanzanian border.

An animal cried in the distance, mournful and discomforting. It sounded both lonely and hungry. Grace worked to calm herself. Listening to Olé's lessons in survival was one thing; living them quite another. Surely the staff at the Ol Donyo Lodge would come looking for her when she failed to make dinner. The couple who managed the place would be worried by now. Help was on its way.

Unless . . .

Someone had obviously planned this for her. She flushed with heat. She did remember now — leaving the clinic with a new driver, one not from the lodge!

So, had they crashed? Broken down? Or had she been left here to wait for her driver's return, or dumped, left to die of exposure? Why couldn't she remember? Had her abductor intentionally left a broken-down vehicle out there somewhere to complete the fiction of her getting lost and isolated? She glanced at her phone; no service.

Grace squatted and pulled herself into a ball, arms clasped around her shins, shivering despite the heat. Her breathing was shallow, her limbs shaking, ears ringing. She pushed to calm herself. She'd gone into shock. She needed water; there was none. She closed her eyes, steadied her breathing. She reminded herself she'd been raised in the rice fields of central China. She'd faced her share of exposure to the elements. Snakes. Wild dogs. Equally wild neighbors. She'd been through boot camp with the People's Liberation Army; had eaten grubs and worms. During her service in Army Intelligence, she'd been trained to survive and escape captivity. She'd scored higher than any woman before her. She was no

U.S. Navy SEAL, but she was no Shanghai shopper, either.

No time for hysterics. Think, plan, act.

As the sun tracked, she would know east from west, north from south. Nighttime presented the greatest risks. Her bodily odors would betray her. Olé had been clear about that: her prey would smell her first.

If not an accident, she'd been dumped with the intention of killing her. Whoever was responsible wanted it to look accidental. Attacked and eaten. Stung. Bitten. Exposure. She couldn't believe that her return trip to the conservation group, Larger Than Life, had caused her situation. Someone had caught up to her there, or had gotten ahead of her and had been waiting. The thought sent a chill through her.

Her real hope remained with John. How long until he acted on that text she'd sent? How effective would the crumbs she'd been leaving since the start of the trouble prove to be? Crumbs too complex for a stranger to decipher, and no piece of cake for Knox, but solid nonetheless.

Another unexplainable chill swept through Grace. Another slow, controlled breath helped her overcome it. None of it mattered. She had only herself to save her. No daydreaming. No false hope. No reliance

on the abstract. One hour at a time.
Think. Plan. Act.

7

Guuleed's lanky frame belied his ferocity. Not only did he possess physical strength, he had the mental fortitude it took to lead a roughshod band of wannabe bandits. He naturally spoke in a growl, the result of years of Turkish cigarettes, hollering orders and a general indifference to others.

He flicked ash out of where there had once been a car door.

The camp consisted of six tents, the largest of which served as the mess. They were tucked side by side along the fever tree-lined banks of a stream of muddy water. It could be easily forded in the trucks. The idea was to present the image of a safari camp, since they did business as one. They ordered supplies, bought fuel and water under the company name. With over four hundred safari operators in Kenya, no one could track them all.

Guuleed's company not only served his

poaching needs but served to launder money by inventing twenty to thirty paying guests each night and reporting much of the phantom income.

"The ambush wasn't coincidence," he told Rambu, his first lieutenant. The two men occupied the front seat of a battered Land Cruiser riddled with bullet holes along its right side. The gas tank had been patched with fiberglass earlier in the day. The vehicle reeked of the fumes. As the sun pushed for the horizon, bugs of all kinds took flight. The threat of malaria flew with them.

Rambu, a brute of a man with near purple skin and a face that had seen too much sun, did not speak. His droopy eyes gave him the look of a young Sylvester Stallone, which accounted for his mispronounced nickname. He knew better than to question Guuleed. His boss had been in a bilious mood of late.

They stood out of the shade, in the direct sunlight, where the insects weren't quite as plentiful. Rambu's acne-scarred face, wide shoulders and massive thighs had helped him earn his position as Guuleed's pit bull, when in fact he was more kind-hearted than his men knew.

"Find me a traitor. Doesn't matter who. You pick." Guuleed intended to send a message to his men about loyalty and leaking information to Koigi and his rangers. His only real concern had little to do with poaching or his men, or even loyalty. His beautiful wife and their six children had been made bargaining chips. "Xin Ha is holding me responsible for the closing of the health clinic."

"Clear down in Oloitokitok? You? Responsible, how?"

"It's believed I overlooked a warning. Completely false. I believe it's because we were sloppy killing Faaruq and the others. They died in the same manner. That will cost us. The clinic's closing hurt Xin Ha mightily. He lost money; he lost an important piece of cover for the exports. You tell the men any of this, I'll cut your tongue out."

"Yes, boss."

"If I do not fix this, my family will be killed."

"Animals! The fucking Chinese!"

"I need tusks, a shitload of tusks. And I need them now. No more traitors short-changing me. Things are going to get bad. Handle it."

Guuleed climbed into the Land Cruiser and watched in the cracked mirror as Rambu called four others to his side and spoke in confidence. Together, these five men singled out a young man named Jakmar and dragged him backward, kicking and screaming. He was stabbed deeply in both thighs, his wrists and ankles bound, his tied hands looped over the tow ball of a Jeep. Rambu and another man dragged him out of camp behind the vehicle, his cries carrying for a full minute until fading to a faint whine that matched the buzz of the insects. He would be dumped, bleeding, a few kilometers away. Stripped to bone by morning. The bush was not a place to be alone at night.

Guuleed looked on with indifference. One did what one had to do. He had liked Jakmar, felt badly that fate should deal the man such a hand.

The others had turned their backs following the first glint of a knife. They pretended not to hear the man's pleas, his proclamation of innocence. One of them, Guuleed thought, knew he should have been the one killed, unless Rambu had made a lucky guess. One of them would not sleep well tonight, or the next. Within two to three days the real traitor would reveal himself in this way, and then he, too, would meet a similar fate.

Guuleed unclipped the cumbersome satellite phone as it rang. CALLER UNKNOWN was displayed on the screen. Not to Guuleed.

"Big Five Safaris," he said, speaking English with difficulty.

He was told an American had been added last minute to Eastland Safari's private list and was scheduled to arrive on an eleven P.M. flight from Berlin. The arrangement had come from England, just like the whore's. The parallel was uncanny and could not be taken as coincidence. Such information was expensive and could always be trusted.

Ending the call, awaiting Rambu's return, Guuleed smoked a cigarette and cursed. If he'd buried Faaruq instead of trying to send a message, none of this would be happening. He had only himself to blame. He thought of home, fought the fear that he would soon receive a package containing his child's hand or foot — or worse.

He needed a good kill, at least ten kilos of ivory; half that of rhino horn would do, though rhino hunting was a much more difficult and risky operation. A good deal of bribery and perfect timing would be required to nail two on the same night.

The tobacco heightened his impatience and tested his already sour mood. His men were locals, mostly poor and desperate to feed their families. A few were simply greedy. Collectively they were bad shots, slow learners and big dreamers. The worst. But Guuleed worked with them daily to improve their skills.

His impatience turned into a kind of hot tar that ran through him as deep-seated anger. Give him a posse of well-trained Somalis and bagging a couple of elephants would be child's play. That would get Xin Ha off his back. As it was, he had to deal with the blood-hungry Koigi, who had well-trained men . . . and a cause. Fucking causes could kill you.

Rambu returned, looking feverish. "It's done."

"I must take a meeting with Xin. The balls on that one! You will come with me to Nairobi and speak to our man in the one-four."

"The senior sergeant?" Rambu sounded doubtful. "Is that wise?"

"There's an American coming in. I told you it was getting bad. We need him gone. It can't attract attention. The sergeant will help us. You'll see to it." Guuleed didn't hold subordinates by the hand, but by the scruff of the neck. Rambu had to step up. "You, me and two you trust. Our best shots.

51

Two vehicles. I will make the call and confirm we're on our way." He squeezed the satellite phone tightly in his hand. "Keep watch for the real traitor. He will expose himself before midday tomorrow."

"Yes. Of course."

"Take care of it the moment you know. Something the others won't forget."

Guuleed praised Allah, and Rambu did so along with him. Guuleed could smell something on the wind. The dead man's blood.

8

Knox took Nairobi's dismal airport as a harbinger of what was to come. Immigration control looked like a row of tollbooths with hand-painted signs for RESIDENTS and NON-RESIDENTS. Baggage claim was a low-ceilinged space with a poured concrete floor and two rusted, noisy luggage conveyors. A pair of plywood booths at the far end advertised LOST LUGGAGE and VISITOR INFORMATION. He saw lines at both.

Knox hadn't checked a bag. He walked past bone-weary tourists recovering from the nine-hour flight who stood now, waiting for bags. Knox hated waiting. Hated misplacing things, not for the fool it made him feel like but for the time wasted in trying to find them again. Put it back where it belongs and it's there the next time. If he ever had kids, he intended to tell them that.

He intended to spend time in the backyard with them, too. To read to them before bed and make sure they ate as a family every night. Music. Movies. A love and respect for all things living. A garden, maybe. A lawn for sure.

I find in my heart both something missing and something fulfilling. Grace's words, not his.

He thought about her then, imagined where she was at this moment. Held in a room? The back of a van? He hoped she'd gone to ground. Situations changed abruptly in the field. A broken phone wouldn't explain forty-eight hours of radio silence, but maybe she'd worked her way into an inner circle of Winston's enemies and didn't dare risk communication. Maybe she was traveling with people suspicious of her. Maybe her phone had been confiscated.

Grace had good instincts and tremendous nerve. More nerve than brains, which worried him, given how smart she was. He wanted, needed, her back.

"Here's the deal. My brother is the most important person in my life." His words, not hers.

"Mister!" A tug on Knox's jacket. "Did you check a bag?" A boy who looked no older than twelve. Boot-black skin. Leviathan eyes. A face adorable enough to win tips, but deceptively ageless. Twelve, four-

54

teen, going on twenty. He topped out halfway between Knox's navel and collarbone.

Knox kept walking, never breaking stride.

The kid wore an oversized orange vest with reflective stripes on the side. Rubber flip-flops clapped the concrete. A piece of string bunched his shorts at the hips.

"This way," the boy said, tugging on Knox's wrist.

Knox flicked him off. "Don't touch!"

The boy held up his hands. It was all part of the act. *I mean no harm — poor innocent me! I want only to pick your pocket and leave with your wallet.* Knox knew the boy's cousin in Tunisia, his second cousin in Amman. Take a number.

"Other green line is here," the boy said, indicating a guarded doorway to their left that had no line. Overlapping safari posters and hotel advertisements served as wallpaper, occupying all available wall space. Knox was familiar with third-world rules, could play by them most of the time. Now he regretted not speaking Swahili.

The busy green exit — NOTHING TO DECLARE — lay straight ahead. Arriving passengers were being checked, their carry-ons searched, despite the green. Knox had nothing to fear from an inspection, but for him waiting in line was right up there with misplacing things. More time wasted.

"He's a friend of mine," the boy told Knox, pointing to a uniformed man, off on his own, guarding another exit from the terminal.

"Is that right?"

"His second wife's son and I go to Sunday school together."

"Sure you do. And you're both in AP Chemistry."

"Please?"

"You're saying he'll let me through?" Grace would handle a kid like this better, he thought. She knew how to say no and mean it.

The boy reached for Knox, reconsidered and, instead, waved him ahead and to his left. "Think about it. How do I get a tip if I make trouble for you, mister? That's not good business."

Knox laughed and turned some heads. Knox didn't do many things small. "A tip, is it?"

The kid signaled to the uniformed meathead. The guard opened the gates for Knox. Knox passed through without incident.

"Eastland Safari. This is correct?"

"Excuse me?" Knox grabbed the kid by the arm, spinning him. He'd misjudged the

56

boy's weight. He turned him hard. Some heads turned. Knox released the boy. "Go away! We're done here."

"Through there. An Eastland driver is waiting, holding a sign with your name." The boy pointed to a frequent-flyer tag on Knox's overnighter that identified him by name.

"What?" Knox said, taking a moment to process that the boy was thinking two steps ahead.

"You want my help, or you want me to leave?" the boy said.

Knox laughed quietly. "You can go now. Thank you."

"Maybe you need a guide in Nairobi. A driver. A woman."

"Maybe you should be in school."

"I'm Bishoppe." He pointed again to the man holding a folded newspaper with Knox's name written in marker across it.

Knox scanned the crowd. Eyes came at him from everywhere. He was entering a country where he was a different color and bigger than the average. People noticed. Knox was used to it. He'd learned to distinguish quickly between random curiosity and pointed interest.

Now he singled out two men in particular who were working hard to ignore him.

Fished two U.S. dollars from his pocket. "Sorry, no shillings yet."

"Dollars. Euros. Shillings. No problem, mister. You need to change to shillings? I can get you the best rate!"

Smirking, Knox handed the boy the money, feeling two dollars was too much, yet somehow not enough.

"Welcome to Kenya, Mr. Knox. Please, enjoy your stay."

"Bishoppe," he caught him by the arm, this time far more gently. "Tell me, is there a car park outside?"

"Of course."

"A taxi stand?"

"To the right, sir. But you already have a driver."

Knox pulled out another five dollars. He didn't like the looks of the two men keeping tabs on him. Belatedly, he snapped off the frequent-flyer tag. His brother, Tommy, must have strapped it on. Answering a sign with his name on it wasn't the best course of action, he thought. Maybe Winston had failed to call off British Intelligence; maybe in Kenya guys like this just stood around waiting for guys like him.

"Tell a taxi to pull around to the far side of the car park. The driver is to wait five minutes. If I don't show, he can keep the five dollars." He gave Bishoppe an additional two dollars for his trouble. It disappeared into a pocket. Knox studied the kid, liking him. "Don't run off with the money. Don't burn me on this."

Knox walked past his driver. He and Bishoppe split as they started out of the building. One of the two men interested in him followed Knox. Another got on the phone, his back turned.

Outside, drivers for hire, hucksters and families waited on a concrete road divider. They wore Western dress — the men, business informal; the youngsters, jeans; the women, dresses and skirts. A mood of excited anticipation hung in the warm air.

Knox coughed against the blue exhaust that snorted from tailpipes. The roar of jets taking off covered the sounds of vehicles. The people in conversation were like actors in a silent movie. Cigarette smoke spiraled from pursed lips; the clouds hid eyes bloodshot with fatigue.

A few lights shone from high atop concrete poles, spreading a canary glow across rows of late-model vehicles crushed together in an overcrowded parking lot. The driver holding his name in his hands called out curiously, "Mr. Knox?"

Again, Knox cursed his height and skin

color. The driver caught up and asked for a second time. He was small, late forties, with graying hair at his temples. He wore gray slacks and a white shirt that had started the day pressed. Knox told him to keep moving and to keep up.

"You drive for Eastland?" Knox said, naming the safari company Winston was using as a liaison.

"Ten years."

"Did you drive the Chinese woman?"

"Yes. Of course."

"Her hotel?"

"I am to take you to the guesthouse, not the Sarova Stanley."

"You will do exactly that," Knox said. "Open the boot like you're putting my bag inside, but drop it and kick it aside. Then get behind the wheel and drive to the guesthouse."

"I drive you."

"Not exactly. You will drive, but I won't be with you."

The man trailing him had been stopped by traffic from crossing the access road. This was no longer just curiosity. He was being followed. He assessed his surroundings. There were two service vans in the lot. Both were tall enough to conceal a crouching Knox.

He spotted Bishoppe talking heatedly to a taxi driver across the busy one-way service road. Could he trust this kid? Over the years of buying and selling in third-world countries, he'd dealt with hundreds of such boys. A nickel for a favor; a dollar for a treat; they'd pick your pocket or steal your bag if given the chance.

"You would like me to call in?" The driver pulled his flip phone from his pocket. "You wish to speak to Tina?"

"Do this just as you would any pickup," Knox said, reaching into his pocket. "Tell me which is your car. No pointing please."

The man described a silver hatchback.

"No need for that, sir!" Offended by Knox's reaching for a tip.

"I'm being watched. Two men, maybe more. One on the phone. They picked me out as I approached you at arrivals."

"You stand quite tall. Police have many questions these days. Many eyes here at the airport. Troubling times, as I'm sure you are aware."

"The bombings," Knox said.

"Exactly. Nairobi is most dangerous at night, Mr. Knox. For you, very dangerous."

"The trunk. Leave my bag. Then drive out of the car park and off to the guesthouse. If they follow you, would they normally see me get out upon arrival?"

"No. There is a gate. A guard. I will drive inside."

"Excellent. Please thank the Barr-Latners for their generosity. I will contact them in the morning." Winston had arranged the husband-and-wife safari guiding service to look after him; Knox had not expected to be a guest in their home.

"My card." The driver passed it to Knox surreptitiously. "You may call at any hour."

They went through the ritual of pretending to put the bag into the back. Knox walked to the far side, kicking his bag farther afield. He opened the door, ducked and closed the door as if he'd gotten in. Then, bag in hand, he slipped behind the adjacent van and began to move, his heart racing. He stayed low and reached the second van, remained in the crouch as he hurried out the far side of the parking lot.

The taxi was waiting. Knox tossed his bag and followed it inside.

"The Sarova Stanley plea—"

His satchel lay firmly in the grasp of Bishoppe, who smiled broadly back at him. Bishoppe rattled off a series of directions to the driver in Swahili. Turning to Knox, he spoke, grinning. "We will avoid the highway. Traffic into the city is very bad this time of night. Too many trucks." The boy shouted something more to the driver in Swahili. The taxi charged off.

Knox leaned back and stole a look into the parking lot. The hired car had pulled up to the exit gate. He'd lost sight of the two men. But the pang of nerves remained, as did more questions than he could answer.

"National Police," the boy said. "The two men."

Impressed, Knox nonetheless didn't speak.

"You are a criminal?"

"Far from it."

"Police?"

"You weren't invited. Here. The taxi."

"I did you a favor. Why are National Police waiting for you?"

"They weren't. Mind your own business."

"I think maybe you are my business."

Knox suppressed a grin and turned toward the window.

The overcrowded, narrow roads were in a state of decay. Axle-wreckers. It was nearing midnight, yet a seemingly endless migration of people on foot filled either side of every road, the men in dark trousers and T-shirts, the women in skirts and colorful tops. Backpacks. Purses.

Knox asked the kid about the boxy vans

that outnumbered all other vehicles. Called *matatus*, they were commuter buses packed with fifteen to twenty in a seating arrangement meant for nine.

Day-Glo-vested motorcyclists serving as single-passenger taxis weaved through the slow-moving traffic. Where traffic in Shanghai had struck Knox as choreographed, Nairobi felt more like a slugfest. Why couldn't Winston have donated money to a clinic in San Diego?

The roads lacked streetlamps, were lit only by vehicles and the glow from billboards and shop signs along the route. Their taxi driver took back streets as he and the boy argued, his eyes periodically finding Knox in the rearview mirror.

Downtown Nairobi still retained some of its British colonial character, the art of marrying landscape to architecture. Almost every city block offered a stark contrast between poverty and affluence, a confused, schizophrenic identity.

The taxi pulled to the curb. A bellman opened Knox's door and welcomed him. The air smelled better here. Knox was about to pay the driver when Bishoppe snatched the cash from his hand, snapped off a ten-dollar bill and handed it to the driver, who argued loudly. The boy returned the rest of

Knox's cash with a huff, saying the driver was a greedy thief.

Knox paid the kid five dollars out on the sidewalk, believing it a small fortune to the boy, and thanked him.

"What time tomorrow?" Bishoppe asked.

"There is no tomorrow. We're all done here."

"There is always tomorrow," the boy said. He shook Knox's hand heartily. Despite the childlike look of the boy's frayed shorts and broken flip-flops, Bishoppe's composure struck Knox as businesslike and solicitous.

"You need pharmacy? Liquor? Woman? Phone card?" the boy called over his shoulder.

"Jack of all trades," Knox said, smiling. A fourteen-year-old pimp.

"You like to gamble?" the kid said, misunderstanding.

"SIM card." Knox showed him his mobile. "At least two hundred megs of data."

"Twenty, U.S."

Knox gave him ten. "I'll wait in the lobby. Make it fast." The boy took off like Usain Bolt.

"Was this boy bothering you, sir?" the bellman asked.

"No, no. I'm fine. He's fine. You know him? See him around?"

The man gave Knox an insulted look. Knox didn't push it.

The luxury hotel shut the ragtag world out. Knox might have been in any city. The lobby exuded an old-world pretense; the service was overdone. At the front desk, Knox withheld any questions about Grace's stay. Night shift; they wouldn't know.

He ate dinner at the bar amid lingering business suits and low-cut dresses. Bishoppe returned with his SIM card and no change. Knox said goodbye; Bishoppe, "See you later."

9

Knox slept for five hours and awoke to a smudge of pink dawn in a charcoal sky. Using the new phone chip, he sent a text of an airplane emoji to Dulwich. That would give Dulwich his private number.

While he awaited a thermos of coffee, he used the television to go online, accessing his own company's catalogue and account information. At 3 A.M., Dulwich's alias had ordered a Jade Buddha. At 3:05 A.M., the order had been canceled.

A bubble — of what? Fear? Anxiety? — lodged in Knox's throat: Grace had failed to make contact for the second night in a row. He spent thirty minutes doing sit-ups and stretches in front of BBC News and then took a long, very hot shower. He had Winston's prioritized list of trusted contacts. He also had a sinking feeling in his gut.

He left messages — with a journalist; an activist; several environmental NGOs; the

British embassy — referring to himself as a small-business owner who was friends with Graham Winston. Then he waited for his phone to ring.

A journalist named Bertram Radcliffe invited him to lunch at the Jockey Pub at the Hilton. Knox loaded up on shillings from a lobby ATM and used the hotel's back street doors. As he turned toward the Hilton Tower, the sound of light-footed flip-flops approached at high speed. Knox stepped aside at the last minute and grabbed the boy by the arm.

"Bishoppe," he said, swinging the boy before getting a look at him, "I thought we had an agreement." He set him down to his right and continued walking. The boy caught his breath and tugged up his shorts. A motorcycle's roar cut the air.

"You would like a tour. Safari, maybe? I can get you a driver very cheap."

"Go back to the airport. Find another tourist. I work alone."

The boy struggled to match him stride for stride. Looking back at him, Knox saw his brother, Tommy, laboring to keep up in the early days of their brotherhood, long before Knox fully understood Tommy's challenges. Carefree kids. No yesterday. No tomorrow.

A pang of want surged through Knox, a

reflexive anger at the unfair and random nature of disease. Normalcy had escaped his brother and him at an early age. Tommy defined his life now.

Bishoppe still hadn't left. In spite of himself, Knox exploded. "Scoot! Go! I'm not buying!"

"I am not selling." The boy stopped, allowing Knox to walk on without him. "Those men at the airport," he called out, paying no attention to the passersby around them. "One was special police for certain. The other, he meets only the British arrivals."

Knox stopped. A steady procession of Kenyans spilled around him, some taking mind, some oblivious. A flag, mounted at a rising angle from a building across the street, snapped in the wind. Down on the sidewalk, there was no breeze whatsoever. Knox took in the sharp human scents; mixed in with them was the stench of burning charcoal. Everywhere he looked, he kept seeing Grace's face.

He eyed the boy, wondering what he was playing at. The two of them, staring, their gaze broken by passing pedestrians. The boy approached in fitful glimpses, postures and poses.

"He follows them out. Never greets them

himself. He speaks to his phone a lot."

"Them?"

"He works with a British High Commission driver. This man, he meets them. Never a taxi, these people, always a Land Rover. Black Land Rover or Range Rover. The special tags."

"Diplomatic tags."

"Yes. Exactly this. Sometimes more than one car. Also, sometimes security. But always this man in the terminal. The same man that followed you."

Knox regarded the child.

"I know the airport and everyone in it."

Knox understood well how small a place could and did become, how familiar one could be with a large group. He'd worked in Tiger Stadium the summer of his senior year in high school. Within weeks he'd known many of the crew by sight and dozens by name. The team remained at large, but the stadium's cleanup crew, food service, the managers, even security and a few police — Knox had considered them friends by the time school started. He didn't doubt a bored boy's ability to see things others did not, even in the chaos of Nairobi.

"The other man. Follows them for how long?"

"Sometimes a car meets him at the curb.

70

Sometimes not."

"What kind of car?"

"Mercedes? Toyota? Shit car. Old car."

"Drives himself?"

"Not always." The boy looked hurt. "You don't believe me? I try to help you and you don't believe?"

"You're playing me. Why?"

"What does this mean, 'playing'?"

Knox tried to penetrate the consuming black of the boy's eyes but found it impossible. He'd dealt with extortionists and kidnappers more easily read. He recalled the boy negotiating with him in the backseat of the taxi.

"Did this man follow me last night?"

Knox had looked for a tail, but it had been nighttime on unlit roads.

"I will help you if you want me to help. That is your choice."

Knox reached for his pocket.

"No money. Americans, it's always money. What have I done? Nothing. Look, I am not done helping you. Where is it you are going? I can watch for other men."

"No, thank you." Knox offered him twenty shillings and the boy took it.

"As you wish," Bishoppe said.

Knox thanked him and continued toward the distant hotel, all the while reading the shadows and determining the boy was still following ten yards back. Knox fought to keep from smiling. Grace would like this kid.

The Hilton, standing like a forty-story toilet paper tube atop a five-story cube of concrete, declared itself at the end of the street. A perimeter of trees was fronted by a row of parked cars. He saw a dry, scrubby-looking park to the east, the trees in need of a water truck. Knox allowed contact with a pedestrian, turned just enough to steal a look behind. The boy had made him paranoid.

He looked for anyone following. Saw nothing obvious. Ahead, more cars, and more cars still in the distance. Knox tasted the dry mouth of fatigue. He hoped like hell his gut was wrong about Grace. Tried to convince himself again that she'd had to lose the phone for self-preservation. She was smart and cunning. She had a plan. They would laugh about it all by the end of the week.

He was lying to himself.

He hated that.

10

Knox watched Bertram Radcliffe struggle from his chair to shake hands. Boyish at forty-five, the man wore a sharp blue blazer that strained around his gut, an open-necked dress shirt and khakis. His rheumy eyes were unwilling to ignore the gin and tonic on the table.

For downtown Nairobi, the pub was bizarrely British. Dark wood and leather. Tinted gel blinds pulled down over the windows. Soccer memorabilia hung side-by-side with photos of Winston Churchill.

Radcliffe carefully measured his drink and took a swig. Knox ordered a Guinness from a gorgeous African waitress, who, like all educated Kenyans, spoke English with a colonial accent. Knox thanked her. Radcliffe did not.

"You met with Grace Chu," Knox said.

"I did. Twice. Charming."

"Mr. Winston is eager to hear from her.

She's gone off the radar. She was staying at the Sarova Stanley?"

"When not traveling. She traveled a great deal. She went off my radar as well." The reporter spoke with an air of superiority. "To be honest with you, I was somewhat put off by the whole thing."

"Because?"

"She stood me up. A dinner."

"This was?"

"Three nights ago? Four, I think. The seventeenth it was."

He might as well have punched Knox in the chest.

"Not what you wanted to hear."

"No."

"To be honest with you, I'm rather relieved I'm not the only one she's stood up."

"Let's say it wasn't voluntary on her part."

"Oh, dear."

"Where would you start looking for her?"

"Don't be too concerned. People change plans, eh? Nothing untoward will happen to a Chinese woman in Kenya. For one thing, they are too important to the government; for another, you fuck with the Chinese here, they fuck you back. The Chinese have carried out enormous construction projects in exchange for mineral rights. They import their own workers. Many are lowlifes who go from the construction jobs to black-market work. They are tough blokes, the Chinese. Kenyans know this. It's hands off, believe me."

Knox nodded. He appreciated the absence of small talk. "You met with her twice. What was the context?"

"She's a lovely woman, that one." The gin was talking now. "Kind eyes. I love Asian eyes, don't you?"

Knox flexed his fist beneath the table. "You discussed?"

"A bright girl, too. You'd better hope she's not in Mathari. You'd rather she be dead than in there."

"Mathari?"

"Psychiatric hospital. Squalid. Horrifying, really. Mental health issues are often thought to be witchcraft here, which will give you some idea of what goes on there. Wouldn't wish it on anyone."

"And why would she be there?"

"This Kikuyu government, horrid people." Radcliffe leaned in over his precious drink, gripping the glass with white knuckles. "Deeply corrupt, in power far too long. They will go to any lengths, my friend, to shut up the truth. Any lengths." His voice grew strained. "Grace is investigating a crime, something involving a bad bit of vac-

75

cine. I have made a career of investigating such crimes. One must tiptoe. There could be so many involved in something like this, and all blood-related to the next — it's so damn tribal here, so incestuous. To cross it, to question it, to challenge it, is . . . believe me . . . if her disappearance is a carjacking, a ransom, then maybe you stand a chance. If she unearthed what she shouldn't have, you *won't* find her."

"But I will find her."

"You damn Americans." Radcliffe chuckled into his glass. "Don't push me. I'm meeting with you as a favor to Graham, just as I did with Grace. You are a guest, my friend. The Lord giveth, and the Lord taketh away. In this case, Lord Graham Winston."

Knox sized up Radcliffe. The man wasn't as drunk as he played. Knox saw a clear-eyed appraiser of men, a veteran journalist who lulled his prey into believing him incompetent and dulled by booze. Find the cracks in others and pry. He felt like Radcliffe was about to pick his pocket.

"Listen carefully. You may want to take notes," Radcliffe continued.

"You're going to lecture me?"

"I'm interesting. You'll enjoy it. As I told Grace, the prevailing wisdom on the vaccine's horrible side effects is a lack of refrigeration. Nothing sinister. When the clinic closed, it was assumed the government had shut it down. But the second time I saw Grace, she thought she might have found something. She asked me about a shipping company called Asian Container Consolidated. ACC all but controls the Mombasa port. Crooks, every one of them.

"Frankly, I was surprised to hear a newcomer talk about ACC. It doesn't pop up when you Google 'corrupt shipping companies in Kenya,' though it should." He squinted at Knox, thinking himself amusing. Reached for the drink, but merely spun the glass on the table. "Look, I advised her not to cross swords with ACC. It has this government's blessing. She asked about any connection, alleged or otherwise, between the health clinic and terrorism. I might have laughed aloud at that. I honestly don't recall. Expats and visitors are so eager to see terrorism in everything. It's hard for them to imagine a country formed solely around everyone-for-himself and the rest be damned. I'll tell you what I told her: Corruption rules here. Profit. Money. Greed. That's all. I've been writing about it forever. It's poison, sometimes fast-acting, sometimes slow. Is terrorism an increasing problem? Absolutely. It seeks to destabilize, and without a strong government working to defeat it — impossible with such rampant corruption — it will out. But in terms of hard evidence, there is little suggesting internal funding of terrorism."

"Her response?"

"She asked if the clinic had ever been tied to poaching."

Ever Grace, ever efficient. She'd run the list of Winston's "gets."

"And?"

"If I had a dollar for every rumor in this place. But none of them ever proves out."

"The third time, she stood you up," Knox said in a leading tone. "Did she call back to apologize?" He knew Grace.

"No. I haven't heard from her, I'm afraid."

"Did you try her?"

"Left a message at the Sarova Stanley. Was told there was no guest by that name. Perhaps I'm not memorable enough. Perhaps I slipped her mind."

Knox puzzled over Grace's possible actions. A trip she wanted kept private? Abduction? Illness?

"What one has to ask oneself," Radcliffe said, "was how a virtual stranger to this country came to inquire about ACC. That kind of specificity is extraordinary. ACC is in the middle of everything, yet it took me six months or more before I began to see the threads leading there. How did your Grace identify the company so quickly?"

Something in Knox bristled at his word choice — the idea of Grace being "his." "There's a long answer to that, but neither of us has the time. And she's not mine. You met her; she's as independent as they get."

"How sweet," said Radcliffe. "You care. I can see it all over your face."

"Your contempt for the government. Did you share that with her?"

"Let me tell you about this place, this government." Again he played with his glass, though did not drink of it. "There are over forty tribes in Kenya. Five of those tribes make up over sixty percent of the population. They have warred intermittently, mostly over arable land, for thousands, maybe tens of thousands of years. The Kikuyu hit a bit of good fortune over other tribes when we Brits arrived to colonize. Their tribe, the largest on the east coast of Africa, was physically the closest in proximity to Nairobi when we Brits stuck our flag in the soil. That meant they got the language first, the favors first, the relationships first. Ahead of all other tribes — and to much resentment. It also meant the Kikuyu were

79

first to tire of the relationship, the first to stage uprisings, the first to run Kenya once the Brits were driven out. It didn't run well. When the wheels finally came off, an international coalition put together the present government, and we all know how such arrangements work out. Take a look at the Middle East."

"You want them out of power," Knox stated.

"Think of me as the Gandhi of the printed word."

"And modest."

"I have no time for false modesty. I, and a few others, are this country's last good hope."

Knox put some shillings on the table. Before he left, he carefully wrote down the phone number of his new prepaid SIM on a bar napkin. Folded the napkin and placed it alongside Radcliffe's gin, where the man couldn't miss it.

11

Kenyan night: as dark as a throat. The few stars couldn't lift the sky from opaqueness.

Grace recalled the day, of touring the former Oloitokitok health clinic and interviewing Travis Brantingham. She remembered their discussion, her ruse to gain Ethernet access to their network, the last-minute substitution for her driver.

Tucked under a fever tree that had been overtaken by an aggressive vine, she shook from fear and the evening chill, squatting on her haunches in an attempt to keep the ants off her bottom. She fought against sleep, afraid she'd awaken to jaws tearing flesh from her bones. She hid well, but it wasn't being seen that worried her. They would smell her. They would come for her as food.

Her mind wandered, a product of the heat, dehydration or a subconscious effort to avoid the present threat by reliving the past. The plan to dispose of her had not occurred spontaneously, she thought. Her hacking had been detected.

When the conversation with Brantingham had ended, she'd climbed into a Jeep with a stranger. She'd been told her guide from the lodge had gone off on errands and would be delayed. One of the locals, a younger guy, Leebo, bone-thin with hollow eyes, had stepped in to drive her back across the savanna to Chyulu Hills and the Ol Donyo Lodge. Together, they had set off from Larger Than Life for the ninety-minute trip down a rutted dirt track back to the lodge. How quickly they'd left any sign of the village behind.

Grace remembered that drive more clearly now. She'd ridden in the open-air Toyota, marveling yet again at the lack of fences in the wide-open plain. In the distance, she saw the majesty of Kilimanjaro rising so high that its ice-topped summit looked like clouds. With the onset of evening, the rich blue sky had slowly gone pewter, silhouetting a few small hills to the west. The air blew in her face, warm and fragrant, and she'd closed her eyes for a while, savoring the solitude and the sense of timelessness. The rhythm of the rough road made her eyes heavy. As they fell, she'd had no inkling of what was to come.

When her driver, Leebo, called out, she startled awake.

"Lions! You wish to see them?" He was shouting, pointing.

"Yes, please!" Grace called — and off they went cross-country. He drove hard and fast, but the vehicle handled well. She squinted, trying to see. "Where?" she asked. He pointed. Grace still didn't see, but that was nothing new: the Maasai could spot game, could track so brilliantly, that they were nearly as entertaining as the wildlife. She held firmly to a safety handle. The vehicle rose and fell. The driver weaved through the vegetation, slower now, his head aimed down at the ground. Tracking.

"Two!" he said. "Young. One year perhaps." Grace continued scanning the open expanse of buffalo grass, cacti, sagebrush and fever trees. No sign of movement. The craggy ravines were lined with outcroppings of rock. Thick shrubs and lines of cottonwood and willows clung to the soil, fatigued by hard sun and the endless wind.

"Where?" she shouted. The driver lifted his hand only briefly from the wheel, pointed across the hood and slightly to the right. Grace still saw nothing. She looked behind. No road in sight. She'd lost track of

time. Had lost all landmarks but Kilimanjaro and the buttes. "It is getting dark," she
called.

"I know where they go. The lions. There is
a wash. A bone wash." He pointed again.
Out. Off. Away.

Several more minutes passed, and with
them a great deal of ground. "What is a
bone wash?" Grace asked. He didn't answer.

A hood of clouds had been pulled over
the savanna. With it, a false dusk. Distance
to the fever trees could no longer be easily
judged. Kilimanjaro melted into the horizon. The truck slowed and stopped. "Here!
We go here! I will bring the glasses." He
hoisted a pair of binoculars as he climbed
down from behind the wheel. Grace stood
and looked down. Her foot found the rail.
She lowered herself out.

Something sharp pricked her — a needle.

Time passed. The truck took off, the
driver back behind the wheel. "Hey!" she
called, feeling woozy. Why would he need to
move the vehicle? "Leebo!" She tried his
name. She sounded drunk. He wasn't moving the Toyota; he was leaving. "Hey! Come
back!" she shouted. Laughing; knowing it
wasn't funny. Her astonishment and disbe-
lief were overpowered by whatever he'd
injected into her. Elephant tranquilizer?

84

Ketamine?

Later, when she awoke, she remembered hardly anything. Brantingham. The clinic. A black void of drugs in her system. The wind. Insects. She clasped her arms across her chest.

If this was an attempt to kill her through exposure, to make her death look like an accident, she believed her attackers would have left a vehicle somewhere in her vicinity. The gas tank would be ruptured, a tire or two flat, the keys missing. She knew the tricks. Scuffs in the dirt leading away.

Death by exposure. She could imagine the stories now. A tourist strays from the vehicle and expires in the bush. Not the first time. Olé, her guide back when she'd been staying at Solio Lodge, had told her that every few years, a safari guest wandered out of camp, usually drunk, and didn't last the night. Between the lions, hyenas, snakes and jackals, a night in the bush was a death sentence.

The sun had just set. *A vehicle,* she thought. *Out there somewhere.*

She set a goal. She had a mission.

12

Rambu's bulk barely fit behind the wheel of the land Cruiser. His eyes may have been on the potholed road in front of them, but Guuleed felt that the man was hyperaware of his boss's presence. Guuleed's temper was as fast and unpredictable as his scrawny limbs, and his men knew it.

The vehicle, outfitted for nine including the driver, had a canvas top and fold-down windshield. Rambu had smeared mud over the line of five bullet holes in the passenger side and had otherwise cleaned the vehicle to help them blend into city traffic.

Several kilometers from Nairobi's city center, Guuleed watched the thick line of pedestrians on either side of the road. There were more people than cars. Blue exhaust rose in waves. Marketing flags on PVC poles flapped with wind from the traffic: VW, Windows 10, a supermarket. The Land Cruiser passed a fortressed shopping mall crowded with hyperclean high-end SUVs. Private drivers. A secure entrance with more uniforms than the airport. Little kids were collected in bunches beyond the eight-foot walls, their bare shoulders glistening, their laughter rising above the groan of traffic.

Guuleed's anger flashed into his chest, a slow and steady burn. Xin Ha was threatening to kill his wife and children.

"You okay, colonel?"

"Just drive." Rambu was trying to loosen him up with the "colonel" reference. He wasn't colonel of anything.

Guuleed rubbed the stump of the missing joint on his finger. Eight days until his family was to be executed. Today he had to face the Chinese bastard behind the threat. He'd been summoned like a common peasant. He wanted to shove his hand down the man's throat and squeeze his heart to stopping. "After you drop me, you'll go to the sergeant. Give him the envelope. Tell him the American's an Eastland Safari guest. It has to be handled professionally. The more legitimate, the better. A passport problem, something out of anyone's control. You will book a flight out before you leave the sergeant. Tell him to get our friend on that flight."

This was the third time he'd given Rambu

the same instructions. "Yes. It's not a problem. I understand." He slowed for traffic. "I hate what this city has become," Rambu said abruptly.

Guuleed didn't speak, but he agreed. Nairobi made him long for Somalia and his family. They were involved now. The thought made him ache. He'd seen whole bloodlines wiped out before.

"Our men are inferior," Guuleed said abruptly. "We need new men. And Faaruq! He started this all!"

"Yes, colonel."

"Don't call me that, for fuck's sake!"

Rambu was smart enough not to mention that Guuleed had been the one to shoot Faaruq in the back of the head, not one of his men; that it had been Guuleed who'd come up with the idea to stage the man's death as a poacher, shot by KGA rangers.

"This Chinese prick dares to threaten my family?"

Rambu twitched. The Land Cruiser nearly sideswiped a *matatu.*

"You get us in an accident, and I eat your liver. With bacon and onions if I can find them."

"Yes, sir." Sweat burst out on Rambu's face, running in the grooves of his acne scars. *Good,* Guuleed thought.

Red dust rose from the pedestrians teeming on both sides of the road. "Look at them," Guuleed said, taking in the people. "What kind of fucking life is that? They look like safari ants."

"Ants or not, my prick goes stiff just looking at some of those women."

"Yes, that's for certain." They laughed not as comrades but as men, no rank between them. Guuleed said, "You will resupply before the shops close. I have the list." He pitched it into the ashtray. "Handle the sergeant first, then the shopping. If I'm still alive, pick me up when I say so."

Rambu hesitated, ventured, "He will no doubt be pleased when you tell him about the Chinese woman."

"If I'm given the chance. He's a terror, this one. All throttle; no brakes. But you're right. It's good thinking, Rambu." He slapped the man on the shoulder, his flat hand hard as stone. He could see Rambu flinch, and it gave him satisfaction. People were constantly misjudging his strength. "Tell me when we're ten minutes out."

Guuleed shut his eyes. He saw his wife's face, her bare breast suckling their firstborn. He saw all six of his children, gathered outside their modest farmhouse in fierce, slanting light, ready to visit the *musalla.* He saw charcoal pits and ladders rising up the rust-crusted hulls of vessels toward blue sky. Grieving women wailing over husbands stolen from their homes by government troops. All these things in a moment, all part of him and unshakable. He was who he was and only Allah would judge him. Not some Chinese prick. He expected divine providence. If he allowed his family to be wiped out, he would be looking at hell and eternal damnation.

Nothing short of forever was now at stake.

The concrete block structure, one of four nearly identical buildings lining a small-business complex cul-de-sac off Jogoo Road, southeast of downtown Nairobi, reminded Guuleed of a school or a prison, the two not being terribly different in his mind. A few cars were parked in the dirt circle.

Guuleed stood before the office building door, feet firmly planted. What to expect? The Chinese egomaniac could be in trouble, might need Guuleed's muscle and be willing to negotiate down the sentence on his family. He clearly wanted to discuss something he considered too sensitive for even the satellite phones, which was stupid, Guuleed thought. No one could listen in on a scrambled satellite phone.

Whatever the man's motives, Guuleed would have preferred not to know them. He walked past a Chinese man nearly as large as himself in the lobby. Another two in the hallway outside the office door. It looked like a former doctor's or dentist's office. No furniture or artwork in the waiting area. The reception desk was manned by a guy holding an AK-47. Guuleed was frisked and lightened of a Glock semiauto 9mm, three ammo magazines, a U.S. Navy–issue knife and a garrote.

Guuleed found their silence disturbing. He wanted to get on with it. He wanted this over.

In the unremarkable office, Xin Ha moved out from behind a desk crowded with paperwork. He was thin and taut, his age difficult to judge. North of thirty, south of fifty. He wore his oily black hair too long, but his eyes were tough, black.

The man had risen to great power in Mombasa. He controlled most of the port, had enough political leverage to remain untouchable, and an insatiable hunger for more. Poached horn and ivory went north into Somalia or south to Mombasa. Drugs and young women flowed in the other direction; no container, no truck ever ran empty.

Now Xin had moved to Nairobi to appear more legitimate, but most knew he continued to run the port. He was said to refer to himself as the CEO of Kenya, his ego knowing no bounds.

He walked up to Guuleed and appraised him like a man at the racetrack deciding how much to gamble on a horse. Nose in the air. Lips pursed.

"I dislike rumors, don't you?" he began. Guuleed hadn't prepared for such inclusion. He'd felt a lecture coming, a berating was more like it. Why ask for face-to-face and take a collegial attitude? The man had promised — not threatened but promised — to slaughter his family! "I have taken on too much, perhaps. We lose patience when we're pressured, don't we?" He backed up two steps and took a wider view of Guuleed. "Tell me about the woman."

"It has been handled. It will look like an accident. A tourist abandoned in the bush. It's over."

"That's good. Better than I thought, at least. Well done."

Guuleed knew Xin Ha primarily by reputation. He didn't offer compliments. There was threat and menace couched in every word.

"You understand the shortfall she caused us?"

"I had nothing to do with that." He said it all wrong, regretted his words immediately. A man of action, talk had not been his forte.

"Is that so? My mistake, not yours? It's not *your* man who reports such people? She was *inside* my company's computers. Do you understand the gravity of this?"

"He's not my man. He's freelance. It's true, he reports to me, but —"

"My point, exactly." Xin Ha sat casually on the edge of his desk. "And did he report to you?"

"I get a dozen such reports a week. Twice that in tourist season."

"You ignored his report about the woman."

Guuleed searched for a way to deflect the accusation.

"She caused my investors to panic. Do you understand the cost of closing the clinic? Hmm?" He smiled, the look prohibitively sweet. "I think not. A very dear cost to you if you don't rectify the situation, to be sure. Please, do not think for a moment I enjoy any of this. A man's family? It's horrible! I detest even the thought of it. But examples must be made, hmm? I'm willing to bet you make such examples to your men as well. We each have a cross to bear."

He was staring in the area of Guuleed's collarbone, as if unwilling to make eye contact. With a huge effort, Guuleed forced his body to stay still.

"You're thinking we could have done this by phone. Hmm? And you would be right, except for the rumor I referred to earlier. Do you know the rumor that is troubling me?"

"No," Guuleed admitted. He'd anticipated a different man, a different conversation altogether. A one-way conversation. "You know what's troubling me? Your threatening my family."

Xin Ha failed to react; it was as if he hadn't heard Guuleed. "First, this American!"

"We are taking care of him. A visa problem. He is being deported. He's not your concern."

The man might have nodded; he sucked through his teeth. "Second . . ." He began moving around the room in no particular pattern. Guuleed never took his eyes off him. "There is a rumor, a trustworthy source, that private drones have been deployed."

Guuleed's bowels went to water.

"That mess with the hunting of the lion

last month. Bleeding hearts to the rescue! An American donated at least three drones! They can see through cloud, read your wristwatch. They carry photo and radio surveillance into formerly unreachable places. On top of the drones, surveillance may now include mobile phones, possibly satellite phones. Do you understand why you're here in person?"

"From the sky we look like any other safari base camp. We are registered as a business. We know what we're doing."

"If a single automatic weapon is photographed . . . a grenade belt . . . a box of ammunition . . . a scope. You understand?"

"Yes."

"You will break camp. Relocate. Your existence depends upon it. Your family's existence depends upon it." His pallid skin turned a dismal pink when flushed. "You must make up for my losses. Do you see what you've done? How many you have put at risk?"

Guuleed wondered if he killed the man right here — regardless of how quickly the man's guards would kill him — might his family be saved?

Xin Ha lunged toward him and Guuleed flinched, something he never did, something that left him feeling ashamed, humiliated.

Xin Ha laughed in his face. Guuleed forced the lid down to contain his temper.

"Out!" Xin Ha said, finally meeting eyes with him.

13

"Mr. Knox, it's the front desk. Just a reminder, sir, of your four P.M. departure to Kibera."

Knox checked the room's clock radio: 16:05. Knox felt the floor shift beneath him. "I didn't —" He caught himself. He hadn't ordered a car to Kibera, wherever that was.

"The tour of Kibera. You signed up with the concierge."

He knew the name now. Kibera, one of the world's largest slums. He hadn't signed up for anything. Had Winston signed him up? Dulwich?

"Is there a problem?" asked the concierge.

Or maybe the damn kid from the airport was trying to play tour guide.

"Right. Sorry, I fell asleep. Give me a minute. I'll be right down." It didn't escape him that an arranged trip, one he had not signed up for, could well be a trap. But staging an abduction while he was in the company of other hotel guests had to be the lamest idea he'd ever heard. Knox checked for messages on both phone numbers he carried, switching out the SIM cards and restarting his phone. Nothing.

Moving through the lobby, he made note of everyone he saw, including a husband and wife in the gift shop. Nothing out of the ordinary, not that he found that re-assuring. He was unlikely to spot a true professional.

Outside, flags hung, lifeless, in the pain-fully hot exhaust-filled air. Taxis waited in a queue, drivers sharing smokes. Hotel guests came and went on foot, some asking ques-tions of the various bellmen. The traffic was as bad as the night before.

Approaching a white high-top van bearing a tour company logo, Knox remained on high alert for a possible attempt to grab him. His gut wrenched at the thought of Grace, coming down these same steps, fac-ing this same street.

The van held a half-dozen anxious-looking hotel guests. Knox spoke his name for the sake of the driver and ducked inside. He apologized to the others, crammed his legs in behind the passenger seat. A bellman slid the van's side door shut, his eyes expres-sionless, his smile practiced.

"Please enjoy," he said.

Knox studied the faces of his fellow passengers. A woman riding shotgun was using the visor mirror, attempting to rub the white of her sun cream away. Knox used the mirror, too; watched for anyone overly interested in him, anyone reaching for a phone. He scratched off his list the retired couple from Ohio who'd been outfitted by Orvis. The African slacker and his Princeton-semester-abroad redhead were too small and self-absorbed.

He assessed the remaining three: solo travelers; a buttoned-up middle-aged woman who showed little joy; and two black businessmen, one in his thirties, the other twice that. Nothing registered. He smelled body odor and suntan lotion, cologne and perfume. He saw camera bag straps and sunglasses and water bottles, jet lag and anticipation and a lot of sweating.

The guide turned out to be the woman Knox had taken for the joyless middle-aged traveler. In guide mode, she snapped into an all-too-cheery robo-caller voice, nasal, with a thick South African accent. Kibera had been created as a land gift for Nubian soldiers returning from war in 1904, she told them. Over a century of use and expansion had left a sea of corrugated metal huts, open drains and overcrowding. The government estimated the population at a tenth of its nearly million souls. She rattled off some do's and don'ts. Don't pay anyone to take their photo; don't buy bottled water from the children, it's street water; negotiate every sale; be respectful; remember nearly everyone speaks English and can understand what you're saying.

Their arrival drew hordes of kids, trying to sell them souvenirs or the aforementioned bottled water. The guide cut a path through them and led her flock ahead. The smell of open sewers carried on a light breeze. Several tour guests clasped handkerchiefs over their noses, a practice the guide discouraged.

The large number of roaming children, like flights of winter birds, followed in waves, adding to Knox's sense of tragedy. He hated being associated with an "edutainment" tour, of curiously inspecting a place where a bottle cap was currency.

The guide led them down narrow lanes between open-stall stands that sold everything from trinkets to Coke. Other Kibera residents had set up souvenir stands on inverted crates, displaying craftwork made from recycled plastic, aluminum cans and bottle caps. The people were clean, as were their colorful clothes. Their smiles genuine. Houseflies outnumbered people a thousand to one.

Knox kept track of the guide as she took a moment with a woman at a souvenir stand. He witnessed an exchange, the passing of a note along with money. It went the wrong direction for Knox's taste, saleswoman-to-guide. He could have taken it as a payoff for the guide steering the tourists in this direction, but the look the guide gave Knox told him it involved him. Another surge of adrenaline. Knox had three exit strategies at the ready.

As the guide herded the rest of the group to a larger shop across the hard-packed dirt, she blocked Knox with an extended arm. Knox stopped, every nerve sparking.

"You, Mr. Knox, are certain to find this other shop the more interesting."

He told her he was in no mood for a sales pitch.

"These particular goods are special. They are important to you, Mr. Knox. This shop is *just for you.*"

"I don't think so." Knox could see himself outnumbered and pushed through the shop's black plastic wall, carried deeper into Kibera. Into a van. Into a pit.

The guide rose to her toes. "You *must*

trust me."

"But I don't," Knox said. He rummaged through some of the craftwork laid out on a board supported by inverted milk crates, ready to run. Dried pieces of eggshells, reinvented as decorations. Paper litter, now sculpture; leopards, gorillas and chess sets made of discarded computer parts.

"Please, mister," said the stall's bone-thin proprietor. He had drooping eyes and a pencil neck. "More in back." He motioned Knox toward the plastic wall at the back. Knox didn't move.

"This was arranged for you," the guide whispered.

"I'll bet it was." Knox reached inside the Scottevest, the Mary Poppins bag of windbreakers. Inside its seventeen zippered pockets he carried everything from money to a switchblade, which he now palmed and hid up his right sleeve.

He couldn't blame the tour guide or hope to get anything out of her. She'd been paid to deliver him. The people behind such arrangements created multiple layers of self-protection.

"You go first," Knox said.

"I must see to the group," she said.

"And you can. Right after you go through and hold open that sheet." To his surprise, she didn't quibble.

"Very well." She stepped forward.

Knox grabbed the back of her shorts. She caught her breath. He held tightly, cinched the shorts into her crotch to remind her who was in control. He nudged her forward, watching the bottom of her short-cropped hairline. The neck was the tell-all of danger. As she drew the plastic sheet aside, the static electricity lifted her fine hairs. But her neck did not incriminate her. Knox glanced over her head to see a fashionably dressed, blue-jeaned African woman in her early to mid-thirties. His first guess was journalist. His second, lawyer. No wedding ring. Hands empty, she carried a messenger bag purse, slung at her side.

The shack had walls assembled of junk-yard materials but was sturdily built. The crate the woman sat on was immediately adjacent to someone's former screen door, now blockaded by an improvised metal crossbar. At first blush, it appeared that the woman was being cautious about their security.

"Leave us," she said to the guide. She spoke with confidence, the tone of one in charge.

Knox released his grip and the guide slipped around and past him. "We will not leave," she told Knox. "You will find me and join us after. She knows where."

Knox swallowed dryly as he looked back at the mud-rutted lane. He propped open the plastic sheet in order to see out.

Before him was a cramped, sour space: a mattress made of three garbage bags filled with Styrofoam peanuts. A tattered piece of a former green-and-white awning apparently served as a blanket. A wall of stacked cardboard boxes held everything from food to toiletries.

He moved closer. The woman had baker's-chocolate skin, haunting brown eyes and a nearly shaved head.

"I am called Maya Vladistok," she said.

"I left you a phone message." She'd been on Winston's list.

"Indeed. And I am answering that message."

The two shook hands — hers were callused, with short nails. Knox angled a remaining plastic tub to allow him a view of the woman, the screen door and a sight line through the open plastic sheet.

"Please pardon the theatrics. Necessary, I'm afraid. I am no friend of this current government, nor do I trust the hotels. As to my name, my father was Russian. My mother Kenyan. So that's out of the way."

"Understood." It was the second time politics had been mentioned in the past few hours.

Vladistok appraised him. "You will be better suited to take a room away from downtown. Something small, in the suburbs. Karen, perhaps. There are small inns. Fewer eyes and ears."

"You're saying —"

She cut him off with a finger held to her lips, and acted out a request for Knox to surrender his phone. Passing it reluctantly, the switchblade still warming in his palm, Knox watched as, to his horror, Vladistok stuck a piece of chewing gum over the microphone hole and, fishing a crumpled sheet of aluminum foil from her bag, wrapped the phone tightly before returning it to him.

"Sorry. I'm a lawyer. Though I'm considered an activist — a label I detest."

Knox congratulated himself on his ability to read first impressions. "I run a small import/export company. I'm on a buying trip."

"Are you? Professionally, Mr. Knox, I am a legal consultant. Corporate security. But my life's work is to get things right in the courts. To get the poachers tried. In five out of six cases, paperwork is lost; the case never comes to trial. Midlevel civil servants, paid small amounts to misfile, shred, divert. They are paid off by businessmen. Arab. Chinese. Somali. Elephant and rhino is big business. They use helicopters now. Automatic weapons. ATVs. It's wholesale slaughter. Big business. And remember, the fewer animals, the higher the price for the tusk and horn. So with each kill, each harvest, they increase the value of the commodity."

"Crime syndicates?" Knox had seen automatic weapons in use on the battlefield; she'd put a picture into him he couldn't stomach. Rhinos were bigger and slower than buffalo; elephants, ten times that.

"That word is overused. Is there organized crime here? Of course. But it's not like what you hear. It's my belief that the influence of outside crime syndicates, not including the Chinese, is almost nonexistent in Kenya. There are certainly organized criminals in this country. The Chinese are the market makers for elephant tusk. Vietnamese for the rhino horn, though the Chinese export it. But overall, poaching is less connected to terrorism and outside influence than others would lead you to believe. This is what I told Ms. Chu."

Knox's throat went dry. "Did you?" Grace would react more viscerally to the poaching than terrorism or corruption. She was made a child by the sight of a stray dog or cat.

Maya looked into and somehow through Knox. Not a dead stare, not a flirtatious stare. More like some of Tommy's looks. X-ray. Probing. "I met with her when she first arrived. We discussed many issues. My work with corporate security and Internet issues, as well as the recent failure of a major vaccination program." Her face remained unreadable. An attorney, indeed. "As she explained it, that program was privately funded."

Knox had no interest in politics, humanitarian aid or theatrics. "Have you spoken to her in the past two days?"

"I have not."

Wrapping his phone in the aluminum foil struck him as overly paranoid. Who was it she feared? Only the most sophisticated agency possessed the capability to listen in on digital phones.

"You were in contact often?" Knox asked.

Her eyes darted more quickly. "Three times, I believe. She sat where you are sitting."

Knox felt a little sick. "Okay."

"The clinic at Oloitokitok interested her."

"Tell me about the Internet protocol."

"She wanted to know the sophistication of

107

spyware employed by the state, the military, outside agencies. I warned her to be careful. Many prying eyes."

Knox's throat remained overly dry. "I'll bet," he croaked.

Vladistok spoke more softly. "A kilo of rhino horn is worth two hundred dollars fresh off the kill, as I said. Ten times that to a Somali broker. A quarter million U.S. by the time it reaches Vietnam."

"Grace wasn't investigating poaching."

"She was investigating corruption. In Kenya, the two are never far apart."

"The clinic has ties to poaching?"

"This was her concern as well. But the clinic is closed now. It no longer matters."

Knox swallowed, clearing his throat. "If she has been kidnapped?"

"Why say such a thing?"

"We're approaching two days of silence."

Vladistok answered carefully. "In Central and West Africa, the paramilitaries will kidnap for political gain. Here, it's for money or show. If she has been abducted, it could be to send a message, to pressure others not to investigate as she did. It could be for money." She grimaced. "How can I help?"

"You can give me specifics," he said.

"Grace implied — she did not state, I

must emphasize this! — that she had reason to suspect a connection between the failed vaccine and a company based here in Nairobi."

"Asian Container Consolidated," Knox said.

Shocked, possibly impressed, Vladistok took measure of him before speaking. "She did not name the company as you just have. It is an interesting choice."

"Why?"

"Asian Container Consolidated is run by a Chinese man named Xin Ha. He's powerful. He has privileged access at all levels of government. No one's going to touch him. He imports containers of Chinese goods, and more than likely either exports ivory and rhino horn or looks away when others do. His men are butchers. Allegedly, he has ties to the Somalis, and therefore the al-Shabaab terrorists. There's no way the government doesn't suspect this, yet they never act. He conducts business with impunity."

Knox nodded, trying to swallow spit to moisten his throat.

"If Xin Ha was behind the vaccine switch, if he discovered Grace was investigating this fraud . . . But that's entirely too much speculation. If Grace is in trouble, she needs you to stay away from Xin Ha, John, believe me."

"What do you know of Bertram Radcliffe?"

Her face tightened. "He was a remarkable reporter in his time. That time has passed. Have you met him?"

"Yes."

"Then you know he drinks excessively."

"Professionally. Yes."

"He lost his wife under questionable circumstances. This followed several columns he wrote excoriating the current government. After, Radcliffe outright blamed the government. His paper distanced itself. Things with him became all the worse recently: a colleague of his was shot up north. They said he was a poacher — as unlikely a truth as there's ever been. He's very near a broken man, John. I would be wary."

"His articles are online? The ones that got his wife killed?"

"You and Grace are not so very different."

"You might be surprised."

Knox saw her eyes track something or someone behind him. He turned abruptly in defense. No one.

"We must go. Both of us. Now!" she whispered. "There's going to be trouble."

Taking him by the hand, she unwrapped his phone and slipped it to him. Then she unbarred the screen door and led Knox out to a muddy lane no wider than his shoulders, through an adjacent dwelling, and out into a different lane.

"We part company here," she said, pointing Knox deeper into the settlement. "Take your first right. Cross three lanes like this. You will find your group there."

"What's going on?" Knox asked. "What kind of trouble? I don't need my group."

"Yes, you do," she said, her eyes frightened. She'd been spooked by something Knox had missed.

"What is it? You saw someone."

"Your group will provide you with cover. The police will ignore you if you are with them."

"The police? Here?"

"They will be soon enough. We must go, now! There is going to be bloodshed."

Vladistok headed off in the opposite direction, deep into the squalor.

14

Loose tarps serving as stop-gap roofs snapped in the breeze like flags. They rattled Koigi. A bushman through and through, he had an aversion to all things urban. He viewed Nairobi as a blight, the slums of Kibera as an infestation.

As a matter of pride, he refused to shed his ranger uniform in favor of civilian clothing when he was in the city. Given that he was wanted for questioning by police and the KGA, it was a bold and premeditated statement. Today, the KGA could shoot poachers and ask questions later. But Koigi had started out in another era, another epoch. Back then, he'd been tagged for murder for his slaughter of five poachers caught in the act of attempting to hack an elephant's tusks from its head with machetes as it lay — alive — paralyzed by a poacher's dart. Six months later: two more poachers. A year after that, a band of eight in a pickup truck with automatic weapons.

Today, a tip had overcome his reservations and brought him to Kibera. He led three of his best men. Like him, they wore protective vests. This was what the city did to you: You left your tribe and your village for the promise of money and material goods, only to find it an empty promise. The work was infrequent, the housing absent. You joined a million souls squatting in the dirt only kilometers from Range Rovers, exotic fountains and excess.

Koigi knew this all too well; knew Kibera as a place of boredom, disease, childhood and work. God, how he resented its existence. He had been raised here, by an aunt who sewed scraps of tarps into grain bags and an uncle who'd had a corner on the recycling market. He knew the lanes, could navigate their wandering inconsistencies blindfolded. Knew the place he would find Guuleed if the tip was accurate.

He and his men moved quickly, assuming the police would soon arrive. Those in the lanes moved aside. Uniforms of any kind meant trouble, even the wrinkled and soiled khaki ones worn by this quartet of determined fighters. To them, the leader, the one with his arm in a sling, looked as mean as a water buffalo. He could see the fear in their eyes. Reveled in it. The weapons slung across their necks but held in hand were well used. Children dodged out of the way, then turned and followed at a distance. Women pulled their handiwork back into their stalls. Grown men scattered.

Koigi hand-signaled one of his men down a lane to the right. Moments later, another to his left. Behind him, another spun fully around every ten paces and walked briefly backward, taking responsibility for defending their backs. The same man tried to discourage the children from following, but failed. In Kibera, a raid was considered entertainment.

A moment earlier, Koigi had spotted a familiar face through a parted plastic sheet. Maya Vladistok was important to the cause. An ally. Her presence confused matters. He wondered if she'd been behind the tip. Perhaps that explained the white man he'd seen her speaking with.

The string of shanties stretched in every direction. Masses of people. Koigi identified the dwelling in question not by the flaking marine-blue corrugated tin that formed its outside wall, but by the bootprints in the mud heading inside. It was sandals, bare feet and trainers in Kibera, not bush boots.

He allowed time for his two unseen men

to gain position. Held his finger to his lips and motioned civilians away. He tightened the vest, more a nervous tick than a necessity. Then he eased forward, and gently tried the door. Blocked from the inside. Motioning his man behind him down to his knees to reduce his profile, Koigi kneeled as well. He hoped they would shoot high.

He had nothing to live for but the elephants. No family. His childhood sweetheart long dead. *Take the fear of dying out of a soldier,* he thought, *and you have a monster.*

From somewhere behind them, a person whistled. A lookout. Their cover blown, Koigi kicked open the door, his weapon at the ready. The clean *pop! pop!* came at a distance. Gunfire, one lane over. His man there returned fire.

Koigi and his backup stormed the empty shanty, moving room to room. He felt the claustrophobia of the tiny space. He nearly fired on two women, huddled on a soiled mattress. In an instant, he exited into a lane. His man lay in the mud to his left. His backup turned toward the injured; Koigi headed to the right, running now, his weapon raised. People scattered.

He saw three men twenty yards ahead. One was Guuleed, he felt certain. The Somali had poisoned villages, recruiting young men who would have never poached elephants and rhinos without him. Koigi raised his weapon.

"Down!" He shouted, and watched two dozen human beings collapse like marionettes with their strings cut. The three men remained standing. He fired. The man to the right spun in a cloud of pink mist and fell. The remaining two darted left into a dwelling.

One down . . .

Koigi took no precautions as he charged into the structure. No pause-and-clear, no police procedure. He would shoot anyone standing. He spotted and avoided a woman and her two children lying on the floor, hands over their heads. He kicked aside a piece of tin, cut through and into the back of a conjoined shack. A mosquito net hung in the corner. He saw the weapon a fraction of a second too late. Took a slug in his vest. Pushed back and off balance, screaming in pain, Koigi fired twice. The second shot found its mark.

Two down . . .

Crashing into crates, tumbling into a tangle of pots and pans, Koigi worked hard to breathe. On top of his painful shoulder, he'd cracked some ribs. Up on his knees, to his feet, he pushed out into yet another lane.

Guuleed was running back in the direction they'd come from. Koigi lifted his weapon, but couldn't get it to eye height. He couldn't manage to shout out a warning to those in his line of sight.

He limped ahead. By the time he discovered a tunnel dug into the black dirt floor of a shack fifty meters down the lane, Guuleed was long gone. Koigi's man, also protected by his vest, was helped to his feet, made to walk as the sirens drew closer. The team hurried toward where they'd left the vehicle. It was a footrace now.

15

Gunfire sounded in the Kibera township. Screams rang out. Knox heard the percussive slap of sandals and bare feet moments before the flowing horde of terrified, would-be victims reached him.

The mass moved far more quickly than he'd estimated. It hit him and knocked him down. Knees and elbows pummeled him as he struggled to stay on his hands and knees. To succumb and lie flat was to drown. The gunfire continued. Hundreds, maybe a thousand people surged down the narrowest of paths between the shanties. Alongside him, a girl of fifteen went down hard into the packed dirt, her shirt torn off, an earring ripped from her right ear, which bled profusely. Knox moved toward her and took a series of knees in his side. Thought he felt a rib go. Rolled. Managed to get back to all fours, but now downstream of the girl.

Swinging both arms powerfully, he stood,

his height providing a view over the heads of the human stampede. He fought upstream, pivoted right and left by ferocious blows. He couldn't locate the fallen girl. He fought and battled against the flow. His feet hit something. He bent to retrieve her. Gathered the girl into his arms, cradled her. He knew better than to go against the flow. Instead, he turned with it and, allowing himself to be driven ahead, shoved his way to the side, where the walls of several shanties had collapsed. Without pause, he moved into a connecting alley, saw up ahead the same insanity on a parallel lane. The gunfire was sporadic now, but the population didn't slow for an instant.

A woman who looked barely older than the girl he carried spotted Knox, broke from the stampede and fought her way into the same alley. She was limping; she burst into tears when she recognized the girl he carried. The girl was alive, her arm possibly broken, her eyes open in shock.

The mother — it had to be her mother, not an older sister — accepted her, tears streaming, spouting a million thanks to God and Knox in no particular order. Knox helped to get them settled.

When he looked down the lane a second

time, there was the boy Bishoppe. He was smiling as he waved Knox to him.

16

At that moment, without fully understanding why, Knox felt Grace's presence. The stampede was something they would have survived together. He guessed that was it. But there was more to it. She was alive. He knew this fundamentally. And she had not simply gone to ground; she was in trouble, the kind of unthinkable trouble one didn't like to consider.

John Knox didn't believe in premonition, didn't ascribe any particular significance to this feeling. At the same time, it was a *feeling,* not some flicker of his imagination.

"Where the hell did you come from?" Knox asked, breathing hard.

"Not hell, Mr. John. I was at the hotel when you joined the van. I came straightaway. Kibera is not a place for you. I can show you much better."

"Can you get us out of here?"

"Please, Mr. John, you insult me with such

questions. Five minutes. All will return to normal. I'll take you to your driver."

"My driver."

"Correct."

17

"Hello there, Koigi."

The ranger stopped, one hand on the grip, ready to pull himself up into the vehicle. The woman's voice, coming from behind him, was familiar. His men climbed into the vehicle. He spoke without turning around.

"Inspector Alkinyi. What brings you to Kibera?"

"My question exactly. In," she said, opening the rear passenger-side door and pushing the others aside so she could take the seat behind Koigi. She was small and frail, not cop material. She wore her hair in a headscarf, street clothes belonging to a graduate student, and black running shoes. She carried no purse, only attitude.

The car doors closed and, for a moment, only the idling engine could be heard.

"Talk to me," she said. "Don't make me guess. I'm police. We don't like to work hard."

"Guuleed," Koigi said. His men reacted like schoolgirls. He dared to tell a cop the truth?

"Here, in Kibera? Why?"

"It's of no interest to me why." Koigi looked straight ahead. All his men were in a full sweat from the activity of the past fifteen minutes. The car smelled foul.

The policewoman reached over the seat and put her hands on both his shoulders. "Who told you? How could you know he would be found here?"

"We explore even rumor when it comes to Guuleed."

"You bring this fight here? My city? These people?"

"I will not pass up such an opportunity."

"Why would Guuleed agree to a meeting in Nairobi? I don't believe that. His face is known to every policeman. There's a shoot-to-kill on him. We'd have done your work for you."

"And did you?"

She frowned.

"Tell me again, Kanika. Why does an inspector respond in such a timely manner to some gunfire in Kibera?"

She didn't answer.

"We all have our sources, yes?"

"It's not like that," she said. "I picked up

the call on the radio."

"Sure you did. And my men and I were just buying Kibera souvenirs."

The two rangers sitting next to the woman smiled.

"There's a man arrived from —"

"John Knox," Koigi said, interrupting.

"Jesus!"

"Is Guuleed in Nairobi for him, the American?"

"I told you," she said, "his reasons for being in Kibera don't concern me. Only that he *is* here — was here. You didn't kill him, did you? If you had, you'd be smiling."

"You will get out now, please," Koigi said. "We must be leaving. There are police in the area."

She laughed nervously.

"He went to ground," Koigi said, throwing her a bone. "There's a tunnel system off Trumpeter's Lane. You might want to collapse it."

"Thank you," she said, tugging the door handle and pushing the door open. "You could be shot if you're recognized. I'd keep my head down. Head south. Come around the city to the east. The gunfire has pulled our cars from those areas."

If she'd been hoping for a thank-you, she left disappointed.

18

Bishoppe led Knox on a fifteen-minute walk through the slum, which was still reeling from the stampede. People were already at work to restore walls, gather goods and look after the injured. To Knox it looked like a refugee camp recovering from a bombing.

They arrived at a gleaming red *tuk-tuk,* a three-wheeled vehicle with an enclosed cab. Knox and the boy took the backseat.

"The Sarova Stanley," Knox said, imagining how the parking valets would greet such a vehicle.

"It is a little more money than a *matatu,*" Bishoppe said, "but much better in traffic. And the police pay them no attention."

Knox grinned. Entrusting a fourteen-year-old street kid to look after his security? It was idiotic. And yet, it felt right.

They drove. Knox quickly broke out in a sweat. The interior of the fiberglass cab was boiling, despite the windows and the open front; its progress through the heavy traffic slow.

"Let me see your phone."

"Why?"

"Your phone, please!" Knox demanded.

"No. I come out to Kibera to help you, and you don't trust me?"

"You followed me out," Knox said. "Why?"

Bishoppe indignantly handed his phone over to Knox. It was a primitive flip model with basic texting. Knox stumbled through the menu navigation. His thumb was the size of three of its keys. All the texts were in Arabic.

"These are to my friends," Bishoppe said. "Do you read Arabic? I think not. I am Muslim. My friends are mostly Muslim. I speak and write three languages. How many do you? Why do you insult me like this?"

The driver glanced back at them. Knox waved him on.

"I've given you enough money by now that you do not need to work for the next few days. Weeks, months, maybe. Do you have friends, maybe family outside of Nairobi? Some place away from here?"

"My sister lives in Korogocho. You know it?"

"No, I don't. You should go there."

The boy laughed. "What have I done but help you? You don't like me, Mr. John?"

"You can't follow me around, Bishoppe. You could have been killed here today."

"My sister is nineteen. She has sex with men." Bishoppe's words swam in the space of the claustrophobic cab. "The men pay her for it. Most. Some do not. They hit her and refuse to pay. I send her money when I can. That's all I can do. You have money, so I follow you. You're a good client. You understand?"

"I'm sorry."

The boy shrugged. "It's not her fault. Our uncle made her do it. She gives him the money. I'd rather buy a pair of Air Jordans. Have you ever had a pair of Air Jordans?"

"No. Your parents?"

Bishoppe pursed his lips and frowned. "The water sickness. Many years ago."

Knox leaned out the window for air. The street was loud with engines of all kinds.

"I'm telling you, Mr. John, you get me a pair of Air Jordans and I will help you find your friend."

Knox had not mentioned Grace or her situation. He blinked. Realizing his mistake, Bishoppe flushed and said, "You spoke to the old reporter at the hotel. Your waitress is a cousin of mine."

"You bribed her!"

"I run a business, Mr. John. Information is king."

"You read that off a cereal box?"

The boy looked confused. Maybe not a big consumer of corn flakes.

"What are you? Twelve? Fourteen?"

"Air Jordans. Red. Do we have a deal?" Bishoppe offered his hand.

"No, we don't have a deal. You're playing me."

"People talk, Mr. John."

"What kind of people?" Knox asked.

"Red. The basketball shoes over the ankle."

"They cost a fortune! Forget it."

In the front seat, the driver — clearly eavesdropping — could barely keep his eyes on the road.

"I can get them black market. Not all that much."

"I'll decide *after* I hear what you have," Knox said.

"I'll trust you." The boy sounded about five. Fourteen had been a stretch. "There was this woman at the Sarova Stanley. Her reservation was also made by Eastland. Like yours. She also took the Kibera tour. Like you. You see? So many similarities."

Knox worked to control his temper. "You

don't work for Eastland. And how could you possibly know if she did or didn't visit Kibera? You're fishing."

"No." Bishoppe shook his head vigorously. "I'm not. I told you, I hear things. My cousin. Maybe he works for the hotel, maybe not."

As in China, Knox thought, *everyone is everyone's cousin.* Like the reference to the waitress, Knox took it to be meaningless. "Go on."

"Maybe he's good with computers. Maybe he has a way inside the Internet at the hotel."

"He's a hacker."

"He's a businessman, like me. Sometimes he asks me to make a pickup for him."

"Blackmail. You're a bagman."

"Sometimes my cousin borrows credit card information."

"Borrows! I like that."

"There are many such businessmen in Nairobi."

"I'll bet there are. Tell me about the Eastland woman."

"She . . . my cousin said she has the kind of firewall only a spy or a thief would have." He paused. "Are you a spy? Jason Bourne? *Mission Impossible?* Like that?"

Again, the boy trying so hard struck Knox

130

as so young.

"There's no way he could have hacked her," Knox said. Racing through Knox's mind was an image, an emoji of a bomb, followed by a question mark. Had it been some punk kid who'd scared Grace off? Had he traveled halfway around the world because of some kid hacker?

"That's the point. The police offer my cousin payment to learn about such foreigners."

Knox had to let it register, worked to keep the incredulity from his voice. "The police pay local hackers to know who can't be hacked." Grace would have taken immediate action if she'd suspected someone had discovered her. But he wasn't sure what those actions would have been, didn't know what Kamat and the others at Rutherford Risk had taught her to do.

"My cousin says this woman was possibly with the ministry."

"What are you talking about?"

"The government ministry."

"Why would he say that?" Knox asked.

"Look, I don't understand computers. He said she might lead him to a prize . . . you see? So I get my prize, right?" Bishoppe stood up, grabbed the rail behind the driver and started shaking the *tuk-tuk* side to side.

The driver reached back and slapped out for the boy. Bishoppe sat down again. "I love that," he said. "Have you ever surfed, Mr. John?"

Knox was in a brain freeze, unable to allow himself to see Grace's work from the perspective of corrupt police, hotel hackers and desperate street urchins. "Call this cousin now. Right now! Pull over!" he shouted to the driver.

The *tuk-tuk* weaved artfully through the traffic, but there was nowhere to pull off the road. Mobs of pedestrians and bicycles formed an undulating wall on all sides. Knox struggled to tune out the noise and confusion.

This "cousin" of Bishoppe's had clearly gotten close enough to Grace to panic her. *Think! What did it all mean?*

Finally, the driver pulled off and stopped. Knox already had his phone out. He awoke Vinay Kamat, in Hong Kong, from a deep sleep. Knox allowed the sound of his voice to introduce him.

"Say Grace thought she'd been caught. She's online, inside someplace she doesn't belong. What's her first response?"

"John?"

"Quickly. What's the training?"

"Abort. Back up your assets. Physical

drive, nothing online. Then zero the hard drive. Boot and nuke. Full wipe."

"How long for that?"

"Depends on the amount of data. An hour. Two, to do it right."

"What physical drive? An external? A thumb drive? What?"

"I told you: it depends on the amount of data. John, I was dead asleep. You can Google this."

"Google didn't teach Grace how to handle a breach."

"No one breached Grace, John. Now, if she thought they were trying — that's another story. She carries multiple thumb drives. There are some very cool SD chips out there that can hold two hundred gigs. Smaller profile, easy to hide. But the upload is slow. I might do one of each. One comes with me, one stays behind."

"Hidden."

"No, I'd leave it on the table with some arrows drawn to it. Yes, John: hidden."

"What could a hacker know if he couldn't actually breach Grace, which I'm assuming is basically impossible?"

"Basically? John, the CIA can't breach us. Not without a week or two on a Cray. No one hacked Grace if she didn't want it. The raider might get the router log, some metadata. But she'd be in stealth mode, John. Proxies. Ghosting. Someone skilled could determine the general area of her target, narrow it down to a neighborhood. Nothing past that."

"An area within a city? Chinatown. Capitol Hill." He was thinking: the Ministry?

"Sure. But only if this person is very, very good."

"Does she leave a signature, something he can keep watch for?"

"Not Grace. Not on her end."

"Meaning?"

"We're talking Snowden shit here, John. Not some Detroit hacker. Okay? Think of it like this. You see a person on a bus. You follow the bus, but you never get a look at the face. So you take a chance. You drive to the neighborhood where you think the bus is headed. You get in front of it. Wait by the side of the road. Maybe you recognize the bus or the face, maybe you miss it. Depends on traffic."

"Motherfucker."

"John?"

"Thanks." Knox hung up and reached toward Bishoppe, who backed away. "Your cousin. Right now. Give me your phone."

The back of the *tuk-tuk* was no bigger than a can of tuna and still Knox couldn't get his hands on the kid. Bishoppe moved like a wraith — under his arms, around his back. He was a cat in kid clothing. The driver never twitched.

"You'll get the shoes!"

The boy stopped, out of breath.

"No texts, no calls," Knox said, holding up the flip phone.

"You touch me, I'm gone. You never see me again."

"You take me to him. No games. No false leads. Do it, or so help me, I will out you and your cousin to the police, national security, hotel security, airport security."

The boy was clearly considering his options, including the door.

"*Now,* Bishoppe. We go straight there. Right now."

The two connected in a long staring contest. The boy was tough to read. Knox blinked first. Time was of the essence.

"The shoes for you. Twenty thousand shillings to your friend if I'm pleased with the information."

The driver sat up sharply, eyes straight ahead.

"Sixty," Bishoppe said calmly.

The driver coughed.

"Twenty-five."

"Fifty. This is a very great risk for me. He

won't like it."

"Twenty-five is final."

Bishoppe folded his arms across his chest. "You treat me like shit."

"Don't swear."

"Fuck you."

"The shoes, and twenty-five."

Bishoppe tapped the driver on the shoulder. "Drive."

19

The car carrying Knox and Bishoppe arrived at a strip mall, the central occupant of which was a 24-hour department store. The sidewalk out front was littered with cigarette packs and candy wrappers. Groups of young men in shorts and T-shirts loitered. Customers came and went in the relative darkness of the dirt parking lot.

Knox entered with Bishoppe, moving through a grocery section at the front of the store, followed by cosmetics and a pharmacy, hand tools, office supplies and paper products. Down a set of steps into clothes and kitchenware. The shelves were mostly vacant, their ragged contents haphazardly presented. Several dozen Kenyans wandered the aisles, from mothers with strollers to well-dressed businessmen.

Bishoppe navigated with ease, making it clear to Knox that this wasn't the boy's first visit. They pushed through a swinging door into an unboxing-and-storage area, dodged a few dollies and stacks of flattened cardboard, and entered the third door in a string of four.

"Yeah? Hang on, I said I'd do it!" a young kid said angrily, not bothering to turn around. Cigarette smoke wafted between his head and the computer screen.

"It's me," Bishoppe said.

The hacker looked over his shoulder. His youth shocked Knox. He was lighter-skinned than most Kenyans; he might have had some Arabic blood, or Mediterranean. He was not pleased to see someone like Knox.

"What the fuck?"

"Twenty thousand to answer a few questions," Bishoppe explained. "Just the questions. No problems."

"Get out! You are in trouble now, kid!"

Knox pulled out the money.

"Fuck off. Keep your twenty thousand."

"There's a life at stake," Knox said. He could do this his way, but he wanted to show Bishoppe some respect. Bishoppe would get pulverized if Knox took over the way he wanted to. His adrenaline was itching for release.

"A white life. What do I care?"

"Chinese."

That interested the guy. Or scared him. Knox tested his theory. "You don't want to be connected to a Chinese getting killed."

"I am not connected to nothing."

"You already are. You just don't know it yet. That's why you need me as much as I need you."

"I said, fuck off."

"I heard you, and I'm still here."

The hacker looked him up and down. More frightened than before.

"Okay."

"You . . . visited . . . someone online. You identified her as a woman. You told the boy something about the Ministry."

The hacker boiled. Said nothing.

"You know what I'm talking about?"

The boy nodded.

"How did you know it was a woman?"

He turned back around. For a moment Knox thought he'd blown him off. But he was typing; the screen before him jumped through hoops for several long seconds, and then he read from what looked like a lengthy file. "Sarova Stanley. Room six-two-four, registered to a Grace Chu."

According to Vinay Kamat, the boy couldn't possibly know that. Knox wasn't about to say anything, though.

"You doubt me."

"No."

"She is something."

"Yes."

"The work is beautiful. Impossible. Highly . . . suffocated."

"Sophisticated. Yes."

"I have never seen such a thing. Not our own government, even. I am telling you, a thing of beauty."

"How many times?"

"You're asking what, exactly?"

"How many times were you with her online?"

"I was never with her. I watched her. I am Peeping Tom." He smiled. "But not pervert. Only joking! I worked hard to get inside her." Knox didn't appreciate the sexual overtones; hacker speak, he figured. Still, he wanted to smack the boy. "Kryptonite, I'm telling you. No way I could do nothing."

Knox took a chance. "You worked the metadata. You got in front of her and waited."

"Shit, man! Who are you?" The guy's eyes were bloodshot.

"Tell me what you found."

"If I am to guess? She sailed through the firewall and into the Ministry. I have no proof. First time was most probably a probe. I was lucky to see her that time,

140

because the next, she was in. She was off-line only maybe one hour and one half. The same work for me? Twelve hours. Twenty, maybe. I admire this woman."

"How many times?"

"After this first time, two more." The hacker sounded tentative now, worried he was in too deep.

"Was she detected?"

"No. The English say, 'A knife through butter.' Like that. She is this smooth, this Grace Chu."

"Did she know you were there? Is that possible?"

"Fuck you. I'm good, mister."

"Yes, but we both know she is better."

No comeback.

"Which ministry?"

The guy smiled self-confidently. "Take off," he said to Bishoppe. Bishoppe left without a word.

"How much did you offer?"

"He told you: twenty thousand to you."

"You just got your twenty thousand, mister. Two hundred U.S. Who do you think you're talking to?"

"Someone with his pretty face intact. Someone with no broken bones and his equipment in one piece. An additional twenty thousand. No more discussion of money, and if I suspect you're holding out on me, I'm not going to ask again. Just so you know who *you're* talking to."

The hacker and Knox could see one another in the reflection off the glass of the monitor and Knox liked what he saw. The guy looked away, suggesting the terms were accepted.

"I think it is the Ministry of Public Works. I cannot prove this."

"Seriously?" It slipped out. Knox had expected something sexier. "Public Works."

The boy spun around on the wooden stool. "I believe so."

"Did you determine a department? A particular office?"

"No. Public Works. I am guessing."

"Do you have a way to know when she's online? An alarm? A signal? Can you tell me who else, where else, she hacked? Raided. Whatever."

"No. Most people, yes, I can tell you all this. I can show you video calls or online order for escort. What I like about Grace Chu, she gave me none of that. She made me work."

Knox didn't understand this techie world at all. Thankfully, Grace had come to it late. In her heart of hearts she believed she was still in Army Intelligence. She viewed accountants, of which she was one, as boring people and wanted nothing to do with that lifestyle.

"If you know her name, you accessed her hotel account." The words bubbled up, unbidden. He didn't like this punk referring to Grace by name. "So you've hacked the hotel's accounts. Many of the hotels, I'm thinking."

The punk didn't contradict him.

"You can show me her charges. Room service. The dates of her stays."

"I can tell you if she bought tampons in the gift shop."

"Shut your face." Knox took a step forward. The kid reeled back. "Her accounts. Now."

The guy could type at superhuman speed; Knox waited less than five minutes.

"Print it out," Knox ordered. He kept his voice intentionally calm. "Now. I'm going to ask you again. Do you have ways of knowing when she comes online again?"

The punk didn't hesitate. "Yes."

"I'm going to give you a local number. You will text it, if that happens. If you so much as think she might be online, I'm going to hear about it."

"Yes. Okay."

"Same thing if anyone attempts to hack

the Ministry of Public Works."

"I can do that."

"If I have questions, I will reach you through the boy, Bishoppe. You're to consider him me. Do you understand? You get rough with him, you get rough with me. You ignore him, you ignore me. Clear?"

"Yes."

"The people who taught her that? They work for me. Do you understand? I'm telling you that within the hour, they will know you. Your digital fingerprint, or whatever you geeks call it. They will know your equipment. They will know your way. You run, I will find you."

"You tell them I will work for them." The kid didn't seem the least bit intimidated; his initial wave of panic had worn off.

Knox collected the printout and stepped toward the door, hearing Bishoppe's sandals hurry away from the other side. He'd been listening in.

"You know, I might have recommended you if you weren't holding back on me," Knox said. "But you are." As feeble as it felt, it was worth a try.

As Knox pulled open the door, the guy called out. "I have messages. The kind they print out and slide under the door." His finger traced the screen. "Reservation con-

144

firmed for Kibera tour. Who the fuck wants to tour Kibera?!" He added as an aside, "People pay for that? Then someone named Radcliffe confirmed a meeting at the Jockey Pub."

He scrolled down, by which point Knox was reading over his shoulder, heart pounding. He could see Grace reading these words in his mind's eye, could hear her internal reactions. He knew her too well, he realized. She was on his brain. "Hotel transportation arranged . . . so on and so on . . ."

"Print it, please."

"Here's one: 'The guest for whom you left a package is not registered with the hotel, nor has a reservation on file. We regret to inform you that it is strictly against hotel policy —' "

The boy's reading was slow. Knox took over. " '— to hold items or luggage for third parties. Please see the concierge or the hotel manager for the return of your property. Regrettably, any such item will be destroyed after twenty-four hours of the issuance of this notice as per our security standards.' "

It was signed by the hotel assistant manager, Clare Umford.

20

From the moment the sun had dimmed on the first day, Grace had worked feverishly to stay alive. Relying upon her military survival techniques and the Maasai lore provided by Olé, she sought first to keep the insects off and the animals away.

"They are attracted to our human smell," he'd said. "Fear causes us to sweat. Running causes us to sweat. From the moment we panic, we are telling the animals where we are and how desperate we are. Mosquitoes can smell humans as far away as fifty meters. They are attracted to carbon dioxide. Some people give off much more of this than others. Maasai wear very little clothing, because clothing holds scent. The animals are put off by the dung and urine of other animals — it is how many of them declare territory. In the bush, Maasai cover ourselves with dung to disguise our human smell."

"Perfume," Grace had mused.

"If you will. Yes. Just that."

Now, despite her reluctance, she stripped. As she shed her clothing, she recognized an opportunity. She could use her clothes to stage evidence of her death. If Leebo or others returned in an attempt to confirm her death, she would leave them what they wanted. It was something she hadn't considered previously, and it filled her with purpose.

Working fast, Grace tore and shredded her clothes, laying them across the ground, dragging pieces into the bushes. In doing so, she told a story. Animals were certain to investigate, perhaps even fight over the remnants. She used sticks to break up the crusted sand, making what might pass for a freshly contested battleground between animals and a desperate woman.

Let them use their imagination, she thought.

Shivering from chill, embarrassment and the fear that accompanied her nakedness, she went the final step and removed her underwear, straining to rip them apart. Arms crossed, tears threatening, she stood in place for several minutes, unable to move. Then, finally, she trudged over to the waiting piles of dung.

The moment came, the moment when she

147

had to dig through the crust of each for the moist, grassy manure within. It was cold, sloppy and horrible-smelling, and it took a good bit of courage to smear it over her limbs. Bugs buzzed around her head. She smeared the foul paste under her arms, over her legs and between her buttocks, onto her neck, chest and belly.

When it came time to spread the horrible stuff onto her face she was crying, her stomach heaving.

But as she rubbed it into her skin, she felt something change. She was aboriginal. Old. Maasai. Olé's teachings came flooding back. Edible plants and grasses. Tools. Weapons. Poisons. Water sources. Navigation.

She kept her high hiking boots on. No amount of risk was going to make her go barefoot. She packed the dung onto and over the boots. She finger-combed dung through her hair. Feeling light-headed, she broke a thin branch from a prickly bush and snapped off enough of the thorns to hold it. Three feet in length, it gave her a dangerous whip with which to defend herself.

The trick with the bugs was to move, and keep moving. She considered the best vantage point from which to watch for her abductor's return. She pushed away despair, invited anger.

This spot of torn clothes was her "kill zone." From here, she would establish a pattern as she searched for the abandoned vehicle, working outward in a spiral. If out there, it would be several kilometers away; it would tell its own fiction. She could search while keeping the kill zone as a center point. She had a plan, a mission.

When her killer returned, she would attack him, wound him and leave him to the elements. Quid pro quo. She set this as a priority. Aware that the mental and emotional toll would be her biggest challenge, she braced for the unexpected, told herself to take failure as motivation, setbacks as lessons.

Start small, she thought. Stay alive one more hour. Keep to the plan at hand. Walk. Bigger ambitions would have to wait.

21

Knox was heading to the front desk to ask after the assistant manager when his phone buzzed. His mood changed instantly; he imagined Dulwich calling to say Grace had been found, alive and well. Gone to ground just as expected. That she was asking after him, wondering what had taken him so long. He viewed the screen.

Not safe. Gather belongings. Side doors. Five minutes.

He casually raised his head, still walking. Maya Vladistok, phone in hand, offered a sideways glance. A uniformed policeman, an officer, was staring at his mobile phone, head down, seemingly engrossed. Knox took the stairs and walked the lobby balcony to reach his room. He never unpacked; lived out of his duffel. Packing amounted to collecting his toiletries, putting his Dopp kit into the duffel, and zipping it up. He was wiping down the room when a knock on the door startled him.

"Police."

The only way out was the door — or to break a window with the desk chair and bail out from three stories up.

"Mr. Knox, you will please open the door?"

The cop knew his name. Not good. Knox checked the peephole. He recognized the sergeant from the lobby. The policeman had been waiting for him. Alone. An arrest would typically involve patrolmen, not a sergeant. Either he wanted only to speak to Knox, or Knox was about to learn firsthand about the Kenyan corruption he'd been hearing about. He moved the equivalent of a hundred dollars in cash into his right pocket.

"How can I help you, officer?" he shouted as he considered the window. He carried one hundred feet of AmSteel rope in his bag; about the thickness of a shoelace, its nearly five-thousand-pound tensile strength was more than enough to support his rappelling.

Forced to make a split-second decision, he elected not to run. He unlocked and opened the door. Took a bathroom towel and dropped it to the floor to prop the door open. Before the sergeant asked, Knox was already presenting his passport.

The sergeant was black-skinned, round-faced and forbearing in his examination.

"It's your visa, Mr. Knox, that's the problem," he said.

Knox waited. Nothing about this was right. Cops didn't chase down bad visas. Sergeants didn't make hotel calls. Knox's visa was standard issue. No wonder Maya had tried to warn him.

"Your visa was executed at the airport?"

Here it comes, he thought, wondering if a hundred dollars would be enough. "Yes. Of course. The stamp is right there. Issued upon entry, just like everyone else's. It cost me fifty U.S. dollars, cash. The exit document's right there. It's all in order."

"It's not right, I'm afraid. You will need to leave the country."

"What? Why?"

"This visa was issued incorrectly. You will need to apply for a tourist visa once you land. At the granting of that visa, you may return to Kenya."

"I just got here. My visa's good. What's wrong with the paperwork?"

"Please collect your things. You will come with me."

152

"Please check that you have the right John Knox. It's a common enough name."

"There is no mistake. I apologize. It's a clerical error. You are not alone in this."

"Obviously, there is. Look," he said carefully, "if it's a matter of the funds not being properly recorded, maybe this can be worked out between the two of us." Knox took a step closer, his hand slipping into his pants pocket. "I'd just as soon handle it here as have to go across town to an office and stand in line." He found the man's recessed eyes off-putting.

"You will collect your belongings. There is a British Airways flight three hours from now. You will be on it."

"Are you sure we can't work this out?" Knox produced the wad of shillings.

"Any attempt to bribe a public official results in a mandatory six months. Are you sure that's the way you want to go, Mr. Knox?"

"Perhaps I got the amount incorrect?"

"Second warning. There will not be a third."

"Then I suppose we'll have to settle this at the U.S. Embassy," Knox said. "If you wish to meet me there, you are invited to do so." Knox returned the man's cold stare. "I will leave the country only if advised to do so by my embassy."

"There is no room for negotiation, Mr. Knox. There will be no trip to your embassy." The sergeant lumbered forward, snatched Knox's small duffel and turned for the door. Knox smelled bitter sweat. "Your paperwork is incomplete and can only be corrected at a consulate or embassy *out of the country.* You will be coming with me whether by choice or by force."

You and who else? Knox wanted to say. Mixing it up with a cop, even a corrupt cop, was a bad idea. The window was the better choice, after all. "I will call my embassy. You will wait outside, please." Knox removed his phone slowly from his pocket, so it could not be mistaken for a weapon. He showed him his phone. "To be fair, sergeant, you may wish to know that I am recording our conversation to the voicemail of my lawyer. Your badge number is 9527. No matter what you do to me or my phone, there is no undoing this recording. If you'd like to reconsider your refusing me access to my embassy — the United States Embassy — now is your chance." He waited, expecting more of a reaction. The sergeant stared ahead stoically, almost comically unimpressed.

"Call whomever you like. You're coming

with me. Now, please." He gripped Knox's bag more tightly. Most of what Knox needed was zipped into the many interior pockets of his travel jacket, but if the man kept his bag there would be the discovery of the go-bag and other circumstantial evidence that might require explaining.

Maya Vladistok appeared in the doorway then, a step behind the policeman, who turned to account for her. Her eyes were frantic; her breathing revealed she'd hurried.

"What's the meaning of this?" she demanded.

"It's nothing, *sweetheart,*" Knox said, trying to cover for her. "A misunderstanding about my visa."

"I know you," the sergeant said to Vladistok. Addressing Knox, he spoke condescendingly. "This is the attorney you called? I should have figured as much." He spoke to Vladistok. "You're lucky I don't arrest you."

"How will your captain feel about such publicity?" Vladistok said, clearly unintimidated.

The sergeant's confidence lessened as he turned and backed up a step in order to keep both Vladistok and Knox in sight.

"Her? No," Knox said. "The attorney I

155

called is in England. This woman is my . . . friend. A close friend, if you understand. That's all."

Vladistok appeared to consider speaking for herself, but Knox gave a slight shake of the head. "I'll catch up with you later, *sweetheart.*"

She refused the role. "What seems to be the problem, officer? You claim to know me, but I don't know you. If you know *of* me, well, that's different. Then you know how good I am at what I do, and that I'm very well connected. Including within the police department. Yes? Which precinct are you with? Allow me to make a call, which is within this man's rights."

"He'll be coming with me. And if you attempt to interfere with my performance of duty, we both know where that gets you."

"Sweetheart," Knox said more deliberately, "I'll be fine. Don't worry."

The officer turned to Maya, his tone condescending. "You make any calls and it's just going to make things harder on him."

Maya moved past the policeman and into the hall. "Well, let's just see, shall we?" She pulled a mobile out of her purse. "You wait here," she said to Knox. "Don't go anywhere just yet."

She dialed the phone and placed it to her ear, walking out of sight. The policeman backed out of the hotel room, never taking his eyes off Knox. "Come back here!" he called nervously down the hall while his attention remained fixed on Knox.

Knox heard it before the sergeant. Wheels moving quickly behind a rattle. The sergeant never saw the baggage cart. He turned his head in its direction, but too late. The cart carried a young European boy, sitting on its empty platform, holding the sides like he was riding a sled. Two older teenage boys were pushing hard from behind. They had the thing really moving.

The thud of the collision, the *whoosh* of expelled air, the call of high young voices and the trampling of light feet as the teenagers hurried away mixed with the casual sounds of the lobby below. Then, what seemed like an eternity later, a telling thud was followed by a hush as the lobby went chillingly silent. This silence was shattered by high-pitched screams.

Knox hurried out of the room. His duffel lay on the tile by the banister. He peered over and down into the lobby. The sergeant lay in a crippled, ungainly, inhuman form, blood splatter surrounding him, a pool of it around his head like a crown.

A woman looked up and pointed.

"There! Him!"

Heads snapped up, took in Knox leaning out over the rail.

The same woman shouted, *"You!"*

22

Knox stepped back, mind reeling. He grabbed his duffel and headed for the fire stairs, descending two at a time.

He considered hotel security barely a step above the Boy Scouts. Their reaction time would be slow. They'd take elevators. Knox reached ground level, punched through an alarmed door to the outside. A side door, as Maya had suggested.

Keeping his head down, he turned left, away from the front entrance. He used the windows as mirrors. Walked fast, but did not run. He slipped his arms through the straps and slung the duffel on as a backpack.

He thought of Grace and what a mess he was making of this.

When a woman spoke as she passed, he nearly missed it.

"Government Lane, River Road, Koja stage." He repeated what he'd heard in order to remember it. Glancing behind him,

159

he saw Vladistok's back. She did not slow, did not break stride. She had given Knox the one chance to hear her, and no more.

Already working his phone's map, he cut between parked cars and dodged moving vehicles to cross. Reaching the opposite sidewalk, he reversed direction and paralleled Maya, now a half-block ahead. Wedged into hundreds of Kenyans, a full head taller, Knox hunched his shoulders, shrank down in order to make less of a spectacle.

As sirens neared, he briefly stepped out of the mob and tightened a shoelace. He counted an impressive five patrol cars outside the hotel. A dozen patrolmen scrambled from the vehicles. Knox turned, kept moving.

The closer he drew to the stage stop — a triangular parking lot formed by the intersection of three streets and crowded with *matatu*s — the more pedestrians crowded the space. A hardware store, a cell carrier, food stalls, clothing stores and an open-air market all competed for the attention of the thousands using the bus stop. Knox slowed, not knowing how to find the "Koja stage."

He felt a hand take his.

"Stay with me. Say nothing. Make yourself as small as possible and be friendly. Are you capable of smiling?"

"I didn't do it."

"Of course not. I saw it all. I'm your only witness, which is too bad for both of us."

"I have to speak with hotel management. Not about this! I have a lead."

"Not now. Probably not ever. Forget that for now."

"I can't."

The *matatu* ride was spine-jarring. Knox sat sandwiched between two passengers, head spinning from the conflicting body odors. The driver talked to himself, into what later proved to be a Bluetooth earpiece; the woman next to Knox threw elbows as she knitted a baby's cap; he caught Maya Vladistok smiling at him from the seat behind. He not only liked, but trusted her. Best of all, he no longer felt at sea. He'd found a navigator.

Maya's apartment, a modest studio with a view of a parking lot, had more books than shelf space. It contained two ladderback chairs, a small round dining table and a galley kitchen. Either she slept sitting up or there was a well-hidden Murphy bed. Knox used the toilet — the bathroom was even smaller than the kitchen — to wash up.

They sat in the two chairs, saying nothing. The sounds of a busy city penetrated the thin glass of the only window. Among

161

the hundreds of books, he didn't spot a single work of fiction. Law journals, biographies, African history.

"I have to get back to the hotel. She left something there. For someone. I don't know who. But whoever it is can help me. I need the name. And whatever it is she left behind — if it hasn't been picked up."

"You do not want to test Kenyan justice, Mr. Knox. Justice in matters such as these is tribal, severe and swift. And though this government will be hesitant to jail or execute a foreigner, especially an American, you have come at an inauspicious time. The current government would be well served by declaring itself judicially independent and able to prosecute its own laws. The killing of a policeman is justification enough. I would imagine you would serve at least a few years." She frowned. "The airport, trains and border crossings are out of the question. Do you have money?"

"Yes."

"Mombasa is your best option. With the right connections and cash, you may be able to arrange stowage on an outbound ship. Ironically, John, this is how the elephant tusk is exported. And by the same people."

"Asian Container Consolidated."

"Or a competitor. Being white will cost

162

you and won't help. Those in the Mombasa port would be more than happy to take a payment from the police for you. It will be extremely difficult to arrange passage, but I think it is not impossible."

"Not exactly a ringing endorsement."

"Few options, none without risk, I'm afraid."

"There may come a time for that, but it's not now."

"Don't be stupid. You cannot remain in this country. Every hour works against you. In the public eye, you have killed a policeman. You are a foreigner. The manhunt won't stop, believe me. You are a trophy now, more valuable than the big game you came to protect."

"You can't harbor me. I understand." *Every hour works against Grace, too,* he wanted to say.

"It's not that! Don't try to switch topics. I know a clean cop called Kanika Alkinyi. She is one of very few. She will help us." *Us,* Knox noted privately. "The pressure will intensify to bring you in. The secret police are everywhere and always in plainclothes. They have a massive network of informers. A single tip can net a month's wages. Add to that the CCTV here in Nairobi and your odds are nonexistent. If we hurry, and stay

163

one step ahead, we might get you to Mombasa and out of the country. Until I reach Kanika, it's best to stay here with me."

"Not advisable. They'll have video of you at the hotel. Look, I appreciate the offer. Any contacts you're willing to share would be terrific. But as far as your direct involvement, Maya . . . No way. As you've said, when I'm caught — and I won't be — they will have to choose carefully how to deal with me. We both know how they would deal with you. It's off the table."

To his surprise and pleasure she didn't argue with him. Instead, she sat, staring at him contemplatively — through him.

At last she rose, reheated some rice and beans, opened a can of chicken soup. Knox ate with her.

"You saw someone, recognized someone in Kibera, just before the firefight — the guns."

"A ranger, a man called Koigi."

"You knew there'd be trouble. How is that?"

"You see a skunk walking around in the daytime —"

"You shoot it because it likely carries rabies," he said.

"Koigi, he's one of the good people. A legend. But it was the same thing as the skunk. He cannot afford to be seen in Nairobi. I cannot imagine what would be important enough to bring him here."

"Should I care?"

"Koigi runs a group of rangers in a particularly lawless part of the country. Not a declared reserve, but it doesn't need to be declared with Koigi looking after it. He is suspected of having killed a dozen poachers or more. And though the KGA has a shoot-to-kill policy, technically what Koigi does is homicide. The government leaves him alone for many reasons, including public approval for what he does, but in Nairobi they would have to arrest him. He gives the police no choice. For him to arrive, in daylight, into Kibera — yes, I knew there would be trouble."

The equatorial sun set quickly. Knox tasted the soup again, looked out over the spoon as he did. "I'm not going to Mombasa. I need to get into that hotel. It's the last place they'll look for me."

"You cannot help Grace Chu. Not any longer. You must think of yourself. Of Kenyan prisons. Everything changed with the fall of that policeman. If you move quickly, you might be able to stay ahead of them for twenty-four hours. No more than this."

Knox tapped his watch. "Then I have twenty-four hours. The hotel."

She hissed. "You are a single man, I believe."

Knox stared at her.

"No great surprise. Tell me what it is you must do at the hotel. I will do it for you."

"I can't ask that."

"I did not hear you ask." She returned his stare. "The hotel, and then Mombasa."

"The hotel," Knox agreed. "First things first."

23

Maya drove a Chinese-manufactured four-door Sedan with minimal appointments. Knox had switched the plates in her parking garage with those of a neighbor. She'd objected, but not too strenuously. He rode shotgun wearing his ball cap, his duffel at his feet.

"Why do this for me?" Knox asked.

"You have to ask?" Maya said.

"I have to ask."

"Your conceit will always hide the truth from you, John. Beware of that. I don't do this for you, but for that woman, Grace Chu. I'm a woman also, like her. If men have taken her . . . I spend my professional life fighting the unjust. Consider her my client, that's all."

It was dark out. She'd parked on the block behind the Sarova Stanley. With the car visor down, a passerby could only see Knox's neck — his head practically hit the ceiling.

"An African woman won't win a second look in the lobby. A white man your size? That's the reason. I'll be right back." She passed him the keys. "In case I'm not."

Without allowing him time to object, Maya entered the hotel through a side entrance. It led along a parade of boutique shops, an all-day restaurant and the hotel gift shop. She asked the woman at the desk to speak with the night manager.

"I'm an attorney representing a former guest. I'm sure this can all be handled quickly and quietly."

Five minutes later, she was shown through an office area to a somewhat larger cubicle in the back.

"I was hoping for Clare," Vladistok said as she took a seat.

"How may I help you?" The man was in his early forties, his temples graying. He wore the kind of dress shirt Vladistok disliked, the weave too busy. His tie was slightly crooked, tempting her to fix it for him.

"There was a misunderstanding." She presented her business card. "A hotel guest, my client, Ms. Grace Chu. A package she left in the hotel's care for a third party."

"We don't —"

"Yes, I know," she said, cutting him off.

"That's the basis of the misunderstanding. Notice of the hotel policy was delivered to her room, by which time Ms. Chu was unable to execute the instructions therein. As she is no longer in Nairobi, and the twenty-four-hour deadline has recently passed, she engaged me to retrieve her property."

He typed on his computer terminal's keyboard. At least a minute passed. An extremely long minute for Maya Vladistok. "Yes, I see."

"We both know the hotel does not liquidate a guest's property after twenty-four hours. We also know the police have better things to do than sort through a hotel's lost and found. So, let's dispense with this formality, shall we?"

The manager, who'd put on a pair of reading glasses before peering at the computer, slid them down his flat cauliflower nose. Said nothing.

"Shall we?" she repeated.

"Have you been our guest before, Ms. Vladistok?"

Maya stiffened. If he'd recognized her, it had likely been from a security video of the cop's death.

"I've had the pleasure of the occasional drink in your bar."

The man nodded. "I'm so glad you enjoy

our hospitality."

"Very much."

"If you please? The name the package was left under," he said, reading his side of the computer terminal. "For verification purposes." His voice cracked. He shot her a look that flooded her with panic.

She felt it a trap, suspecting it had been left for Knox. To identify with that name was suicide.

"I wasn't given the details. I'll have to make a call. You'll excuse me, please." She dialed Knox's number. He answered. "Grace? It's Maya. They're putting up a bit of a fuss, I'm afraid. Could you please give me a description of the packaging and the name of the recipient?"

Vladistok paused.

Knox asked if she was all right.

"The hotel is insisting," she said. "They are treating me like a common criminal. As if I intend to steal the thing! Yes, I know. But you must remember? Seriously? Well . . . if that's the best we can do, then yes, I'll explain. I'll call back in a minute. Thank you."

She tapped the screen as if to end the call and placed her phone upside down on the man's desk — the connection still live. "It was a frantic day for her. It could have been either of two names. As to the packaging, she believes she used a hotel envelope."

"One name, not two."

"It's the best she can remember. It's either addressed to Rutherford Risk" — he shook his head — "or David Dulwich."

"I'm sorry," said the night manager. "I'm afraid I can't help you."

"Won't help me, you mean." She wasn't sure what to do next. "I don't understand why you're making this so difficult." She worried the manager was going to notify the police about the package. She'd made everything a lot worse.

A closed folder on the desk caught her eye — a crisp, new folder, a partial sheet escaping, a triangle of gray black. A photo. Maya assumed the worst: her image, as well as Knox's, in that folder. A photocopy of a photograph or video capture? Her face in an elevator or the lobby?

"Listen, I'm sure we can resolve this." He sounded insincere. "Let me check the packaging, please. That should be enough. I'll be right with you. Excuse me a moment."

He smoothly scooped the folder off his desk and stood to leave. But something stopped him.

"I beg your pardon," he said, turning.

"But we do dispose of such property, Ms. Vladistok. Though the typical grace period is often, but not always, closer to thirty days. Wait here, please."

He wanted her to hold out hope, to stay in the chair, to sacrifice herself to the police. He headed back in the direction from which she'd come. She watched his head move through the maze of cubicles.

At last he leaned over and disappeared. Stood up again. They met eyes.

"It may possibly be out front." Another lie. She'd heard a drawer open; had heard the crinkle of paper as he'd pocketed something. The moment he passed through the door to the front, he'd be blocking her only exit.

"Wait!" she called out, standing and grabbing her phone. Holding it in her hand rather than returning it to her purse. "Please! There's another name! I should have thought of this. We can clear this up."

"Sit tight. Just a moment."

The man took a step toward the swinging door, half in, half out — and then moved backward with extraordinary speed. Knox had him by the neck with one arm, the manager dancing backward on tiptoes.

"Pocket," she said.

An instant later, an envelope in Knox's

hand. He threw it to Vladistok, spinning the man, cupping his mouth and aiming his and the manager's faces at the black plastic eyeball of the ceiling security camera.

"Read the name," Knox called out.

Vladistok flipped the envelope. "John Knox."

"You tell the police," Knox said, aiming the man's face upward, "that had your hotel done a proper job of things, someone would have noticed that a family, possibly two families, checked out immediately after the tragedy. That both families had at least one teenage boy. That's because — and you'll have footage of this somewhere, though possibly not in the hallway, where you should have cameras — three boys were playing with your luggage carts. No one stopped them.

"These boys? They rode that cart right into the police officer I was speaking to. They knocked him off that balcony, and their parents changed plans the moment it happened. Their prints will be on that cart. My prints are only on the banister, where I rushed the moment I saw it happen. This woman, whom I'm holding against her will, is my witness. She saw it, too. You tell them that they have this completely wrong, that they are an embarrassment to law enforcement."

Knox pushed the man forward. With a free hand, he jerked open drawers, taped his prisoner's mouth shut with a roll of fragile tape, the word marked out in bright red letters.

"The desk?" Vladistok asked.

"Empty," Knox said, finishing the job, binding wrists and ankles. "I'm sorry about this," he said to the manager. "No intention of hurting you. I hope I haven't."

He grabbed Vladistok roughly by the arm, acting out his role as her abductor. She worked to get free, not understanding.

A woman stood at the front desk. Knox aimed his head down.

Vladistok said, "Please thank your manager again. He's been most helpful."

Back in her car, Knox tore open the envelope, running his fingers over the words, written in Grace's hand. His name.

He tipped the envelope. A thumb drive slid out. Knox caught it.

"My name," he said, mostly to himself.

24

"We need to create a cover for you. I will tie you up," Knox said.

Maya Vladistok laughed. "I'm really not into that stuff." She added, "I can play ignorant. I can say I threw you out when I realized the trouble you were in."

"In your apartment," Knox said, ignoring her suggestion. "We make it look like I abducted you. Something believable but leaving you a way to get out of it with some difficulty. You will then call the police. Maybe this friend of yours. Tell them about the hotel. Back me up on the cop's death, and tell them I made you work the manager. You live here, Maya. We've got to make this right for you."

"The upside is, you can steal my laptop after I back up some files."

"That's extremely generous of you. I'll return it, I promise."

"A friend — a couple friends, actually —

have guesthouses. If I call from your phone . . . You can't very well check into a hotel or boarding house. They all require passports."

Knox elected not to share that he traveled with several such documents. "Fine. Good. Thank you."

25

Knox's taxi driver dropped him off at a turquoise sliding gate in the pitch dark. He pounded, and the door opened to reveal a lanky black man with a .22 slung over his shoulder. He wore shorts, sandals and a sleeveless shirt for the Liverpool football club.

Knox was shown into a three-bedroom guesthouse and greeted by a personal cook, a woman in her forties who couldn't stop smiling. The rooms were all rustic luxury, the living room's vaulted ceiling thatched reed, the beams African ironwood and the floors gray tile with Oriental rugs to cover. The furniture was a motley collection of shabby-chic antiques, well-loved and comfortable.

He was led to the covered patio. Kerosene lanterns burned at the four corners. The skinny guy built a small fire in the corner fireplace, smiled good night and disappeared into a darkness so profound he vanished within two strides.

He withdrew her letter from its zippered pocket and read from where he'd last left off.

As you know, I am not given to the outward expression of my emotions. This, I fear, is a product of my culture and my upbringing. I struggle with such things. So perhaps here, in a letter, not a phone call, I have that opportunity. I can write to you as a man, not as a professional partner.

Our friendship has seen many tests and trials that most never would. We have come to rely upon each other in ways few know or will ever understand. These experiences make us different. They form us.

What I can — need — to tell you is that when I was on my solo, I found myself thinking of you. I promised myself I would write to you. These kinds of things do not happen to me, John. Not ever. I am not given to sentimentality, and yet I am emotional writing this.

I have tried to listen to my heart and to be honest. I am deeply fond of you, your humor, your gallantry, your kindness. I miss you when we are apart. I believe that under the surface of John Knox lies a person rarely glimpsed. This is the John Knox I want to know better, the John Knox I have come to treasure.

I do not expect an outpouring of love from you, John. But I would hope for no jokes either.

I am thinking of you, often, and will continue to do so until such time as you tell me to stop.

Yours,
G

Knox smiled ruefully, tucked the letter away again, set up Maya Vladistok's laptop and pulled out the paperwork provided by Bishoppe's hacker. He plugged in the thumb drive and accessed it. The screen presented a question with an empty box to the right. He understood immediately why it had been addressed to him. Had Dulwich retrieved it, Knox would have received a phone call.

Amsterdam Brothel:

Knox typed: Natuurhonig
Had to enter it twice, the second time with two "u"s. It translated "natural honey" — a

phrase that had proven difficult to forget. His only time having seen Grace without her clothes — also difficult to forget.

The screen refreshed. He'd been admitted through her firewall's first test.

Shanghai B&B:

He answered: Quintet
Another refresh. Another layer in.

Played nurse in what hospital?:

Knox entered: Florence Night— but the box wiggled and cleared his entry — too many characters.
He typed: Nightingale
Another refresh.

You constantly criticize my:

Knox's fingers hovered. Did she actually take as criticism what he meant as teasing? He felt a pang of disconnect, of miscommunication, of regret.
He typed: smile
She covered hers far too often and he complained unmercifully about it.

The screen displayed a directory listing containing twelve files, including one .txt file marked "READ FIRST." He was in.

Knox read.

The files herein present solid evidence of what I would term "a convincing case" that a corporation DBA Asian Container Consolidated likely influenced or actively managed a fraud involving the shipment of vaccine arriving to the port of Mombasa.

Asian Container Consolidated was on contract to the Oloitokitok Health Services Clinic and Field Hospital. Trucking manifests confirm regular shipments of refrigerated medicines, medical supplies and medical equipment. An anomaly is present that suggests malfeasance: on an intermittent basis — every six to twelve weeks — fuel costs for return trips, Oloitokitok to Mombasa, listed on the bill of lading as empty are three times that of other empty legs, suggesting an unaccounted-for heavy cargo and therefore the trafficking of contraband. Contraband weighing a ton or more with the highest probability of shipment from the port of Mombasa is rare minerals or ivory.

The movement of Asian Container Consolidated funds indicates a sophisticated network of financing and the use of a series of shell corporations, wire transfers and cash management to effectively obscure the trail of certain funds. I was able to access many, though not all, of those records.

My interpretation of the funds is as follows:

- However and whenever the original shipment was intercepted, it likely involved an ACC ship sailing on a Panamanian registry: Pristine.
- A substitute vaccine (source currently unknown) took the place of the measles vaccine, which was shipped overland to the DR Congo. Cash withdrawals suggest a cost of 8,000 USD for the refrigerated transportation of the authentic vaccine.
- A party in DR Congo, through multiple wire transfers and laundering techniques, returned a payment of between 200,000–250,000 USD to ACC expensed as shipping services. Laundering services would appear to have been approximately 25 percent, consistent with current global practices.
- 75,000 USD of the laundered cash was redistributed by ACC within ten business days — difficult to prove but easily inferred. This is obviously a payoff of some sort. I thought it would be to a minister able to influence safe passage for the vaccine out of the port city of Mombasa.
- I uncovered the approximate equivalent of 75,000 USD deposited — as cash — into

six accounts that share only one overlapping signatory: Achebe (Archie) Nadali, Minister of Public Works in Nairobri.

- I detected an attempted breach on my system at 00:35 5/17; access was denied. No data loss. A second breach was detected 02:17 5/19, using the same cloaking technique as the first. I have no choice but to consider both attempts intentional and the work of the same individual. Note: not government or law enforcement. Of this I am certain.

- I have, thus far, been unable to compromise the clinic's computerized records, including their finances. I am in pursuit of a hardware solution that seems promising.

- I have followed procedure, including the disuse of all wireless communication, including mobile. A wired connection I can trust may be unavailable for twenty-four hours. John or David: If I have failed to make regular contact twenty-four hours past the last expected contact, consider me blown and in harm's way.

Grace

Knox reread it a half-dozen times, thinking it so clinical compared with the letter he'd zipped away. This was the other Grace, the Grace of Rutherford Risk.

Then he opened some of the accompanying files. Though able to read them, he could make little sense of how she'd come to her conclusions. Nothing personal had been written, and there was no indication of a planned itinerary.

Something stood out: the misspelling of Nairobi. The extra "r" didn't sit well with him. Grace, a perfectionist, a computer expert, would not have missed the error unless in an enormous hurry. He cross-referenced the times on the files and that of the text he'd received from her. The spreadsheets had all been copied to the thumb drive, their file times hours or days prior to the text she'd sent him. Only the letter implied a chronology. She'd backed up her files, had texted Knox she'd been blown and had written the explanatory letter — in that order. Her writing could have been rushed; she'd saved the letter for last.

Knox was in the process of convincing himself that the misspelling was a rare Grace mistake when he isolated the word a final time.

Nairobri

He stared at it long and hard. Letter combinations jumped out at him.

Nai**rob**ri

Robbery?

Nairobri

Air? Flight?
Nairobri
Railroad?
Nairobri
Initials? NA AI RO OB BR RI
His mouth hung open. *BR.*

The cook emerged from the darkness, the skinny gatekeeper at his heels. The fire was prodded. Food was placed before Knox. A beer. His caretakers, all smiles, retreated inside the guesthouse to await the completion of his meal.

Nairobi, but with *"br"* added. Bertram Radcliffe. It made all the more sense to Knox, given that this line of information had to do with a Kenyan government official, one based in the city — where Radcliffe was also based. Grace was talking to him from the other side of a Knox-only firewall, leaving a flyspeck of a clue to direct him to her source. Radcliffe had ranted about government corruption. It fit. It was all Knox needed.

He pushed the plate of food aside without taking a bite and raked open the door to the guesthouse.

"Can you drive?" he asked the spindly man.

The man nodded.

"Can you drive me?"

The gate guard shook his head, no.

"I can arrange, sir," said the cook. "Please, you will eat something. The car is perhaps ten minutes."

"Please tell the driver to hurry."

He half bowed. "Please." He motioned to the patio.

Knox didn't know how to tell him he'd lost his appetite.

26

The drive to the Nairobi suburb of Karen was short. This was a place of grand homes, of sprawling estates dating back to the colonial era. Radcliffe arrived at the door, looking like a man who'd fallen asleep on the couch and didn't appreciate the visit.

"Come in," he spoke gruffly.

Knox sat in a sturdy chair with zebra cushions. Radcliffe indicated the couch he occupied. "I lost my wife. Can't seem to bring myself to use the bedroom anymore. Cowardly, I know, but a man is who he is."

"It's not. I'm sorry."

"Traffic accident." Knox had lost him; perhaps Radcliffe was still half asleep. "But it was I who got her killed. That accident was meant for me, or at the very least as a warning to me and the columns I was writing at the time. This is how they do things here, John. This is why it must be changed."

"I can't imagine what you've been

through."

"I know that look. You think I'm a drunk. Don't equate sorrow, regret and guilt with alcoholism. I'm not that bad off, believe me."

"I should have called."

"You should have left the country. Cop killing is frowned upon here. But you haven't, have you? That tells me you're either in love or so well paid it's worth the risk. Either way, you're a threat to yourself and to people like me who are obliged to report you."

"I can't leave."

"Whatever it is you want, make it quick."

"Achebe Nadali," Knox said, leveling his gaze at the man. Radcliffe blinked rapidly and appeared to wake up some. If there had once been kindness in his eyes, Knox didn't see it. "Public Works minister."

Radcliffe returned a long, pensive look. With an effort, he forced strained humor onto his face. "You'll find he's gone missing. With government ministers that means either early retirement because of a kickback so enormous one can't hide it, or misfortune that typically involves torture and a permanent loss of assets."

"I hadn't heard."

"Your best and only bet, John, is to get

the hell out of Kenya. No amount of money is worth it. Ah! It isn't money, is it? You poor sod."

"She hasn't been heard from for —" Knox checked his watch, nearly overcome by what he saw. "Forty-seven hours." *God,* he thought, *we've lost her.*

"You must leave. Have Graham send someone else. This government is a virus. They will seek you out. It's in the wind, man. You can't quarantine them one at a time. You have to round them all up at once."

The man advocated a revolution. "You're an anarchist."

"I'm a pragmatist."

"You don't hold back information when a person's life's at stake!"

"You don't lecture a man from whom you want information. Sit tight. I'll make some coffee."

"I'll take mine black," Knox said.

Knox sought out a bathroom and discovered Radcliffe's home office on the way back. Radcliffe had earned a degree in journalism from City University London. Had won the David Astor Journalism Award, another from CNN and one from the Media Council of Kenya. There were photos of a younger man with a woman

Knox took to be his wife, white politicians, black tribesmen.

Coffees in hand, Knox stood, while Radcliffe perched on a stool at the counter beside him.

"How could you possibly know about Archie Nadali?"

"Grace left me a present."

"How could she —"

"— know?" Knox interrupted. "Because that's who she is, Radcliffe. You just come to accept it with her."

The man wouldn't make eye contact with Knox. "I hate women like that."

"Not me."

"Different generation."

"Not really. We're both breathing. You, barely."

Radcliffe raised his coffee as a toast. He'd have needed a Red Bull to feel a pulse, Knox thought. Radcliffe swallowed and grimaced. He straightened his back, settled his shoulders.

"The rumor," Radcliffe said, pushing back his disheveled hair, trying to make his point, "from one of my *helpers*," he stressed the word, "was that Archie Nadali was acting like a man who'd come into money. These government ministers, this bloody government is all about who can grab the most the quickest, isn't it?"

"I've already heard this part," Knox said. "Let's get past it."

Radcliffe wasn't to be bullied. "A minister's salary is less than mine. Far less. But still they're driving a Mercedes AMG, wearing Zegna and golfing the Windsor. When Archie moves up a rung, it's my job to see who built the ladder.

"The problem, you see, is that the better one performs at one's respective occupation, the more one's colleagues enjoy knocking him down a peg. Hmm? After my wife, what was there to lose? I got too close to the quick in a few of my columns. Next thing I know, I'm unpublishable. My own paper fears this government. When one door opens . . . am I right? So I passed the mantle to Daniel."

"Clock's running," Knox said. He thought it cruel what had happened to Radcliffe, admired him for what he'd once been. But he worried the man's depression was unshakable. "Let's try again: Grace coded your initials into a message about Achebe Nadali. A Public Works minister of all things. Why?"

"No need to be rude."

"If you're Grace, there's every need."

"The answer is: Daniel Samuelson. I

191

passed the Archie Nadali lead to my colleague and friend. A fine reporter was Daniel." *Was,* Knox noted. "My protégé. A most
excellent young man who understood old-
school journalism. Roll up your sleeves, yes?
Screw Google. Put some shoe leather into
it. A month later, he's shot dead as a
poacher in Mount Kenya National Park. He
and another man, a common laborer, a
Kenyan from here in Nairobi. Both killed.
What's that, you say? How does a top-notch
journalist end up two hundred kilometers
from home, facedown in a game reserve,
shot in the back of the head by wildlife rangers employed by the same bloody government that's been on the take here for twenty
bloody years? Well, I wonder, man."

Now red in the face, Radcliffe looked
fragile and suddenly old. Knox poured him
more coffee.

"A touch of the king's water wouldn't
hurt."

"Do any Brits actually serve themselves?"
Knox fired.

"Not those of us who fled to Africa. Not
if we can help it."

Knox spiked the coffee with Scotch. Radcliffe nodded; took a swig. The man wasn't
drunk or hung over. He was sad.

"You told Grace about Daniel Samuelson?" Knox said, thinking aloud. "You told Grace that Samuelson's investigation into Nadali got him killed."

"It got Daniel killed and Nadali to vanish."

"Presumably Samuelson's investigation was aimed at uncovering Nadali's accepting cash from Asian Container Consolidated. She's trying to follow the money from the bad-vaccine mess. Seventy-five thousand dollars of that scam's profit reached Minister Nadali. The two investigations intersect."

"She might have first considered where it got poor Daniel."

"He was shot on Mount Kenya?" Knox stood, his legs twitching. The coffee was strong.

"Doubtful. The bodies were found there. You're wasting your time. The game agency investigated the deaths. But who do you think's behind most of the poaching? The exports? Nothing on that scale can happen without the ministers' blessing. They bribe a few KGA rangers over to the dark side and who's to stop any of it?"

"Let's stay on topic. Nadali accepts a bribe from Asian Consolidated. Daniel Samuelson goes after the story."

"Ivory is the topic, John. It's the poor elephants in the middle of everything."

"Okay. I'll play."

"It started with charcoal, believe it or not. The Somalis controlled the charcoal export market. True story. Funded their pirating with it, among other exploits. The international community, in a rage over the pirating, shut them down, eventually took the charcoal exports away from them. So they turned to a more lucrative export."

"Ivory."

"And rhino horn. You see what happens when international committees decide things? Remember this, John: there's never been a monument to a committee."

"Noted." He'd felt the lecture coming. Radcliffe had too much time on his hands.

"Days before he died, Daniel paid a visit, thanking me for the lead. He let slip that he thought Archie and this money he'd been paid was tied somehow to the missing ivory."

"What missing ivory?" Knox stressed.

"More coffee, please. Let's skip the Scotch." He hoisted the empty mug. Knox obliged him. "It was execution-style, you know? Single shot, back of the head. Both men, Daniel and this other chap. I showed Grace the crime scene photos. For the record, you don't shoot poachers on their knees in the back of the head. More like a

194

long rifle at sixty meters. But there it is, Bob's your uncle. Got the photos from a reliable source. I promise you these were not the crime scenes shown to superiors.

"Of course, you shoot a chap in the back of the head, there's no face. Takes longer to identify. Gives everyone more time to effect the cover-up.

"As to the ivory. It's a mythical amount — several millions' worth — recently disappeared from the government vaults."

"Forgive me, sir," Knox said, feeling increasing respect for the man. "But we're off-topic. Nadali," he pressed, "ACC."

"You must listen more carefully. Money is currency. We are following the current. You said yourself Grace suspected some of the money from the vaccine switch ended up with Archie. Daniel then connected Archie to the robbery from the vaults. At least he thought he had."

Follow the money, Knox thought, realizing Grace would have been hanging on Radcliffe's every word. *In this room?* he wondered. On the couch? On the stool where Radcliffe sat?

"Every African nation has their treasure. The South Africans have their diamonds, don't they? And gold. Others, gems. All keep ivory. It's the same as your Fort Knox.

Ah! How ironic! John Knox." Knox had been plagued with that joke his entire life. "No need to explain national treasure to you."

"Someone robbed Kenya's Fort Knox?"

"Four million euros. That neighborhood. But that's how rumors go, isn't it? The vaults are spread around. Carefully guarded. The currency used to be supported in part by that ivory."

It didn't make complete sense — Grace, following this lead. Knox could understand her interest in following the money trail, but she was tasked with recovering the money from the illegal sale of the vaccine. Beyond that, why bother?

"The point being," the man continued, "Archie takes a bribe. In short order, one hell of a lot of ivory goes missing. It is my life's goal to bring down this government, and Daniel was no doubt perilously close to indicting at least Archie, if not others with him."

"Grace doesn't care about Kenyan politics," Knox blurted. "If she'd suspected some of the seventy-five thousand dollars had gone on to fund the theft of ivory from a government vault, that should have been enough for her. End of story."

"She said she was attempting to connect

the profit from the vaccine switch to wherever it led," Radcliffe said. "It led to the inner circle of the government and the likely theft of elephant tusk."

"Graham Winston's million pounds ended up funding over four millions worth of tusks," Knox said.

"Grace's expressed interest," Radcliffe said, "at least to me, was getting to the source — the start of it all. That included the theft of the substitute vaccine, the cattle vaccine." Radcliffe was waking up from the coffee. "Don't you see, man? Whoever provided that cattle vaccine was either the source or was the closest to the source of this whole catastrophe." Radcliffe appeared astonished to have heard himself speak these words.

"Go on."

"There'd been a prior killing with a similar MO to Daniel's. Also a reported poaching incident. Also done execution-style. And the timing — very significant. No one paid much attention because the man was African. Another dead black man. Not like Daniel. I had the original crime scene photos, didn't I? And your Grace stopped in her tracks at the sight of the bloke's tattoo. Got all hot and frothy. I printed a copy of it for her."

Knox resented the description. He resented Radcliffe expecting him to keep up. "May I see it?"

Radcliffe climbed off the bar stool. He led Knox through the old house to a library and map room better suited to a museum. The home went back to the early twentieth century and was full of ornate woodwork, animal skins and oil paintings. Radcliffe rifled through some files and led Knox on to his study. Seemingly in his element now, he fired up a laptop computer and found the photo of a man's black-skinned arm. Knox made out an India ink tattoo of Arabic symbols.

دائما

"That's the only photo she took away with her?"

"The only one that interested her."

"Let me guess," said Knox. "You mentioned the timing. It was just prior to when the vaccine would have been switched — the cattle vaccine for the measles vaccine."

Radcliffe froze. When he spoke, there was an air of reverence. "Well, I'll be damned," he said. "And here I was taking you for the muscle."

"This dead guy was a witness? Maybe a co-conspirator to the purchase or theft of the cattle vaccine. He has second thoughts. He's killed execution-style and made to look like a poacher. Why? They could have just buried him."

"Same reason as poor Daniel. To send a message. You don't fuck with these people."

"Because they're organized," Knox said, "and they're everywhere."

"Every-fucking-where," Radcliffe said. "Your Grace asked me if I knew a police-woman, Kanika Alkinyi. If she could trust her. I've known Kanika for years, I told her. One of the few good cops left."

The bogus vaccine, Knox thought. *Closest to the source of this catastrophe,* Radcliffe had said.

"I'm thinking Grace wanted to use this tattoo to link the dead man to a specific group. She has a mathematician's mind. A equals B; B equals C; A equals C." Knox held the printout tightly. "Wild guess: Kanika Alkinyi's beat is counterterrorism."

27

Knox hesitated only a moment before calling Bishoppe.

He had no time to plan and scheme, to wait for things to be perfect. He'd often worked under such pressure — always for Dulwich — often with the same stakes: a human life in the balance. Hostage extraction. Ransom payment. Yet the Rutherford Risk ops paled in comparison, and he knew why, exactly why, even if he refused to acknowledge it fully. Searching for a friend and colleague was a wholly different experience from searching for a person he knew in name only — and for a paycheck.

"You know who this is?"

"Of course, Mr. John. You're in trouble with the police. I don't like the police. It will cost you more."

He could sound streetwise and boyish in the same breath, Knox thought. "One thousand shillings." Ten American dollars.

"I need you to contact a police officer. No phones. It must be done in person."

"Are you listening to me?"

Knox smiled to himself. He liked this kid. Very much. They negotiated and settled on fifteen hundred. "Her name is Kanika Alkinyi. You will need to find the precinct she works from. You will tell her, only in person, face-to-face, that you're speaking for a friend of Maya Vladistok." Knox worked through his instructions. He had the boy repeat them twice. "If you sense it's going wrong, run. Got it?"

"I have no problem running away from police, Mr. John."

"You're a good man. In terms of the place and time, she needs to give me at least an hour. You understand?"

"Two thousand shillings."

"You can't renegotiate. We have an agreement."

"I just did."

Knox wiped the smile off his face; composed himself so the boy wouldn't hear the grin in his voice. "Done."

He disconnected, wondering how it was he'd entrusted his security to a fourteen-year-old.

28

The sound of the jackals scared her the most. In the dark, Grace heard the animals following closely, too skittish to attack — she hoped — but too hungry to ignore her.

At times too terrified to continue, she would stop, turn and shout out. The jackals would scatter. She would move on, relieved, but not for long. Soon, the horrid panting would return. The dry, insistent reminder that she was prey.

Beneath the skim of dried dung and dirt, gooseflesh rose on her chapped skin. In this fashion, she moved through the chill night for hours, tracking stars, disturbed by the mysterious sounds around her. She dared not stop.

As the edges of a sky bruised purple, then royal blue, she began to sort out her immediate surroundings. She spotted what she believed to be some of the edibles Olé had shown her. She took extra care inspecting the leaves in the light of the graying dawn, measured the height of the plants and examined the berries closely. She gathered what she thought to be jackalberry and black monkey orange and, following Olé's rigorous routine to establish the safety of each, crushed and smelled the fruit, on alert for the scents of almonds or peaches or latex, any of which meant discard it.

At last, she dabbed a tiny bit onto her lip and waited to see if the skin went numb, stung or burned. After the lip, she tested the corner of her mouth, then the tip of her tongue, then under her tongue. Finally, she chewed a small amount. She waited. No pain or numbness. She chewed and swallowed. Then she collected bunches of each and moved on.

The rule was to wait five hours, but she didn't think she could. The black monkey orange was distinctive enough that she gave in to her hunger and thirst and ate the insides of three.

Locating a source of water — the most urgent necessity — presented a greater challenge. *Forget the jackals,* she thought. Dehydration was her most feared enemy.

Navigating now by landscape, she continued in her ever-increasing spiral outward from the thick bushes where she'd staged her own mauling. Hours later, she neared a low escarpment that fronted a wide section of dry riverbed, fifty yards across, cut by spring runoff, the gravel interspersed with tall islands no more than a few yards wide. A vehicle lay on the far side of the wash, smashed, rolled up against a tree.

Ducking and hiding behind the rocks, Grace ate half of the berries and monkey oranges and felt better for it. After a time, convinced it wasn't occupied, she dared to approach the vehicle. She found the keys in the ignition, the battery dead. A smashed starburst in the windshield, she imagined, was meant to tell the story: the driver's head, collided on impact, giving him the later excuse of forgetting where he'd lost her.

Grace inventoried any and all materials available to her, not surprised to find the spare tire toolkit missing. She knew the engine would have oil in it, possibly petrol. The car had four good tires and a fifth mounted to the back; two windshield wipers in front, one in back; a radio antenna that would serve as a whip; under the hood, a sheet of flexible insulation backed by aluminum foil that could serve as a small blanket. The variety of mirrors could be detached and used for signaling. She tore loose an elastic net from the back of each front seat; they could be used for storage. The owner's manual gave her hundreds of pieces of paper she might use to start a fire.

Fire. The idea had barely occurred to her. She knew the wood-on-wood technique, but in the dark had found no wood thick enough. The escarpment plateau was heavily treed. She broke one of the mirrors and used its glass to slice the seat upholstery. She hit a layer of plastic and spent time delaminating it. She kept the plastic and fashioned a skirt out of the upholstery.

Working fast, determined to set the vehicle on fire as a signal, she stripped out the plastic ceiling fabric. From beneath the listing vehicle she collected black grease that she smeared onto a few pages torn from the manual. By cutting rubber hoses in the engine compartment, she struck oil and captured it in the plastic sheeting. Digging a hole, she set the bowl of oil inside.

Euphoria coursed through her. She'd made it through the night alive. The rising billow of black smoke would . . .

. . . signal whoever had left her here.

Before she burned the vehicle, she had to have a damn good plan for self-defense. What if they brought dogs to hunt her?

Grace paused, reconsidered. No matter

how tempted, she was not prepared for the possible consequences. "Victory in battle is as much about preparation as it is execution" — her army drill sergeant had told her that repeatedly. Her enemy was counting on her dying of exposure. By shredding her clothes, she'd begun a ruse. To attract attention now could easily backfire.

Undaunted, she spent more time stripping the vehicle. She gleaned lengths of nylon thread from the seats, several meters of wire from under the hood, two long dipsticks, shards of glass from the lightbulbs. She gathered her take into a piece of seat upholstery, tied it off and threw the sack over her bare back.

If her driver returned to confirm the kill, he would come here first. He would see that someone had salvaged the vehicle. Burning the car would prevent that, but would reveal her. She needed a plan — and quickly. The man wouldn't allow much time to elapse before he checked for her. The longer it took, the more difficult it would be to find her remains.

Grace prioritized. She would remain close to the vehicle, hopefully with a distant view of the kill site. If dogs were brought, the smear of mud and dung might keep them at bay.

As she worked over the vehicle, she found herself wondering again where she'd gone wrong, who had betrayed her. She'd taken a circuitous route, to be sure. Nairobi. Then the Oloitokitok Clinic. Back to Nairobi. Up to Mount Kenya, in pursuit of the substitute vaccine. The breakthrough she'd needed. Again to Oloitokitok.

Now, alone and abandoned. Discarded. The spider silk connecting and binding each piece to the next appeared as fragile and tenuous as the facts at the start of any investigation. This uncertainty was part of the thrill of what she did. Grace thought her exposure had likely come from whoever had tried to hack her. Either from that person directly, or from wherever he or she had managed to sell the information.

Asian Container Consolidated or Archie Nadali came to mind. Had her investigation into Samuelson tipped the scales? Had she shared Radcliffe's photo of the tattoo with one too many? And what of the embittered and embattled Radcliffe himself? To what lengths would he go to avenge the death of his wife and his fellow reporter?

And then there was the country at large — the vast open sore of distaste over the Kikuyu government, hoarding public funds at great cost to the Kenyan people, the wildlife and the country's future, all while allowing the Chinese to take over everything but the Parliament House.

What did any of it, or all of it, have to do with the missing cache of elephant tusk? Ironically, Grace had believed she'd been close to uncovering the mystery of the missing cache.

I'm the one person who knows how to find it, she thought grimly, *and I'm stuck in a desert with no way to communicate.*

And what of Travis Brantingham, the head of Larger Than Life? He'd been her last interview before this. Someone in his ranks had switched drivers on her.

The dry wash of the seasonal stream created a warren of erosion eight to ten feet deep. A desolate, barren pit, void of anything green or living. Grace felt something evil about it, but recognized it as a good place to hide. It was easy to move through without being seen.

Beyond it, the escarpment rose, the ground of the savanna lifted by volcanic upheaval. Atop its plateau grew twisting shrubs and struggling trees. She would find more to eat there, and possibly water. The wash ran left to right, parallel with the face of the escarpment, which continued half a kilometer farther. The rock face drew a line that pointed toward the kill spot where she'd left her clothes.

Grace made for the end of the outcropping, wanting the higher ground and wondering if it might afford her the ability to see both the vehicle and the kill site. As she walked, she mentally inventoried the items in her knapsack, deciding upon a use for each one. She struggled to better recall Olé's teachings. And for the first time since the horror of undressing and slathering herself with animal shit, she felt a ray of hope.

29

As he entered Nairobi's Uhuru Park, Knox took note of the woman sitting next to Bishoppe on the molded plastic bench. Wearing black pants secured by a wide black-leather belt with a bold silver buckle, and an army-green, loose-fitting boat-neck shirt that spilled off her right shoulder to reveal a strong collarbone and a sky-blue bra strap, she didn't look much like any detective Knox had ever known.

He saw her come off the bench, her strength masked by a controlled gracefulness. Thin face, small eyes. A strong neck and square shoulders. Not for the first time he wondered how smart it was to take a meeting with a policewoman when he was wanted for the murder of a cop.

The woman joined Knox but kept an arm's-length away. Bishoppe trailed behind. They remained on the park's central path. The cop impressed Knox with her ability to match his long strides.

"I am Inspector Kanika Alkinyi."

"John Knox."

"Yes. We have your face pinned to our board. You've got yourself in a bit of trouble, haven't you, Mr. Knox?"

"I didn't do it."

"I phoned Maya after the boy found me. She told me your story. I'm inclined to believe you both, or I wouldn't be here."

Was the tone of concern normal for her? Knox didn't know. He was out of his depth. Hell, the minute he'd entered baggage claim, he'd felt that way. And he wasn't comfortable following on a dance floor. He liked to lead.

Eyes trained forward, mouth dry, the smell of dirt and dust commingling with automobile emissions in his nostrils, he grew impatient.

"Should we need to speak again, we will not use telephones," she said.

"Agreed." He had no idea what she was proposing.

"The boy can be our go-between, if needed. That was a wise choice. Why do you risk seeing me?"

"Maya said you were trustworthy. If there's a hotel video, which I assume there isn't, it'll show a pair of kids knocking that cop off the balcony with a baggage cart."

"There is no such video. I am under the impression that you are requesting transit to Mombasa, passage on a freighter."

"Not yet, I'm not. Maya and I don't see eye-to-eye on that one."

The policewoman reversed direction, heading back toward the gate she'd come through. Ahead was burned-out grass and a few plastic benches, litter like fallen leaves.

Knox caught up with her. "You're counter-terrorism!"

"I don't discuss assignments with anyone. Certainly not you, Mr. Knox."

"Please." He was able to stop her — barely. "The sergeant at the hotel told me I had visa problems and plane reservations in three hours. Who could arrange such a thing?"

In profile, Kanika Alkinyi was strikingly pretty. An upturned nose and pouty lips. Earthy and sophisticated at once. Urban chic. "There was a man rumored to be in the city. Very risky, his coming here. It is possible the two are linked. But it will take time to prove, if such proof is even possible."

"I'm out of that commodity, time."

"Yes, you are."

"You've seen this, I assume?" He unfolded

the printout of the tattooed arm from Radcliffe's illegally acquired crime scene photos. It showed the dark-skinned arm bearing a roughly circular three-inch medallion with an Arabic word tattooed over it.

دائما

"This man was shot execution-style," Knox continued, "two months before Samuelson, a reporter for —"

"I'm familiar with the Samuelson shooting. What is the significance of this photo, Mr. Knox?"

He wanted to be careful, didn't want to report Grace as a missing person. It was one thing for Winston to have alerted British Intelligence. What happened from there was up to them. Involving the mostly corrupt Kenyan police, on the other hand . . .

"Execution-style. This man. Then Samuelson and the man with him. The work of terrorists made to look otherwise? Corrupt rangers?"

"You're familiar with gunshot wounds, I suppose?"

"I drove supply convoys out of Kuwait. I've seen my share of bodies, including those lined up on their knees and shot from

213

behind. It's not pretty."

She nodded, spoke. In spite of himself, Knox appreciated the singsong of her colonial British accent, the rhythmic, almost musical, cadence to her speech.

"The tattoo translates, 'Always. Constantly.' It is Arabic, as I assume you know." She returned the photo. "I can, perhaps, help you leave the country. I can advise you on how to secure relatively safe transit to Mombasa. These are the limits of my involvement. You understand?"

"Of course. But the photo," he said, waving it. "That's all? Nothing more?"

"The problem with foreigners, especially Americans, is that you move too fast. You are smart, but impatient. And always so independent." She slowed their walking pace. "I am aware of your missing friend. Maya told me. Do not be alarmed. I will not act upon this information without your request, but I tell you this: not all Kenyan police are corrupt, Mr. Knox. Far from it. We can help in these matters."

Knox took in the stark park grounds and its carefree visitors. A pair of older men planted like sculpture on a bench. A woman entertaining a young child with blowing bubbles. *The farther you travel,* he thought, *the less distance separates us.*

"Get away while you can. This is my advice. Leave the missing persons to us."

"She came to you. She was looking for a terrorist connection." He had no idea what he was talking about, but it was worth a try. "Bernard Radcliffe sent her."

"Smart but impatient, just as I said."

"The tattoo is tribal? Gang? Militant? Help me out here. Please."

"I told you what it means. It is an Arabic symbol. It is . . . we see it worn a great deal by those with allegiance to al-Shabaab, Boko Haram and al-Qaeda."

Knox sorted out possible explanations. She wasn't about to volunteer information. "So, in this killing, they apparently killed one of their own in the same method used on Samuelson and the other man. Why? Was this man with the tattoo an informer of yours?"

"I could never confirm such a thing. Let me say my best guess is betrayal. His execution was a message to others. If not, there was no reason to allow the body to be found."

"Understood."

"I can get you to Mombasa. I can give you the name of one who can arrange passage. From there, you are on your own. Every police officer in Kenya knows of you.

You are a cop killer. Most would gladly gun you down."

"My friend was tasked with connecting certain funds to terrorism. The funds led to Achebe Nadali." She snorted. "You know him. Daniel Samuelson began investigating Nadali two months prior to his murder. He was executed in the same manner as this alleged terrorist. You can see why it would have interested my friend."

"Her interest ran deeper than this. The tattoo does not mark him a terrorist, per se. It's of interest, certainly, but nothing close to evidence. If your friend traced illegitimate funds to Minister Nadali, she should have shared such information. Too independent, you see?"

"She's not American. A Chinese national."

"All the worse. Much worse."

"You said her interest ran deeper." Knox heard the exasperation in his voice. *What to hold back? What to reveal?* Winston had tasked Grace with three objectives: trace the money, recover it if possible, and connect the clinic to terrorism. "Please. She shouldn't have tried it alone. On that, we agree."

Inspector Kanika Alkinyi leveled Knox with a look of frank disappointment. "She is a smart woman. She has likely gone to ground."

He shook his head. "Yes, she's brilliant, but no. She's an accountant. Ambitious to a fault. She had no business taking this beyond the computer work. Radcliffe put the reporter Samuelson onto Achebe Nadali. Then he put Grace onto him as well."

"Archie's had a hell of a time."

"Radcliffe drew a timeline between a payoff to Nadali and the disappearance of the ivory from the government vault."

The woman sucked air through her teeth, whistling. "Did he? That's the first I've heard of any such connection."

The idea came to Knox like a premonition. Out of the ether and into his lap. "Tell me something: is there a reward for the ivory?"

"Indeed. It's the new national lottery. Twenty-five percent. The government, no matter how complicit, must take a stand, must attempt to recover this ivory and keep it off the market. This theft is an embarrassment of epic proportions, Mr. Knox. A demonstration of the depth of corruption. It's catastrophic, politically."

She turned to him and leveled another of those looks. She wasn't a woman to waste time. She drove home her points and expected Knox to think them through on a variety of levels. She was a marathon runner who expected him to keep up.

"If what you say is true about Nadali, he's a dead man. He'll have an accident. A house fire. Something. The government will want to destroy the ivory in a very public setting. Returning it to the vault is not an option."

"Twenty-five percent," Knox said. "That's a million U.S., or more." He fell silent, his mind spinning. The sum nearly matched the exact dollar figure of Winston's loss, the amount Grace had been tasked to retrieve.

Grace was after the ivory to complete her assignment trifecta. And to think he'd chided her for being Winston's lapdog. Trace the money and leave the rest to Winston and his staff? She just couldn't do it.

He felt violently angry. Grace never stopped pushing.

"What is it? Are you not well?"

"Samuelson would have had a laptop, papers."

"I wouldn't know."

"Cloud storage."

"She's clever," the policewoman stated. "Look. The stories about the health crisis resulting from the bad vaccine included references to a vaccine intended for cattle. Miss Chu asked me about bigger cattle operations in the vicinity of —"

"Samuelson's killing. Mount Kenya."
Knox nodded. "Smart." *Shit,* he thought.

"There's a ranch called Solio, out of the
village of Nanyuki. No theft was reported to
police. No insurance claim has been filed."

"The first victim. This man," Knox said,
shaking the printout of the tattoo. "Is the
timing right to connect him to a theft of the
vaccine?"

"Speculation." Kanika shook her head.
Her short hair held to her head like a
helmet. Her upturned nose lent her a
haughty impression. She was clearly considering Knox's question. "My offer to get you
out of country won't stand for long. Please,
accept it."

"I can't," Knox said. He took a breath,
asked, "Is there someone, anyone, in
Nanyuki or this Solio you trust?"

"The people at Solio are good people.
They are part of the Eastland group."

Eastland had arranged Knox's airport
pickup. The owners were friends of Winston's.

"There is a ranger on the Solio reserve,
I'm sure. I can't speak for him. And there's
another man, someone called Koigi. But he
won't see you. And listen, going up there is
out of the question for you. You're wanted."

"You said the provincial police might be a

219

day or two behind."

"That's not a risk you want to take."

"Do you know Koigi personally?" he asked.

"I know of him." Kanika blinked. It was the first lie she'd told him. "He is a complex man," she added. "Passionate. Single-minded. The Kenyan government has been talking about the menace of poaching for decades. Koigi takes a more . . . proactive stance. It puts him at odds with people in my department and the KGA. He's caught between the laws and the lawless. He will take every measure to ensure self-preservation."

Kanika stopped, took in their surroundings and sat down again on another park bench. This one was made of recycled pink plastic. She covered her mouth as she spoke, her voice barely above a whisper. "Where Koigi's rangers and tactics have been installed, the elephants are on the return. This is no coincidence. Folklore abounds, but his stories need no exaggeration. As a policewoman, I turn a deaf ear, as do a few others. Poachers who find their way into Koigi's territory do not find their way out. In fifteen years, he has arrested three that I am aware of. Three. All under sixteen years of age."

Knox wondered if she was putting him on. Folk heroes arose from rumor and want.

"There is a story that says Koigi once entered a newly formed Muslim village on the border of one of the reserves under his protection. Alone, he cautioned the residents that anyone found across the park boundary would be beheaded. He said he would drink soup from their hollowed-out skulls. To the people of Islam, this is the ultimate threat, for they cannot reach the promised land, the afterlife, without proper burial. It is said that no one from that village has ever tested the threat. This is because it is Koigi. His reputation is the stuff of legend. He has given his full life to the elephant and rhino. His whereabouts, and that of his team, are rarely known. His kills are never found, never investigated. The people of Kenya, people like me, will protect him, Mr. Knox. Believe me."

In the distance, Knox saw children playing on brightly colored jungle gyms, heard the traffic overcome by birdsong, felt a breeze cool on his sweaty face. He dried his palms on his thighs.

"Koigi was ahead of his time. There is a group in the south, Larger Than Life it's called, a conservation NGO that was started by an American photographer, Rick Rand,

221

who saw through his lens the effect of poaching on our Big Five. Larger Than Life now employs two hundred and fifty private rangers. It's run by a South African called Travis Brantingham. They're financed by international grants and donations. Entirely different than Koigi, a black African financed by God knows who. Larger Than Life patrols over three million hectares. Whether or not they employ shoot-to-kill protocol is unknown, but it's believed they do. They've had tremendous success protecting the elephant. Similar to Koigi's success, but without nearly the same amount of controversy."

"Because Koigi is himself wanted," Knox said. "So meeting an American trying to find a Chinese woman won't exactly top his list."

She laughed for the first time. The sound was husky, yet feminine. "Mombasa, John. Not Nanyuki. And today, while it's still an option."

"If the boy comes to you, he represents my interests. If he asks you to arrange a meeting, then I've made it safely."

"Shot on sight. You understand, John? My offer is short-lived."

"Let's hope I'm not."

She chuckled, leveled a disparaging gaze

at him, then stood and walked away. She glanced back once, the smile now a smirk of satisfaction.

"Whatever you do, don't stop moving," she called out.

30

Sarge was in the lead truck. We were on a delivery — that's what we called them, whether it was a full convoy or just a few trucks. Kuwait to one of our bases in Iraq. This one was small, three rigs. A Humvee front and back, the one in front taking an extreme forward position to sweep for IEDs. The one behind stayed in tight to the last rig.

"There are abandoned vehicles along any route. Burnouts. Casualties of war. You don't notice them after a while. The lead Humvee pays attention so we don't have to.

"They think it had to be radio-controlled, probably cell phone–activated. It may have been our own radios. That can happen. But the precision suggests we were being observed. It skipped the Humvee and blew up the cab of the lead truck. They try to time it like that so they can salvage the contents of the trailer. Big ball of black smoke. Flames. I can't remember it most of the time. When I do, I get parts of it wrong. It's like switching to a television channel that's just static. My brain shuts down and I don't remember.

"There may have been gunfire. They tell me there wasn't, but something sure sounded like it. Maybe a second IED. No one knows because the cab blew up. Apparently I got Sarge out. I wasn't playing hero because I wasn't thinking. Something like that happens, you just react. You move. Maybe I was running scared. I have no idea.

"It wasn't until the hospital in Switzerland and therapy that it started coming back. To this day, like right now, if I try to think about it, it isn't there. It comes in nightmares. Car wrecks. Any loud noises. I avoid the Fourth of July. Seems cruel to put vets through explosions like that once a year, not that I'm a vet. Not even close.

"The second explosion did in my left ear. Blew out my eardrum. I was bleeding from it. Sarge was a mess. Whatever genius put a medic in those Humvees, Sarge owes his life to him.

"From the moment the first bomb went off to sometime later, when a medic was waving salts under my nose, my one thought, the one thing I remember, is seeing Tommy. My brother. I'm his guardian, his legal guardian, and I remember thinking about him, about

225

seeing his face. I thought I was going to die. I was convinced that after the bombs, we'd be ambushed. It's how other attacks had gone. Bomb on one side, attack from the other. Kill everyone. Pilfer the goods. In and out, over and done. We were a good three hours from the border at that point. Another two to the base. It's not like the cavalry was coming.

"They didn't get us. But it screwed me up. To this day, I'm still screwed up because of it. I can't watch violent movies. Don't even want to. The smell of smoke, oil smoke, makes me sick to my stomach. I'm half deaf in my left ear. I never tell anyone that. I shouldn't have told you, Grace, because if you tell Sarge about my impairment he'll take me off the list."

"I would never do such a thing. You must know that, John. How can you not know that?"

"I felt things before that delivery. Love, compassion. Not so much anymore. I feel for Tommy. I love that kid and I hate him at the same time because he's defined me.

"I was scared for you in Amsterdam." The abrupt transition made it sound like a confession of sorts. His eyes went soft. "When you went into the Florence Nightingale Hospital in Istanbul, I was terrified you wouldn't come back out."

"I always come back."

Grace recalled the conversation nearly

226

word for word. Yet she couldn't remember exactly when they'd had it. Wasn't sure if she hadn't lied about returning. Had it been leaving Istanbul after the op? Over Skype? It didn't matter. It was a moment of endearment for her, one she hadn't forgotten. Knox had allowed her in.

For a time, she'd begun to think there was no "in," just a man crushed by living too long on the edge of war, by caring for an invalid brother who often dragged him down into depression. Whether a moment of weakness or something intentional on his part, she wasn't sure. But she remembered feeling good in the hours that followed, incredibly good, while simultaneously upset at herself for allowing another's tragedy to result in her own happiness.

An ancient Chinese proverb kept recurring to her when she thought about that talk. Roughly, it went "An invisible red thread connects those destined to meet, despite the time and place, despite the circumstances. The thread can be tightened or tangled, but will never be broken."

That day with John convinced Grace Chu of the existence of a red thread, a treasured discovery she kept close to her heart and even more closely protected.

She wasn't feeling good now, hidden

among boulders with a view of the listing truck to her right and the kill spot well in the distance. Just below were the three holes she'd dug. She'd lined each with plastic and sealed an additional sheet of plastic over the top, like a lid.

Her need for water was growing fierce. She'd sucked a few tablespoons' worth of aloe from a plant; any more would make her sick. If she could kill something, she'd drink its blood, repulsive as it seemed. To that end, she'd strung a length of wire from the engine across a rabbit path. One foot beyond, she'd dug a hole deep into the sandy soil and stuck carefully split sticks into the bottom. She'd covered it fully with loose leaves. A long shot, but one worth trying. She'd created the same trip-and-pit two hundred meters north, where a few small-game trails intersected. She kept the thorn switch, the antenna and one of the two dipsticks by her side, alert for low-flying birds, moths, moles or mice. And then she waited, as still as the rock that concealed her mud-and-dung-plastered form.

For a time, she dozed. Then, startling awake, she went in search of the yellow and red berries that curbed her appetite and worked as a mild stimulant. Back to her sentry position.

Her urination stung. The thick stripe of forest behind her frightened her, and for good reason. After hours of looking out over the wide, dry riverbed, she'd decided to collect some of the white driftwood it contained, in case she could figure out how to start a fire.

Drawing closer, she'd determined it wasn't driftwood, but sun-bleached white bone. Hundreds of pieces scattered randomly in small piles, each representing a kill. A graveyard. Gorgeous, majestic animals, twenty — no, more like forty, she realized — preyed upon most likely by lions. The cats used the rock outcropping where she now hid to spy arrivals, then sneaked down into the deep ravines of the wash and waited, unseen around the curves. The most bones were clumped at either end of the deepest cuts — areas where the impala or other gazelle had no chance of climbing out.

Grace sat atop her rock outcropping, shaking, one eye trained down the line of boulders. She anticipated the arrival of a set of ears, or the profile of a large cat's head. Dawn and dusk would be the most likely times for lion attacks. Dusk of her second day would soon arrive. She'd extended her life expectancy by a full day. Surviving this night — any night — would be the real challenge. Just as in cities, that was when the violence occurred.

During the past thirty-odd hours, her senses had clarified. She felt able to see longer distances, to discern changes in the smells carried on the breeze, to hear faraway things. The slightest change of temperature brought chills or sweat. Her nakedness — but for her skirt — her skin covered in dried mud, was a new and not unpleasant experience. She thought of herself as a lion, patiently awaiting sight of her prey.

Just in case, she'd found a space between two huge rocks that offered a degree of shelter and protection; if she slipped down, she could fit herself into a deeper cavelike hollow. She'd practiced her retreat several times; the first gap was so narrow it scraped off some mud each time she squeezed through. There was no way she could do it quickly. If attacked, she would need fifteen seconds or more to reach safety.

How much safety, she wasn't sure.

Nor was she sure how, or if, she would attack should someone return for her. Further complicating matters was the question of whom to trust. Certainly her would-be killer might come, but any number of people and agencies might be out searching as well. By now, she hoped the lodge would have put out an alert. If a ranger showed up, should she trust him, or attack? An attack would require a weapon, and the only foolproof one at her disposal, beyond a rock and hand-to-hand close combat, was from an Olé lesson. He'd shown her the poison arrow tree and the white milk that gushed from its leaves or bark with the smallest cut, a few drops of which killed nearly instantaneously upon entering the human bloodstream. The Maasai tipped their hunting spears with it. The tree grew abundantly and was easily identified.

If Grace could get up the nerve to enter the forest behind her — the lion's lair — she felt confident she'd find at least one such tree. A fallen branch with its tip honed and she'd have her weapon. But she couldn't bring herself to do it.

The rumble of an airplane overhead caught her by surprise. The wind must have held off its sound; by the time she heard it, it was nearly upon her. Could she trust it? Could she afford to let it pass?

Grace grabbed one of the mirrors and, one-handed, scrambled down the lattice of slippery rock, jumping and sliding in an effort to reach the flat ground below, where her waving would be more easily seen. She wiggled the mirror, trying to find an angle between the sun and the single-engine plane.

In her frenzy, her left hand slapped onto a rock and touched something soft. She jerked back instinctively, but the bush viper was faster. It struck, biting her on the wrist. The snake's scales were brown and yellow, its eyes a vivid green. As it lunged for a second strike, she clipped it with the mirror and sent it tumbling off the warm rock. Her backward momentum carried her down, too, casting her off balance. Her left ankle rolled and pain shot up her leg.

In a long, agonizing slide, Grace fell to the sandy floor, crawling and squirming, still trying to flash her mirror into the sky overhead. The plane had passed. Dropping the mirror, she writhed in reaction to two distinctly different pains.

Her wrist stung chemically, like the worst of a bee sting; her ankle throbbed, instantly hot. A slight sprain, but nothing more. Her wrist, on the other hand . . .

It was difficult to breathe through her fear. Grace felt faint. Steadying her breath, having no idea how toxic the snake might be, but somewhat mollified by how stout it had been — the general rule being: the bigger the venomous snake, the less lethal its bite — she pulled herself painfully back up into the rocks, her left foot useless, debating whether to tourniquet the bite.

Back at her station, a length of engine wire wrapped but not yet tightened around her forearm, she scratched away the mud, spat to clean it off her skin, and watched for any sign of inflammation and redness to begin creeping toward her elbow. In this environment, without water, to tighten the tourniquet, cutting off all blood flow, would likely mean losing her hand.

It was not a decision she wanted to make.

31

Having been told to keep moving, it occurred to Knox that Bishoppe, working the airport as he did, might know a pilot in general aviation with a single-engine plane and a mouth that could keep shut. He now found himself riding in a car arranged by Bishoppe, on his way to a plane arranged by Bishoppe.

His fourteen-year-old personal concierge talked incessantly from the front seat, saying little, if anything, of interest. Knox tuned him out, instead studying the printout of the tattoo by the sliding rectangles of streetlamp light. The image was the one piece of evidence connecting Knox back to Grace. He wasn't going to let go. ·

Bishoppe turned a shoulder and looked into the backseat.

"I should come with you, Mr. John."

"Right. Of course you should."

"We agree?"

"I was being sarcastic," Knox said. "You understand?"

"You are not funny. We are a good team."

"You've been a big help, Bishoppe. If I return to Nairobi I'll call you. How's that?"

The boy pointed through the seats. "Many men have this same tattoo."

Knox worked to contain his astonishment before speaking. "You've seen this same tattoo before?"

"I just said so, didn't I? Many times." Bishoppe opened his hand. "Let me see." Brash. Ballsy. Knox passed him the photo. " 'Forever.' This is what it means. It is a statement. Arab forever. You understand?"

"Yes. 'Constant.' 'Always,' " Knox said, quoting Kanika Alkinyi. But the kid's combination of 'Arab forever' hit home. It wasn't a spiritual statement, but a nationalist slogan.

"One symbol, many meanings. It's the same in English. Yes? Hot food. Hot woman."

Knox laughed automatically.

"This other part, the circle, this is not common. Tell me, what does it mean?"

Knox unbuckled to lean forward. "Always. Constant."

"Not the writing! I can read, Mr. John!" Bishoppe leaned to point out the dark

235

medallion the calligraphy covered. "A burn, maybe. Some villages mark a boy when he is a man. No one is going to burn me. I want a tattoo of LeBron James."

Knox asked the driver's permission to turn on the overhead light. The driver nodded; the light was burned out. He used his phone's flashlight app. "Let me see."

Again, the boy pointed out the dark circle of skin. "The tattoo runs across it, you see? Maybe he makes the tattoo to cover it. Maybe he doesn't like the look of it, so large and ugly. Recent, I think. You see the pink at the edge?"

Knox reached over and took back the printout. He shined the light close to the paper. "You have good eyes."

"You must be blind. You know I speak the truth. You need my help, Mr. John. I know much more than you."

Knox laughed aloud while folding up the printed page. It felt impossibly good.

32

"That one had buffalo balls," Guuleed told his lieutenant, Rambu. They stood just outside their relocated camp. Observing Xin Ha's warning about overhead drones, Guuleed had split his team into two, setting the camps several miles apart. Weapons were kept hidden at all times. The men from both camps were sent out daily on wildlife reconnaissance, binoculars only. From the air they would look like rangers or conservationists.

Radio contact was kept limited; messengers delivered written notes between the two camps. Guuleed appreciated the old tradecraft. He'd had enough of technology.

"We dragged that poor bastard out into the bush . . ." Guuleed searched for the name of the man they'd sacrificed; he couldn't find it. "To make a point . . . and you know why no one has surfaced as the real traitor? Because the fucking traitor is up there." He pointed into the sky. "We weren't betrayed in Kibera. We were seen going there. It's been those damn birds all along. The elephants get drones. Who could imagine such a thing?"

"If I may?" Rambu ventured. Guuleed nodded his assent. "Could we use this to our advantage?"

"I'm listening."

"These drones. They can see us. They can see our body heat in the night. But they come and go, and they don't do well in foul weather. The afternoon thunderstorms, for instance. Very bad for them. And the spring migration. A great many safari companies, same trucks as ours. We wait our chance. We move with them, leaving our tents and all else in place."

"I love to hunt at night," Guuleed said. "It's good thinking. We will do as you propose."

At his side, Rambu seemed to grow a few centimeters taller.

"But I have important information that cannot wait for the pace of the migration. I need volunteers. One truck. It can be made to look like resupply. Four in the morning. Like you said, they can't watch us at all hours. It's worth the risk."

"I will volunteer, of course. And as many

others as you need."

"I appreciate that, my friend. We have made a mistake." Rambu looked troubled by his boss's use of that particular pronoun.

"What is it?"

"You look like you're going to shit yourself, man! Can't we make mistakes?"

Rambu picked at his ass. "You may be right." He was kidding, and the two laughed.

Guuleed sobered first. "I've just heard the American killed the sergeant. Tossed him over a balcony into the lobby of the Sarova Stanley. Like I said, brass bollocks on that one. Now he's on the move. Nothing we can do about him for the present."

"Is this the mistake you refer to?"

"No. It's the Chinese whore. It's possible she has — or had, if we've killed her — information vital to our cause. There is hope yet for my family."

"For this I am thankful."

He stepped closer to Rambu. "But we must get her back."

"What? But we — Leebo left her in the bush. Is this possible?" Rambu had learned the art of turning statements into questions, the better to allow Guuleed to make the conclusions. Guuleed had personally instructed Leebo to get rid of the woman.

"Find her."

"It was two days ago. The bush. She's a woman. A Chinese tourist —"

"I don't give a shit. I want her alive. Failing that, I want everything she's got. Her clothing, notes, computer, phone. Everything left behind at the Ol Donyo. Tell Leebo to take you to her. Or everything that belonged to her, if she's dead."

Guuleed unlocked and handed Rambu the treasured satellite phone. It was a symbol of power and Rambu accepted it reverentially.

"Go on," he said. "Make the call. A coded message. Tell him you're on your way. That should light him up."

"It's a day's drive."

"Damn it! Am I asking? Call Leebo! Get this thing started. I will not be happy if you fail. You are to make it look like a rescue. But no matter what, I want answers by tomorrow night!"

Rambu looked shell-shocked by the imposed deadline and his sudden involvement. Guuleed felt the need to motivate him.

"It's the Nairobi ivory, Rambu. It is said the woman was getting close to it." Rambu's eyes grew enormous in his blue-black face. "But listen up! If you repeat what I just said, repeat it to anyone, I will nail your tongue to a poisonwood tree and watch the ants eat you alive."

33

The Macadam road leading from the Nanyuki airfield was bordered by small farms, forest and the occasional village of cinderblock one-story buildings painted turquoise, rose, purple and green. Pickup trucks passed frequently, carrying harvested crops, farm animals and children. Boys with long switches herded goats, sheep or cattle along a well-worn roadside path. Women wearing colorful long skirts and sleeveless tops walked in pairs.

Knox, in the front seat, used the driver as a tour guide. Healthy sons were herdsmen from age ten, he learned. Girls lucky enough to be married off did so between thirteen and sixteen. A lucky man lived to sixty.

Despite a road sign that listed its population as over thirty thousand, Nanyuki was a blink-and-miss-it town, little more than a crossroads of two paved double-lane highways. A majority of its residents appeared to be constantly afoot, hordes walking along the roadways, just as in Nairobi.

Three structures rose above two stories, all hotels. Trash, detritus and red dust as fine as baking flour swirled about, carried on the wind.

"Jesus." Knox let the word escape absentmindedly. He'd been expecting a mini-Nairobi.

"Ah, there are five churches in town," the driver said happily. "Several more along this road. Take your choice."

Knox shook his head and slipped on his sunglasses.

The town's main road had been patched so many times it was nearly impassable. Vehicles crawled. Randomly placed speed bumps added a touch of irony. On all sides, the men wore blue jeans and, inconceivably, Nike running shoes and Under Armour shirts. Knox rolled down the window — then quickly rolled it back up. He didn't want to think about the source of such smells.

He checked into an older hotel along the main road. The Kirimara Springs had lost its veneer of pretension the day construction was completed, perhaps some thirty years before. Knox's second-floor room had a dust-encrusted ceiling fan, complaining at one lazy speed, and a hard mattress on a low wooden bedframe beneath a veil of what had once been white mosquito netting. There was a mirror, two ceramic elephant trunks for hooks on the wall, one of them chipped, and a wooden dresser that looked like a high school freshman's wood shop project. A corner sink played host to a parade of small black ants and two tiny bottles — shampoo and conditioner, the printing of which was so well worn from refilling that only the double *o*'s distinguished between them. Down the hall, a community toilet had the disinfectant smell of an Ohio travel center off Interstate 80. There was no phone, no magazines, no tourist brochures. No hotel map mounted inside the door displaying the nearest fire exits. Presumably the window won. Or, you'd be so depressed having stayed here that when it lit on fire you'd just remain in your room and suffer your lumps.

Knox felt like a tick in an armpit. He secured his phone inside one of the interior pockets of his windbreaker, which he carried over his shoulder as he left the hotel for a walking tour. The jacket also contained a Maglite, Rolaids, a ten-dollar roll of quarters for his clenched fist, and a Swiss Army knife bought on the streets of Nairobi.

His shirt hid two parcels of cash; a thin leather wallet carrying credit cards and IDs warmed itself alongside that area of the body Bonnie Raitt described so articulately as: "Down where it's tangled and dark." Three passports were Velcroed into an added interior pocket of his jeans. He wore a pair of matte black Wayfarer sunglasses and a warning expression: *Fuck-with-me-and-you'll-be-sorry.*

Outside, he joined the pedestrians on his side of the roadway, matched pace and walked. Knox towered over everyone, winning an endless round of curious looks. They seemed to suggest that, as a white man, he belonged in a vehicle.

The stores were mostly shacks with a small dark window through which orders could be placed and goods delivered. Shadowy figures moved within, selling gum, cigarettes, phone parts and fruits. Mini-pickup trucks piled absurdly high with hand-tied bales of *khat* lumbered past. The plant was chewed as a mild stimulant. Knox could have used some.

He arrived at the center of the village and found his way to the town market, led by farting motorcycles, belching trucks and the drone of a Bruno Mars song. A wide dirt street with dozens of competing fruit and vegetable stands lining both sides opened out before him.

The open-air market attracted barefoot kids, women of every age and shape, and an abundance of houseflies. Each small stall offered nearly identical produce in vivid colors — carrots, beets, melons, green onions, tomatoes. The occasional stall of nuts and fruits or fly-crusted meats broke the monotony. Knox walked slowly, answering inquisitive eyes with a smile, all the while keeping track of anyone and everyone within twenty yards.

Keeping his pace slow and easy, he continued down a small hill to an open field filled with tables heaped with color. It took him a moment to grasp that what he was seeing were mountainous piles of clothing, organized by vendors who advertised their prices on hand-scrawled posters.

"English? English?" Knox called. A young man in his early twenties appeared. He wore a St. Louis Rams jersey, black trousers and scuffed penny loafers without socks. His complexion suggested younger than thirty but older than twelve.

"I speak the English," he said.

"What is all this?" Knox asked, gesturing to the field of clothing. The area was thirty yards wide and over a football field long.

"Nanyuki market," the man said.

"So much."

"It is always like this. Everyone from Nanyuki and many villages for many miles buys the clothes here."

Wandering among the tables, Knox observed that every shoe, shirt, bra and pair of jeans was used. All American brands. He mentioned this to his interpreter.

"Yes, of course. These are clothes sent to Africa by American charity."

"But they are for sale. Clothes sent from the U.S. are meant to be given away."

"Not here in Kenya. The clothing arrives by ship to Mombasa. It is sold in large . . . how would you say 'tied together'?"

"Bales."

"Very large bales. These bales are resold once onto the dock. This buyer then makes smaller bales and sells to these people here. Same, all over. You see such clothing markets everywhere."

Chicago Bulls, World Series, Nike — Just Do It., Lee, Wrangler, New Balance . . . The closer Knox looked, the more he saw the American suburbs face-to-face with this underground Kenyan economy.

"You wish to buy something?" the man asked. "I may help you?"

"No, thank you." Knox wished to be seen,

to stand out in the crowd. "I'm just looking."

He was idly searching for an XXL T-shirt when a voice sounded behind him. The speaker was a tall, elegant blond woman of indeterminate age who projected a high-minded forbearance.

"I'm called Ava. We spoke."

"John." They shook hands. She could wrestle alligators, he was guessing. "South African?"

"Bravo. Thirteen years in Kenya in September. My fourth at the lodge."

"Solio."

"I apologize for the dramatics. It's just that hoteliers can talk. Better for you not to be overheard hiring a car for the lodge."

They rode in the second bench of a stretched safari truck — an open-air Toyota Land Cruiser — passing huts marked by hand-painted signs advertising eggs and fruit, churches, small farms and the occasional collection of dilapidated shacks. When the colorfully dressed Maasai driver turned off the main road, it was onto a gravel and dirt track that rolled across an open plain of dry grass on both sides. Shortly thereafter, a high, reinforced fence topped with barbed wire appeared on both sides of the track.

"Jurassic Park," Knox said.

Ava winced in amusement.

The brown safari truck crested a hill. Looking down on a green line of cottonwood, Knox saw live rhinoceroses for the first time. He marveled like a little boy. The pair looked like cows from a distance, but evolved into massive gray beasts, their signature upturned curving horns held quizzically toward the sky. "Unreal," he muttered. A dozen Cape buffalo came next, followed by Thompson's gazelles, eland, and more rhinos.

"Do you . . . I mean is this an everyday occurrence?" Knox wanted to shout to stop the car. "Can I get out?"

"There will be time for that." Ava grinned. "It never gets old, believe me."

"I've never seen anything like it." Knox couldn't help sounding awed, wondered why it embarrassed him. "The size! They're *right there*!"

"The cattle operation is on this side," Ava said, indicating the fenced land to the right. "Reserve, here on the left."

Knox couldn't contain his inner tourist. "How big is it?"

"The reserve is seven thousand hectares. The entire ranch, twenty thousand. The cattle operation helps fund the reserve. It's a wonderful symbiosis."

Soon they entered the more forested area and slowed at a KGA checkpoint, Knox slouching and pulling his hat down on Ava's command. The gate was opened before the vehicle fully stopped.

Ahead, a dirt track meandered through dense, lush forest. Soon the lodge emerged, Solio, elegantly designed with a flowing thatched roof and whitewashed stucco walls. It belonged both to its surroundings and on the cover of travel magazines. A line of three staff awaited, all African. Backs straight, heads high. The display was slightly off-putting to Knox, who didn't like being kowtowed to.

Once inside, his freshly wet warm hand towel returned to the tray, Knox looked through the open-air wall onto a panorama of marsh, forest and grassland. A giraffe stood no farther than thirty yards away, by a deck constructed as a dining island.

"The Barr-Latners, the owners of Eastland, built this. Rusty designed it."

"Impressive."

"Yes, we get that a lot. Shall we take some tea? I've arranged a meeting with Benson, our head of security, as you requested. But we have forty minutes or so if you like?"

"Wonderful. Thank you."

She led him to the outside deck. Iced tea and pastries arrived. Ava caught Knox admiring the giraffe, still only a matter of yards away.

"Amazing," he said. "So close. I can see her eyelashes."

"His. He's called Girafa, after Rafael Nadal, my tennis hero. He took a liking to us. He doesn't spook easily."

"It's . . . otherworldly," said Knox. "He must be twenty feet tall."

"Quite nearly six meters. Yes."

"Grace must have loved this." It was the first time he'd mentioned her. "His movement is so elegant. So fluid."

"I would have offered for you to stay with us as well, but because of the uncertainty you expressed . . ."

"Yes. I think this best. That is, until I saw what I'm missing."

"We have the largest herd of black rhino in all of Africa. Larger still, our white rhino population." She smiled at him; he nodded for her to go on. "Rusty and Lana Barr-Latner are both fourth-generation Kenyans. His family was the first to transport wild animals. It's quite a small community, the expat travel industry. But a most trustworthy one. Graham — Mr. Winston — is a regular guest at Solio."

Something lighted upon her lips, not quite a smile, but a rosy warmth of satisfaction. Her eyes softened as they had when she was talking about Girafa.

A herd of Cape buffalo passed slowly far beyond the marsh. A procession as old as the dirt at his feet, Knox thought.

"You like the view?" she asked.

"It's a time machine."

"True."

"How much did Grace tell you?" he asked.

"That Graham had sent her down on a fact-finding mission. No details. She asked if I knew where Samuelson had stayed prior to . . . the tragedy. I told her she'd have to ask the police. That it wasn't here."

"Do you believe he was poaching?"

"Don't be ridiculous. Of course not. Mr. Samuelson wrote about corruption. No great surprise he met his end. But still, an enormous loss."

"Grace was interested only in Samuelson's lodging?"

"And she wanted to meet with Benson. Same as you."

"After that?"

"She checked out two days ago. First flight out. You won't raise her by phone. I've been trying."

"Because?" Knox suppressed the shudder

he felt ripple through him.

"She left an item behind in her room." Ava paused to make eye contact with Knox. "Happens more often than you might think. Although this was a little unusual. It was sealed and on her bed. Out where we couldn't have missed it."

Knox considered the look she gave him. "An envelope," he said. "Something small inside. My name on it."

"No. It's marked 'Private — Do Not Open.' But yes, there is something that moves around inside."

"I'd like to see it, please."

"Drink your tea," she said. "I'll fetch it."

The envelope Ava's housekeeper had retrieved from Grace's room had contained a
second thumb drive. Now, once again, the
screen presented Knox with a question.

Pulled from the fire (nickname):

He entered: Sarge. He didn't like being
asked to remember that day.
The screen refreshed.

The bottle opener:

Knox had gotten stuck on this second
question. He'd sat there for ten minutes,
wondering what Grace was asking, if he was
the right one to try to answer the question.
Fearing the program would only allow a
finite number of tries — three? — he'd withheld from wild guesses.
The small drive was currently zipped into

his Scottevest. Until he could solve the second clue, there were better uses of his time.

Olé wore ceremonial Maasai dress, a colorful waist skirt and a sleeveless scarlet tunic decorated with beads, bone, carved wood and gems. He wore neck bangles, too, which set off his fierce but handsome face, all chiseled, aristocratic bone structure and blank dark eyes. He carried a small, menacing machete in his waist belt.

Another guide, so far nameless, rode standing in the far back of the truck, also dressed in a tribal costume. He carried a bludgeoning weapon, a lump of metal attached to a strong handle. The two spoke intermittently in Swahili.

Heeding Ava's advice and insistence, Knox was on his way to vacate his Nanyuki hotel room — false passport or not — and take a guest room at Solio, where he would be an unregistered guest. The interview with Benson, arranged for later, following the man's afternoon rounds, necessitated the quick trip into town.

"Everything okay, John?" Olé asked.

"Not exactly okay, no," Knox answered honestly. "I'm on a bit of a schedule. Behind schedule."

"This is just the place to forget such things."

"I appreciate that." Knox looked over again at the man, wondering how transparent he could be with him. No; why was he hesitating? Grace didn't have time for subtlety. "A Chinese woman visited, last week. Do you remember her? Grace Chu?"

"Miss Grace. Of course, sir."

"You drove her then?"

"I did, yes. My pleasure."

"She's a close friend of mine. You two talked."

"Of course, sir. A most interesting woman. Very curious."

"She is, isn't she?" Knox's stomach knotted. He didn't trust the tense he was using. He appreciated being reminded of her endearing qualities and how easily likable she was. Painful at the same time. Knox took in the surrounding landscape, all grass and mountains, sky and clouds. No structures. A few fences. A hawk, its wings set, gliding low over the swale.

"What'd you two talk about, if I'm not being rude?"

"Not at all! She asked questions" — Olé gave him a wide smile — "but not like the other guests. Miss Grace is a special woman."

In spite of himself, Knox wanted to snap at the man, tell him to shut up. "In what way did her questions differ?"

"Guests usually ask only about the animals. Similar questions, all the time. We are happy to answer these. This is the joy of Solio Ranch, so many animals, so beautiful."

"But not Grace."

"She was more interested in . . . me, sir. As a man. A Maasai." *No great surprise there,* Knox thought. Grace always turned the conversation away from herself, always made Knox feel interesting, even as he was also the target of her condescending humor.

"Your costume."

"My dress. Absolutely! Right you are! That is where we started. She was much less interested in the Big Five," he said. "She was curious about my life. How it was I found my way to this position at Solio Ranch."

Knox felt her sitting in the same seat as him. Heard her voice. Saw her wearing a hat to hold her whipping hair at bay, one hand constantly on her head.

"She inquired about living off the land, as my people do. What it was like, how we go about it. How it has changed. Most curious."

"She grew up in a small farming village in

China. Did she tell you that?"

"She did not, John. She asked about the Maasai. We have survived well for quite some time. This intrigued her. She wondered what we ate, how we treated disease and birthed our children. She expressed a genuine interest in our way of life."

"Comparing her upbringing to yours," Knox said.

"I suppose. We didn't talk of her. She asked all the questions."

Knox found himself smiling at the thought.

"She asked about Charcoal as well," Olé said, gesturing into the back, toward his silent passenger. "You work together long enough, you grow a fondness. It is true."

"Charcoal? You call him that?" Knox asked, horrified.

"Yes. His skin is gray. You see? His tribal name — it is far too difficult for the guests to pronounce."

The man smiled at Knox from the back.

"He is working on his English," Olé said. "He understands some of what we are saying. But he can speak very little. I am training him. Another five years, he'll be a guide himself."

"She wanted to see plants," Knox said, drawing the conversation back to Grace.

"Just so! Instead of the lion, we stopped to look at trees and plants we Maasai use. I would tell her stories from my boyhood. Miss Grace is most enjoyable."

"Poachers use these same plants and trees?" Knox asked.

"If they are to spend any time in the bush, then of course."

"Or hiding in a reserve."

"Hiding. Waiting. Setting traps. We live off the land. We all know its uses."

"She wanted to know about poachers, what might be found in a poacher's stomach." Knox was thinking autopsy, wondering what other documents Radcliffe might have supplied her.

Olé sounded excited. "You could be right about that, sir! Her concern, to be sure, was medicine and health care, how Maasai, Kikuyu and other tribes find the medical care when needed. I explained we have medicine men and traditional medicines. That over one hundred African plants are used as the basis for important European drugs. Many are simply synthetics of the original plant-derived chemical. This interested her, I think. She wanted any examples I could give, and so I showed her. We talked much about vaccinations and how villagers didn't trust them."

"Vaccines," Knox said, thinking of the work Winston had assigned her.

"Yes."

"And they aren't trusted because . . . ?" Knox asked.

"So many times these injections make our children sick. Some have died. Others, adult and child alike, never improve. For decades, Africa has been used for clinical human trials. Our villages were paid — not well. We have come to associate free medicine with disease. This, while our own medicines cure dozens of illnesses."

The talk of Grace had put her in the vehicle with them. Knox could imagine her in the seat where he now sat, having the conversation he was having. Being awed by the landscape just as he was. *Alive,* Knox thought. Olé had brought her alive.

35

Grace had yet to tighten the wire tourniquet. A raised red welt surrounded the two holes in her skin. The size of a large coin, it was not expanding. Warm to the touch and intensely painful, the snakebite reminded her of a twinned wasp sting — horrible, but nothing fatal.

She struggled to remember Olé's lessons, the Maasai treatment for pain, but couldn't. The symptoms of her increasing delirium were familiar to her: light-headedness, sensitivity to light, daydream hallucinations that mixed with memory. Adrenaline had kept her going for the first twenty-four hours — or had it been longer?

Again, while she still had strength, she scampered down the rocks favoring her rolled ankle. She reached the three holes she'd dug. Two remained lined and covered with plastic; the third had been disassembled. The heat inside the hole increased by day; by night, the cool air in contact with the top piece of plastic caused condensation. The condensed water dripped and fell to the bottom of the hole, collected on the plastic lining. She, or perhaps an animal, had clearly sampled the first hole.

Two days, at least, Grace thought. Time was blurring, slipping away from her. But she believed she had retrieved this water herself. She saw no tracks or signs of animals to convince her otherwise. Carefully, she reset the first hole, sipped the few drops from the second and third, so that the day's hot sun didn't evaporate her winnings. From the second, she captured enough to wet her mouth and throat; the third, better sealed, offered her a small sip that actually ran down her throat. She reset all three more carefully, trying to duplicate the third.

Next, she checked her trap lines. The first, closest to her perch, had not been tripped. But the wire set at the intersection of two small game trails was no longer in place: the ground coverage disturbed; dried blood on the pikes. She followed the irregular track of what she thought might be a small hare, dragging one leg. Drops of blood had spilled with every step, in increasing volume. Fifty meters down the thin trail, Grace cursed: she'd killed a rat. Worse still, it was warm to the touch. Though she knew what had to be done, it was hard to contain her disgust. Shuddering, she cut through the animal's skin with a shard of broken mirror and eviscerated it. Finding its tiny liver, she cut it loose of the entrails, dropped it into the back of her throat and swallowed. She kneeled for several minutes, expecting to vomit, but nothing came up.

On her way back to her lookout, she eyed the rocky plateau, covered in the inviting gray-green of bush and trees. She knew she might find nuts, roots and fruits to eat within — or that poison arrow tree — but could not summon up the courage to try. Imagination, or fairy tales, or the piles of white bone in the wash, held her back.

Sitting again on her perch, she resigned herself to fatigue. Shuddering, she forced her body through the small slit at the bottom of the boulders and crawled inside. It was cooler there, almost entirely in shade. She closed her eyes and within seconds was swallowed into deep, dreamless sleep.

36

Knox asked to be dropped off two blocks from the small hotel. Hyperaware of his color and height, he kept his head low and his face tucked beneath a Tigers cap. He found his way to the back of the hotel and entered through an open door to the kitchen. He passed a distrusting dishwasher who averted his eyes when challenged.

"You can't be in here, sir." The man was a Kenyan his age. He wore a stained blue bandana tied around his sweating brow and carried a two-foot-long spoon in his right hand. "Not for guests."

"Oh, come on," Knox said, seamlessly picking up the conversation as if longtime friends. "How am I supposed to catch her cheating on me if I enter through the lobby? She paid off one of the bellmen; I know she did."

The man seemed tempted to capitulate but wasn't fully buying it. "Health laws."

"I'm sure." The kitchen was in fact surprisingly clean.

"You can't be in here."

"So throw me out, just throw me out through that door." He pointed.

"You try this again, it won't happen." The man stepped aside.

"You must not be married," Knox said, charging through.

He took the stairs, forgoing an elevator he didn't trust anyway. At the top of the stairs, he paused and listened. The talk of Grace and pharmaceuticals, the discovery of the thumb drive left him jumpy. He heard a TV, some water running. He moved slowly ahead.

Upon entering his room, he immediately backed up to the door, his heart racing. He swiftly secured the door with a travel rod, never taking his eyes off the room's interior. No one could enter now without Knox removing the rod.

Someone had been in his room, possibly still was. Not a maid, not unless her job description included searching his carry-on. He'd left the bag's twin zipper pulls drawn all the way to the left rivet, as he always did.

They were currently centered.

The only decent place to hide was between the bed and the wall. The roll of quarters gripped in his right fist, Knox crossed the room in two strides.

Empty. A bead of sweat streamed from his sideburns across his unintentional beard. Burning with tension, he opened his bag. No bomb. No body parts. No ransom note. He wanted badly to attribute the search to a bellman or maid on the take but, except for the zippers, it had been a pro job; he'd have been hard-pressed to know anything had been touched.

He reached for his phone, driven automatically to warn Grace. The reflex startled him.

He'd been away from the hotel for two hours, had unpacked only his toiletries. It took no time at all to collect them.

What might a person learn about him from the contents of his bag? The unusual first aid supplies and medications he carried would be a tip-off. The needle and suture weren't on everyone's vacation list. Hotel staff were known to steal prescription drugs. But his meds were all there, he realized. Cipro, Ativan, surgical scrub, lidocaine cream, Pennsaid, aspirin, Advil, Tylenol. Don't leave home without them. Nothing had been pinched.

The person might have noticed his preference for dark clothing, for Scottevest garments with hidden pockets. The very few dress clothes he carried. That he shaved with a razor, avoided any deodorant with alcohol, carried a dozen protein bars and a go-bag containing vital necessities for seventy-two hours on the run — canned tuna, freeze-dried meals, water purifying straw, Maglite, face black, Leatherman, fire-starting tool, space blanket, duct tape, and nearly two dozen other items, including batteries, maps, a compass and more meds.

Upon inspection, he would come off not as a tourist but as ex-military or paramilitary, or someone on The Circuit — mercenaries who moved between conflicts. He took extra care checking out the window. No uniformed police at the front of the hotel, though that didn't mean much. The lobby desk would be on alert for him if the police were involved. His passing through the kitchen had been a mistake.

Leaving his room, he moved from the stairs to the end of the long hallway, where an alarmed door gave way to a metal lattice fire escape. Power to the panic bar's alarm was supplied through an aluminum flex conduit. Digging into his duffel, he insulated his hand with a neoprene knee brace and sawed through the conduit. He averted his eyes from the blinding spark as he cut the live wire inside. Then he opened the door and was out, scurrying down the fire escape, dropping his bag off the side and hanging before falling the remaining ten feet.

He ran down the alley, feeling like a fugitive and wondering who the hell had searched his room — and why.

37

"What's he like, this Benson?" Knox asked.

The safari truck moved along a rutted dirt track that ran through the green of thick foliage and the gray of fallen trees. Gangs of baboons scattered like startled grackles. Knox had the sense of being watched, of animals lurking. Olé's initial silence, his constantly moving head and searching eyes contributed to Knox's unease. A blast of sunlight gave way to open, dry-grass fields reminding him of northern California. More dead trees lay splayed across the land like skeletons.

Olé drove. Charcoal stood in the back of the truck as scout.

"You will like Benson. The head ranger before him was believed to have cooperated with poachers. The temptations are very great. But I believe Benson to be an honest man. His job, my job — we all rely upon the game in this reserve. It is shortsighted to think otherwise. And he is Kikuyu. His people migrated south and settled around Mount Kenya five hundred years ago. He has this place in his blood. Many times, Benson has expressed to me his dedication to this place and to the preservation of all who live here. I have no reason to doubt that."

"That's quite an endorsement," Knox said.

"I am Maasai. He is Kikuyu. The Maasai warred with the Kikuyu after the British arrived. My ancestors won this war, but eventually lost control of the government. Since this time, the tribes respect one another. We are brothers, Benson and I. We depend upon each other. Without the animals, we have no tourists. Without the tourists, we cannot pay to protect the animals. We are like the ants on the flowers, the vultures on the carcasses. We all rely upon the other."

The truck climbed out of a muddy river bottom marked by a meandering stream and stamped by thousands of animal tracks. The road opened up to bright, searing light and a series of hills.

It was nearing sunset. As they reached the top of the highest hill, Knox saw two army-green SUVs. Range Rovers or Land Cruisers.

"I will just take a moment." Olé parked and left the truck to speak through the passenger window of the lead vehicle. Behind the glass Knox saw a wide, exceptionally round head, a tree-trunk neck and shoulders too wide for the seat to contain them. Olé waved Knox out of the vehicle. The head ranger met him halfway, reminding Knox of some kind of prisoner exchange. Together, the three men stood in the red powder of the dirt track.

Following some formalities and small talk, Benson addressed Knox with a keen intensity.

"So, John, how may I help?"

"Grace was interested in the killings on Mount Kenya. The execution-style murders. Did she ask you about those?"

"She did. I will tell you what I told her: it is all rumor. The only man I would trust to be impartial in such matters is a ranger called Koigi. If anyone knows, it is this man. He has no allegiances, no alliances."

"She asked if you could arrange a meeting for her."

"She did."

"And did you?"

"I may have. I am not a tourist guide,

270

John. Do not ask me to do the same for you."

Knox had been about to ask for exactly that. He lacked Grace's charm, her ability to slowly bring you around to her way of thinking. He pushed himself to think like her, act like her. "Can I ask your opinion of the killings?"

Olé shuffled his sandals in the dirt, head down.

"Let me say," said Benson, "that this man, Faaruq, the first man found, was known to Koigi."

Knox unfolded the printer photo. Benson told him to put it away.

"She showed me this photograph as well. I will not comment on this." Benson looked away from the photo and out into the landscape. Knox gazed out along with him.

"What do you think?" Benson asked.

"Beautiful."

"Too common a word," Benson said.

"Endless. Timeless."

"Better. Yes."

"Untouched."

"Exactly! The same now as then. We Africans take great pride in being the origin of man. Our landscapes, our wild animals."

"We have views like this in America, but there is always evidence of man — a plowed field, a power line, a road, a fence. It's the absence that gives it substance."

"You see? It turns us all into poets." Benson smiled. Not to Knox, but to the reserve and the distant majesty of Mount Kenya that raided a sky of pink-tinted cumulus clouds.

"You get paid to oversee all this," Knox said. "I envy you such a job."

"I am a lucky man." Benson's widely spaced eyes were hidden behind a pair of aviator sunglasses, but the skin at the corners compressed as he squinted.

"She is important to me," Knox said abruptly. "She's gone missing, Benson." It sounded odd to hear the words coming out of his mouth. He rarely took measure of Grace's importance in his life; he wasn't given to sentimentality, his emotions long since burned and buried by Iraqi IEDs and the nearly 24/7 care of his younger brother. Now his simple statement provoked a stream of thought that might have occupied hours, but flashed by in fractions of seconds.

Benson appraised Knox thoughtfully. After a moment, he asked Olé to return to the truck, which the guide did. Considering his words carefully, Benson said, "What I tell you now is in the strictest confidence."

He smiled, showing off uneven teeth.

Knox's chest pounded at the thought of what Grace might be going through. Terror. Abuse. Starvation. Torture. He fought the chemical reaction, knowing firsthand the poison of pent-up adrenaline.

The ranger continued facing the landscape. "There is a Somali called Guuleed who organizes poaching raids here in Kenya. It is believed to profit the terrorists — no proof — but must involve the Chinese as well. He is my sworn enemy. And Koigi's as well. Koigi believes Faaruq, this dead man with the tattoo, was one of Guuleed's most effective enforcers. An expert in torture of all kinds. His execution had to be at Guuleed's hand. It was meant as a warning to others."

Alkinyi had told him the same thing, nearly verbatim. "Torture gone bad?"

"It would not be the first time. Guuleed's men are cruel. They often go too far. This other man killed with the reporter, he too showed signs of having been beaten badly about the face. I have no way to know if this is the truth. I would say Guuleed's men beat this man. A common laborer from Nairobi. Why?" Benson shook his head.

Knox felt the meeting drawing to a close, the brief moment of revelation slipping away with the sunlight. He decided to hazard a

273

guess. "Grace asked you about a break-in here, a theft on the cattle side of the ranch."

Benson remained remarkably unreadable, though he sneaked an admonishing look in Olé's direction. He retained the sunglasses despite the sun setting.

"He said nothing," Knox said. "I haven't mentioned it to Olé. Grace asked you about a large quantity of vaccine. I'm guessing you wouldn't acknowledge it, much less discuss it."

Benson stood so still Knox wasn't sure he'd heard him.

"I ask you to reconsider. Her disappearance has to do with that theft, as well as this photograph. It has to do with Faaruq and a corrupt minister in Nairobi."

"All ministers are corrupt."

"The thieves got away with the vaccine," Knox pressed. "If you intercepted them, and I'm assuming you did, you thought they were after the cattle. You didn't notice the missing vaccine, not for a while. By then you worried about the reputation of the reserve. You realized how little good it would do anybody to report it."

Benson's eyebrows arched above the sunglasses. "Like you, the woman was a storyteller."

Olé's radio clicked, nearly simultaneously

with Benson's. Running toward them, Olé called out. "We must go now, John. The rangers come!"

"KGA have entered the reserve, in pursuit of an American wanted for the killing of a policeman." Benson addressed Olé. "A wanted man. Are you mad? Why was I not told?"

"I've killed no one," Knox said, stepping in front of the man. "I give you my word on that."

Benson spoke softly. "Never ask the right questions of the wrong people."

"Are you going to help me, or turn me in?"

"My friend here," Benson said, gesturing to Olé, "knows this property well. Better than even the KGA. It will take at least fifteen minutes for them to reach us here. If they think to block the east gate, and they may, then your situation is not good. My men and I could conceal you in our vehicles, but that might require lying to the rangers, and that is not my way. I need them more than I need you, Mr. Knox."

"The lookouts —" Olé proposed.

"Will eventually be searched," Benson said. "Hiding in one of them would merely delay the inevitable." Knox appreciated the calm of the two men. "My advice is this."

275

Benson spoke to only Olé, his voice low, authoritative. "Those kids and their damn sheep."

"Ah! Of course!" Olé sounded impressed. He turned to face Knox. "There are shepherd boys always here on the west border. Our friend Benson is very smart. You will please get in the truck, John. I will be right along."

Olé and the ranger spoke as Knox looked on from the open-air vehicle. It was a relaxed and easy conversation between friends. At last the men shook hands, displaying no urgency whatsoever, and Benson strode slowly to his waiting rangers.

"The KGA is ten minutes out," Olé said, climbing back behind the wheel. "You like Benson?"

He sounded as if he was still in guide mode.

Off-road, at the bottom of the next swale, Olé shut off the vehicle, called out up the hill and waved to a small figure. The bone-thin man waved back, and Knox jumped out.

Ahead was a twelve-foot-high electric fence, built with wires wide apart and meant to contain rhinoceros, Cape buffalo, impala and giraffe. Knox heeded Olé's warning of the high-voltage wires, took his time, slipping very carefully through the eighteen-inch gaps between the wires. The air was gray with insects.

Safely on the other side, Knox quickly hiked up a barren hillside toward a band of ragged sheep and their three herdsmen — all young children. The man Knox had seen was about thirteen and clearly the one in charge. An emaciated sheepdog, down on its belly, its front legs extended in prayer, back haunches ready to spring, kept an alert eye on Knox.

"English?" asked the leader.

Knox nodded, stealing a glance at his watch. He expected the KGA to pass by at any minute. Olé's plan remained unknown to him. If anything, he felt set up yet again: high on a hill, his six-foot-three frame towering over these children — he could be easily spotted.

"Here, please," said the boy kindly, leading Knox into the midst of the flock. The sheep parted begrudgingly, bleating and jumping, more than a few of them kicking out their hind legs. "Sit."

"Here?"

"You will sit, please," said the boy.

Through a combination of light breeze and the noise of the animals came the distinctive groan of approaching vehicles.

277

Knox dropped to the ground. He was told to bend forward, to hold that position and not move. Without any more explanation, the boy moved away and emitted a series of ear-piercing whistles. The dog yipped.

Bent forward over his crossed legs, Knox heard the call of high voices and the constant yapping of the dog. In no more than a few seconds, the flock compressed around Knox. Where there had been space between the animals, there was now none. In considering a close-up look at the animals of Africa, Knox had not bargained for sheep. With him in the mix, the animals became agitated. Several walked over him or landed on him as they startled.

Through the groaning of the animals and the tamping of their hooves, Knox heard at least one — possibly two — vehicles draw close to the fence. The engines died. Voices called out loudly. The oldest of the children shouted back. The conversation sounded amiable enough. It went on for perhaps thirty seconds before the engines started again, and the sound of them slowly faded.

Minutes passed before the flock began to thin and a pair of dirty feet in tire sandals appeared in Knox's field of view.

"It is okay now, sir. These rangers are gone. It is best, I think, if you stay as you are in this place. The KGA rangers are devils. I will watch the hills for them. Just in case."

Knox sat up to relieve his back, keeping his head at the height of the sheep for good measure. He also kept watch into the reserve for the wink of binoculars or movement of any kind. With no trees nearby, or terrain to hide in, he had little choice but to stay among the flock.

He crawled several yards on hands and knees, moving along with the animals, avoiding the oval stains from their urine. The fresh pellets he could not dodge. The sun was hot, the sky clear. The smell, overpowering. Thirty minutes bled into forty-five.

"You will keep moving, please!" The lead boy's voice was distant. "Not far now."

Knox felt as if he'd gone a hundred yards on hands and knees. A pair of thin legs appeared. "The rangers return now. We must hurry." Knox hastened with the boy to a copse of trees ahead, where a rusted bicycle lay on the ground.

"Down this path to the main road. You will turn to the left. Our village is then two kilometers. You will leave my bicycle behind the store with the red wall. It is the only one. Wait there for the Maasai. Ride fast.

You must watch for the KGA trucks. They are green like the British army."

Knox thanked him. The bike's front fender had rusted off, along with the brake wire. It had once been three gears; now it was stuck in the lowest. Knox climbed on, the tires squishy under his weight.

"The bell works," the boy said. Knox one-handed the handle bar and lifted his arm to thank the boy.

38

Grace woke to the view of a cat's paw the size of a bread plate. She blinked rapidly, realizing the chill covering her body had nothing to do with hiding in shadow.

Something intangible had brought her out of her sleep. She awakened sick to her stomach, dizzy and finding it hard to breathe.

The lion paw — a front paw — was pressed at an angle against a rock visible through a slice of space formed by her two protective boulders. The giant paw had wisps of feathery auburn hair on its pastern and rising toward its elbow. Grace could have pushed her hand through the crack to touch it.

The cat stood directly over her, sniffing. It was a glorious creature, awkwardly lanky and thin but clean, strong and stealthily silent. Only the faint clicking and scratching of nails to her left suggested a second cat, an inference confirmed only a moment later as it slinked past the wider gap through which she'd come. This bigger cat swung its head across the entry, whiskers twitching, but never gave Grace a second thought. She closed her eyes in appreciation — and reopened them as she heard one of the two urinating. It sounded as if someone had turned on a faucet.

Eye to the crack between stones, she watched as both cats gracefully slipped down the rocks off the plateau and sauntered toward the dry wash. They were rangy and scruffy, with paws that didn't seem to fit their tall bodies. *Juveniles,* she thought. A pair of one-year-olds out in the wild, fending for themselves.

The snakebite no longer stung, but itched like mad. She willed herself not to scratch it. Quietly, carefully, Grace squeezed out into the daylight and, keeping low, moved to the rocks wet with cat urine. Her ankle was tight and sore but functional. She rubbed her hand along the wet rock and transferred what she could to her arms and stomach. Just below, a smooth bowl in one of the pockmarked boulders had caught a few ounces. It was horrid-smelling, but she used it sparingly, like the most expensive perfume: under her arms, between her legs, down her ribs, onto the base of her neck. It turned the dried dung and mud dark and damp, its odor stinging her eyes and testing the strength of her stomach. The stench gave her good reason to be grateful she hadn't eaten.

Turning to retreat to safety, she was stopped by the distant sound of a motor. *Airplane or vehicle,* she wondered, and was amazed anew by how finely tuned her hearing had become. Her sense of smell and vision, too. She felt as if she'd taken a drug to enhance her senses; everything had come so alive, from the buzz of an insect to scents of all kinds carried on the wind. She knew at once that she was hearing a vehicle, traveling toward her from a great distance.

39

Having walked the bike as much as ridden it, Knox arrived at the crumbling village two kilometers from Solio Ranch amid stares and smiles. He felt like the tall man in a carnival act.

The streets were caked with dried mud, the block buildings suffering from leprosy, the women colorful and busy, and the men crouched, smoking, chewing *khat* and looking bored. Knox left the bike behind the red building, moving fast, well aware that the police might have already alerted the village to the reward for his capture.

He identified what he hated at this moment — the loss of control. He ran his import/export business as a one-man show, with Tommy tangentially involved; his jobs for Rutherford Risk had struck a balance between him and Grace that he'd come to rely upon. Without her, with strangers like Benson and the quick-thinking Olé determining his fate, Knox was well out of his comfort zone.

He hid himself between two head-high piles of trash and debris at the muddy end of a lane. Despite the stench, two wayward dogs and the sight of an animal carcass covered in maggots, he attracted a group of ten to twelve kids. They stood a few yards away, smiling at him. They weren't begging, just curious, amused and abundantly entertained by this tall white stranger.

Knox tried to ignore them, to focus. With the KGA patrolling the reserve, returning to Solio Lodge was out. Public transportation under any alias was out, too. Grace's "first forty-eight" had slipped past.

His phone buzzed. A text from Dulwich.

crossed border. your 20?

Nanyuki

the package?

progress. "bottle opener"
mean anything to you?
a puzzle from her.

Enough time passed that he thought he'd

285

lost Dulwich. But then his phone buzzed again.

World Financial Center
building in Shanghai

Knox grinned, standing by himself, a dozen small black kids staring up at him. The financial high-rise dominated the Pudong skyline, its top stories looking like a giant bottle opener.

thanks

puzzle?

Knox wondered how that information would strike Dulwich.

crumbs to follow

that's her

yup

rendezvous?

Knox consulted his phone's map.

Nakuru? possibly tonight?

The exchange with Dulwich put him in a better frame of mind. Going on seven A.M. in Detroit, he called Tommy, apologized for missing the past two days and listened to his brother's excitement over a supermarket job he'd gotten recently, bagging groceries. *Twenty-six years old, going on fourteen,* Knox thought, but smiled again, proud of Tommy's sense of engagement and independence. The call ended with both brothers the better for it, a rarity.

To Knox's surprise, the same young herdsman who'd loaned him the bike rounded the corner an hour later. Knox's youthful audience had not given up on him, sitting cross-legged in a semicircle ten feet away, as if Knox were reading to them.

"You come with me," the young herdsman instructed.

"Where?"

"Benson. You understand?"

"Why didn't he come himself?"

"It is not safe here. Not safe in Solio. You understand?"

"Come with you to where?" Knox repeated.

"My cousin is to drive you."

"To Nakuru. I need to reach Nakuru by

287

nightfall." Knox's patience had long since expired.

"Not possible. Police on roads look for you. You understand? My cousin, he . . ." The boy searched for a word. "Left you."

"He'll leave me? Where? No, he won't. Nakuru."

The boy shook his head. "The ranger make the plan."

"Benson."

"Just so. Good man. You must trust the ranger."

The boy was right, but Knox didn't like it.

"The wildlife rangers, the police, will come here soon, I am afraid. They wish to find you."

"Nakuru," Knox repeated, knowing the answer.

The boy shook his head. "Police on the roads."

"So why would I get into a vehicle with your cousin?"

The boy appeared delighted. "Yes, exactly!"

Knox struggled to contain his temper. "Where is he taking me?"

"If you wish to walk," the boy said, repossessing his bicycle, "it is your decision. You tell my cousin when he comes here."

40

Grace considered the approaching SUV from two opposite motives: a search-and-rescue effort . . . or a search for her dead body.

Her head ached, her wrist continued to itch. She pulled a piece of aloe from her sack and chewed. She hadn't anticipated indecision; didn't know herself in this state. Her former plans to stay put and observe from her perch struck her as unreasonable. If she ran out in the direction of the vehicle, waving and shouting, she might be inviting her own execution. If she did nothing, she might never have such a chance again.

Forced to consider the vehicle hostile, she decided that the closer she could get to the abandoned Jeep, the better chance she had of staging an ambush. With the lions somewhere in the wash, she kept against the sharp edge of the outcropping that formed the plateau. She hurried, hunched over and limping slightly as she favored her ankle.

Run. Stop. The ankle warmed; stiff, but no longer painful. She studied the wash, looking for the lions. From where she stood, she could not see down into most of the dry wash, so any animal within could — hopefully — not see her.

Run. Stop. The vehicle seemed to be moving closer, though sounds in the bush could trick you.

Run. Stop. Search. Appraise. The listing Jeep was farther away than she'd estimated. That, or her legs were moving far more slowly than she thought. With each short, limping sprint and the pumping of her arms, her snakebite hurt more. The ankle, in contrast, felt a bit better.

All of a sudden, it was clear to her that the vehicle was headed toward the abandoned Jeep. Toward her.

Another fifty meters and she felt her balance failing. Her lungs weren't providing enough air. She didn't need to compute distance to come to grips with the obvious: the vehicle was going to reach the Jeep well before she could. Yet another choice — up into the rocks or down into the dry wash? If she was spotted unintentionally, escape from the rocks would be difficult; she'd make an easy target for a rifle. The dry wash, a labyrinth of gullies weaving between a lattice of sand islands of varying sizes and shapes, would provide far more cover.

If she could only look past the lions.

This internal dialogue took no more than a second or two. Her legs moved toward the dry wash and, as she caught sight of the SUV from the side, she dropped and rolled, spear in hand, down a sand-and-rock incline, coming to rest in a pile of bleached bone.

Grace slithered across the dry riverbed to the cut wall of one of the many rock islands and tucked into the slanting shade. Her mud-covered body blended in well; only her black hair gave her away, and even then only while moving. Holding still, she became a camouflaged chameleon.

Following the raised bed's uneven line, she crept forward, hoping for a view of the vehicle. But the wash was several hundred meters wide by a half-kilometer long, the space cut by a maze of channels. Faced with a dozen possible routes around and through, Grace chose central corridors, the deeper and more steeply eroded paths. She found a rhythm of run-and-pause, her heart thumping, legs weak, spear at the ready.

For her breaks, she threw her bare back to the dirt wall, lessening her profile and providing her with a 180-degree view in both directions. Reaching the end of each small island, she took extra care before crossing the more open areas.

The rumble of the slow-moving SUV continued. A matter of minutes now.

Grace hurried, pressing on with more determination, abandoning the shady side for the more direct, sunlit bank. Halfway along this island, she froze.

Directly across from her, hunkered down in the shade, was one of the two lions. The other was on her side, lying behind a large rock. Both were looking straight at her.

41

The rattletrap Japanese pickup dropped Knox off on a dirt road in a sea of low, dry grass. Mount Kenya loomed in the distance, a majestic backdrop.

A cool wind lifted Knox's collar, its corners flapping like flags against his neck. The air smelled of grass and dirt and the inescapable sense of primordial history underfoot. Perfectly spaced cumulus clouds marched across the horizon, occupying the rich blue sky; a bird of prey soared effortlessly, wings set.

As instructed by the driver, Knox called the phone number provided. It took only seconds to identify the voice that answered as that of Sergeant Kanika Alkinyi.

"It's me."

"Stay where you are." The call disconnected.

Despite this warning, after ten minutes, Knox began to walk in small circles, up and down the road. Of everything he abhorred — incompetence, political correctness, making excuses — being made to wait cut the deepest. He was nearly coming out of his skin by the time the first tendril of dust coiled in the distance. When a second rooster tail appeared behind the first, Knox considered running. Instead, he hid his private SIM chip in the hidden pocket on his briefs, held the roll of quarters in his right fist and waited.

The trucks were safari green, and equipped with a snorkel, front winch and bull bar. Not the Chinese models used by the KGA, but not the kind of open safari truck driven by Olé, either. Flooded by a sickening chill, Knox saw uniforms behind the windshields and realized that first instincts were almost always correct: he never should have trusted the herdsman.

The soldiers — if that's what they were — had been well trained. One truck slowed to a stop; the second skidded through the grass and blocked the road in the other direction. Two uniforms jumped out of each, automatic rifles in their hands. They established positions that covered Knox while not putting each other into the shot.

When they shouted for him to lie down, arms and legs outstretched, he had no choice but to comply. It was senseless to resist. Better to play along and look for a later opening.

Two men patted him down. They took his jacket. A sack was pulled over his head; they strapped his wrists behind his back with cable ties, pulled him to his feet and pushed him in the direction of the vehicles. Blinded, Knox thought of poor Samuelson. Faaruq. He thought of Grace, too, hoping beyond hope that she had not been put through this same ordeal, that the stunning view of wide-open space had not been the last thing she'd seen.

The drive was long, in a direction away from Nanyuki. The road turned rough after twenty minutes and required several stretches of slow travel, suggesting a remote destination.

This was confirmed when he was led from the vehicle and the hood lifted. Knox found himself in a heavily wooded area that gave no view of the outside landscape. Nor would it be easily spotted from aircraft. He counted seven tents, one of the two largest used as a garage, a curious use that told him secrecy was a top priority — nothing glinting or mechanical to be spotted from above. The camp was well worn and had been in place for weeks if not months. Paths cut between the tents suggested the other oversized structure was a mess hall. He counted eleven soldiers, guessed occupancy at over twenty.

As a whole, they were big men with unforgiving, distrustful faces, and the physical confidence of seasoned veterans; their boots alone told Knox they'd been in service for years. Never mind the scars, the mended uniforms, the faded camouflage of the tents, and the full maintenance shop in the right bay of the garage.

The moment Knox saw the broad-shouldered man emerge from the mess tent he knew it was Koigi. He looked to be in his late forties. His war-weary face revealed a man both thoughtful and distrusting. He had the confidence and forbearance of a giant sequoia.

Knox pushed away the bit of awe he felt. He didn't believe in living legends, yet that belief was being tested. This man was maverick, savior and cult hero in one. He appraised Knox without a hint of kindness.

"I met her only briefly. I owe her and you nothing. You have five minutes."

"I have as long as it takes," Knox said. "I've come a long way."

"Take him back," Koigi said, turning away.

Knox called out. "We're twenty-five kilometers north-northwest from where you picked me up. We gained two hundred meters in elevation and crossed two streams, the first thirty meters in width. We entered dense forest three kilometers prior to arriving in camp. You have a dozen or more men, thousands of rounds of ammunition and you resupply with the white Chevy pickup truck. Your men went through my hotel room in Nanyuki, searched my bag. Did a piss-poor job of it, I might add. I obviously passed muster or I wouldn't be here. So let's stop playing, you and I."

Koigi spun around, pivoting on the ball of his right foot like a military man. He walked forward, slowly. "How could you know of the ammunition?"

"The final tent is well off on its own. If it was a latrine or a kitchen tent, I'd smell it — and it wouldn't require two sizable fire extinguishers outside, one on each corner."

Koigi looked in the direction of the tent under discussion. Then he nodded. "I'm impressed, Mr. Knox. You've earned your extra time."

He extended his hand and they shook, Koigi's skin as rough against Knox's palm as a cat's tongue.

"If you are indeed an import/export man, as I'm told, then is it arms?"

"It's trinkets, souvenirs, the occasional piece of art. We all have our pasts."

"And futures, if we're blessed."

"Amen."

There was no offer of hospitality, or even a chair. This was going to be done standing on pine straw somewhere in the hills of Kenya, not far from a tent loaded with ordnance.

"Grace Chu," Knox said.

"I didn't know her name. As I said, hers was a short visit."

The printout of the tattoo had seen better days. Knox unfolded it carefully and passed it to the big man — then startled as Koigi barked out two words that proved to be names.

Two of his rangers came running from the big tent. He rattled something off in Swahili. Both men tried to roll up their sleeves, then took their shirts off instead. Turning sideways to Knox, they displayed their muscular arms, bearing nearly identical three-inch circular scars. *Like medallions,* Knox thought. The background scar upon which the tattoo in the printout had been written. Bishoppe had mentioned a burn; Knox chided himself for having missed the cause. Grace's interest had not been in the tattoo, but the scar upon which it had been drawn.

Forest for the trees, he thought.

"Vaccination scars," Knox stated.

"Yes! The Oloitokitok health clinic did this to my men," Koigi said. "Tetanus. Measles? One of those. Four months ago."

"Why were your men vaccinated there? It's not close, is it?"

"It is a free clinic. We work closely with rangers there. We meet often to review our successes and failures. There are clinics in Nairobi, but we avoid Nairobi as much as possible. You understand?"

"Radicals? Insurgents? How could they use the same clinic?"

"The clinic services tens of thousands. Kenyans. Tanzanians. Any adult with an ID. All children. They serve people, not politics."

"IDs?"

"Those of age. Yes. For proper record keeping. Justify their budgets, I imagine. What of it?"

"You told that to Grace. You showed these men to Grace?" Knox asked.

"Correct."

"Her reaction?"

"She reached out to touch them. They are Muslim. It is not permitted."

Knox nodded. It sounded like Grace. "She asked about this tattoo. I'm told it means 'forever.' "

"It means 'constant.' But yes, she asked."

"So this photo suggests that this man likely visited the same health clinic as your men." Knox tried to pronounce it, but failed miserably. "If he was killed as an act of betrayal, and left to be found as a warning to others, an example, then we can infer that he might possibly be one of Guuleed's men."

"You impress me again. What do you know of Guuleed?"

"Nothing, really."

"He is vermin. A poacher of the worst kind. Automatic weapons. Wholesale slaughter."

"How does he get the ivory out of the country?"

"If only we knew . . ." Koigi said. His forearms and cheeks showed raised black scars of all sizes and shapes, like a man who'd once climbed through barbed wire. "Mombasa, certainly. There have been arrests and seizures there. Also, overland through Tanzania, we believe."

"If Grace had found proof the Oloitokitok Clinic was connected to the export of the poached ivory, would that surprise you?"

"Little if anything surprises me, Mr. Knox. But the information interests me, of course. I would very much like to see such evidence."

"A company called Asian Container Consolidated manipulated a batch of vaccine."

"Xin Ha" — the large man nodded — "has been long suspected of controlling the export of the ivory. He has a partner in Guuleed. The clinic is closed now, was never associated with the poaching. It served many thousands for years. Without concrete proof . . ."

"I may have the proof. If I could get to a computer . . ."

Koigi appraised him thoughtfully. "I will not put a total stranger onto the Internet, Mr. Knox."

"No Internet. Just a computer. I can supply you with all the financials Grace uncovered."

Koigi was clearly tempted. He excused himself and made a call on a satellite phone some distance away. Several long minutes passed. Then Koigi approached Knox and handed him the heavy phone. Knox looked at it, puzzled.

"It is a secure line," Koigi said, "but no names, please."

"Go ahead," Knox spoke into the phone.

"My friend tells me you have financials." It was the voice of Graham Winston.

42

Grace couldn't face both lions at once, so she chose the closest, the cat directly across from her. Staring it down, she raised her arms overhead, feeling particularly naked as she did so, and spread her legs while waving her arms.

The cat shied, tucked in on itself, stood to all fours and slunk away, circling counter-clockwise, putting itself to her left. The other, just coming to its feet, moved to her right.

Pinned. She held the spear in her right hand as she continued swinging her arms. The idea was to present herself as game the animals did not recognize. Lions often shied away from the unfamiliar.

Not these two, she realized. Seen up close, they were definitely adolescents — all spindly bodies and oversized paws — whiskers twitching, eyes curious. Grace growled and grunted, keeping an ear out for the approaching SUV.

Nothing stopped the steady advance of the cats. They seemed more curious than aggressive, but Grace knew that could change instantly. She shook involuntarily the closer they came; her arms froze, refused to move. She stood like a criminal presenting herself to police — legs spread, arms up overhead.

The cat to her left drew within three meters, nose twitching more noticeably.

"That is your piss," Grace said. Speaking softly to the lion. It stopped. Speaking, yelling, clapping were all known to cause a cat to back off. But she couldn't draw the attention of the driver. "We smell the same, you and me. You like that, do you not? You like that smell. It is your smell. We share that smell."

The cat stood its ground, but did not advance. She glanced to her right and swallowed a scream; with her attention on the other cat, its partner now stood within a meter of her. It had golden eyes that shimmered in the sunlight, a scruffy monochrome coat, a white-haired collar, white chin and dark ears. Its legs were spotted. On top of its head was a tuft of fur — the beginning of its mane — a male. To her left, a female.

Grace continued talking gibberish and moving her arms. Both cats now seemed overly curious. The male advanced to within a half meter, its nose working furiously. She jerked down the spear and aimed it at him.

He jumped back like a kitten. Too late, Grace caught sight of the female leaping. She cowered and shrank to a squat, knowing it was the worst possible reaction. The cat lifted as high as Grace's shoulders and landed with practiced ease. On the ground now, two meters away from her. The male sprang, and Grace barked out an unwitting cry.

The SUV was slowing now, approaching the wash.

The male lion landed just behind the female, who turned and slapped the ground in front of him with a swift paw. Grace saw it then: a sparkling white light, moving across the earth. Her first thought was divine intervention; some miracle had torn the cats' attention off her.

Just as quickly she realized it was the reflection of sunlight off her spear's slice of mirror. It was like using a laser on the floor for a house cat. As Grace directed it, the cats pounced. She flashed a spot of light up onto the opposite bank; the cats attacked it playfully. Left, right. Forward.

Away . . .

Flash by flash she herded the pair of leaping and slapping cats in the opposite direction, moving them out from the end of the wash, where the abandoned vehicle rested. As she did, she slipped forward, increasing the distance between herself and the lions, who had clearly forgotten all about her. Moving the bright starburst reflection in jerking, jagged lines, she led them to the end of the opposite island, turning them completely away.

Reaching the end of her own island of sand, Grace lowered the spear, cut around the end, and, crouching, shot down a different streambed, running hard in the direction of a Jeep that she stood too low to see.

43

Knox was not one to surprise easily, but Winston's voice released a rockslide of implications, each tumbling over the next and dislodging the others in its path.

"Yes, sir," Knox said, answering his question. "But not those you requested. Not yet."

No names. He kept the thought ever present in his mind.

Kanika had told him that Koigi had known his name. Because Winston had told him, Knox realized.

"Our female friend?" Winston asked.

"We're well past the first forty-eight."

"I'm aware. And?"

"She's left a trail to follow. That's the positive takeaway."

"Clever girl."

Woman, Knox thought. "Yes, that she is. It's layered, complicated."

"Hardly surprising."

"She . . . that is . . . I think there's a good chance she was — is!" — he corrected himself, feeling guilty over the slip — "close to tying off two of the three objectives. The third, the final objective . . . I think she believed that within her reach. It's a creative solution. No surprise there. In her mind, it's tied into everything else. Seems to me it may have been responsible — this pursuit of hers — for her current situation, whatever that is."

"There has been a satellite phone intercept."

Knox's heart rate increased palpably. "Excuse me?"

"Who do you think keeps an operation like Koigi's running? You think this is without costs? And how is it that a man hidden away in the African bush can put his finger on abhorrent creatures like the Somali?" No names. Knox thought: *Guuleed.* "Information is power, my boy, and I can provide the former. I'm not without friends. Lyon, Brussels, London."

INTERPOL, EU, MI-6, Knox heard. He ruminated on the idea of unspoken alliances, the arming and funding of groups like Koigi's. On the passions and interests of men like Winston, who have all the best intentions, and money and power as their tools. He thought of The Circuit — mercenaries; the recruitment of ex-military as privatized soldiers, how close he'd come to choosing that direction for himself.

A world of war beneath the surface, out of the news, away from the parliaments. He looked around, taking in anew the extent of Koigi's operation. Fifteen men fighting a private war on poachers. *A million a year?* he wondered. *Two?*

"We all need a helping hand," Winston said.

"Yes, sir," Knox said. "We do at that."

"We've had a drone, a private drone bought and paid for by an American, over the Somali for several weeks now. His communications were monitored before that — twenty-four/seven. We know for a fact he's killed his own men, believing them traitors. The only traitor is himself. Every time he picks up that satellite phone, every time he drives away in a vehicle. The beauty, the elegance, of technology."

"You mentioned a call." Knox's heart, still racing.

"From the Somali's camp, to a location a quarter-kilometer outside of Oloitokitok. The message . . . our friend there with you will provide the message once you've transferred the financials and anything else of

hers you have. You understand, John Knox?"
No names. Knox swallowed dryly. "You are
reckless. You are wanted. I will not have my
investment recovered in the course of your
capture. You should have sent it all the moment you had it."

"The timing . . . it wasn't intentional."

"I'm sure it wasn't." Sarcastic. "But let's
take the guesswork out of it, shall we? Our
friend will provide you with what you need.
Upon confirmation of its receipt, he will
pass along the message. Transportation is
being arranged. Good luck."

The call disconnected, though Knox held
the receiver to his ear for a while after, trying to give himself time to think.

"For how long do you plan to stand
there?" Koigi asked. Knox felt like a fool.
"The transmission light went off over a
minute ago."

A beat. Then Koigi smiled. "It's okay, I
know the feeling."

44

The sound of an idling engine droned around her, invading her thoughts. Grace crawled up the island bank on hands and knees, struggling upward until she could just see out to the perimeter of the dry wash. She couldn't stop herself from checking behind as well, terrified the cats might double back on her.

The SUV crept along, approaching the abandoned vehicle at a snail's pace. The driver, on the right-hand side, was leaning out, eyes trained down. Grace had been in a vehicle a half-dozen times with a guide who'd used this same rolling method to scout for animal tracks.

The driver sat up and glanced out front — the windshield was folded down — clearly trying to keep himself on course. Grace stifled a gasp as she recognized him: the driver who'd dumped her. She even remembered his name: Leebo.

A more clear memory of the ride returned. The sudden switch of drivers after her tour of Larger Than Life. The amiable conversation she'd had with Leebo. His spotting lion tracks — or claiming to, she now realized — and turning the vehicle off-road. The thrill she'd felt. She'd never suspected him; he'd held her captive through his own excitement, his pointing, his explaining.

Reaching back, she touched the sore spot where he'd pricked her with the needle.

At least she'd thought to shut the vehicle's hood and close its doors. Unless he stopped and climbed out to look inside, he wouldn't see the scavenging she'd done. If he paid strict attention, he might notice the missing antenna, but his focus was aimed down, at the ground. She'd been careful to brush out her tracks.

But how far away from the vehicle had she swept? She couldn't recall. Grace's stomach turned; she'd lost a day or more in dehydrated delirium.

The SUV rolled past the abandoned vehicle at a walking pace, the driver's head still trained down. Grace wanted badly to punish him, to take the SUV away and leave him, just as he'd stranded her. At the very least she planned to follow the vehicle. She'd have to keep well inside the driver's blind spot — behind and off in the bush on the passenger side.

She lowered herself down to the dry riverbed and did her best to estimate and parallel the SUV's movement. Scrambling up another island, she took a careful look. Searched behind her for any sign of the cats. The SUV continued forward, staying clear of the wash, fifty meters away. A moment later, the brake lights flashed. She watched Leebo retrieve a pair of binoculars and hold them up to his face, then swivel in her direction. She ducked. Waited. When she sneaked an eye over the rim, the binoculars were chasing tracks in the dirt.

The SUV backed up at high speed. Grace slipped down below grade, adrenaline cutting into her blood, poisoning her already weakened body. It wasn't lions that interested him. He'd spotted a boot track, her boot track.

The sound of a car door brought her back to the top of the island. She peered over the rocks and saw Leebo, out of the SUV and carrying a machete in his right hand, the binoculars clasped in his left. He approached the lip of the wash and raised the binoculars. Grace slipped back down the embankment.

Aware that she had a momentary advantage, she seized it. She knew the route she'd taken when inspecting the dry wash, a route he would likely follow. A larger threat existed there: the cats.

Grace moved without hesitation, without fear, her spear in her right hand, a naked, dung-smeared woman in hiking boots wearing automobile upholstery for a skirt. She kept the mirror side of the spear tip aimed to the ground to avoid an accidental reflection. Having spent a day or more atop the plateau, she'd subliminally memorized the layout of the wash. She could picture its structure in her mind's eye, its many cutout islands cohering into a single pattern. She visualized her location, moving to the center of the wash, where the dry river bottom was deeper, the walls sheerer. The shadows darker.

As she ran, she recognized her own transition, her regression. She felt part savage now. The woman who ate rat liver. The woman who buried her urine and excrement in deep holes and carefully packed down the dirt. The woman who gladly smeared lion urine on herself, who now credited that act with possibly saving her life.

With the driver so close, within range of an attack, she was angry with herself, too.

She should have had the nerve to enter the plateau's forest and search out the poison arrow tree.

But the regret was useless. Her thoughts focused on the keys to the SUV. She would do anything to get them. Killing or wounding Leebo was a means to this end. Surprising him so that he didn't use that machete on her, a necessity. She hurried, running a jagged route, searching for the lions, listening for the driver, for any sound from the SUV. She was part of the landscape. She belonged here and, at that moment, wouldn't have traded her situation for real clothes and a gun.

It all made sense to her, her situation, her prey. She almost felt sorry for the driver. He had no idea what kind of shitstorm he was walking into.

45

The inside of the tent showed the camp to be truly well established. There was a cot, some rugs and a bench table on collapsible sawhorses. Four car batteries powered a single lightbulb and a strip of outlets, which connected to a laptop and small printer. A modem wire could be plugged into Koigi's satellite phone.

Knox sat at the laptop and typed: Pudong. The box following the query: "the bottle opener" danced and cleared. He typed again: SWFC, for the Shanghai World Financial Center.

The screen refreshed.

The amount paid Danali?_____

Knox didn't know anyone named "Danali." Nor did he appreciate Koigi and another man, both of whom smelled sour, watching his every action. Their presence

315

distracted him, slowed his thoughts.

"In 2013," Koigi said, "some African-Americans formed a group to climb this peak in your state of Alaska. Their adventure was covered well in Kenyan news."

"Spelled differently," the other man said. "The mountain is with an 'e.' "

Knox saw it then. "It's an anagram. Thank you!" He grabbed a pen and paper from Koigi's desk and began attempting to unscramble the word. His second try was Nadali — Achebe "Archie" Nadali. Only someone who'd read the contents of her first thumb drive could open the second. *So Grace,* he thought.

When he input the word, the screen revealed a file list of dozens of names. Word documents for the most part; a half-dozen Excel sheets intermixed.

Knox copied and moved the files to Koigi's computer. He opened the first few, skimming them quickly.

"The reporter, Samuelson." He spoke aloud for the sake of his voyeurs. "She either found or hacked his files." He tried and failed to keep the excitement out of his voice. "His articles, his research, his finances. It's all here." He opened and closed file after file. "This may have been what Samuelson was killed for. This may be

316

enough to bring down the minister."

He opened and scrolled through several of the spreadsheets. A number of ATM card cash withdrawals were highlighted in green. A small red triangle filled the upper-right corner of several of the cells. Knox hovered the cursor over a triangle in the cell of one of the green withdrawal amounts. A comment box popped up: See phone records 3/20; Subject 17 3/22.

It took Knox ten minutes to cross-reference the documents. There had been several meetings with "Subject 17," and Samuelson had made interview notes of each, including March 22. Photocopies of call records for March 20 had been highlighted by hand in yellow. Grace had connected Samuelson calling someone and, two days later, likely making a cash payment. There was a note in the margin written in her hand: *laborer?*

He opened a set of photocopied receipts and travel vouchers and the accompanying expense accounting. One highlighted expense was to Safarilink. Under notes was typed: Nanyuki.

"That's what got her up here," Knox said. All she lacked now, something he didn't intend to share with Koigi, were the health clinic financials.

317

"We can upload all of these to . . . your friend," Knox said, meaning Winston.

"The satellite connection is slow. We will get started."

"The intercept," Knox said, reminding him. "I was told you would share the contents of the intercepted call."

"When the files are received," Koigi said.

"Now," Knox said. "You have to trust me. These are all the files. Five minutes? Thirty? I don't have the time. Grace doesn't have the time."

Knox executed a quick series of cursor moves. The small arrow hung suspended over DELETE ALL. His index finger hovered over the mouse.

"You tell me. What's it going to be?" he asked. His voice utterly steady.

Koigi's sidekick drew a revolver and pressed it to Knox's temple.

"He can shoot me," Knox said, thinking the man might be doing him a favor. "But what if my finger twitches when he does?"

46

Grace spotted her own boot tracks, moving from right to left in the dust of the river bottom. She positioned herself for ambush, tucked uncomfortably behind a fallen rock. The placement of her spear was difficult. If held at her side, it was too long and stuck out into the river bottom. If placed behind her and into the rocks, it would take longer to move and was likely to make noise that she could ill afford. She settled on placing it mirror-down at her side, wiggling it into the dirt to help disguise it.

Then she waited. As she did, she spotted more boot tracks — the ones she'd just left in making her approach. The impressions came up the riverbed to behind the rock where she hid. She'd left a neon arrow pointing directly to her hiding place.

Time played tricks on you. An army sergeant had once reminded Grace that within the passing of a single second there were one-thousand thousandths of a second. It had seemed so Confucius at the time that she'd hardly paid attention. But now it made all the sense in the world. If the driver was moving in seconds, she would move in tenths of a second. Defeating an opponent had little to do with strength and everything to do with leverage and training. A woman her size could drop a beast of a man before he knew what hit him. She had such training, and felt certain he had not. Advantage: Grace.

She heard the crunch of sand underfoot, amazed by her heightened sensitivity. It seemed as if she could hear the rubber of his flip-flops bending and stretching; as if she could hear his labored breathing; could smell his pores expelling sweat. Fifteen meters . . . ten . . . five . . .

She didn't dare try to steal a look, refused to give Leebo any kind of advantage. Instead, she burst out from behind the rock, crouching low, the spear held in both hands. She hadn't realized it had only taken her two days to learn how to walk or run so quietly.

He didn't turn at first. When he did, she saw him in full profile — a more difficult target to strike. He must have caught her movement in his peripheral vision, for he slowly pivoted, the machete lifting overhead.

It became immediately apparent to Grace that it wasn't simple surprise that froze him; it was shock, followed by incredulity. A crouching, shit-slathered, bare-chested Chinese woman, with chapped lips and bloodshot eyes, was charging him with a spear. By the time it registered as more than a hallucination, she'd sliced his forearm deeply, causing the machete to fall. It fell onto his right foot and, judging by his reaction, cut or severed a toe or two. As he bent, Grace spun a full circle. The edge of her spear caught the side of his neck. Blood poured from the wound. As he came up, she plunged the spear into his belly and yanked it out with such force that the shard of mirror stayed in him.

She held a blood-tipped branch in two hands. Her reaction had been primordial. Only seeing the man stagger and bleed did it hit her what she'd done.

Leebo wavered unsteadily on his feet.

Grace picked up the machete, held it aloft, her teeth gritted and showing. She brandished the machete, ready to hack him to pieces — wanting to hack him to pieces. He dropped to his knees and started crawling on all fours, wailing, bleeding, dying.

"I didn't want to," he moaned. "I'm sorry.

Help me. Please . . . How . . . is . . . it . . . possible?"

Grace screamed as the first lion sprang, knocking the man over. She backed up into the shadows, shaking in terror, yet still able to see what she'd done. Able to feel the machete raised overhead, too. This was her doing.

The male lion came from her right, jumped onto the man's back and bit down into Leebo's neck, killing him instantly. He dropped, his legs and arms twitching as if he'd taken hold of a live wire. His arm came off in the jaw of the lioness. Grace turned away — then looked back, unable to take her eyes off the savagery.

She was the lioness, she thought; she was the victor.

A pair of jackals stood observing with her. Soon, hyenas and vultures would follow, each taking their turn. Olé had told her the bush could strip a rhino to bone in four to six hours. She wondered how that worked with something as small as a human.

The keys! She backed up more quickly, pausing behind rocks, not wanting her movement to attract attention. The two lions glanced in her direction several times; she stopped, slowly raised her arms high overhead, and the animals turned back to their feast.

Once out of sight, she cut through the labyrinth of islands to the far bank and scrambled up toward the SUV, startling the two jackals, who darted off.

The key was not in the ignition because there was no ignition. A button read PUSH TO START. She searched but did not see the fob. He'd carried it with him, this man currently being shredded by the jaws of two young lions. More depressing, the existence of the electronic ignition meant the car model was highly computerized and difficult, if not impossible, to hot-wire.

Grace grabbed the wheel — also locked. If she couldn't turn the wheel, the SUV would make it only thirty meters or so before plunging into the dry wash.

"No, no, no." She heard her own voice inside the vehicle, dry, raspy. She hadn't spoken in days. A few yells were all. She kicked the open door in anger. And there it was: a clear plastic bottle, two-thirds full with some kind of loose-leaf tea. Alongside the bottle, a leather pouch filled with green leaves.

She fought every instinct she had, battling back her desperation to chug the tea. Instead, she uncapped it and wetted her parched throat. She coughed. Gagged. The first several sips went down like vintage wine. Before she could overreact, she recapped it.

The leaves, she knew. She'd asked Olé about the pickup-truckloads of vegetation on the roads. He'd told her of *khat,* chewed as a stimulant. It gave great stamina. She tucked it into the waist of her skirt. The water bottle begged to be reopened. She fought against this with all the willpower she could summon, and still nearly succumbed to it.

She had to have the keys. There was no choice. She marched toward the rim of the dry wash, lying down to get a view of the lions. Immediately, she looked away again, unable to stomach what she saw. A horror to humans, yet it was as natural here as the passing of the sun in the sky.

If the keys were down there, it would be hours before she could look for them. She lay prone to screen herself from the jackals, and she waited.

47

' "Save the wounded gazelle. Return her to camp.' This was sent less than eight hours ago." Koigi said the words with no feeling, just resignation.

"I don't understand," Knox said, taking his hand off the mouse. The lieutenant retired his sidearm.

"We don't save wounded gazelles, Mr. Knox. But what choice was there? An elephant or rhino mentioned in such a communiqué would trigger intense scrutiny. I am told the origin of this message was one of two camps controlled by Guuleed."

"You know his location?"

"We have been watching, yes. Both his camps have gone quiet since this message was intercepted. They may have fled when we weren't covering. If so, it's a terrible loss. You understand?"

"The gazelle is Grace?" Knox felt physically faint. He couldn't remember the last time he'd eaten. "You wouldn't happen to have some food around here, would you?"

Koigi sent his man out. Knox drew a breath sharply.

"They have her held hostage. They want her moved or returned? She's alive . . ."

"We will presume so."

"The call? Oloitokitok, you said?"

"Voice recognition is being undertaken. We should know within twenty-four hours." Koigi shifted on his feet.

"Grace doesn't have twenty-four hours. If they're bringing her in, it's for ransom — or to sell her for any number of uses."

This was his wheelhouse, Knox thought, *kidnapping, extortion.* He felt oddly comfortable for the first time in days, yet still sick to his stomach. *She's alive,* his mind cried for the umpteenth time.

"We'll have the one shot at her, that's all. I'll need you and your men. I can gather the intel with some luck. If her keeper is working it solo, I'm good. If not . . . if it's multipersonnel . . . I can't do an extraction like that alone."

"I can send you some men overland."

"I don't have the time for that."

"I would advise you to request help from Larger Than Life. They have many rangers."

Knox shook his head. "I'm not sure I can trust them."

"What do you propose, then?"

"I should fly down to where she was staying. Pick up her trail from there."

"I cannot arrange this for you. Mr. Winston cannot arrange this for you. Nanyuki airfield will be guarded. Nairobi, the same."

"There must be a stretch of road that could be used to land a small plane," Knox said. "A field? A ranch?"

"Yes, of course. But the pilot? This will not be easy, Mr. Knox."

"I know a guy," Knox said.

48

Witnessing the dismemberment of a human finally proved too much. Grace backed away from the edge of the dry wash, moved into the SUV, out of the sun and away from the predators. She had no intention of attempting to interrupt their symbiotic system. Lions, spotted hyenas, black-backed jackals, hooded vultures, each appeared in order, seemingly from out of nowhere, each taking their turn at the trough. It was a thing of beauty, a thing of horror.

How long did it take to strip a man to bone? she'd wondered. The body at the bottom of the wash required only ninety minutes.

When at last she dared, Grace slipped over the edge and slid down to the dry river bottom, waving her arms and scaring away the vultures, though the big birds didn't go far. They flapped and settled only meters away from the mangled bones and blood, spread around in an unimaginable scene of horror. There was nothing left, not even the piece of mirror Grace had lost. To the naked eye, even Leebo's clothing was gone. A few scraps of cloth remained, a belt, one sandal.

She used the stick end of her spear to move pieces of bone and fabric, to search for the ignition fob. She envisioned grids, searched each painstakingly. Halfway through, she no longer saw the gore, only colors and shapes. Thirty minutes. An hour. No fob.

In all likelihood, she thought, it had gone down a throat with a bite of clothing. It would appear in scat sometime tomorrow. The crushing defeat drove her to start again.

Grid by grid. Another hour. Two. Eventually she turned away; the SUV, so full of promise, had ended up being nothing but a tease.

Other thoughts came to her. One stayed: She had never killed a fellow human being before. She felt bad that it felt so good. Hated that she'd enjoyed it.

None of that mattered now. She'd done it. The driver was no more. She could feel the mirror slicing his arm, the plunge of the blade into his gut. She moved back toward the SUV, the guttural sound of vultures picking at bones rising from the wash behind her. A few of the birds flew away, lifting out of the pit to reach the trees cluttered with their kind. All waiting their turn.

Grace sipped the dead man's tea, and thanked him silently for it.

But it was hard to stay calm. She pounded on the steering wheel, cursed in Chinese and screamed into the cab so loudly she hurt her own ears.

With her cry, some of the vultures startled out of the trees. They rose nearly in unison, flew to the next tree and settled in for the long wait.

49

"You remember me?" Knox asked into his mobile, returned to him by one of Koigi's men. Somewhere along the way, Olé had handed off his jacket and duffel bag recovered from the crappy hotel, the act of which implied a connection between all these men that Knox found unsettling.

"You ask this every time, Mr. John. Please!"

"I want to hire a private plane. Single prop. A bush pilot. You understand?"

"Why do you call if you think me stupid?"

"Tonight."

"It will be expensive."

Knox didn't have the kind of cash required. He would have to hope for the Koigi/Winston alliance to supply it. "Call me back with the pilot's number."

"I will negotiate this for you."

"I'm sure you would. The pilot. This number, within the hour."

Ending the call, he spoke to a concerned Koigi. "I will need cash. A good deal of it."

Koigi nodded. "I will confirm with Mr. Winston."

"And we'll need a reasonable landing strip," Knox said. "Something a pilot can check on a map and see will work. But not the strip we're going to ask him to use. We radio that location once we determine if I've been betrayed."

"You've done this before." Koigi smiled for the first time, suddenly impressed with Knox.

50

It took her several tries to get it right, but once she did, Grace filled her mouth with the infamous "Nectar of the Gods." Warm milk seeped from her lips and ran down her chin; her tongue flashed sensually through the warm liquid, lapping it up, coaxing it into the back of her throat and coddling it between her tonsils before a gentle swallow and the long, slow trickle toward her empty belly.

The cow stood complacently, chewing on a bit of nothingness, some dry grass forcing itself up between rocks. Grace was bent and twisted partially beneath the beast. She squeezed the teat again. A spray of milk shot out and blasted the back of her throat.

Grace had heard all the jokes about praying to God and God never answering. The punch line was that the one doing the praying never opened his or her eyes to see that God had been responding all along —

they'd been too resistant to the idea to see the opportunities before them.

For herself, she had no trouble understanding and acknowledging the source of her good fortune; she'd found the cow just standing there, all puckered body and protruding ribs, but a full udder. Might as well have had a neon sign pointing in its direction.

Grace drank until she threw up, then drank some more to wash down the foul taste in her mouth. When she was finished, the cow ambled away. As it did, a curtain to the landscape behind seemed to open itself.

Two Maasai herdsmen in their late teens or early twenties stood not ten meters away, an African version of *American Gothic.* The taller one held a ten-foot aluminum spear at his side, its sharpened tip stuck into the cracked earth. The other was significantly shorter. Their faces were as drawn as the cow's belly, their black eyes oversized and haunting. The tall one wore a tattered and stained white T-shirt bearing the Nike swoosh and JUST DO IT in bright red letters, below which a yellow *shuka* wrapped his waist and hung to his knees. The smaller, sturdier boy wore a red *shuka* shoulder to calf. They were barefoot and carried no sacks or bags. Both carried machetes from ropes lashed around their waists and empty plastic water bottles hung over their shoulders on chains of rubber bands.

The tall man's eyes were cold and distrusting. Fear and curiosity marked the smaller one, who did nothing to conceal his prominent erection, pressing up against the *shuka*. Grace remained squatting, bare-chested, absolutely still, her makeshift skirt riding high and showing more than she would have liked, her mud-and-dung-crusted skin giving her the appearance of a female shaman, or a wild spirit from the afterworld. But at her core she was an outnumbered, naked woman with a broken spear, a pair of antenna whips and a lumpy bag over her shoulder.

Taking a chance, she bared her teeth, hopped side to side and hissed like a snake. The smaller boy stepped back. It was the Nike man she was going to have to contend with; he held his ground, the spear immobile, and smiled, entertained by her antics. The look in his quiet eyes was unmistakable. So was his white-knuckle grip on the spear.

She continued her chimpanzee dance, appreciating the continued retreat of the smaller man. Winning the numbers game, she focused on fight or flight. To run invited

335

the spear.

Wild and alive with adrenaline, drained by the horror of the driver's death, she elected for the unexpected: to charge the man with the spear. He stepped back to hoist the weapon. Grace knocked it aside with the front of her stick, while thrusting the butt end into the man's chest.

She hit him hard in the solar plexus, stunning his lungs, then head-butted his right shoulder, sending a stinger down his arm. He dropped the spear. Her right knee found his crotch; her right elbow his jaw. She had a rhythm now, her right limbs punishing his left side, her left hand used to slap his head back to face her. She screamed, a terrifying, painful wail that seemed to come from elsewhere.

Her opponent found his machete; it took both her hands on his forearm to prevent him from hacking down. This freed his left hand. He threw a punch, full force into her bare breast. Grace's knees went out from under her.

He was atop her then, fighting to pin her arms while he held the machete to her throat. He shouted, and Grace felt the other man's hands on her legs. A split-second decision pushed her again to the unexpected. She fought every instinct, every natural response, and followed a former instructor's teachings. She went limp, dropped her head, her eyelids closed as she feigned unconsciousness.

Count to two. One . . . two . . . She felt the man's hold on her relax ever so slightly. Enough. Grace jerked her head toward the handle of the machete, avoiding its blade, and sat up sharply, kicking the smaller man in the face. Her teeth bared, she sank her jaw into the neck of the one atop her and bit down. She locked her jaw, his salty, sour flesh in her mouth. He let go of her arms. She thumb-gouged both his eyes and rolled, dumping the bellowing man off her.

She grabbed the spear. The boy ran away hard and fast. She stabbed the tip of the spear into the writhing man's foot, ensuring he couldn't follow her.

The cow had hardly moved. Grace saw the herd now — brown dots in the distance. The two men had been chasing down a stray.

Carrying the spear, she jogged off, following the boy. *When panicked,* she thought, *we all head home.*

51

Bishoppe waved from the passenger seat of the single-engine Cessna.

Despite his making the arrangements, Knox couldn't believe the pilot had allowed the boy to come along.

Koigi and Knox occupied a well-hidden vehicle with a view of the roadway where the plane had landed.

"The boy is yours to deal with," Koigi said before Knox could ask. "You will not leave him with me."

Knox accepted the money and once again shook Koigi's hand. "I hope I won't have to see you down there," Knox said.

"It is my wish as well."

Knox thanked him a final time, grabbed hold of his duffel and made for the waiting plane. His ears rang from the roar of the blade as the pilot turned into the wind on the roadway. Despite the noise, Knox turned in the seat to address Bishoppe, who'd quickly climbed into the back.

"What the hell were you thinking?"

"I want to be paid," the boy said, smiling widely. "If I don't join you, how do I know I will be paid?"

The plane took off, charging through the black of night, a waning moon rising on the horizon. Knox pulled on the cumbersome headset, adjusted the microphone and waited for the pilot, a weathered South African in his sixties, to complete his procedures. They leveled off at five thousand feet. Knox spoke softly into the microphone, so only the pilot would hear him.

"Our destination is Oloitokitok. And someplace between here and there, where we can drop the boy."

The pilot nodded. "There's a grass strip used by the Del Monte pineapple farm in the village of Thika. North of the Mathare slum. The boy can easily return to Nairobi in the morning. I didn't want to bring him."

Knox glanced over his shoulder. Bishoppe, unable to hear the discussion, looked deeply concerned.

"We will land at either Chyulu Hills or Amboseli, not Oloitokitok," the pilot added.

Knox didn't appreciate people messing with his plans or delaying him. If Grace was being moved, it would be at night. That gave him less than eight hours. "Oloitokitok."

"It's not safe. The village is too near the border. It's policed. Small planes like mine are searched for drugs and contraband. It's random, but much more regular at night. These arrangements we've made . . . my transponder's off, as you wanted. I'm giving you as much radio silence as possible. And I'm taking your money, gladly. But I won't go to prison for you. Grass strips are okay. Roadways, fine. But nothing bigger."

Knox unclenched his fists, roiling at the thought of delay. "I will need transportation."

"The lodge can supply you."

"You'll radio them?"

"When we're closer. Our mobiles will have signals intermittently if I fly the roads."

"Do it. And I'd like you to ask some questions about the lodge."

They flew for ten minutes. Just the flashing lights on the wings, the glow of the instruments, the reflections off the glass and the pitch-black night outside. Rarely did Knox see a single light below.

"How do you know the boy?" Knox asked.

"Bishoppe? He's an errand runner for a friend of mine. Keeps tabs on everything at the airport. He's a good boy, just a little aggressive. One of so many in Nairobi, but he's wise beyond his years, eh?"

"He's helped me out. This is the last I'll see of him."

The pilot looked over. Said nothing.

"Are you familiar with the Oloitokitok Clinic?"

"Very. I flew its biggest contributor more than once, when she missed a Safarilink or needed a direct flight."

"She?"

"An American, like yourself. From Baltimore, Maryland. I'm told it was very old money. Chemicals, I think."

"It closed recently, the clinic."

"Yes. Her doing, I imagine. Told me she accounted for over thirty percent of the funding. But the current government wouldn't support her. Claimed the place was servicing mostly Tanzanians. It's not true, but that's politics for you."

"Why would she withdraw her funding?"

"Controversy. The usual for Kenya."

Knox wanted to believe the clinic had closed because of Grace — that Grace had had time to celebrate a victory. Something about the vast black night absorbing the small plane made her situation seem all the more grim. He'd seen it in Koigi's eyes, felt it in the man's handshake: you don't fuck with men like Xin Ha and Guuleed. Grace had made one too many hacks, one too many connections, pulling a thread between the clinic, a trio of executions and the funding of insurgents.

Sooner than Knox expected, the pilot radioed and the plane began its descent. The boy leaned forward.

"Check your belt please," the pilot advised.

The strip was lit dimly: a motorcycle headlight at one end, a man waving a flashlight on the other. The landing was rough.

Knox climbed out and allowed the boy to follow before saying anything. He didn't want to wrestle him out of the backseat.

On the rough strip of grass, he handed Bishoppe a roll of bills. "You can get into the city from here. This should be enough to help your sister for some time. Use it for that, you understand?"

"You're getting rid of me?" Despondent and upset, the boy tried for puppy eyes. "I've helped you more than once."

Knox wasn't buying. "It's too dangerous. If I'm caught, you would be considered an accomplice."

"I don't care! We are a team! Take me with you. It is my decision, Mr. John. Please!"

"You stay here. You're a good man, Bishoppe."

"How can you do this, Mr. John? You and all the others, just like the men with my sister. Hello. Goodbye. Get lost."

Knox's chest knotted. "Take care of your sister like you've taken care of me, and she'll be fine."

"I can help you."

"You already have, Bishoppe. Trust me, you already have."

Tremulously, the boy backed away from the plane. Knox climbed into the seat, pulled the door shut and turned its handle. The act itself seemed so final. He understood the limitations from here. Grace was being held in or near Oloitokitok. She was being returned to an unidentified location. Knox didn't know the area, speak the language or have any backup.

He waved to the boy. Bishoppe did not wave back. Instead, he lifted his hand and flipped Knox his middle finger.

52

Beneath a cloud-shrouded, moonless sky, Grace squatted to urinate. The bellyful of milk had sustained her during her attempt to keep up with the fleeing boy, but his Maasai heritage and endurance soon showed, and he left her well behind. By nightfall even the fleeting sight of him had slowly but steadily disappeared, a boat sailing over the horizon.

He'd been aimed directly at Kilimanjaro. As she pursued him, she'd tried to outrun her own incredulity as well: there was no nearby village in this direction. The two herdsmen were a hundred kilometers from home, had probably been in the bush for months, living on cow's milk and root vegetables.

Olé had spoken of such an existence, but at the time his stories had seemed more lore than reality: an encounter with a lion; a friend dying from a soup he'd made that could have killed them all; hunting gazelle with primitive, poison-tipped spears. The stuff of film.

Slumping down, Grace scraped the hard-packed dirt with the tip of her attacker's aluminum spear, trying to break up the surface. Crumbling chunks of sandy dirt began building up in a pile alongside her. The loosened dirt would weigh down a blanket of salvaged car upholstery while she slept.

The night promised to be cool. Running had exhausted Grace; her chills warned of a fever. She'd used up the last of her energy, had begun hallucinating, a vision clouded with red and purple that frightened her. Too much information was a dangerous thing, she realized, trying to ignore the warning signs of her body shutting down. Despair chased away her courageous optimism. Depression replaced hope. She wanted to sleep and never wake up.

Though she could no longer see her hand in the thick dark, she saw herself digging her own grave. She was two people now: a woman who'd been well trained; and another woman, at the whim of the devils and ghosts her superstitious mother had warned her about.

As she thought of her family, Grace broke

into tears. Yellow and orange joined the swirling colors. She willed it all away, but to no effect. Closing her eyes tightly, she shook her head in an attempt to clear the canvas. The colors remained, now spinning to create vertigo and push her out of her squat. She fell back onto her bottom.

Lying down felt worse, and she feared that without a substantial layer of dirt atop the car seat fabric she would be at risk of hypothermia. Eyes open, eyes shut. The yellow glow came and went. The purple and red remained.

Focusing on the difference — open, shut — she strained to explain the yellow's absence when she closed her eyes. The color reappeared when she opened them, stayed in place while the red and purple colors shifted and flowed in her periphery like northern lights.

Eventually she determined that the small yellow blur actually existed in the landscape. It burned, real, steady. A campfire.

53

The Chyulu Hills airstrip was lined with five road flares, black smoke billowing upward as if from long-wick candles. The wind was from their right and slightly ahead. The plane bounced only once and taxied. Knox, consumed in thought, nearly missed seeing the tall Kenyan wearing khakis and a windbreaker standing alongside the army-green safari vehicle.

He was focused on two words in the intercept: "wounded gazelle." He'd pushed that aside without thought, but now he'd locked in on it. Was it an expression to allow the full meaning of the message to resonate, or was it literal?

"Nice landing."

The plane shuddered to a near stop and turned a full 180 degrees. "Pleasure," the pilot said, extending his hand. A dazed Knox took a moment to meet it with his own, then held the man's hand a little too long.

The pilot throttled the engine down lower, quieting it. The plane rumbled beneath them, as if eager to fly. "Well, it was a pleasure flying you — and the boy, too, I guess."

"You said Bishoppe ran errands and supplied information for a friend of yours. Do you mind me asking who?" Knox blurted out.

"Not at all. A journalist, Bertram Radcliffe. Bert's got ears and eyes all over Nairobi." The pilot reached out and put his hand on Knox's shoulder. "What is it, man?"

Trying to mask his shock, Knox thanked him and climbed out clumsily, struggling to squeeze his large frame through the small door. He felt sick. Bishoppe connected to Radcliffe, Radcliffe with his bizarre political agenda, his association with the dead reporter, his enlistment of the boy's services and the trouble chasing on its heels.

54

A steady and foul wind blew out of the northwest, drying Guuleed's tongue. He could still feel grit between his teeth, nubs worn to the nerve from years of chewing *khat.*

His prickly mood matched the weather. Eyes stinging, he knew better than to be outside in such a storm.

He moved for his truck. The remainder of his men huddled inside the two other vehicles, gambling away their meager earnings. A driver sat alone behind the wheel of Guuleed's truck, monitoring the CB and shortwave radios used by police and KGA rangers.

From the moment the sandstorm had risen and blown across their camps like a dry fog, Guuleed attributed it to Allah. He had ordered his men into the three best trucks and, driving separate routes, they had made for the forested hills in Aberdare

National Park, a swath of land east of Kijabi. Allah had provided them cover at a time of need: they'd been hunkered down under the watchful eye of an overhead drone. The camps had been left intact, along with several vehicles to sell the ruse of their still being occupied.

"Anything?" he asked his driver.

"No mention of us. No deployment. I believe we're in the clear. Praise Allah."

"I have already," Guuleed said testily.

"There is this, on the website." The man spun the laptop, which was wired to the satellite phone. Guuleed read. Blinked. Read again.

"Do we trust this source?"

"Yes. Absolutely. He works the hotels, same as the others."

"This is the American?" Guuleed suggested.

"I believe so, yes."

"A private flight? As soon as this shitstorm clears we head south, the lot of us."

The driver looked deeply troubled.

"Fucking Leebo's gone AWOL. Rambu's shorthanded. Cheer up, man. There's a woman who's going to make us rich. The Larger Than Life rangers travel in pairs. We can overpower any of their patrols. In and out. Quick strike. Ten, twenty times the money for you and the men. Our luck changes here."

55

Knox apologized to the hotel driver/guide who'd met him at the grass strip. "I'm fine with paying for a night's stay in the hotel — two, three, whatever your minimum is — but I need a ride to Oloitokitok now."

"It is I who is sorry, sir. It is not possible, this request you make. My instructions are to deliver you to the hotel. In the morning, such a trip can be arranged."

"It can't wait until morning."

"Then I am sorry, but you should have instructed the pilot to drop you off in Oloitokitok, sir. This is Ol Donyo. Chyulu Hills. It is seventy-five kilometers on dirt track across the bush. It is slow enough by light. At night, it would be four hours or more. My advice is for you to arrive to the lodge. Wake at sunrise. You will arrive to Oloitokitok at approximately the same hour. It will be my pleasure to drive you."

"It has to be now. It has to be Oloitoki-

tok. There's a man there named Brantingham, Travis Brantingham. Director of
Larger Than Life. You're smiling. You know
him?"

"Mr. Brantingham lives five minutes up
the road from the lodge, sir."

"Travis Brantingham? He commutes
seventy-five kilometers?"

"Several times a week. Oloitokitok is not
so pretty as Chyulu Hills, I think."

56

Grace's initial hope, that the two men around the campfire might be rangers sent to rescue her, was crushed by what she saw. Dressed in ratty bush clothes and car-tire sandals, they sat close to each other, as if for protection. Both looked hardened, and far too comfortable. A blackened saucepan was balanced on stones over a fire no bigger than a fist. It amazed her that she'd spotted it from so far away.

While one of the men cut up a tuber, the other smoked a foul cigar. Its smoke nearly made Grace sick. She left her hole, shed the skirt for fear of it making noise and belly-crawled twenty meters to the edge of the firelight.

In the flickering glow, she saw a backpack alongside the man smoking. He carried a Kalashnikov 74 across his back, the strap pulled over his head and under his opposing arm so the weapon ran on the diagonal.

She was close enough to the fire to see what might have been her own small boot impressions in the sand. They were trackers. They were hunting her.

Both wore equipment belts around their waists, laden with bulging ammunition pouches and Velcro pockets. If there was a second gun, she couldn't see it.

A light breeze blew. Each time the wind shifted, so did the men.

Seeing the supplies and the rifle, experiencing the dementia brought on by starvation and exposure, Grace nonetheless began plotting. They had water. Every fiber of her body ached at the sight. She would leave with it, or die trying.

She could crawl back into the dark and get as far away as quickly as possible. But they'd tracked her. She wasn't going to lose them. It was kill or be killed. It was water.

There were opportunities here. She knew Kalashnikovs well, had trained on a Chinese-made replica. But the rifle was out of the question. She'd have to fight the man to get a hold of it.

She sat back, mind whirling. Seeing them there, the camaraderie, the pot waiting to boil — it evoked in her a story Olé had told.

"We were a long way from the village. The grazing was much better there. There were three of us that day. Our friend gathered the roots to make the soup, while my other friend and I looked after the goats. Each day we fixed a meal for ourselves when the sun was at its height. It was his turn. But my friend and I were delayed. One of our goats encountered a snare trap and was in a bad way. We were no more than thirty minutes past the time we had wanted to return to the meal. When we arrived, our friend was dead, the tin he was eating from still gripped in his hand. All the veins in his arms, neck, head — everywhere — bulged to four or five times their size. His eyes were as big as stones in his head. My friend had seen it before. He drew his knife on the dead one's arm where the veins stuck up like tree roots. The blood was hard, almost dry. I have never seen anything like it. He explained it is — like what you call a potato. A root that can be mistaken for another you can eat, if you don't look carefully at the shape of the leaf. We used a goat to drag him back to the village. He was greeted like a leper until an old woman explained what my friend had told me."

Later, he'd shown her the poisonous plant. Its leaves were like those of a holly bush, distinctive.

"The plant is itself abundant. Its effects

are lethal. You must learn this one, Miss Grace."

The cook was brushing off and cutting the roots and stacking them in a pile at his side. He was going at it slowly, a few slices, some talk, more slices. The discussion was in Swahili and Grace wished she understood it. She assumed they'd tracked her. Perhaps they could read her shortened strides and knew of her exhaustion. She was deeply troubled by the apparent confidence that allowed them to stop for some soup and a midnight smoke.

Again, she considered her choices. Fight or flight? Again, she came to the same conclusion: to slip away and allow them to follow her by daylight was suicide; they'd be on her in a short time — and on their terms instead of hers. Currently, she had the advantage of surprise.

But how close could she get to the fire without being detected? How much was she willing to risk for that water?

She crawled slowly backward, as silent in her retreat as she'd been in her approach. Working at the very edge of the haze of light, she moved stealthily in search of the holly-leafed bush Olé had shown her. Twice she thought she had a candidate, but the feel of the leaf was wrong; she was looking for a firm, waxy leaf, one that might snap if folded. She kept one eye on the camp. The cook took a smoke off his companion and stoked the small fire with a few twigs, conserving what little fuel existed.

Grace had moved nearly halfway around them when she spotted a taller bush, raised up in silhouette, out farther from the fire. She cursed her luck; the moon was rising. She was going to have to act quickly.

The taller bush was indeed the one Grace sought; she recognized the feel of its leaves. She dug at the dirt around its base one-handed, glad for the crackling of the renewed fire.

Like nearly all plants in the bush, its roots were very near the surface, ready to take advantage of the slightest of rains. Grace twisted and broke off a length. It cracked.

The man with the gun turned his head. Already on hands and knees, Grace crawled slowly away from the bush, root in hand.

The man slipped the gun off his back with far too much ease and familiarity, stood and moved to the edge of the light.

She'd already put ten meters behind her. She continued ever so slowly, a wolf on the prowl. He'd given her an idea . . .

The men had an extremely brief exchange, by which point Grace had moved a full

ninety degrees clockwise around the campfire's perimeter. As the cook stood, grum-
bling, and moved toward the backpack, he
provided her with an opening.

She belly-crawled as quickly and silently
as possible, her sound partially covered by
the rustle of the cook digging through the
backpack, and the other man's movement,
the sound of fresh twigs snapping. With
both their backs turned to her, she knelt
and threw a rock high above their heads in
the direction of the bush.

They startled. Grace felt emboldened by
her success. This was the turning point in
her plan. She slithered to within two meters
of the cook's back, reaching for the pile of
tubers.

The cook called out, pointing. The rifleman turned. Grace froze, hand in the air,
fully within his field of view. But the gun-
man was looking at his partner for direction, for an animal or intruder to shoot, not
a shit-smeared, naked Chinese woman, bare
bottom to the sky. The cook switched on
the flashlight and blinded the rifleman. The
cook tossed the flashlight; the rifleman
missed the catch and cursed.

Grace slipped the root into the cook's pile
and crawled backward as fast as she could.
Sliding back into the dark, she lay still on

her stomach, focused on the root she'd left among the others.

And, moments later, the cook's hand as he reached down to continue filling the pot.

57

Brantingham swung open his front door with all the authority of a man unhappy to be disturbed.

"You're wanted by the police."

Somewhat round-faced and kind in the eyes, he wore his graying hair long and unkempt. His flamboyant bathrobe hung open, revealing a white T-shirt and boxer shorts. His skin had seen too much sun. He was clearly not a man to awaken at midnight.

"You must have me confused with someone else."

Brantingham shouted to the driver. "Do I invite him in, Thomas?"

"I believe he was about to force me to drive him to the clinic, sir. You would be doing me a favor."

"Come in and get yourself a tea, Thomas. This won't take long."

The driver entered and headed to the back

of the house, a contemporary, low-profile adobe structure built into the hill. Like Solio, the entire wall was windowless and open to the savanna.

Brantingham said, "You are advised that our rangers, all two hundred and fifty of them, have seen a photograph of your face. We are a private agency, which means all police, all KGA rangers are ahead of us in the pecking order. Understand? If we know your face, they know everything about you."

"It was an unfortunate accident," Knox said. "Some kids."

"That's original. Let me see your passport, please."

Knox hesitated, but he didn't see a lot of options. He withdrew and opened the document, retaining control. Brantingham gestured to hand it over. Knox did so reluctantly. Brantingham studied it and handed it back.

"Sir?" Knox said.

"Who the hell do you work for?" He moved to a side table that held mail, an iPad and his mobile phone, which was charging. He picked up the mobile. "If that's counterfeit, you paid a king's ransom for it; if it's authentic, as it appears, then I need to know what agency I'm speaking with. What American agency, I presume."

"A woman, a Chinese woman —"

"Grace Chu. Answer the question, Knox. Which agency?"

"I'm in global import/export. Crafts, mostly. The occasional piece of art."

"Sure you are. Thomas!"

"No, no, no!" Knox said hastily.

Thomas appeared behind them, approaching down a short hallway that, like the living room, had walls covered with enormous art photos of African wildlife.

"I'll explain," Knox said.

"Enjoy your tea, Thomas. Sorry to bother you."

"No bother, sir," Thomas said, and retreated.

Knox resigned himself to the truth for Grace's sake. "I contract — only occasionally — for a company out of Hong Kong called Rutherford Risk. Missing persons. Negotiation and recovery."

"Kidnappings. Extortion," Brantingham said. "We are all too familiar with such things here in Kenya. Didn't used to be this way."

Knox nodded. "Grace and I have partnered on a few projects. I'm here on my own. I'm not under contract. It's personal." Hearing it put that way surprised Knox. Was that the first time he'd admitted it to someone else?

"You're here because — ?"

"You last saw Grace two days ago. Before that, maybe three weeks earlier."

Brantingham raised his eyebrows, impressed. He motioned Knox onto an animal-skin couch. Knox had no idea what animal. "Don't expect me to tell you anything about it. She asked for confidentiality, and she will have it."

' "She hasn't been heard from since."

"Thom-as!" Brantingham shouted.

Again, the driver appeared. Brantingham spoke boldly, like an employer. "The guest, Grace Chu. Chinese woman."

"Yes, sir."

"She was with us two nights ago. She headed back to the lodge, correct?"

"No, sir. She took a side trip into Tanzania."

Brantingham grinned at Knox. "Well, there you have it. No wonder. Happens all the time."

"Thank you, Thomas," Knox said. "Nice to get that cleared up."

Again, Thomas retreated. Knox wondered how much it might anger Brantingham that his guest had dismissed the driver. It was nuance that steered an interview.

"She's not in Tanzania," Knox said. "Nor

364

is it likely she was ever in Tanzania. She was abducted and held and is now being returned — possibly as proof of life, possibly because of illness or some other factor unknown to us." Knox tried to sound definite as he explained the recent intercept of satellite phone traffic to Oloitokitok and the reference to a "wounded gazelle."

"Return a wounded gazelle?"

"You see the problem? We believe she's being moved tonight. Dawn at the latest."

"And you waited to tell me in person? What the hell, Knox? I have the third-largest army in Kenya at my disposal, second only to the military and the KGA. You didn't think you could trust me? Did you ask anyone about me?"

"Until a few hours ago, I had no idea where to look. No idea who to call."

"You need food."

"I'm all right."

"Thomas!" The man reappeared, smiling this time. "Would you mind terribly preparing some food for our friend here? Anything will do."

"My pleasure."

Brantingham's brow furrowed. He stared off into space for a long moment. "You believe she's being returned to Oloitokitok."

"It seems so. Yes."

"By her kidnappers."

"Again, a strong possibility."

"You said the gazelle message was recent. So what changed?"

"As I said, I'm not sure. The hostage's health? Outside pressure? Internal discord among the kidnappers? We had one case where they'd planned so poorly, they ran out of food."

"You intercepted this communiqué? Why do I find it difficult to believe that a wanted man such as yourself has those kinds of contacts? If you did, someone would have arranged to get you out and install another man or woman in your place."

"I have to keep my source confidential."

"If you want my help, if I'm supposed to trust you, you will tell me what I need to know."

"It was a ranger named Koigi."

"You spoke to Koigi? Face-to-face?"

"I did."

He barked out a laugh. "Do you drink, Knox?"

"Not tonight, sir."

"Pardon me." He poured himself a dark whiskey. "A great man, our Koigi. A kind of national treasure."

"So I've heard."

"There's no chance you spoke to him. So

you lied to me, and I don't take that lightly. A brazen lie, I'll give you that."

Knox explained his abduction, the sack over his head, the drive — but not the location. Nor did he reveal the number of tents and vehicles. "Koigi's a very stocky six feet. Looks more like six-foot-two."

"Anyone could tell you that."

"Has hands like a cat's tongue."

"Well, I'll be damned."

Thomas delivered a poorly stacked sandwich and a cold beer. Knox asked for an iced tea instead.

"What the hell were you doing with Koigi in the first place?" Brantingham asked.

Knox passed him the crumpled photo of the tattooed arm. "The tattoo is drawn over a vaccination scar."

"Yes, I see that."

"A couple of Koigi's men had similar scars," Knox said "Bad vaccine, just like the one Grace was chasing. Koigi said a number of his men had been vaccinated while in Oloitokitok."

"I wouldn't doubt it. Free health care. The clinic drew hundreds a day at its peak. But I don't follow."

"He told that to Grace. The clinic keeps records. She would have been after a man named Faaruq." Knox pointed again to the photo. "I don't know what Grace may have told you, sir. But she came down here to access the clinic's records. She was looking for the man's records."

"Which were taken or destroyed, or both, when they shut down shop."

"She wouldn't have come back if there hadn't been some way for her to confirm that this Faaruq had been vaccinated there."

"This is the same Faaruq shot at Mount Kenya. The alleged poacher?"

"It is."

Brantingham hung his head. "Shit. She tricked me."

"How's that?" Knox said, leaning forward.

"She's a clever one, your Ms. Chu."

Knox was tired of so many people calling Grace "his." *It isn't like that,* he wanted to say. But the more he heard it, the more he wondered if he was projecting something he was unaware of, wasn't intending.

"God!" Brantingham shook his head as if clearing it and poured himself more whiskey. "The first time, I mean, who would have guessed? But the second? I should have caught it. She's into computers, isn't she, John? IT work? Computer security?"

"Yes, sir. That's right."

"I'm called Travis. She played sleight-of-hand with me. Not once, but twice."

"That sounds like her."

"She engaged me in a discussion of our antipoaching, our relationship with the clinic — nonexistent beyond our taking over some space as they moved out. Thirty minutes in, she asked for Internet access. Wouldn't take the wireless I offered. Had to have Ethernet. Thing is, and this is the part that frosts me, she'd managed to get me to explain that we'd assumed many of the clinic's utilities after the hurried closing. We paid some of the back bills in order to avoid an interruption of service."

"Including the Internet provider," Knox said, guessing.

"Yes." Brantingham exhaled dramatically. "Would that have helped her somehow? Their computers were gone. First things they took away."

"I don't know enough about it."

"Well, I know a little, just enough to get me into trouble. I know for a fact she couldn't hack their computers. They were gone. Removed. But we're using their router, their account. We took over their account."

"The cloud," Knox said. "She probably compromised their cloud storage or even e-mails." He tried to keep the awe out of his voice, but it wasn't possible. "She's very good at it."

"And then she came back and did it again. A second time." Brantingham sounded astonished. "That's humiliating."

"To get at their patient records," Knox said. He swallowed hard. The sandwich tasted far better than it looked. He was still awaiting the iced tea. He wiped his lips. "Tanzania or not, she's being moved to-night," he said flatly.

"If it came from Koigi's sources, it can be trusted. He and my people share a great deal."

"Maybe not enough this time."

Brantingham didn't appreciate the rebuke.

"Thomas claims I have to wait for daylight to drive to Oloitokitok."

"He's right about that," Brantingham said. "You can ride with me. I'll pick you up outside the lobby at four thirty."

58

Watching the two men die was no kind of sport.

At first, Grace had cheered on the cook's hand, reaching down blindly into his pile and grabbing hold of the root she'd slipped him. She'd celebrated each slice of the knife and the steam that slowly rose from the pot. The soup took time to cook.

Then came the moment when the two portions were poured out. The other man tossed his cigar into the fire; Grace watched the amber sparks rise from the coals and take flight. The men drank their soup and talked in the casual, comfortable tone of two friends, and Grace wondered at what she'd done.

When death came — first to the cook, who much to her alarm had taken early sips from the broth to taste its readiness — it arrived as a seizure, a cramp that locked the whole body as if it were a single muscle.

Despite the agonies she witnessed, Grace felt no remorse. Unable to stop herself, she walked from the dark into the rim of light thrown by the fire, standing close to the Kalashnikov. She was possessed with desire, the need for them to know this was no accident.

In her mud-slathered nakedness, she stood watching, the cook likely dead already, the other man wild-eyed and terrified by her visage. The veins swelled just as Olé had described, more like a special effect from a comic book movie than anything real. People didn't die this way, alarmingly fast, their eyes bulging, the veins growing from their arms and neck and face. The bodies looked like road maps.

She didn't know the woman who savored this moment, didn't recognize herself.

The poison took the second man more slowly. Paralyzed, he twitched and tried to speak, his tongue swelling to the size of a cow's. He fought to move his right arm. Grace picked up the rifle and aimed it at him in case he found his pistol. She could have — should have — ended his life then, but instead she savagely looked on, savoring his agony. His hand found his pocket. Grace aimed for his head. His final effort showed a surprising will and strength; he not only pulled a phone from his pocket, but he managed to throw it into the fire.

Grace, not wanting the sound of the gunfire, smashed his face with the gun stock, driving him back. He was dead before he hit the ground. She dove, threw her hand into the fire, burned it trying to retrieve the phone. Furious, she scooped its withering plastic husk out and threw it onto the dirt at the dead man's feet. She kicked the men to confirm their condition. The poison had made them solid with rigor.

The phone's keys were melted and inoperable, the clothing she stole ill-fitting and sour, though as welcome as a hot bath. The backpack held two thin blankets, mosquito netting, a few spare magazines for the Kalashnikov, some pieces of fruit and, most important, three liters of bottled water. Grace knew better than to gulp, though the temptation was there, just as it had been with the dead driver's tea.

Sobbing dry tears, laughing, dressed in the stinking clothes of the dead men who now lay naked by a dwindling fire, she left the useless phone behind, not wanting an ounce of added weight.

With the hint, the suggestion, that she might yet make it out of this place came the unwanted realization that she had lived more fully in the past few days than at any other time in her life. In a strange, sickening way, she didn't want to leave.

At that moment, she heard the trumpeting of an elephant.

59

"We need better men!" Thomas announced as he climbed out of the safari truck to open the electric fence gate. Task completed, he got back behind the wheel and drove the truck through. "We put the fence up at night to keep the game out."

Again, he left the truck and replaced the gate. Back in the car, he looked around searchingly.

"There's supposed to be a guard here on duty all night. He will be reprimanded, if not fired, I promise."

"Not on my account, I hope."

"You're in number six. I'll bring your kit down to the room while you check in."

Knox was dropped off at the open front doors of the main lodge. He saw through the open wall to the pitch black of the savanna beyond. The truck motored off. Knox paused a moment and then headed inside.

It was late, after eleven. The lobby was quiet. He called out a greeting. Earlier, he'd asked Thomas to see that Grace's belongings be delivered to his room; he'd overheard him radio in the request. He reminded himself to check on that.

After two more unsuccessful attempts to summon the staff, he grabbed a complimentary flashlight and turned back toward the entrance. The beam caught on something in his path; he stopped and bent down to retrieve a flashlight that had fallen. It was sticky to the touch — a kind of sticky familiar to Knox.

He reacted immediately, letting go and wiping the blood off his hand onto his jeans. Guarding his back, he moved along the wall, toward the drinks bar at the far end of the large pavilion, which was divided into sitting areas by furniture. The bar was unattended. He didn't appreciate the sixty feet of open-air wall and the dark beyond; anyone could be out there, watching him.

For safety's sake, he moved in rapid, irregular jaunts. At the opposite end of the pavilion a series of split-level drops began, each descending to a more intimate dining area. The last led to a pool. From the pool, a long, steep staircase descended to the "hide," a camouflaged wildlife viewing area only yards from the largest of two watering holes.

Knox saw a few drops of blood leading to the first terrace. Low, romantic lighting lit each successive level. Down, down. Pumped and breathing shallowly, Knox moved in the direction the blood pointed, not wanting to use the flashlight to announce himself. The night sounds were reminiscent of summer in Detroit; they played peacefully in his ears, giving a false sense of security. He wished Thomas had stuck around. Knox was unfamiliar with the layout, and no doubt outnumbered.

With no way of knowing otherwise, discounting a dozen other scenarios that ranged from simple robbery to random violence, he had the hubris to assume the invasion had to do with him and Grace.

A hurried search of the dining levels left him at the pool. Its circulating, bubbling water looked pleasant, seductive. Yet Knox felt pulled down the stairs to the hide. A pair of torches threw flickered flames of light; their jumping movement marked the top of a gravel path cut into the dirt hill. Knox's own shadow danced, too, distracting and rattling him.

He moved rapidly, avoiding the gravel for its noise. Slipping over the log stairs set into the hill, he headed down through the rising walls of dead tree limbs erected to screen humans from the sight of elephants. It was a much longer path than expected, drawn out by the discovery of blood, by the eerie quiet and the impenetrable African night. Under the glare of the torches, the walls of dead limbs took on the form of human and animal bones, shadows moving with Knox's motion, a kaleidoscope of skeletal fingers pointing in all directions.

At last he reached the hide, a rustic space with a wooden bar and stools also screened by an array of sticks. At the back was a split-level elevated viewing deck, its floorboards rotted. He made it to the center of the small space before catching sight of the bodies. Living, twitching bodies, hog-tied and gagged. Four staff and the two young managers. The male manager had taken a blow to the side of the head that was going to need stitches. Barely conscious, the man groaned as Knox touched him.

Knox apologized as he tore a shirt off one of the male staff and tied it around the bleeding man's head. Knox then rolled the young woman manager over, dropped his own face to within inches of hers.

"Listen carefully. I'm here to help." The woman manager squirmed and wiggled, eyes like those of a wild horse. Knox pressed down gently onto her chest. "Easy. I will untie you all, but I need you to listen!" The woman quieted. "They mean you no harm or they'd have killed you. Let's keep it that way. Nod, if you understand." The woman nodded — what choice did she have? "Okay. Good. Quiet, now." Knox loosened her gag. She said nothing, breathing hard as if starved for air. "How many?"

"Three."

"Did they say — ?"

"Miss Chu's possessions," she said, cutting him off.

"Thomas called in after I landed for you to —"

"Yes, we delivered her bags to your room." Knox appreciated the woman's relative calm. "Rob gave them the wrong room number." Rob's forehead was covered by the tied shirt.

"How long ago?"

"Not long. A few minutes at most," she said.

Knox had just missed them. The time lag explained the still-sticky consistency of the blood he'd found, and the quiet of the place. The noise of his arrival had likely hurried the intruders away.

"Untie the others. Head into the bush;

don't stay here at the hotel. Keep down, get far away and regroup."

She nodded vehemently, tears spilling. "Thank . . . you."

He loosened her bonds. "Do not return to the hotel tonight. Promise me."

"Yes. Promise! Thank you! Thank you!"

In what felt like a matter of seconds, he was back up the stairs. He moved across the pool terrace, bent at the waist, senses heightened. He imagined hearing things to his right. The central pavilion split the suites, four to each side. Knox's was the last to the left.

Another sound from the same direction.

He thought the arrival and departure of his truck could have panicked them. At least one man would be sent to investigate. So either two were searching for Grace's belongings and one man for Knox, or the reverse.

Electing to stay out of the building in the dark, he left the terrace immediately. He skirted a fire pit, dodged bushes, navigating by the waving orange light thrown by kerosene torches.

The dry, bare earth descended sharply. Knox cut a straight line below the first three split-level suites. Hot tubs threw shimmering blue light up onto the walls, the glow worming through the thatched roofs like something alive. Whenever he slipped, he paused and listened intently. His head hurt.

Below the penultimate suite on this side, he heard a door click shut. Something light: a cabinet or armoire. He stood some twenty feet below the bedroom's open wall. Choices. He moved on.

He reached the area below his suite and scrabbled up the embankment, startled by a warthog's black eyes, curving tusks and long snout — as ugly a creature as ever there was. Behind it stood three more.

In an instant, the group shot off together down the hill, the drumming of their hooves reverberating off the buildings. Knox dropped flat.

A man's silhouette appeared in the gray span of the open wall to the center suite. A brute, tall and broad-shouldered. Knox could imagine him dressed in camouflage, though he could not see well enough to know.

The figure stood contemplatively; he'd identified the warthogs, but was presumably scanning to see what had caused the sudden stampede. A patient man, unmoving and stoic. One minute passed. Two. Three. Knox couldn't believe how the man waited, marveled at such tenacity. The greedy urban misfits he'd faced in kidnappings came off like children compared to this. His adversary was a practiced hunter, composed and unexcitable.

Five minutes. Six. Jesus! A rabbit ran within inches of Knox, darting and jumping almost soundlessly down the hill. The man's head swiveled — he'd heard it from thirty yards away — and, Knox thought, followed it down past the second water hole, where the warthogs huddled. Perhaps the rabbit explained things to him. The man stepped away from the edge and back into the darkness of the suite. Knox waited two full minutes before he dared move.

As he rose, a door banged shut next door. Knox felt it like a starting gun. He climbed the outer wall of his bedroom and hauled himself up through the open space. He'd been told Grace's bag had been delivered to his suite. Turn-down service had left several lamps glowing softly. Knox hurriedly checked the bedroom. No bag.

He moved down the few stairs to the sprawling living area. Like the bedroom, it had an entire wall open to the night air. He locked the front door and turned around. There, on a circular card table near the deck, was a roll-aboard suitcase and Grace's gray carrying case.

Despite his best efforts, Knox had not been prepared for the impact of seeing these things, this evidence of her. He felt it like a blow to his chest. *Three days,* he thought. These bags couldn't be all he brought home of her.

The door thumped — a shoulder not expecting it to be locked. A key, fumbling. Knox sprang to the card table and snagged the bags. Two strides, and he lowered them off the deck and let go. He was on his way back when the handle turned. The key scratched. The deadbolt spun.

Knox slipped into a chair at the card table and picked up a magazine.

The door swung open. The man wore green camouflage with no identification badges. His waist belt was heavy with a large-caliber handgun, multiple magazine pouches, and a decent-sized Maglite that could be used as a club. He appeared momentarily surprised by the encounter.

"What the hell?" Knox said. "May I help you?"

Rambu recovered well, his gaze unflinching. "Military police. A guest's belongings were misplaced by the staff. They were brought to this room by mistake."

They'd searched all the other rooms, Knox realized.

"I believe you're mistaken," Knox said, standing as the man stepped into the room. "I've seen nothing of the sort." He gestured toward the door. "If you please?"

Rather than leave, the big man eased the door shut behind him, never taking his eyes off Knox.

"I said you're mistaken," Knox repeated. "Please leave." He took a step toward the man, closing to within ten feet of him.

"I'll just have a quick look," Rambu said. But more than his comment, his demeanor had changed when Knox stood. For a moment, Knox thought he'd been made — which suggested his visitor was a policeman privy to the warrants issued by the Nairobi police. Tying up the staff seemed extreme, but as he'd learned, the police here made their own rules.

But no. The absent guard at the electric fence tipped the scales for Knox. Military police would have no reason to subdue or kill such a guard.

"Sure," Knox said. He gestured widely. "Have at it."

"I'll ask you to sit, with your hands on the table."

"Seriously?"

"If you please." Rambu's hand lightly grazed the handgun as if reminding both men of its presence.

"I don't please. You're going to shoot me if I don't sit down?" Knox sounded incredulous.

"In the chair, hands on the table." The man's eyes were not searching the room; they had yet to leave Knox. He withdrew his weapon.

"Oh, come on." Knox hadn't moved. There were few things that frightened him more than a gun aimed at him. Rattlesnakes and scorpions ranked high, drunks on the highway were bad, too; but the muzzle of a gun loosened his bowels. "You're going to shoot me fo—"

"Now!" The voice shook the room, though not Knox. Without so much as a tremor, he stepped back and placed his hands on the table. Sat down.

"For the record: you're making a big mistake. I'm a guest in your country. I don't know what it is you want." He worked hard to play the innocence card, but the look in the other man's eyes did not waver. Again, Knox suspected his cover was blown.

"On your head."

"Say again?"

"Hands on your head. No more talk!" Either the man was high on *khat,* easily upset, or exhausted to a flash point. For one so big, he moved remarkably fast, snaring a lamp, trapping it beneath his oversized boot, and tearing the cord away as if it were a balloon ribbon. And all the while, he never took his attention off Knox. "Okay. Hands through the back of the chair. Slowly."

"This is unnecessary! You can search the place! I don't care. I'm sorry."

The gun wavered. Knox winced. This man's weapon — a bulky .45 — wasn't new to the firing range. Its surface was worn to a pale patina, its handgrip stained dark where it contacted flesh.

"Let's be reasonable," Knox said, searching for an opening.

"Through the back of the chair."

Knox obeyed, leaning forward to fit his left arm behind him and through the carved chair back. He needed to break the man's concentration just long enough to challenge him. Had to wait for it; couldn't rush it.

He feigned soreness in his right shoulder as he rocked to fit his arm through. If he completed the move, his arms would be separated by a piece of hardwood carved as a giraffe. If the man tied his wrists together, he was stuck. His feigned cooperation, along with projecting soreness in his shoulder, drew his opponent a half-pace closer. He'd failed to measure Knox's wingspan.

Knox slowly rocked his chin over his shoulder, making sure to lock eyes with the man. "My friend found the ivory." He spoke with a keen familiarity, as if sharing a secret.

For just a nanosecond, the fire in the man's eyes dimmed.

Knox shoved back the chair and began a pirouette with his long right arm, extending it to slap the gun away. His momentum allowed him to crane forward and separate the chair from the card table. As he rotated, the chair hooked in his left elbow whistled past and took the man down. Knox dropped to pin the man, but too late. Pistol-whipped in the back of the head, he faltered. The man heaved him aside, but the act sent the gun spinning across the floor.

The two came to standing, Knox semiconscious, Rambu working out a numb leg. They charged like bull elephants, heads lowered, each throwing punches into his opponent's gut. Knox stretched to kick the man's weakened knee but missed. He took a blow in his bad ear, his head ringing like a bell tower. Threw a knee and caught some ribs; heard the man choke for air.

There was a hunting knife on that belt as well; Knox saw the flash of steel and blocked with his forearm. He threw an ineffective elbow to the man's jaw. Knox feinted to his own right, throwing his opponent onto the hurt knee. As he went down, the knife's blade flashed. Knox's arm bled.

Grace came to mind. Knox attacked recklessly. He took the man into a chokehold. The knife fell.

"Where is she?" Knox whispered. "The Chinese woman? One wrong word . . ." He eased. "Where?" He tightened.

Rambu squirmed, trying to break the hold. But Knox had him now. There was no undoing it. He tightened the grip, thinking of this man and others with Grace, imagining what they might have done to her. "Where?"

"Lost her!" Rambu choked out.

"Where?"

"Olio—" Rambu threw back his head and caught Knox in the jaw. Knox lost his grip, pissed at being lured into a stupid mistake. The inside of his cheek bled, an all-too-familiar metallic taste.

Both men reached for and held the knife, the blade's tip alternating its interest like a water witcher. Rambu used his considerable weight advantage against Knox, rolling and working to lie fully atop him. Knox bucked to keep him off. And still the knife tip winked.

In an instant, Knox drove his knee up

between the man's legs and took possession of the blade. He punched it into the man's thigh — it was like stabbing a tree. The man rocked forward. Knox kneed him in the forehead, and the man was out cold. Knox tore the radio off the man's belt and cut through his pants to expose a cell phone and wallet. Took them both.

He hurried to the balcony, vaulted and landed well onto the hardpack. Grace's bags were nearby. Grabbing them, he clambered up the dirt hill and into the hotel's lush landscape, running hard for the car pool.

Spotting a filthy, muscled-up SUV in the driveway, he skidded to a stop and knifed the front tire. The blade lodged in the steel belting; unable to extract it, Knox left it.

He found a key rack in a staff shed and, third in the line of eight, the vehicle it fit, a Korean crossover. He threw Grace's bags into the passenger seat. Lights out, he drove slowly through the compound's electric fence gate, snapping and sparking its wires before leaving the Chyulu Hills and descending onto the flat gray span of the moonlit savanna.

60

News of a Nairobi market bombing hit Koigi hard. Seventeen confirmed dead and sixty-eight wounded, a dozen critically.

He had little doubt al-Shabaab would soon claim responsibility. The country he loved was coming apart before his eyes. And his precious elephants and their tusks were financing it.

Koigi called Graham Winston. He waited nine minutes to be connected.

"You heard about the Nairobi bombing?" he asked without preamble.

"Yes. Just now."

"I need real-time GPS coordinates. The intel I've been given puts me in the man's exhaust."

"I don't have that information."

"Please, I need it. Now."

"We've lost visual. No movement at either camp for the past two passes. There was a storm. They could be hunkered down, but it looks otherwise."

Koigi processed the news. "The satellite phone?"

"I'm told it's turned off."

"You know they have his coordinates. They can read the phone's coordinates when it's off *and* the battery's disconnected. Please, call someone."

"It doesn't work like that."

"I met with Knox. He's headed south. I'm sending men to support him. Depending on Guuleed's location, I may join them. Listen, if Guuleed has fled his camps, there's got to be good reason. If he's in or near Nairobi, then maybe we can connect him to this bombing. If he's headed south, then Knox is in trouble." He waited for some response. "Hello? Please?"

"What you are asking me to do is no easy thing, my friend. I have someone inside sympathetic to our cause. Real-time co-ordinates is at another level. It requires me to reveal what I know. And I know more than I should."

"I won't ask you to put yourself at risk of criminal charges. And I understand the value of informers at every level, believe me. What I can say is this. Guuleed is a poacher, first and last. If he and his men are on the move, there's a damn good reason for it, a reason dear to both of our hearts. Of this, I have no doubts. He is on the hunt. They have information, and they're acting on it. There is only suffering to come of that."

Winston took a long time before speaking. "If I'm to pull this favor, and I intend to do so, it could very well be the last time we are in this close to operations. You understand what that means?"

"Given the American and the missing Chinese woman. Factor in Guuleed's sudden movement. It's an important risk to take."

"But you understand?"

"I do. Yes. I understand."

"Do whatever you must. God's speed." Winston disconnected the call.

Less than an hour later, Koigi received the first e-mail detailing Guuleed's real-time GPS coordinates.

The poacher was headed south on the road from Ngong to Kajiado.

61

Grace's clothes and personal items lay in a heap on the passenger side of the Korean car. Knox was driving one-handed. He had yet to turn on the headlights; the view from Ol Donyo Lodge's hillside location was vast. He didn't want to reveal himself. For the same reason, he avoided the brakes, finding a speed that allowed him to navigate the barely visible dirt track at a steady pace.

Grace's bag had been packed neatly. Tidy. In a way that tightened Knox's chest. Something about touching her clothing, having a visceral connection to her skin, her smells, her presentation of herself, caused the emotions he'd been suppressing to rise to the surface.

What he had not told Dulwich in England, what he'd not fully admitted to himself, was that the exchange of two short, handwritten letters had changed his situation with Grace, had propelled him onto that jet without so much as a second thought. He would not be able to handle her loss.

For nearly ten years, Knox had worked hard to allow feelings only for Tommy. When he'd found himself under the spell of a woman, he cut the relationship off before it could develop further. He'd been an intentional asshole, or settled into big-brother mode with female friends who clearly wanted more.

Grace? Grace had sneaked up on him, coming through the job, surprising him, impressing him. Pissing him off. Driving him crazy. Calling him out. What had provoked her to write him an unsolicited letter expressing affection — in her backhanded, Chinese way — he had no idea. He'd resented it for its honesty, resented her for sending it.

And then, sober and sleepless, he found himself unable to shake it. Her words had sunk into him like nails, demanding a response. He promised himself he'd never give it to her.

A day later, reading her letter for the fifth time, he'd picked up a pen and started to write.

Dear Grace:

Thanks for the letter. That took/takes a lot of courage. I could pretend you mean nothing to me, but that's all it would be, pretending. We could go on, seeing each other once or twice a year for Rutherford as we have, doing our jobs and going back to our corners. Maybe that's the smart thing to do.

Here's the deal. My brother is the most important person in my life. He's also an adult and someone who hangs around my neck like a flashing sign: DON'T GO NEAR. I'm no use in a relationship, which is why I catch women when I can (something I know bothers you) and never look back. I am by definition a one-night stand, a weekend fling. I'm like a divorced man with children, only my child is twenty-six, has seizures and is mentally around fourteen. No one signs up for that. No one. Not even an angel, Grace. And you are that!

Look, you've been involved in a relationship for years now. From what you've told me (which isn't much), it goes back to when you two were kids. So we both have baggage. Mine is ongoing and indefinite. Yours is in need of resolution, if I may be blunt. You need to go back to him, or move on. It's unfair to anyone else you become interested in (including me, potentially) to leave that unresolved.

Our lives are complicated. No news there. Because my contact with women is typically physical and short-lived, I rarely reach the point of caring too terribly much. Then you came along. In Istanbul, when you went missing, I went nuts. And I knew. You are not just another woman to me.

What this means, I don't know. But I wanted you to know along with me. For what that's worth.

Yours,
John

Her clothes, collected on the floor, reduced to a small pile, looked so insignificant. The contents of the bag revealed nothing. It seemed impossible and drastically unfair that this should be the last he knew of her. A pile on the floor of a car, bumping across a rutted dirt track.

As if hearing his thoughts, the clothes shifted and danced with the subtle jostles of the floorboards, worming lower. A sliver of white appeared. The corner of a piece of paper.

Knox leaned for it, caught a tire in a rut

and felt the car pulled violently to the side of the track. The car bounced up and out into the bush before he caught hold of the paper and straightened out, gripping the wheel tightly and directing the vehicle back onto the road.

An envelope. He leaned on the brakes — something he'd promised himself to avoid — and skidded to a stop, throwing up a billowing plume of dust that carried slowly forward and swallowed him. By the light of his cell phone, he turned the opened envelope over, desperate for some message from her, intentional or not.

It was his handwriting. Her name. Her Hong Kong address. His letter to her. He dug through the pile of clothes, unsure how he'd missed this, a wave of despair and frustration, of irony and unacceptable emotion choking him.

His letter was her one possession beyond some laundry and makeup, lotions and toothpaste. His hand shook as he pinched the letter itself, pulled it from the envelope. Unable to bring himself to confirm its contents, he slipped it back inside and dropped the envelope onto the passenger seat.

He'd not heard back since he'd opened up to her. Had found the wait agonizing, palpably painful. But she'd kept the letter; had kept it close. He felt overjoyed, angry, alone. He felt her, there, on the floor, there, in the envelope. In his thoughts.

He put the car in gear and drove, switching the headlights on and gaining speed.

62

It was not her imagination. The closer Grace drew to the sound of the elephants, which were now less than fifty yards away, the more their pace quickened. No matter how delicately she moved, the rhythm of their movement also increased.

Blinded by the absolute darkness, she gave up and walked slowly, arms outstretched, moving around thickets, trying to avoid stumbling. At first the parallels to her tempo had seemed coincidental, or at most the result of the herd hearing her. Soon it became apparent that the trigger for their movement was something far subtler. Unable to catch up, to even close the gap, she remembered Olé's warnings about predators like lion, hyena and jackal. The elephants' keen sense of smell and easy identification of humans had in part led her to strip and routinely smear animal dung in layers over her body.

She stopped, shed the foul-smelling clothes and backpack of the men she'd killed, tied a piece of the remaining car seat upholstery to a bush as a marker. She put the water bottles into the sack she'd fashioned, slung the weapon over her shoulder and tried again, hurrying to catch up.

It took her nearly twenty minutes to relocate the herd. Without her pursuit, the elephants had stopped. Free of everything but the gun, Grace was able to draw much closer. She smiled ruefully in the dark; in her natural element the elephants now allowed her company.

Awed by their magnificence, their size and stature — they seemed to have no fear — she stayed with them. They moved as a group, their trunks swaying, huge ears flapping. She could hear their raspy breathing, low and sonorous. Found it comforting. Their loamy scent was as sweet to her as that from a stable of horses. Among them she no longer felt alone.

One of the elephants evacuated; Grace crept forward and coated her limbs and belly, grateful for the warmth and thankful for the chance to erase any traces of the clothing.

The horizon behind her glowed gray, then a rich blue. When the sun finally rose, it did so exceptionally fast. She took sightings for compass landmarks and counted six elephants, five adults and a juvenile. The tusks of one were sawed off to stubs. Another had one broken tusk, its spectacular twin curved long and low to the ground. This older elephant wore a heavy-duty nylon collar, filthy, torn and fraying. Fixed to the collar was a beat-up black brick the size of a lunch pail.

The Larger Than Life rangers had explained the collar monitoring. Grace had probably seen the signal from this collar on a computer screen. From headquarters, they tracked collared elephants live, plotting their course by the day, week or month. Some elephants walked in relatively straight routes, others wandered randomly.

If only she could lead the collared elephant around the bush so its tracking device wrote SOS or HELP on the monitors! Like walking messages into wet sand at the shore. Or if she knew electrical engineering — then she might have been able to rewire the collar to transmit a message.

Sighing, Grace studied the burns on her right hand, where she'd fished the melting phone from the campfire. Each opportunity brought her within inches of rescue — only to be denied. She caught herself crying, fought to stop.

The elephant with the collar meandered over to her, as if to comfort her. She looked up and spoke softly to the giant, and he stepped closer still. Grace held her hand out. The elephant sniffed and then coughed through its trunk, wetting her hand. It sniffed more and stepped back, giving her a good look at the battered GPS transmitter.

Grace had been raised by a Buddhist father and Christian mother, but had never found much use for either faith. Her days in the bush had changed that; she'd succumbed to prayer and an impractical reliance upon a greater cause at work in guiding her actions. She'd begged for forgiveness for the lives she'd taken, wondering if the nightmares would ever leave her. She feared that she'd condemned herself to a living hell, that, like the elephant, she would never forget.

Something a ranger had said during the tour of the radio shack echoed in her mind. She could recall nearly verbatim his explanation of the collars:

"Tracking collars allow us to pass along to our rangers in the bush the animals' real-time locations. Should a collared animal stop moving for over twelve hours, we issue an alert. It has three possible explanations:

the collar has malfunctioned and is no longer transmitting; the collar has fallen off; or the animal is dead — poached for its ivory. In any case, we respond after twelve hours. Usually Mr. Brantingham flies directly to the site."

The rangers waited because the elephants could remain stationary for long periods, but rarely over twelve hours. Could she last that long? And a more critical question: how to destroy an indestructible box strapped to a five-ton mammal, the neck of which was well over her head?

The gun strap, heavy on her shoulder, announced itself. Grace adjusted it before she fully realized what she was doing. Touching the weapon, feeling the stock's smooth wood, its clean balance, she shuddered. How could the same gods that had led her to her best chance at rescue now lead her to think such a thing?

Had it come to this? To save herself, would she have to kill the very animal Graham Winston sought to rescue?

Grace squatted, staring at the only elephant wearing a collar, trying to reconcile her predicament, weighing one life against the other. The huge dark eye, fringed by dark, soft eyelashes, stared back as if reading her thoughts.

"What would you do?" Grace said softly. "If you would allow me to cut the collar, I would not have to do this. Do you understand? But even with this machete, it will not be easy. It is a thick collar and it is designed to withstand such attempts. It will not yield easily to the blade." The elephant blinked. "I will need time, you see? No, you do not see. You understand none of it."

To the elephant, it was but another warm day. An odd-smelling creature squatting on her haunches beside him was making noise.

Grace succumbed to the oppressive fatigue, the irony and the inevitability of what she must do. First, her shoulders shook, then the laughter rose in her throat and bubbled out as despair. The snakebite on her wrist had swollen into an ugly purple bruise; her ankle throbbed, her skin was so caked and dried she wanted to cut herself out and shed it. She had a spear, a machete and a Kalashnikov. Some soiled clothing and a backpack a kilometer behind.

A copse of trees lay ahead. Grace wondered how the elephants traveled. She knew them to be as smart as whales — trainable, and capable of long-term memory — but did they follow specific routes, like migrating birds, or did they travel randomly? They slept standing up, often in the heat of the day. Could she take advantage of that? How?

She looked up into the sky, closed her eyes and listened. Where were her rescuers? Why was no one looking for her? She spoke a Chinese curse at herself for deliberately masking her travels over the past ten days. The more she'd uncovered, the more she'd feared becoming an object of government surveillance or the target of the black marketers using the clinic. The visit to the Kibera slum and her carefully choreographed meeting with Maya Vladistok had signaled an unexpected level of caution among the locals. She should have understood then what kind of trouble this could lead to. But she'd ignored it for the sake of her own vanity and the opportunity to work an unusual case on her own.

Ambition digs its own grave; it needs little help beyond ego.

Tears formed. Grace wiped them away so that she could see more clearly. Carefully, quietly, she double-checked the Kalashnikov before pulling the weapon to her shoulder and wrapping her hand tightly in the strap to secure it. Again, the tears threatened. Again, she held them at bay. A single shot. To be fair, it had to be the best shot of her life.

63

"Where are we?" Brantingham asked the three rangers in his radio room. Knox sat up, startled awake.

The rangers had allowed Knox through the locked gate and into the compound, but wouldn't answer a single question until Brantingham arrived. Mobile phones didn't work in the bush; the signal extended to less than a kilometer out of the village center.

In terms of its grounds and buildings, the clinic was far more than Knox had anticipated. It looked more like a private school campus or military barracks, a great surround of cream-colored, one-story concrete block buildings. Sidewalks, leading through large flats of brown, burned-out grass. Several vehicle sheds with uniformed rangers milling about.

"We've stopped seventeen vehicles, all headed in our direction, all within a two-hour perimeter. No luck," the middle ranger said to Brantingham.

"No sign of her? No weapons?"

"Three of the vehicles carried weapons. Handguns. We did not confiscate."

"Show us," Brantingham said. Then, belatedly, he introduced Knox as a friend of the missing woman. He introduced the three rangers to Knox, though Knox didn't catch a single name.

The man pointed out the stops made on a digital map on one of three flat-panel displays. All but three had been on a numbered road from the north — an unlikely choice for kidnappers.

"Earlier this week, the day she visited," Brantingham said, "who drove her into Tanzania? It wasn't Thomas or any of the Ol Donyo guides. So who?"

"Leebo, sir."

Brantingham nodded. "One of our part-time mechanics," he explained to Knox. "They pick up work where they can get it. What vehicle?" He directed this to his man.

"I can check."

"Do that, and have Leebo here within the hour. And check — what, Tanner's outfit? Blake's? Find out where he dropped her off. Who guided her once she got to Tanzania. That shouldn't be hard. A day trip, right?

407

She didn't have bags."

"I assumed a sunset meal, something like that. I only heard of it after she'd left."

"Follow up."

"Yes, sir."

"Coffee?" he offered Knox. "Maybe a little first aid. How'd the other guy do?"

"You heard?"

"How do you think I'm barely an hour behind you? I ended up with half a dozen very frightened staff members at my front door. You told them not to return."

"Intruders. They were after Grace's possessions."

"Yes, I heard that as well. Seems your Grace has stirred the nest, John."

"Your Grace" was about all Knox heard. Everyone kept saying that. This time, Knox nodded. "Yeah, I think she did."

"We'll get you patched up, get some coffee in the both of us. The bright side? They didn't move her last night. We'd know about it."

"There's a lot of land out there."

"There is. And we know it better than anyone."

"Excuse me, Mr. Travis." It was Thomas, the driver and ranger from the radio shack.

Forty-five excruciatingly long minutes had

passed. Knox sat up too quickly, sloshing lukewarm coffee onto his pants. "It's Snaggle Tooth. He's gone black."

Brantingham's eyes saddened; there was no mistaking it. "You've double-checked the —"

"Yes. Satellite's up, other signals are strong."

"Battery?"

"At least six months remaining."

"Time?"

"Just now, sir."

Brantingham checked his watch. "All right. Start the clock. Let me know if there's any change."

"Of course."

"And find fucking Leebo! I want him here!"

"Yes, sir!"

"Bloody hell." He addressed Knox. "One of our oldest ellies. Massive tusks, one broken in a sparring match ten years ago. A real prize, a friend to us."

" 'Black' means . . . ?" Knox asked.

"Transmitter's down. If the ellies stop for more than half a day, we investigate. Transmission failure . . . poachers often destroy the black boxes, you see, believing it buys them time."

"That sucks," Knox said.

"You've no idea. He's our George Washington of elephants, if that's not insulting your sense of history."

"Not at all."

"You might want to join me."

"Excuse me?"

"At the twelve-hour mark — around six this evening — I'll fly to the site where we lost track of him. Try to spot him from the air. Land if necessary. Hopefully not. Hopefully it's only technical. I'd be happy to fly the roadways if there's time. Do a flyover of some of the safari camps my men haven't yet reached. If I were holding her, it would be there."

"Your rangers?"

"Sure. They've begun, at my orders, a grid search. The roadblocks, as we've discussed, including the better-used tracks. Others will be working overland into the camps. It'll take a week, at the least. We could scout a few, you and I."

"Absolutely."

"What is it?" Brantingham inquired.

"Do you ever make exceptions to the twelve-hour rule? Would you, in this case?"

"The twelve-hour rule is in place for a reason. The system isn't perfect."

"I wasn't thinking about the elephant. I should be, I know. I'm thinking about the view from the plane. Early morning. Good long shadows."

"You've done this before."

"From the tops of buildings. Up on a hill. Not airplanes. Fact is, I can't wait twelve hours. Look, I know your guys are thorough. I'm grasping at straws. Their vehicle broke down? Maybe they're moving on foot? I don't know. But I can't sit here."

Silence for a long moment. Knox caught himself holding his breath.

"There's usually at least one police officer at the strip," Brantingham said. His face gave nothing away. "How are you at belly-crawling?"

"I'd show you, but your office is a little small."

Brantingham picked up his phone, dialed a number. "Jamba! It's me. Top off the tank and prep it. I'll be there in quarter of an hour . . . *asante.*"

He turned back to Knox.

"You'll love it. It's beautiful this time of day."

64

Riding alongside Brantingham on a rutted dirt road, Knox felt his phone buzz. He recognized the caller ID as the kid, Bishoppe. Excusing himself to the driver, he took the call.

"Not now!" Knox said. They were within five minutes of the airstrip.

"I have done a bad thing. You must hear me."

"I hear you."

The vehicle beneath him was in another place, another time. Tommy's voice rang in Knox's ears. He, too, had appealed to his brother. Tommy had soiled himself at school and run away. Only the kindness of a grandfatherly gentleman had saved him. His brother, fifteen years old, had no idea where he lived. The man had read the notes sewn into several of the boy's pockets.

"What the hell, kid?" Knox growled into the phone.

"You made me angry, Mr. John. Not taking me with you."

"I can't do this now."

"I tell my cousin all about you."

Told, Knox wanted to correct. His chest was tight. "Which cousin? Told him what?"

"Hakim. The computers."

"The hacker."

"It is not a nice word."

"I'm going to hang up."

"I told him about the plane, about landing on the road. The rangers."

"The rangers?"

Brantingham glanced over at Knox. "I'm going to drop you in two. Be ready."

"I told him you were flying south to Oloitokitok. That the Chinese woman must be there. Your girlfriend who's after the ivory."

The landscape blurred. The blow to Knox's head had left him woozy and nauseated. Brantingham's offer of coffee had only exacerbated the pain. *One minute,* he thought.

"He told the police?" Knox asked.

"The police? No. Someone much worse. Someone who pays better. I've made trouble for you, Mr. John. It's bad. I'm shamed."

"How long ago? When, Bishoppe?"

413

Knox suffered through a prolonged silence.

The boy was sobbing.

"Go to your sister. Do you hear me? The bad men will come after you, too. You must go. Tell no one." Another long pause. The truck coasted. "Promise me."

Bishoppe only cried into the phone.

Knox ended the call, wondering how the boy's betrayal would affect him, if at all. If Bishoppe had associated him with the missing ivory, had named Oloitokitok, Knox could expect even more trouble. If they wanted more detail, they'd go after the boy.

Knox zipped the mobile into his pocket and opened the door as the truck slowed but did not stop. He jumped and rolled, started crawling, using the flashing light atop a rickety tower as his guide to reach the end of the grass strip.

65

"Guuleed is approaching Kiserian. Snaggle Tooth has gone off-grid."

Hearing this, Koigi felt as giddy as a child and as tormented as a priest. The grandfather of the great elephants was missing, the elephant with the most massive tusks in all of Kenya. And Guuleed was running in that direction, which meant he or his men were responsible.

The tusks would fetch millions. Koigi would deny him that with the last fiber of his worn-out body. It was nothing short of war. And for once, Koigi knew his enemy's precise location.

His best map man plotted the GPS coordinates from Guuleed's laptop. The connection was not fast, but it was reliable. INTERPOL or British Intelligence — he wasn't sure — was sending him real-time intel. Winston had come through.

Koigi followed Guuleed, now less than

forty kilometers behind. They would have to close the gap — and before the terrain worsened. He directed his man to remain on the two-lane paved road despite it taking them farther away from Guuleed. He resented the disapproving looks from his men. *Let them try to lead,* he thought.

"I know where they're headed," he told his men with commanding authority. He checked over his shoulder, ensuring his other three trucks were still following in convoy. "We have a chance to save Snaggle Tooth. Fifty years old. Three-meter tusks. One of the great bulls left. This is Guuleed we hunt. We know their tactics. We have a history with them I am not proud of. We don't defeat them by coming up from behind. We must leapfrog ahead and ambush them. It's going to be hell."

"Faster," he instructed. Project confidence; hide your own fears. "We turn south on the road from Machakos. They have no choice but to head east from Kajiado. It's the only road."

"Aha! Where the three roads meet!" the driver called out, satisfied. "Brilliant! I know the place!"

The truck gained speed. Koigi knew it would be a letdown to the driver and others when he chose not to ambush, but his hand had been forced. The Chinese woman was the variable. She deserved a chance to live. On the off chance Guuleed was in pursuit of the "wounded gazelle" and knew nothing of Snaggle Tooth, he would give him some rein in the early going.

He rubbed his painful shoulder absent-mindedly; a reminder of the stakes involved. With a sigh, Koigi closed his eyes and pretended to take a rest. He wanted his men to think he was relaxed. "Wake me as we near," he said, his limbs sparking cruelly with anticipation.

66

Knox rode in the copilot seat. He was too tall, and his headset struck the ceiling of the small cockpit.

By morning light, the bush appeared a vast, empty place. Auburn grasses gave way to shrubs, which gave way in turn to rock outcroppings. At one point, Brantingham pointed out giraffe in the distance. Knox would never have seen them.

The land beneath was all sand and scrub, a harsh place of burning sun. The stark reality struck Knox anew: survival for any length of time in such an environment was unlikely.

For the first time since his arrival, his hopes of finding Grace alive faltered.

"You are looking for shadows, as you said." Brantingham's voice crackled in the headset. "This time of day, you can often see a line of tracks. Movement is more difficult to spot at altitude." He indicated a canvas pouch screwed into the dash. "Alternate between the naked eye and the glasses. It helps keep you sharp."

"How long?"

Brantingham checked his instruments. "Ten, maybe twelve minutes."

"That's nothing!"

"We will patrol after I've had a look at Snaggle Tooth."

Even given the electronic distortion of the man's voice, Knox could hear his sorrow. They both faced grave losses, he thought. "I hope he's alive," he said. It sounded stupid hearing it in his headphones. Brantingham's attention was out his side window, as he searched for signs of Grace's kidnappers.

"There is a camp not far from where the signal was lost. Porini Camp. We will do a fly-over first, at a great distance. It will be off my side. If there is any sign . . . that will change our situation. It could be the poachers responsible for Snaggle Tooth. It could be your kidnappers. Either way, we will take great care."

"Understood."

Six minutes later, the plane slowly lost altitude. Brantingham held his binoculars up to the side window.

"We are two kilometers east of the last signal from the collar." He slowed the plane.

419

"I do not see Snaggle Tooth. That's good. I'll need to fly lower. But not before Porini Camp. It is . . . another kilometer, northwest . . . just there." He flew the plane slowly to the left. "Take the yoke. Easy pressure. No movement." Knox appreciated the chance to fly, however briefly. "Steady. Straight ahead." Brantingham craned to get a look out his side window. "No vehicle. The camp looks empty."

"But . . . ?" Knox could hear the equivocation in the man's voice.

"Two men by a campfire, half a klick due north of the camp."

"Men, no woman?"

"Men? Women? Figures." Brantingham took the yoke and banked the plane sharply. "Behind. You see the camp?"

It took Knox time to locate the buildings. It looked tiny in a sea of gray gravel and scrub. The landscape foreboding, he hoped like hell Grace wasn't one of the two bodies. "Yeah, I got it."

The plane leveled off, then banked again, straining on Knox's seatbelt. "Coming fully around. Your side. Ahead of us by —"

"I see them. Not moving. Sleeping?"

"Look for —"

"I don't think . . . I think at least one's undressed."

"What?"

"Just his shorts."

"It can be warm in the bush at night, but not hot. Not this time of year. Went to sleep drunk, I suppose. The bush leads quickly to drink."

"No packs. No weapons," Knox said.

Brantingham looked at the ceiling of the plane as if it might hold answers. He flew the plane while scanning with the binoculars. Knox watched him.

The plane banked and came around lower. "There!" Brantingham said to himself. "Five in the herd. Headed east toward Tsavo. It's the next water. It makes sense."

"Snaggle Tooth?" Knox asked.

"No. I didn't see him."

"What's it mean?"

"Failed transmitter, I'm hoping. We must pray he's not been hit. Battery, more than likely. What a relief. Hopefully, he's hidden by a tree. Strange he's not with the others, though. It's worth a closer look."

The plane sped up significantly and began to climb. The wings tipped and, according to the compass, headed north.

"Now what?"

"I'll send my rangers to have a closer look."

"I meant us. What now?"

"You didn't see them, did you?"

"See what?"

"The bushes near the camp with the two men."

"What bushes?"

"Vultures, John. A dozen or more in the bushes."

"Missed it. Them."

"They aren't asleep, John," Brantingham said, banking the plane yet again. "Make sure your belt is tight. Landings in the bush can be rough."

67

"Faster," Koigi instructed the man driving.

"We'll break an axle, boss, the way this road is."

The word "road" was itself an exaggeration, thought Koigi. The route didn't qualify as a dirt track, given the huge gaps between any signs of other vehicles having driven it. It was ruts, rocks and weeds tall enough to catch beneath the truck chassis. "So be it."

"Our dust will be seen for miles."

His man next to him, the one with the map unfolded on his lap, was reading his personal e-mail to gain Guuleed's latest coordinates. The navigator placed his stubby finger well down the road from Kajiado, then placed a second, its fingernail broken and black, onto a spot nearly equidistant from the upcoming intersection of three dirt tracks.

The confluence would put them on the same southern track. It was paramount to

Koigi that he arrive first and unseen. He swore in Swahili, then called on the radio for the two trailing trucks to slow down and pull off no closer than a kilometer out from the intersection. It would reduce their dust and provide cover in case Guuleed surprised him and turned north.

In one of the brief spurts of cell coverage, three of his six men and Koigi himself received texts concerning the lost transmission from Snaggle Tooth. If the information had reached his men, then it had reached Guuleed.

"That's what he's after," Koigi said as his men's faces lowered to their cell phone screens. "It must be his men that killed Snaggle Tooth." He felt the loss as a palpable pain in his chest, a shortness of breath, reacting physically as he had in the most recent firefight. A dead elephant was a dead relative; he knew so many by name all across the country. He kept a memorized list of those lost: Satao, Magna, Keyhole, Goliath. Each an animal he'd seen either close up or through binoculars; he felt a kindred spirit. "We capture those tusks and we burn them. We post another video."

"This is Larger Than Life territory, boss. Is the Somali so stupid?"

"He's never stupid, but always greedy."

"Faster," said another of the men.

The driver tested the accelerator and increased the truck's speed by a full third. The men were thrown about in their seats. They braced, rising and falling in unison.

"You sure, boss?" the driver asked. The vehicle was taking a beating.

"Yes. And we go off-road before the intersection. Through the bush. Leave no fresh tracks on the road." The roads could go untraveled for days or weeks. To drive through the intersection would signal the presence of a vehicle.

"Fuck the Somali!" said the same man. Another laughed and joined him. *"Fuck the Somali!"* his men began chanting.

Koigi leaned back, smiling. After a moment, he joined in the chorus.

68

Brantingham carried a long rifle slung over his shoulder and a pistol in a belt holster, with an army canteen, a sat phone and a radio clipped to the opposite side. He handed Knox sunscreen and a canteen; told him to be liberal with the first, and conservative with the other.

"Did you see them?"

"I saw one. The truck?" As they'd landed, Knox had seen a 4×4 out his window. No sign of a person.

"Two. Stay with me." The man was an extraordinarily fast walker. Knox, with his longer strides, could barely keep up.

They reached the two vehicles. Finding both abandoned and one scavenged, they hurried on, hiking for forty minutes in silence toward the Porini Camp.

Throughout their journey, Brantingham never consulted a map or a compass.

When they arrived, they found two

preyed-upon carcasses, their brutalized condition not visible from the plane. One wore nothing but plaid boxer shorts.

What remained of the two dead men around a black smudge of a campfire caused Knox to swear mightily, a long string of expletives. The bodies — both African men — were swollen from the sun, their veins bulging grotesquely. They'd been scavenged, with a good deal of flesh left on the bone. It was a sight and a smell that Knox knew would linger for a long time. *No way to die,* he thought.

"Jackals and hyenas," Brantingham said, studying the tracks around the bodies. He stuck a stick in the only pot and stirred.

"Their veins," Knox said.

"They poisoned themselves, I reckon. Happens more often than it should. Usually it's the kids. A bit surprising in men this age. They should have known better." He spoke in a professional but strangely unsympathetic way, and continued to walk the area, head down. "Odd to see nothing more than a single machete. I'd like to know where they dragged his clothes off to. A rucksack, too, I should think. Usually, it's no more than a few meters away."

He stopped and kneeled. Backed away from the fire circle, head down. His mood had intensified. Moving faster now, he circled in the opposite direction from Knox.

"What?" Knox asked, moving toward him.

"Circle around, man. KGA will need to investigate." Concern had filled his voice. "Look: do me a favor. Search the area. Find the clothes, a rifle. Something." He pointed into the bush beyond the two corpses.

"Something was dragged here," Knox said.

Brantingham stuck a stick in the sand where he'd been standing and joined Knox. The man kneeled and touched a few spots, the sand crumbling easily.

"What do you think?" Knox said.

Brantingham had tuned Knox out. The man was clearly in his element. He shuffled away from the camp in a squat, following the disturbed ground. Then he stopped and turned, still on his haunches, looking back at the camp, where a few daring vultures had returned to feed. Knox looked away.

Brantingham stood and slapped his palms together. "Stay where you are, please, John," he chided. "I don't want to disturb it."

Knox felt a bubble in his throat. "Tell me they didn't have a hostage," Knox said. "Tell me we're not going to find a third body."

"Mother of Christ," Brantingham groaned. He stopped back toward the upright stick. "See my prints?"

"Yes."

"Follow them. Walk in them if possible."

Moving fast, but precisely, Knox reached a series of circles Brantingham had drawn. Each one contained a bootprint. It took Knox a moment to spot the obvious. "Small."

"Yes."

"Too small for either of them. Small, as in a woman's boots."

"There are plenty of small men."

"These guys were wearing sandals," Knox said. "Their prints are all over the place."

"See this . . ." Brantingham used the same stick to point to an impression in the sand. "Here and back there as well. That's a woman's bare breast."

"We don't know that. You can't possibly know that!"

"She's topless and wearing boots."

"That's not true." Knox felt his gut clench. He squatted, trying to catch his breath and quiet the dizziness.

"She wasn't dragged. She crawled out of camp. Crawled backward."

"Alive," Knox gasped.

"If she ate whatever they did, probably not for long."

Knox felt his throat constrict. Brantingham circled the campfire. Knox remained squatting, unable to move.

"She killed them," Knox proposed, wondering on the effect it would have on her. He knew well the depression and torment that came from such an act, even if delivered in self-defense.

"Found them, more likely. Understood not to share the soup if she's lucky. Took their clothes. A rucksack . . . This will require a few minutes," Brantingham said. "I need your eyes."

Knox rose and followed along robotically as Brantingham walked a long, ever-expanding spiral out from the camp, following the line of small bootprints.

"She's walking fairly well," Brantingham said encouragingly. "Sore left leg, but no staggering. No stopping. No blood. It's all good, John."

The boot tracks joined elephant tracks fifteen meters later.

"You're good at this," Knox said, feeling stupid for saying so.

Brantingham took the compliment indifferently. He wasn't talking at the moment.

They walked for several more minutes, this time following the wide swath of elephant tracks. At last, Brantingham raised his binoculars, trained them in the direction of the plane. "We're what, three or four klicks from our lost collar signal? I think we should trek it. Is that good with you? You can wait by the plane, if not. The point being, I may not find as good a place to land."

"I'm good," Knox said.

"She's alone, John. No other prints. No evidence of anyone else. It would appear she got lucky. They likely denied their hostage food, and they both died for it. The only curious thing — contradictory evidence, you could say — was the melted mobile."

"I saw that, too."

"I don't understand it, I admit."

"She's on foot. They're dead. There were no ropes or ties suggesting she'd cut herself free."

"I noticed that as well. She's only a matter of hours ahead. The state of the bodies tells us as much." Brantingham slipped the radio off his belt and called into his agency's dispatch. The KGA would be put on notice. Brantingham's Larger Than Life rangers were mobilized. "They're two hours out," the man said. "I suggest we don't wait."

"That's not an option."

69

It wasn't the axle, but the wheel and rim that Koigi's vehicle lost as the driver set off to shortcut the intersection of the three dirt tracks.

The earth caved in beneath the left tire; a blowout. Koigi radioed one of his trucks forward, leaving the last of the three in a position to ambush if Guuleed ran north unexpectedly.

It took fifteen minutes to change the wheel, fifteen minutes to discover it wasn't just the bent rim, that the truck wasn't going to drive. By the time their truck arrived, delayed by the passing of Guuleed's convoy several hundred meters to the west, Koigi's plan had gone from the shit heap to the crapper. He stomped impatiently, awaiting the truck, and piled his men in quickly once it arrived.

Guuleed was ahead of him.

"So we play catch-up now! Same as always! Who cares?" He wanted his men staying positive. "Call back and bring them along."

To try to catch Guuleed from behind would risk being caught in an ambush. He needed a plan. He leaned over to his navigator. "We need a shortcut across the bush." The track matching Guuleed's coordinates eventually died in the middle of a vast nothingness.

"Yes, boss."

Complicating matters further, Koigi had a love of the mountainous north, had never warmed to the grasslands of the south. He'd established camps all over Kenya in the past fifteen years, had a love of Maasai but not the arid land they often inhabited. From his first childhood trip, a church service trip for Kibera children, the mountains had owned him — the changeable weather, the cool, and forests so thick they blotted out the sun.

"May I suggest . . . ?" his navigator inquired.

"Speak!"

"If the Somali is heading to Snaggle Tooth, and if Larger Than Life won't supply us with the coordinates, perhaps your lady friend, the policewoman, could help?"

The man's mention of Inspector Kanika Alkinyi hushed the car. She was the great unspoken. No one talked of Koigi's interests outside of the cause. The wind whipped, making them numb.

"She could find out for us, eh? That might tip the scales, boss. I map us a route along here." He traced his wide finger along a line of dashes. "There are only two ways to go. Both terminate in the bush. But look here." His finger found and followed a dry creek bed — all such creeks were seasonal, active only during the monsoon — to a vast fan of dry swamp some distance south. "This splits the two tracks right down the middle, boss. We take the creek bed, and they never see us coming. If your friend can get us the co-ordinates, then we also know where they're heading."

Koigi thought back to the message involving the wounded gazelle. He weighed this against Guuleed's brazen entrance into Larger Than Life territory, a place where the odds were stacked against him and his men.

Perhaps, he thought, *Guuleed is after Snaggle Tooth; perhaps, Grace Chu, the wounded gazelle.*

He lit up the satellite phone and dialed, his men looking on.

70

Apprehensive, Knox trailed a few feet behind Brantingham as they followed the disturbed sand and earth left in the wake of the five elephants. The trail looked as if it had been made by a tractor, dragging a heavy implement. Alongside, the occasional small bootprint appeared.

"You see this?" Brantingham said. "Small strides. Walking slowly. She's following the ellies at their pace. Smart girl. She knows they will head to water. Knows the safari guides will be looking for such sightings."

"Smart girl," Knox echoed. In contrast to Grace's steady tracks, he was having trouble walking, overcome by the discovery of the campsite.

Fifteen minutes later Brantingham picked up his pace. Knox saw why. A scrap of fabric, hanging from a bush. They reached the marker and saw what turned out to be a backpack and a pile of clothes. The items

Brantingham had theorized about.

"Well, sir," Brantingham said. "I'd never have expected this. She stripped the man down to his shorts. You see?"

"Not really."

"The shirt. A pair of trousers beneath the pack. I'll wager another set of clothing's inside. Shall we take a look?"

"Sure." Knox forced the word out. He could barely speak, was struggling to understand what any of it meant. Grace wouldn't abandon warmth, or the storage offered by the pack. His gut wrenched as reality sank in. "What's it mean? Why leave it?"

"That is the question." Brantingham had taken photographs at the campfire. Now he studied the back of his camera. Took several shots of the clothing and backpack before approaching the bag.

Knox stayed with him as Brantingham carefully emptied the backpack, revealing a second set of filthy clothes and little else. "Well, there you have it."

"Have what, exactly?" Knox asked.

"Smart, as we've said. Bush smart. She understood the ellies could smell her. Brilliant! They'd kept her at a distance, you see. A distance she wanted to close."

They walked another thirty minutes. Knox felt the desolation of the landscape, the exposure and isolation. The plane was miles behind them now. Brantingham was in his element. Knox barely existed to him.

"Christ to hell!" Brantingham cursed. The words cut sharply into Knox's thoughts. Beside him, Brantingham went down on one knee. He took a photograph, then used the arm of his sunglasses to hook and capture a brass shell from the sand. "Five-four-five by thirty-nine millimeter. Kalashnikov seventy-four. Single shot . . ." He dropped the shell into a leg pocket of his cargo pants and began taking additional photographs. "Kneeling shot. Close range. For fuck's sake, she shot him!"

"Your men told her about the collar," Knox suggested. "She saw a way out. She took it."

"They scattered here. See?" Knox nodded. The elephant tracks fanned out in several directions. "I expect we'll pick up blood within a few meters. Damn it all to hell. We separate. I'll take these three. You follow each of those. The blood may look like water, like a piss spot. You'll have to handle it." He rubbed his fingers together. "The sun dries it quickly."

"Understood." Knox started with the one farthest to his left. "How far?"

"Start with fifty meters. Hard to imagine

she missed, but if she did, we'll need to stay with this."

Brantingham walked off, head down.

Knox walked the first track for fifty yards. He was well into following the second when Brantingham called out. Knox joined him.

"You see?"

"No."

"Just there." Brantingham pointed.

Even being guided, it took Knox a moment to spot the boot heel mark.

"This is the ellie she's following. The one she shot."

"Blood?"

"Not yet."

"Shouldn't we see blood?" Knox asked.

"Depends on the shot. They're big animals. Blood can dry on skin before hitting the ground."

"Let me ask you this," Knox said. "Why a single shot? If she's desperate enough to shoot it, why not take advantage of an automatic?"

"Ellies can run over twenty kilometers per hour, John. There may not have been time for a second shot. Maybe another ellie blocked her. The gun could have jammed. Kalashnikovs can be temperamental. We won't know until we find him."

Her, Knox thought.

On they walked, following both the elephant's long strides and the boot impressions that followed.

"They can't sustain a run for more than half a kilometer," Brantingham volunteered.

Either the sun or the discouragement or both took the talk out of them. Knox applied more sunscreen, pulled up his shirt collar. A line of ants, interrupted by the elephant tracks, drew a broken calligraphy in the sand.

It was another twenty minutes before Brantingham spoke, and then it was in a whisper so faint Knox wasn't sure if he was imagining it. Extremely slowly, Brantingham lay down prone. Knox followed, again not seeing whatever it was Brantingham saw. The man hauled the binoculars to his eyes, propped himself up on his elbows.

"Alive," he said. "Standing. Four hundred meters. Collar's on."

"Snag—"

"Yes!"

"Four hundred meters is within the range of a Kalashnikov."

"I beg your pardon?"

"She's been captive for days," Knox said. "Possibly out here in the bush. A lot can go wrong with a person's mind. We go in quietly, and we go in carefully. For her sake, and ours."

The landscape was crusty with rock. Grasses and bushes were bunched tightly before them. Brantingham spoke in a whisper.

"Whether he's been hit or not, he won't let us get within a hundred meters. You can call out for her, but I'd appreciate a closer look at him first."

"To see if he's wounded."

"Yes." Brantingham belly-crawled to Knox, handed him a Glock 17 with a spare magazine. "We've come a long way, John. Give me the extra ten minutes I need."

"I don't need this," Knox said.

"It's for Snaggle Tooth. Fire into the air if he charges. He likes to charge, that one. Stand your ground. *Do . . . not . . . run.* His legs aren't nimble, but his head and trunk will surprise you. You can jump . . . dive out of the way. But only at the last second. You understand?"

Knox nodded.

"Head a hundred meters straightaway in that direction," Brantingham said, pointing into the thicker bush, "then ahead another hundred until you're even with him. If she's here, she's hunkered down."

"She could easily shoot at us, mistaking us for the enemy," Knox warned. "We do not return fire."

"Keep an eye out. You inspect him from this side. I'll look from the other. Raise one arm if no sign of a wound. Two, if he's been hit."

Nodding, Knox crawled into the shrub, rising up on all fours where the vegetation stood higher. It was slow and difficult going. He quickly lost track of Brantingham and the elephant he had yet to see.

71

Knox crossed the bootprints, his nerves jangling, his senses heightened. He scanned the area for Brantingham, having immediately lost his own interest in anything to do with the elephant. Nothing. The guy was a ghost.

Mindful of Grace's fragile state of mind, and of the Kalashnikov, he stayed low on hands and knees, though everything in him was desperate to stand and call her name. The ground became rock hard. He lost the bootprints.

He heard the elephant before he saw it. The animal was using its trunk to slap dust and dirt over itself in a noisy display thirty yards to Knox's right. He still couldn't see Brantingham, but Knox pressed ahead anyway, dropping into a belly-crawl. He raised the binoculars and scanned carefully, frame by frame. No visible wounds.

He raised his right arm.

When he saw Brantingham, it was because the man wanted him to — three feet up an acacia tree less than twenty feet from the elephant. Brantingham carefully and slowly hoisted a single arm. No wounds on the elephant. Knox had been granted permission to call out.

Knox lowered his arm and took one last look at the beast to make sure he hadn't signaled prematurely.

That's when he saw it.

A perfectly round black hole faced him from a bush. At first it looked like a berry that didn't belong. But it was too perfect a circle. Machined. The muzzle of the Kalashnikov.

He refocused, trying to separate the shrub from the rifle.

"Grace," he whispered, so dryly the word fell only feet in front of him. He cleared his throat and tried again. To the naked eye, the gun barrel appeared to be suspended, propped inside the shrub maybe. Knox looked around, fearing it was being used as a diversion.

Nothing.

"Grace. It's me."

He kept his hands out in front of him. He would not provoke a shot. When he finally saw the unflinching eye, he gasped aloud.

Right there, the whole time, at the end of the rifle looking back at him.

He imagined he could make out a hairline. One ear, perhaps. No chin or shoulders. No body. Just the eye, floating inside the shadowy interior of a thorn shrub alongside the Kalashnikov.

Slowly, the form of an arm and elbow emerged, materialized from within the puzzle of branches and leaves. A shoulder. A piece of a woman's chest. She was sitting, the Kalashnikov resting on a knee.

Again, he called her name. Again with difficulty. "Gr . . . ay" it sounded like.

The muzzle twitched. For a second he thought she'd pulled the trigger. Then she pushed forward, rose out of the thorny shrub without any apparent sensation of it scratching her.

She was kneeling, naked in hiking boots, her skin smeared brown with mud. Her limbs were scratched and bug-bitten. Her wrist was swollen horribly. The one eye he could see looked distrustful and savage. Wild. She held a metal spear under an armpit and across the gun stock, while still managing to hold the rifle.

"It's me: John," he coughed out. "It's me. I'm here. I'm going to stand now. Slowly. I'm here to help you. There is another man with me. You met him. Travis Brantingham. He is a friend, Grace. We are both your friends. You're safe now."

He'd seen shock in hostage victims, been taught how to deal with it. But all the training went away. This was Grace; this was different.

Knox had also been traumatized on the battlefield, had seen others much worse off than he. Doctors spoke of adjustment periods, of giving the brain time to forget. *But some things are never forgotten,* Knox thought.

The weapon remained aimed at his chest.

He screwed up his courage to speak the first words that came to him.

" *'I find in my heart both something missing . . .'* " he coughed, " *'and something fulfilling. Missing, when too much time separates us. Fulfilling when we are together. It is a small thing, perhaps. I cannot say. But its very existence interests me.'* Your words, Grace. Your words to me."

The gun dropped dangerously, pointing toward the ground. As she reached to cover her eyes, her shoulders shook.

"No . . ." She backed away, crab-walking on all fours, her eyes bloodshot and jaundiced in a sunbaked face smeared with mud. She cried out for a second time. But this time the cry was his name. *"Jooohhhnnn!"*

"Good God!" Brantingham said, surprising them both.

Grace hoisted the spear over her shoulder.

"No, Grace! No! He's a friend. You know him."

"Travis Brantingham," the man introduced himself. "You're one hell of a shot, Ms. Chu." To Knox: "Single shot through the transmitter. If it isn't perfect, she either kills him or scares him off. Brilliant!"

Gently, Brantingham set down his rifle. "Brilliant," he repeated. "I'm telling you, John, you or I could try that shot a dozen times and only get it right once." Now he addressed Grace. "How difficult it must have been, how hard to make that choice, take that risk."

Grace lowered the spear.

Knox spoke. "Grace! *'I miss you when we are apart . . . This is the John Knox I want to know better.'* "

Her shoulders shook. He moved toward her, slipping off his jacket as he approached. He held it out to her. Trembling all over, she set down the spear and slipped into the oversized windbreaker.

"Thank you." She leaned into Knox's arms. He held her. Their fingers webbed together. "I knew you would come."

446

Knox felt his throat close off.

She repeated it several times.

Brantingham retrieved the spear and the rifle, pulled her improvised sack from within the bush. Neither man spoke. Though Grace staggered, she was surprisingly steady on her feet. Knox moved her out of the shrubs as Brantingham offered her water from his canteen. "Slowly at first."

She drank. He offered her a fresh orange from his pocket and she bit into it, skin and all. The juice dribbled down her chin, running over badly chapped lips swollen twice their normal size.

"I have a first aid kit in the plane. I should have thought of it."

Knox removed his shirt and, bare-chested, tied it onto Grace's body as a skirt. "There," he said. "Better."

"I can carry her," he added to Brantingham.

"It's too far, and would take too long, even with the two of us sharing the burden."

"Your men."

"Yes. I can call in our location. They're already on their way. Wait here. I'll return to the plane. I should be able to land out there," he said, pointing to the desert. "Better . . . much better for her if we can fly her out. It would be hours overland." He added,

"Or I can wait, if you'd rather."

"How long?" Knox asked.

A series of calls were made. Brantingham came off the last one and shook his head gravely at Knox. "We are advised to hurry," he said. Knox translated the undertone. "My men are at least ninety minutes out. We can beat that easily. I will pick you up in the plane. I'm thinking we're two to three kilometers away. Give me forty minutes at the outside. Move her to that stand of trees there. That will be my landmark." He searched Grace's sack. Came away with three magazines of ammunition. He left Knox with his lever-action Marlin 1895 with an extended barrel and scope. "Holds six," he said, handing Knox a box of shells. "It's fast, and accurate to two hundred meters. You might want to practice loading. It can take a few tries to get it right."

Grace groaned, half asleep in Knox's arms. The men shared an ominous moment of eye contact.

"Three trucks," Brantingham said. "No safari markings. Poachers, more than likely. If not, something even worse."

"Keep low. Run fast," Knox said.

72

The surprise presence of the plane threw Guuleed. He watched openmouthed as it lifted, taking off smoothly over the plains.

He and his men had traveled a full day to reach this barren shit heap of marsh and gravel. Now Brantingham and his fucking plane had beaten him to it. Two of his men got off shots, but they were only throwing bullets into the sky. Guuleed motioned them to bring their rifles down.

Brantingham was a crafty motherfucker. A white man, no less. And so the question remained: had Brantingham taken off because he was done here, or had he seen Guuleed coming and flown off in an attempt to lead him away from Snaggle Tooth?

The location of the last signal from the elephant collar was now just three kilometers south, five if they rode the dirt track to better ground. "Off-road!" he ordered, pointing due south. The truck slowed and lumbered into a dry channel bed.

"It will be slower."

"Shut the fuck up!" Guuleed snapped.

His mind was spinning. Brantingham would have landed as close to Snaggle Tooth as possible. If he'd flown away in an attempt to lead Guuleed away from the elephant, the ruse would fail. Snaggle Tooth's single tusk, an aesthetic prize, was worth in weight alone a million U.S. dollars; twice or three times that given its uniqueness. His broken tusk? A half million. Together, they represented a vast fortune.

If Brantingham's actions had to do with Rambu's report of the American at the Ol Donyo Lodge, then his presence here might involve the missing girl as well — and, indirectly, the missing stash of government ivory. He'd assigned the humiliated Rambu the task of locating Guuleed's two other men, who'd gone missing since entering the bush in search of the girl.

If those two had harvested Snaggle Tooth's tusks and run — another of the reasons for Guuleed's rush to reach this godless place — he would take their tongues for dinner.

73

Knox heard the single report from a rifle echo across the desert like a distant crack of thunder. The dozing elephant spooked, running hard for several yards before pausing and looking around, his ears flapping.

The gunshot caused Grace to twitch awake in a spasm of panic. Knox consoled her, held her close, his left arm around her. After a moment, he felt her relax. It might have been Brantingham trying to signal, though he doubted it.

More likely, it was the poachers.

The next sound began as an insect hum, but quickly revealed itself to be the buzz of a single-engine plane as it arced a turn, its wings steeply pitched, so far to the west that to Knox it looked more like a seagull. Brantingham was flying surprisingly low — *A hell of a time to show off,* Knox thought — no more than seventy-five feet above the gray wash of sand and swamp that comprised a wide, dry delta. The plane pointed in Knox's direction, the wings leveling out.

Fucking maniac, Knox thought; wrong time for acrobatics.

The man's bush pilot skills were evident and on display as the Cessna turned again, this time away from Knox's position, out over the desert terrain at the same dangerously low altitude. Each time a wing dipped, the plane sank lower, slipping away from the force designed to keep it aloft.

Knox thought he heard a backfire, or a sputtering engine. The danger in flying so low was that one brief moment of engine trouble could cause a crash — it denied the pilot any glide time. But it wasn't the engine. It was more gunfire. A lot more gunfire, much of it from automatic weapons.

A firefight. A skirmish . . . or a battle, and a mile or two away at most.

In the near distance, the Cessna flew erratically, slowed and bounced across the desert floor in a rough landing.

"Come on," Knox said, cradling Grace in his arms and standing. He grabbed the sack she'd been carrying, along with the spear and guns, and trudged off toward the copse of trees.

Brantingham had made the rendezvous. The plane, still a long way away, taxied toward the trees. It was going too fast — way too fast.

An instant later, Knox thought he understood the poor flying: he spotted an army-green truck, coming at them from the direction in which they'd found the two dead bodies. Brantingham had flown low because he'd been trying to use the hills to screen the plane.

Cursing under his breath, Knox set Grace in the shade, the plane still approaching, and took the rifle with him as he ran toward Snaggle Tooth. The elephant fled. Knox raised the gun and fired into the air twice, to drive home his point. The elephant charged deeper into the brush, running now. Running out of sight.

He turned to see Brantingham behind him, awkwardly lifting Grace. Knox hadn't realized how far he'd run — two hundred meters or more. He had no way to judge the identity of the approaching truck as friend or foe, but Brantingham's apparent lack of composure told Knox to run. He grabbed the spear and the sack on the way to the idling plane, reaching Brantingham as the man was kicking a rock out from in front of the forward tire.

"You're shot." The man's blood stained his left side from his lower ribs to his belt.

"Yes. Right through the door. Bad luck, that."

Knox looked away, saw the safari truck barreling toward them.

"In!" Brantingham ordered.

Knox ran around the tail of the plane and climbed into the passenger seat. Grace sat awkwardly on the back bench, her eyes open the smallest slit. "I can help," she said. "John? A rifle!"

The truck sped closer. Knox heard a gunshot.

"Shit."

Knox struggled to work the Kalashnikov into his arms, a difficult task in the tiny space. The plane bounced and rocked as it gained speed. Knox propped the door open with his knee and aimed.

"The engine block," Brantingham advised.

Knox raised the rifle. The plane's jostling made sighting through the scope impossible. A man rose out of the SUV's side window, exposed to his waist, an assault rifle snugged against his shoulder.

Knox fired, the repeating rounds deafening, the cordite swirling bitterly.

"Wait!" Brantingham called loudly over the roar of the wind through the door. "Wait for takeoff!"

Seconds later, the plane lifted and steadied. Knox squeezed off three additional sprays of rounds. Then the rattle of the gun stopped, the magazine empty.

From the backseat, Grace, wild-eyed and frantic, passed him the rifle. "One in the chamber," she said.

Knox took the gun, aimed and fired six consecutive shots at the SUV. It swerved. He didn't have time to see what kind of damage he'd done.

"Okay," Brantingham said, his voice guttural but alarmingly steady and calm. "It's all yours." The plane dipped.

"What the hell?" Knox grabbed the yoke. The plane settled back to the ground at a high speed. "You fly!"

"Injured!" Brantingham said, trying to coach him. "Flaps! Speed!"

Knox got his foot onto the right rudder pedal and braked, trying to avoid a group of rocks. The nose wheel hit hard, the plane lurched to the left and dragged a wing.

"Yoke back!"

Airspeed was lost. The front wheel was bent or its tire flat. The plane skidded forward. Knox cursed, pulled back the throttle but kept the plane moving. Shoving down the rudder pedals, he turned the nose slightly right and aimed the plane for the distant trees.

Brantingham was unconscious, his side bloodied.

74

As Koigi's crowded truck hurried along the twisting dry creek bed, one of his men shouted out above the roar of the motor that he thought he'd heard a gunshot.

On Koigi's order, the truck slowed. He saw a single-engine plane lift into the sky to the south. *Travis Brantingham,* he thought. *Snaggle Tooth.* All listened intently, hearing no weapons fire.

Koigi's phone buzzed. Kanika Alkinyi had come through for him with coordinates for Snaggle Tooth's lost collar signal. He and his navigator conferred.

"It's close, boss. Four klicks."

Ground zero, Koigi thought. Guuleed. Snaggle Tooth. The wounded gazelle. His men. Blood would be spilled here today.

They'd come to a stop at the mouth of a labyrinth of islands, a wide dry wash through which the seasonal flood had cut many deep, narrow channels. The banks were steep.

"Boss!" One of his men pointed behind them to ground level, toward an SUV, listing on its side. The vehicle's paint and condition implied it had only been there a short time. The Kenyan sun was unforgiving. Koigi questioned his map man. "Time?"

"It's tight, boss. They're close. Ten, fifteen minutes. The road is six klicks."

Guuleed would have also seen Brantingham's plane. Would the sight of it and the suggestion of Larger Than Life rangers scare the poachers off? Or make them more greedy?

"Plot a route from their last-known position to the spot where that plane took off. You've got two minutes," Koigi said tersely. He ordered three of his men from the truck, decisive and sure. "Cover us," he told those remaining.

Koigi took his sniper with him. The two hurried up the bank to the capsized vehicle. They spotted a second SUV not twenty meters away.

"What the fuck?" his lieutenant said, weapon at the ready.

They split up, Koigi taking the crash. A decomposing body would be signaled by colonies of bluebottle flies. Koigi saw nothing of the sort on the windows as he cautiously approached. He tried the door, pulling it open, anticipating the unforgettable odor of death. He smelled only hot air.

Someone had surgically attacked the interior upholstery and ceiling fabric, removed the mirrors, even the lightbulbs. He thought of all the sights he'd seen in the bush — the bestial savagery of species on species, the tearing of raw flesh from bone nearly a daily sight. Never anything like this. It wasn't Kenyan. A woman's touch, the cuts careful and precise.

"Anything?" he called across to his man.

"No, boss. Empty."

"Engine?"

"Cold. And there's a skim of dust, boss. She's been here awhile."

Koigi found the mention of "she" unsettling. "The interior? Is it cut apart?" He focused, trying to account for the presence of the second vehicle and its driver. His internal clock warned him: they had to get moving.

But if the crash had been an accident, where were the remains? If it was staged, why a second car? By her actions, the Chinese woman had ensured that whoever found the salvaged vehicle would know she'd survived. A massive risk to take if she thought they might return to confirm her death.

"No, boss. The inside's all good."

Together, they slid down the embankment and hurried back to the trucks.

"Mark this spot," Koigi told his map man. "Weapons ready!" he ordered. "We shoot to kill . . ." he said, starting the chant.

"There's blood to spill!" called his men.

"We shoot to kill."

"There's blood to spill!"

"No matter the cost," Koigi said, "no one gets those tusks."

75

Koigi's men double-checked their weapons. They were running south now, following a parallel dry bed separated from Guuleed's GPS identifier by a long low hill covered in fever trees, acacia and bush grass.

"We are close to even with them," his man said, "but their route is more direct. Our best option to cross is here." He pointed to a thin dashed line nearing the end of the hill. One of many such off-road trails that spiderwebbed the area.

Koigi didn't like the thought of falling behind them for a second time. "They will head directly to the elephant." There was no longer any doubt as to Guuleed's intentions. It had nothing to do with the Chinese woman, he realized. He'd wasted precious time at the crash site.

Koigi understood that his one enormous advantage was the element of surprise. Falling behind Guuleed was not an option.

"That wash has got to be slower than these tracks."

"Agreed," his navigator said.

"So drive faster," he advised the man behind the wheel.

"This road is shit. And we're heavy."

"Okay, slow down!" Koigi called to the driver. He pointed at two of his men. "You! Out! Wait for the others."

The chosen men looked bewildered. The second truck was following by a distance of twenty meters.

"Out!" Koigi hollered. They'd slowed considerably. The three men jumped. Now only Koigi, his navigator, his sniper, Blackie, and the driver remained.

"Is that better?" Koigi asked his driver.

He slapped his navigator on the shoulder hard. "Good work. Check your weapon again. His, too. This is going to get cheeky."

76

"Easy!" Guuleed hollered as the truck he was riding hit a rock. The creek bed had widened, the span of it littered with stones. "Go easy, man!"

The truck slowed. Fever trees clogged each bend, giving the driver tough choices.

"The plane is landing," a man called out from the backseat.

Guuleed radioed his men in the trailing trucks to remain in the dry creek bed. They were to quickly search the area where the plane had taken off and rendezvous with him at the landed plane, some three or four kilometers away.

Guuleed could hardly believe his luck. Brantingham — it had to be Brantingham! And Snaggle Tooth, the prize of all prizes!

Though his rival had flown less than five minutes, he appeared to be landing again. Engine trouble? He shook his head. To be safe, his truck would pursue the plane, while the others made sure the takeoff was not intended as a ruse to draw Guuleed and his men away from the elephant.

"Take us out of this godforsaken creek bed, now!" he told his driver, pointing up into the scrub.

77

Seeing the back of John's head from the seat in front of her, recognizing Brantingham passed out in the pilot's seat, lent a dreamlike quality to what Grace was feeling and experiencing. On some level, she understood she'd been rescued; on another, her blood pulsed like she'd drunk Tunisian coffee.

Her muscles tweaked and flexed of their own accord. The space was too small and claustrophobic. She longed for the open air of the bush. The plane's instruments and equipment struck her as man-made and unnatural, something she'd not felt before.

They, and this plane, didn't belong. Her thoughts battled with an instinct to flee the plane and run. How, she wondered, could she think such a thing? Where did such thoughts come from?

"I am frightened," she said, making sure John heard her.

"You're the strongest one in this plane, Grace. Believe it. We're all right. We're heading for those trees." He reached back and took her hand in his. "You amaze me."

The plane shook so badly over the rough ground that Grace feared it would come apart.

"It is not the plane," she said. "Never mind."

"What?" He glanced back. That was all she needed — his eyes. Concerned, caring eyes. "We're going to be okay."

"I want to help," she said. "I can help."

He squeezed her hand. "There's a surprise," he said sarcastically.

"I cannot laugh, John. I have forgotten how to laugh."

"I don't believe that. We can find it again."

We, was all she heard. "Okay."

"That's my girl." Knox laughed to himself loudly. "I didn't mean that the way it sounded."

"What? How did it sound?"

"Sexist."

"Bullshit." Grace seldom cursed. Knox fought back a smile. She placed her hand gently on his shoulder. "John. It sounded good to me."

78

Koigi ordered his driver and navigator to search the immediate area of the plane's tire tracks and then to take up a defensive position, guarding the truck. He and Blackie hiked quickly up a hill overlooking a natural choke point in the creek bed. A pair of fever trees crowded the route, narrowing it to no wider than two truck widths.

He radioed the second truck. His men took up position on the opposite slope. They owned the choke point. Guuleed and his men would be trapped, the only way out behind them, and Blackie's lethal skills could prevent that option.

Stalking their way up the hill, Koigi and Blackie ducked lower as tendrils of rising dust swirled, threatening to reveal their position. To be safer, they dropped, lay prone, Koigi adopting the role of Blackie's spotter.

Quietly, Koigi again radioed his men,

alerting them to Guuleed's approach. *"Kila la kheri!"* "Good luck" in Swahili.

The slow speed of the two trucks was to Koigi's advantage. If he hadn't wanted his opponent forced into the ambush, he would have had Blackie start picking off men. As it was, he and Blackie would serve as cover. He placed the binoculars down and readied his own rifle in case it was needed. His sore shoulder wasn't helping. Still, his heart pounded in his chest. Adrenaline. Always the same. He looked over at Blackie, whose eye was pressed to the scope as two trucks rolled into view.

"I've got them."

79

Koigi, weapon at the ready, watched through the binoculars as the driver's head exploded. Blackie had taken him out from two hundred meters. Through the spray of blood and quaking bodies, Koigi searched for Guuleed.

His rangers made quick work of the ambush. Guuleed's men returned a lame attempt but, sandwiched as they were, and unable to maneuver the trucks, they took multiple rounds each.

Two fell from the trucks. The rest died sitting down. Ten, maybe twelve men. Forty seconds at the most. Four men with raised hands.

Koigi felt no remorse, only a huge sigh of relief. These men, who had killed numerous elephants, rhinos and his own rangers, who had eluded him on three separate occasions and put a bullet in his shoulder — Kenya was rid of them now. Their departure offered a better chance of survival for his beloved animals.

The only missing piece of the celebration was to identify Guuleed's body among them.

"Boss!" Blackie had his rifle's sight trained away from the ambush.

Koigi swung the binoculars south. A third truck had emerged from behind the opposing hill. It was speeding across the flat in the direction of the plane that had landed.

"Bastard," Koigi muttered. "Too far for a shot?" *A moving shot,* he thought.

Blackie with a rifle was akin to a painter with a brush. Koigi watched the truck's three passengers through the binoculars. He could feel Blackie find the vehicle and lead it. His rifle barked. One of the three small figures in the distant truck slumped, a fine pink mist rising like a halo above him. An impossible shot.

He and Blackie scrambled down the hill, running toward their truck.

80

Guuleed heard the sudden burst of gunfire. KGA? Larger Than Life? His men had driven into a shitstorm. He wanted to think it was his men doing the shooting, but when a lighter volley followed a few long seconds later, he knew as any leader knows that the second burst belonged to his team — and by the light volley, he knew they'd already suffered serious casualties.

It erupted then like a fireworks finale, the exchange of gunfire so furious it sounded like rocks rolling down a hill. To try to give backup now would be suicide. His driver and navigator looked at him expectantly, anticipating that order.

"The plane," Guuleed said. "Now. As fast as this shit heap will go!"

The look on the other two faces, as they reacted to his decision not to support his other men, shook him to the core. But he kept his own face still. The sacrifice of the others would not be in vain.

At that same moment, the man between him and his driver lost his head to a bullet. It was like a melon exploding, blood everywhere. Guuleed ducked down low.

"Faster!"

81

Knox maneuvered the damaged plane to the far side of a stand of fever trees, wanting cover. The safari truck was closing in on them, fast.

From their left appeared a thin line of rising dust. "Those are my men," Brantingham said, his head swiveling with difficulty. Knox blinked; he hadn't realized the man was conscious. "Five kilometers. Too far. Too late for us."

Ignoring him, Knox scrambled from the plane, rifle in hand. The Larger Than Life rangers needed at least five minutes to close the distance. The safari truck threw shots at him, peeling chunks of bark and wood from the fever trees. Knox dropped to one knee, steadied the long rifle against a tree trunk and squeezed off three more rounds. He reloaded quickly, stealing glances at the opposition bearing down on him.

The truck's engine died and the vehicle

glided into an area of sparse trees, the driver cutting sharply to put the truck perpendicular to Knox's position.

The two men — that's all he saw — hunkered down inside the vehicle. They aimed and fired in his direction. Knox checked to his left: the plume of dust had barely grown higher, putting the rangers still well to the southeast.

Knox did not return fire, but waited. Soon, the firing stopped. In the distance, a second truck approached at high speed.

Thirty yards of scrub and rock separated the two copses. The man in the front seat lifted his head to have a look. The truck rocked forward on its springs; Knox sighted the head of the man he was about to shoot — and then he gasped audibly.

There, in his line of sight, came the massive gray elephant, its black ears flapped out wide, its massive head leading its lumbering charge. Once again the mass of the thing stunned him. The deep crags in the skin, the scars and stains and age. The wild eyes. As bewildering as anything he'd seen.

He had to hold the attention of the two in the truck. If they looked back, they would see the elephant and drop the beast immediately.

Knox had heard stories of elephants' keen

memory; how some could return to a pile of bones three years after a poaching and shed tears over the remains; how they learned smells to avoid and could recognize the human form in silhouette.

Snaggle Tooth had not shied at the weapon fire as he should have. He had waited nearby and now, with a prolonged cease-fire, had taken it upon himself to avenge, threaten or protect. Perhaps it was a misguided suicide mission. A kamikaze elephant. Perhaps he had smelled Brantingham and knew him as a friend. Knox saw only a bold, heroic charge, the elephant's one glorious curving tusk nearly scraping the ground.

Knox darted between trees to hold the attention of the two in the truck. No shots.

The elephant reached the truck. The men startled and turned; the passenger struggled to raise his rifle. But before he could aim, the elephant slipped his tusk beneath the vehicle, lifted and heaved. A gun fired. The vehicle rolled up onto its side, as if made of cardboard. Both occupants were thrown out, sprawled onto the earth ahead of the truck, which tumbled upside down and on top of them.

A voice cried out. The elephant heaved again, lifting and rolling the truck angrily, ears out, eyes enormously wide. Knox saw one of the men reappear, flattened to the ground, nearly cut in two by a roll bar that had crushed his body beneath his ribs. To Knox's astonishment, the second man, noticeably wounded, slipped between the elephant's rear legs and scrambled away. Knox sighted down the barrel. Slipped his finger to the trigger. Squeezed.

The man lost a piece of his leg in a rose-colored spray. Knox pulled away from the rifle scope, his finger still on the trigger. He hadn't fired the weapon.

The elephant roared and fled the gunfire. His moving aside revealed the second vehicle. There, alongside of it, was the unmistakable profile of Koigi.

For Knox, it was as if this second vehicle and Koigi had closed the distance magically, moving in seconds.

Koigi, not Knox, had shot apart the man's leg. He called out to the wounded man in Swahili. The man struggled to his feet and stood defiantly twenty yards away.

82

Koigi advised Guuleed to stand down, that to reach for his sidearm would get him killed. Guuleed was bleeding from his head and his legs.

And now that Koigi had the opportunity to study him, he realized that this man, this murderer he'd sought for nearly two years, wouldn't be reaching for his gun. Formerly infamous for the missing finger he'd lost in pirating a tanker at sea, Guuleed now had only a fleshy stump where his right hand should have been. The rolling vehicle had crushed it.

"Have you ever seen such a thing as that?" Koigi asked.

"Never so close," replied Guuleed. "Cheeky bastard, that one."

"He saw you coming."

"Yes. You may be right there."

"It pains my heart that we have a witness in the trees," Koigi said. "Without him, I would kill you here, cousin, without a second thought."

"And I would thank you for it." Guuleed fell to his knees, unable to stand any longer. He cried out as his wounded leg hit the earth. "My blood is in the soil, as it should be," he said, his head hung down. "I wonder, cousin, if I can manage to turn my back, would you allow me to reach across for my weapon?"

"No, cousin, I would not," Koigi said, moving closer now. Suicide was too good for this bastard. "I'll take the other leg and your balls first. Your decision."

A knife hung on the man's belt as well, but again, his hand was of no use to him. Koigi adopted the slow walk of a pallbearer. He'd imagined this moment a hundred times. Never like this. He'd wanted the challenge.

Justice did not exist in Kenya. He said as much to Guuleed.

"There is justice here, cousin. In the soil. The sunlight." Guuleed squinted, looking up. "You'll never win, you know? They will be hunted until they're gone. The rhino, also. Easy money, that's all they are."

He was intentionally provoking Koigi and both men knew it.

From ten feet away, Koigi put a bullet into

the man's groin and two more into his abdomen. Guuleed collapsed to the side. Koigi rid him of his weapons and, with the man bleeding out, looked down into his eyes long and hard, his cold gaze expressing his sudden indifference. Then he walked toward the woods and the plane that was cocked down onto one wing.

He left Guuleed alive — but just barely. The lions and jackals were certain to follow in the hours to come.

Even that fate was too good for him.

83

Knox never left her side. He sat her on a chair in the shower at Larger Than Life's headquarters and sponged her clean, never a moment of embarrassment between them. They'd been through Amsterdam together. So many secrets lay behind them now.

Grace showered for forty-five minutes. Washed her hair three times. He tended to her cuts and bites, abrasions and rashes. She kept down the fresh fruit. Didn't want anything more than that, just water and sports drinks.

Brantingham's gunshot wound required a flight to Nairobi. Knox and Grace joined him, leaving behind the only four of Guuleed's men to have survived. They would be turned over to the Kenyan Game Agency.

En route, the medics administered a variety of shots and put Grace on an IV drip. She slept. In Nairobi's Karen Hospital, she went through two days of tests and examinations and was treated for dehydration, malnutrition, a sprained ankle, an infected snakebite, numerous contusions and lacerations. Knox heard a Swahili word repeated by the nurses and was finally able to get a translation: "miracle."

In private moments while she lay sleeping, breathing softly, he would take her hand. It was during one such tender moment that he realized he'd allowed her in.

No one, he thought, would understand the significance of this inclusion. But for a man who'd blocked out the world — save only his brother — behind multiple layers of sarcasm and bravado, pseudo-independence and aloofness, it was a watershed moment for Knox. He felt connected to Grace, and more important, he wanted and welcomed that connection.

He had not a single strand of temptation to sever the emotional ties that had formed. Indeed, he thought, he would work tirelessly to maintain and strengthen them if given the chance.

Several times over the next two days, she came awake to see him leaning over the side of the bed. "Hello, there," she said on the first of these occasions.

"They're calling you a miracle. No surprise there."

No smile.

She nodded and slipped back into sleep. And so it went, each conversation a little longer, a little more in depth. She wanted to know the fate of the elephant with the broken tusk, was horribly worried she'd wounded him. She had, in fact, inflicted a surface wound that neither Brantingham nor Knox had seen. The LTL rangers were monitoring Snaggle Tooth and planned to tranquilize him, dress the wound and re-attach a working transmitter.

Grace started talking business practically before eating her first meal, but for once Knox wouldn't play along. He pushed away such talk for a future time.

That time arrived on the third day of her hospital stay, by which point Knox looked to be the one in need of medical care.

Through various discussions separated by naps, first for her, then for him, Knox caught her up on what he thought he knew of her investigation. Speaking was not easy for Grace. Her voice was raspy and hoarse; when she did talk, it was more of a whisper.

"I got your thumb drives," he told her. "Clever of you."

"David?"

"Sarge and I missed a rendezvous. He's here now in Nairobi, working with the police and the U.S. and Chinese embassies. I have a few charges to get around. Winston has stepped up. It's all good. Kamat says hello. You've given tech services a field day.

"No, it's the Nairobi City Water and Sewerage Company paperwork that's stumped me and the geeks," he said. "The second thumb drive. The one you left in Solio."

"I was counting on you," she said. "Do not tell me you let me down." She smiled, but he could tell it hurt.

"In Solio you were after a connection to the stolen vaccine."

"Yes."

"To make the connection between the man Faaruq and the clinic."

"Yes. Good!"

"Was Samuelson trying to make that same connection?" he asked. "Is that why they killed him?"

She shook her head. "No. He was interested in corruption. He was after the government minister or ministers that had allowed the vault of ivory to be robbed. Only in the way they killed Samuelson did I connect the theft of the vaccine to the poachers and the clinic."

"Brantingham said you tricked him. What was that about?"

"The key, John, was the ISP, the Internet service provider. Brantingham told me that Larger Than Life had kept the same high-speed line used by the clinic. If service had been disconnected and reestablished, I would not have been successful. But it was indeed the same service. LTL simply took over the contract. I suppose I did trick Mr. Brantingham into giving me an Ethernet line. I needed access to the router. Once I was in, it became interesting."

"You went there the second time to pull Faaruq's records."

"Nothing is ever lost once on the Internet, John, as you know. One must simply know where to look. When the clinic closed so quickly, they believed they had erased or destroyed all their data. But I recovered most of their records, all of their e-mails. If you looked at the contents of that thumb drive . . . there was far too much data. I opened up some doors, you might call them, so tech services could access the same material."

Knox walked her through his relationship with the boy, Bishoppe. "In the end, he betrayed me through an intermediary to Guuleed, the man Koigi left to die."

"I know of Guuleed."

"That had to cement Guuleed's belief that

either you were still alive, or I was heading after proof in Oloitokitok of who was responsible for your death. All things even, I'm not sure the betrayal hurt me. But at the time I was only too happy to get onto the plane with Brantingham and out of the village."

Grace lifted up on her elbows. "I am strong enough. No more bed."

But Knox intercepted her and eased her back down. She swore in Mandarin. He told her to cool it.

"Do you understand now, the paperwork on the Solio thumb drive? Nairobi City Water and Sewerage Company?"

"Only that Samuelson was killed alongside one of their employees. I assumed you were trying to figure out the other guy's role."

"Correct. A reporter of Samuelson's stature with a common water master. They had been moved, you know."

"Yes."

"No autopsy. They were cremated."

"Yeah. Look, maybe you should rest. You're getting all worked up."

"There were KGA rangers on the scene. Read what I gave you! Does anyone read anymore?" She strained at the IV tube, clearly irritated. "One ranger did; he knew to read rigor, lividity. At least twenty-four to thirty-six hours' difference in the times of death. The water master was beaten. Likely tortured. He was killed first. He could have been killed anywhere, even here in Nairobi. They tortured him because Samuelson thought him important. Samuelson, who had written about the stolen ivory."

"Maybe you should rest."

"Maybe you should listen."

"You're feeling better," he said.

"Listen to me, John. Samuelson writes articles about corruption. He learns of and exposes the huge losses from the government's ivory vaults over the years, one quite recently. Now, as to my supposition, it goes like this. He is being watched, this reporter. He meets with an unimportant water master, perhaps more than once. Whoever is watching him takes an interest in the water master. They abduct and torture the man; there is little doubt of this. Let us presume this man is stronger than they expect, or, more to the point, the person behind the torture —"

"Faaruq —"

"— is not so professional. He goes too far and kills the water master."

"Before the man tells them anything."

"Precisely, John! So next —"

"They abduct Samuelson."

"A riskier venture. An expat. A white. We can fairly rule out the government at this point. Someone else."

"They say everyone in Kenya is after this ivory. Faaruq had ties to Guuleed, so it was Guuleed."

"Samuelson does not talk, does not explain his connection to the water master. Maybe he dies of a heart attack, maybe again they go too far. How is one to know? In the end, he too is killed — a white man — and now they must cover it up, so they stage it as a poaching."

"They could have just buried them. They staged it to send a message. They wanted the next person they took to talk."

"Perhaps. I do not understand the precise threat I posed to them. It was Guuleed who put me in the bush, though I may never prove it."

He continued to find her occasional naïveté endearing. For one so brilliant, she could sound so childish. "But they came back for you."

"What are you talking about?"

"Guuleed ordered that you be brought back."

"Leebo," she said, shivering. "That is why he returned."

"Because you made the connection," he

said. "You connected Samuelson and this water master to the stolen ivory, and you intended to get Winston his money back with the reward."

"I do not know why David always makes fun of your intelligence, John. He really should be hearing this." She smiled.

"That's the first smile I've seen," Knox said. "And you didn't try to cover it up."

Her eyes softened. "Thank you."

He wasn't sure how to take that.

"For noticing," she said. Then she was back to business. "The problem such people as these have, John, is that they don't read the newspaper. If they had, it would all be so apparent. For me, it required archival work, Internet searches of back issues. Everything needed to locate the missing ivory was right there."

"Now you're sounding arrogant. You must be feeling better."

She didn't comment. Remained silent for a long time. Knox nearly apologized, but then she started up again. "There is an article — it is on the second thumb drive — reporting that Nairobi City Water and Sewerage, a private company contracted to take over the city's supply of potable water, was observing water shortages in the Kibera slum. That was it: a tiny reference on a page

488

deep inside a single day's issue. Clean water to the slum was among the first of NCWS's projects. The article reported a drop by half of the usual volume. But who pays attention to the problems of a slum? The water master quoted in the piece was —"

"Samuelson's man."

"The same. You see, John? Samuelson obviously read his own paper cover to cover each day. He was a true journalist."

"So he interviewed the water master responsible for Kibera. You hacked their water company's records to cross-reference the date of the water loss to the theft of the ivory from the government vault. The Kibera problem occurred after the theft."

"Again! Where is David! You like to pretend you are not so smart, John. This is something you will need to work on."

"Is it really?"

"Oh, yes." She reached over and squeezed his hand, reminding him of the airplane.

84

The operation went down on the first cool day in the two weeks since the bush. Knox and Grace, both guests of the British Embassy and living on its grounds, had differing status. Grace was allowed to leave and move about Nairobi. Knox was not, the warrant for his arrest still outstanding, and still being negotiated. Slowly.

The raid was led by the Nairobi police, observed by representatives of the British and American embassies. The key bargaining chip offered by Knox's attorneys had been his knowledge of a hacker connected to both police and criminals.

Working off a location and information provided by Knox, a Nairobi SWAT team raided the backroom office of Bishoppe's hacker. They seized two computers, three mobile phones, optical disks and three external hard drives. It was over in ten minutes. The store was back in business fifteen minutes later.

85

Grace made only a veiled attempt to contain her contempt for the woman driving her. Her mother considered jealousy a sign of true affection; for Grace, it was more a true affliction. John had spoken highly of Inspector Kanika Alkinyi. He brought her up often. That was enough.

The early going was solemn, two women together in the front seat of an unmarked police car, one making assumptions the other had no awareness of.

"A Chinese woman and a Kenyan cop," Kanika said. She smiled. "The people who see us will think we're buying an apartment building or starting a business."

They rode in silence for several kilometers. Grace thought they could have been driving through the industrial sprawl of Shanghai or Guangzhou. The world was not so very different. She had less desire to see more of it since her time in the bush. She wanted to be in one place, for a long time. She wanted space. Air to breathe.

"We'll probably have to wait," Kanika said. "These municipal guys live by their own clocks."

"There are others? You have other workers available if we should need them?"

"I've done as you asked. They're all reliable. Most are even trustworthy. You will make me famous, you know, if you are right."

"My pleasure."

"Rich, if I were that type of policewoman. Do you ever regret what you are not? Or are you able to live with what you are?"

"I think maybe we Chinese do not think in such terms."

"Count yourself lucky." Kanika grew pensive. "Sometimes I wish I'd been born male. Then I see what idiots they are."

Grace paused, then spoke more openly. "In the bush I came to think of things as far more simple, yet far more complicated. I think it will be a long time, perhaps a lifetime, before I am able to . . . compile that, as we would say in computers. To understand."

"I'm amazed at what you went through. I'm a Kenyan and I still can't imagine how you were able to survive."

"I didn't try to survive. I tried to exist. I think there is a difference. I believe that is what saved me."

"I'm not sure I understand that. But clearly your time was not up. That's what we say to each other. Police. When it gets close."

Grace nodded. "My time was not up."

The worker met them surprisingly close to on time. He was grumpy and unhappy about helping two women in any manner; he showed no respect for Kanika's badge and was openly disdainful of Grace's racial heritage.

Sighing, lips twisted in a sneer, he unlocked a padlock on a heavy steel plate that covered the first six feet of a ten-meter steel rebar ladder fixed to the side of the water tower. The plating prevented anyone without a key from climbing up.

Before they ascended, Grace pulled out and unfolded a photocopy of a blueprint belonging to the Nairobi City Water and Sewerage Company. Had the worker thought through the process, he might have wondered what a Chinese woman was doing with such a blueprint. Instead, he told them both he was in a hurry to get home to his family — it was his wife's mother's birthday. He would catch hell if he was so much as five minutes late.

Grace clarified that the tower above them supplied a specific portion of Kibera with its fresh water supply. The man nodded.

"That much is true," he said.

Kanika offered to lock up behind them.

"You wouldn't mind?"

"It's not a problem," Kanika said. "If you would like to take down my badge num—"

"No need for that. You going to steal some water?" He laughed at his own joke and handed her the padlock without thanking her. Then he trudged off, quickly joining the thick procession of Nairobi walkers heading home.

"He must walk five kilometers or more," Kanika explained to Grace. "We got lucky."

"Not too lucky," Grace said. "I am not keen on heights."

"I was hoping you were. I am terrified."

"I will go," Grace said.

"Not alone, you won't."

The two women climbed slowly and carefully. Grace did not look down. She gripped the rough metal until the color left her good hand, her snakebitten wrist throbbing with the effort.

At last they pulled their bottoms onto a catwalk surrounding a third of the tank's circumference. Another ladder was attached here, running high to the lip of the open tank.

"Do you swim?" Grace asked.

"I never learned."

"Then it must be me."

"You don't like it?"

"It is not the water I mind, I am afraid I will not like the darkness. Since my time in the bush I find myself needing to sleep with the light on. I am like a child."

"It must have been horrid."

"It was beautiful. Truly beautiful. At the time I was at peace with it. Now it is different. I do not understand."

"The water will be dark."

"Yes."

"And you obviously think it will be necessary to swim?"

"I do."

Grace had left her purse in the car, but she handed Kanika her cell phone, a hair clip and her shoes. She faced the ladder.

"How can you be so convinced you're right about this?" Kanika inquired.

"It is the only explanation," Grace said matter-of-factly.

"Oh, I see."

Misunderstanding the sarcasm, Grace said, "Yes. Good." She put one tentative foot on the first rung. Climbing without shoes was going to be painful.

"Because? It is the only explanation because?"

Holding the sides of the metal ladder, Grace turned. "The water supply to this portion of Kibera was cut in half. Cut suddenly, in a system that was quite new. Certainly a water master was dispatched to check the tank, as we are doing now. What he saw was a tank filled with water. Dark, I am sure.

"Daniel Samuelson read of this in his own paper. Curious by nature, and by occupation, he conspired with the water master to gain access to this tank — the logical tank to check first. It supplies the area in question, the area with the sudden drop in water volume. You see?

"But his plan went awry. Before he was shown to the tank, the water master disappeared. Then it was Samuelson who vanished. His theory died with him." Grace's throat tightened, choking her words. "You see the scratches there?" she said. "I'm guessing ivory tusks."

"So many . . ." Kanika whispered. "My God. All slaughtered."

"A corrupt minister like Achebe Nadali . . . If you crossed a man like Xin Ha after he had paid you for services, where would you hide several tons of ivory? Everyone, including Xin Ha, would think to look in shipping containers or warehouses. It is a great deal of weight."

"The kind of weight a water tower is built to hold."

The tremendous number of scratches in the paint stayed with Grace. Each, a tusk. Every two tusks, an elephant. "It's a mass grave," she moaned. "I suppose some of the ivory must have blocked the drain, causing the water shortage. It is the best — perhaps the only — explanation."

"I agree! But in that case — let's just wait. I can call the others, the men I have on standby. There are a few other police we can trust to protect us. You don't need to swim."

"But I must. I must face my fear. There is no personal growth without facing one's fears."

"Are you for real?"

"I think you are joking."

Grace climbed. In five minutes she was staring down at black water and an internal ladder leading into its depths.

Taking a deep breath, she descended, rung by rung. As she climbed down, she saw the jackals tearing apart Leebo. The cook's veins rising from his arms. She felt the warm milk spilling down her chin.

She let go and sank into the cold darkness.

86

Another six days of languishing negotiations for Knox's freedom. This batch included demands for a U.S. presidential visit to Kenya to show support for the Kikuyu government. A sense of desperation began swirling around the embassy, something Knox was not supposed to sense.

The following day, Kanika Alkinyi sent Knox a note via Grace. She'd arranged a seaman's berth for him on a Greek-flagged container ship out of Kiunga in the Lamu East District, sailing to Egypt.

David Dulwich agreed Knox should take the out.

"Unfinished business," Knox said. He, Grace and Dulwich were alone in a small library in the guest residence. Chintz drapes were strapped to either side of the oversized double-hung windows. Oil portraits and battle scenes filled the spaces the bookshelves allowed. The room smelled of rose and leather and binding gum. Knox had made his home here recently, reading through the works of Rudyard Kipling, which he hadn't touched since his teens.

"Unfinished?" Dulwich arched an eyebrow and shut the door, taking the cue.

"Xin Ha." Knox looked between the two.

"No, no. At this point," Dulwich cautioned, "you are — both of you — tangentially tied to Mr. Winston. What you're thinking, Knox, is unacceptable."

"What I'm thinking is nowhere near as sinister as what your deviant mind assumes."

"While I appreciate the compliment, I recognize that look of yours, and I know you're not planning on throwing the man a party, so let's hear it."

"He has to go. Grace, why don't you tell him?"

She focused on Dulwich, her eyes glassy and yet dull, a befuddling combination. Knox wondered if Dulwich could see the damage done to her, as he could. He doubted it.

God, she could act, this woman. She could put on her Chinese airs of stoic complacency in a way that would do the eleven generations of Chus before her proud. But Knox saw into her now in a way he'd never done before.

To make matters more intriguing, he was fairly confident she knew it. And to add to his confusion, she wasn't afraid to let him see. A first. Women were too fucking complicated.

When she spoke, softly as ever, she owned the room. Grace Chu was a marvel, Knox thought.

"It was Xin Ha who intercepted Mr. Winston's shipment of the measles vaccine. This I can now prove. From Mr. Winston's contacts in intelligence, we now also possess the satellite phone transmissions confirming an ongoing relationship between him and the man we knew as Guuleed, born Assim Guuleed to a Somali mother and Ugandan father in 1984.

"Whether we will be able to prove it or not, Xin Ha contracted Guuleed to steal the replacement vaccine from the Solio cattle operation. He then used partial proceeds from the sale of the measles vaccine — what he considered untraceable funds — to bribe Minister Achebe Nadali. Xin Ha wanted access to the ivory vaults. Nadali had other ideas. He crossed Xin Ha, removing the ivory ahead of schedule and hiding it here in Nairobi.

"It gets theoretical here. I am sorry, but

there is little hard evidence from here. We can assume Xin Ha took care of Nadali, but not before torturing him for the location of the stolen ivory. Guuleed's man Faaruq may have been involved. I would doubt we will ever know."

"Along comes Samuelson, via Bertram Radcliffe. We all know how that turned out."

"This is where Grace comes in," Knox said. "She starts digging, so Xin Ha has Guuleed put her out to pasture. Enough with the staged poachings. Her death is supposed to look like a tragic tourist mistake, if she's found at all." He waited for someone to say something. No one did. "It all starts and stops with Xin Ha, who, by the way, just happens to control the export of poached ivory to China — one of the illegal trades Grace was sent to expose."

"He also happens to have close ties to the very people we're trying to convince to let you go!" Dulwich said, scarlet-faced.

"Sarge, easy. I'm just saying."

"Saying what, exactly?"

"Bertram Radcliffe."

Dulwich clearly couldn't fit the pieces together. "Yeah?"

"We'd have to convince him to leave the country. If he stays, he'd be killed for sure."

"Not following."

"I have the paper trail. It is long and detailed and damning," Grace said. "There's no way Xin Ha survives it if it goes public."

"No, no, no!" Dulwich said. "Those were obtained through illegal means and financed by one of the more powerful men in England. They would have to include intelligence records of electronic eavesdropping by — I can't even tell you two who! People connect the dots. Companies like Rutherford Risk exist to keep those doors and windows shuttered."

Grace looked to Knox. He nodded. "Go ahead."

"WikiLeaks," Grace said. "I can put so many layers on top of this that it will never be sourced."

"We give Radcliffe a heads-up," Knox said. "When and where it's going to post on the Internet. He's an award-winning journalist whose reporting will be taken seriously. He's the first to see it, the first to publish. He avenges his friend's death. Xin Ha goes down. If the government lets him escape, it's a disgrace. If he goes to ground, he's radioactive and won't last long once Winston offers a reward. Nice and neat, the way you like it, Sarge."

Dulwich's blank stare was confounding. "WikiLeaks. Jesus."

"Right?" Knox said.

"It is an exposé on the vaccine, corruption within the ministry and the financial link to poaching and terrorism, long suspected but never proved — all proven," Grace said.

Dulwich spent a long minute considering the suggestion. "WikiLeaks," he said again. "Graham will love it. He sends his thanks to you both — you, Grace, especially. Can't contact you directly. You understand. He's going to pledge the reward money to support Larger Than Life and community conservation. He hopes to help open a scaled-down version of the health clinic. It's all good. He's greatly impressed."

Knox said, "Technically, we don't need your permission. The WikiLeaks thing."

"We are not asking you to condone such an action," Grace said. "However, I for one do not wish for it to result in our severing relations. I do not wish to jeopardize my contract with Rutherford Risk."

"You kidding? Brian Primer will pin a medal on you both, and you know it." Dulwich said this to Knox. "He loves nefarious shit like this. End runs. Countermeasures. He'd be all over it."

"But he'll never hear about it," Knox said. "I don't mean to speak for you," he said to

Grace, "but I think that's what Grace is asking."

"I got it the first time, Knox." Dulwich sighed. It was an intentional act, one to express disdain as well as admiration. "Fucking WikiLeaks."

87

Knox and Grace shared an unceremonious farewell dinner in the British Embassy cafeteria, eating off of plastic trays and indestructible ceramic dishes carrying the stamp of the Monarchy. Grace had barely spoken for the past forty-eight hours, since the meeting with Dulwich. To his credit, Knox had not pushed.

He'd brought along a news story to share with her — nineteen people killed execution-style in six raids outside of Mogadishu. Al-Shabaab was claiming responsibility. In Dulwich's handwriting, a note along the top: "M-I6 reporting all relatives of Assim Guuleed." Knox felt it in his jacket pocket and crumpled it. What had he been thinking? She'd seen enough death.

"I have to know if we are going forward," she said, "or if we are to stay here in this place — I do not mean physically; I mean mentally, emotionally." Two days, and this was the first thing he'd heard her say. "Because if we are to remind one another of all that has happened, then what is the point, John? Maybe this is impossible to escape. Maybe we are bound to live the past, just as the boy and his sister, who may never escape hers."

At Knox's urging, Inspector Kanika Alkinyi had made some calls for him. There was a rumor in the sister's town that a known pimp had come into some money. The sister had not been seen in several days. That was where the information began and ended. It seemed as if Bishoppe had invested wisely.

Either that, Knox thought, or he'd gotten himself and his sister killed.

"He deserved better than I gave him," Knox said.

"You said he is resourceful."

"Very."

"So it is."

"You know what I imagined, Grace? I imagined us adopting him. Of giving . . . of him . . . of adopting him." He couldn't believe he'd just said that. A moment of weakness.

"Us," she said wistfully.

"Yeah."

"Maybe we start there."

Knox studied her face, the cosmetics barely covering the sun damage, chapped skin and abrasions. He nodded. "Yeah, maybe so."

"I poisoned two men for no reason."

"They were Guuleed's men. I have no doubt about that."

"I did not have to kill them. That will never leave me. I . . . enjoyed it, John. I was not sorry then, I am not sorry now, but I must live with it all the same."

"I faced one of Guuleed's men at Ol Donyo."

"Yes. You told me."

"He'll pick up where Guuleed left off, have no doubt of that."

"We both changed the subject. You see, John. We must decide, here, now, if this continues. If either of us, if both of us, are to work with David again, and if so, together or separate. If together, it will not be like it has been, John. I wrote you the letter. You wrote to me as well. We have said things man to woman, woman to man. Not worker to worker. You understand?"

He felt his eyes smile. "My brother complicates everything."

"You love your brother. Love complicates nothing."

"It complicates everything, are you kidding me? Look at us!"

"I am," said Grace. "Looking. At you. That is all that matters to me. All that is important. It is present."

Knox swallowed. "It is."

"So we stay in the present," she said.

She smiled, making no attempt to cover her mouth.

88

Knox opened the door, found his brother watching television. He kneeled alongside the recliner, took Tommy in his arms and held him.

"I'm watching, Johno."

"I've been gone for three weeks!"

"It'll be over in seven minutes."

"Seven. Okay." Knox sat on the couch and watched his brother as his brother watched the television. The seven minutes felt like sixty. At last, Tommy shut off the television with the remote.

"How long are you back?"

"A long time, I hope. Longer, this time."

"I'm glad."

"Me, too. How's it going?"

"I have a job, Johno. I have a job at the grocery store, and I'm good at it. I like it."

"I'm so glad."

"It's not that I don't like working with you, for the company. I do. But I like this better. I fill the bags. I talk to the customers. They like me."

"I understand. It's great."

"Really? I thought you'd be mad."

"I don't get mad at you, Tommy. I love you, man. I mean it. Brothers, you know?"

Tommy looked at him curiously. Knox wasn't sure Tommy would ever fully understand, and that hurt in a way he'd never be able to articulate.

"I have a surprise for you. I know you like surprises. You're going to like this one. It's different than any surprise ever. It won't always be easy. It won't always be perfect, but you're going to like it."

"A dog?"

Knox smiled. "Not hardly. But something like that." He stood and walked over to the recliner. Put his foot onto the footrest and pushed it down, sitting Tommy up. It was a routine for them, something Tommy enjoyed.

"Do it again!" Tommy pleaded, sitting back.

"One more time," Knox said, repeating the process. Then he offered Tommy his hand and helped him up.

He led him to the front door.

AUTHOR'S NOTE

How You Can Help

The fight — and it is a fight that includes sophisticated weaponry aimed at defenseless wild animals and rangers — continues. It does so only with contributions, big and small. I am pledging twenty percent of any royalties or film contracts to assist those "in the trenches" of Kenya, working to stop the poachers. I urge you to research those non-profits and organizations dedicated to wildlife preservation. Sadly, not all efforts are equal. Some use funds to support more administration than boots on the ground. Others are doing stellar work in Kenyan communities, on reserves and in the range-land, to protect and defend wildlife. Any amount of donation (no matter if you think it too small!) goes such a long way. "This is Africa." Among those with which I had direct contact and can highly recommend:

African Wildlife Foundation (finances responsible nonprofits across Africa to preserve wildlife)
1400 16th Street, NW
Suite 120
Washington, DC 20036
USA
www.awf.org

Big Life (manages more than 250 armed private rangers in the bush)
Big Life Foundation USA
24010 NE Treehill Drive
Wood Village, OR 97060
USA
www.biglife.org

The Gorongosa Fund (supports conservation of Gorongosa National Park in Mozambique)
www.gorongosa.org

Northern Rangeland Trust (oversees rangers, community outreach)
Northern Rangeland Trust
Private Bag
Isiolo 60300
Kenya
www.nrt-kenya.org

Wildlife Direct (works within the court systems, doing some of the most important work in this effort)
WildlifeDirect Inc.
306 5th Street, SE
Washington, DC 20003
USA
www.wildlifedirect.org

ABOUT THE AUTHOR

Ridley Pearson is the *New York Times*–bestselling author of more than two dozen novels, including *The Red Room*, *Choke Point*, and *The Risk Agent*, as well as the Walt Fleming and Lou Boldt crime series, and many books for young readers. He lives with his wife and two daughters, dividing his time between Saint Louis, Missouri, and Hailey, Idaho.

The employees of Thorndike Press hope you have enjoyed this Large Print book. All our Thorndike, Wheeler, and Kennebec Large Print titles are designed for easy reading, and all our books are made to last. Other Thorndike Press Large Print books are available at your library, through selected bookstores, or directly from us.

For information about titles, please call:
(800) 223-1244

or visit our Web site at:
http://gale.cengage.com/thorndike

To share your comments, please write:
Publisher
Thorndike Press
10 Water St., Suite 310
Waterville, ME 04901